# WATCHER AT THE CROSSING

ASH FITZSIMMONS

# WATCHER AT THE CROSSING

## THE CROSSING

1

WATCHER AT THE CROSSING. Copyright © 2023 by Ash Fitzsimmons.

Print Edition ISBN: 978-1-949861-51-8

Cover design by MiblArt.

www.ashfitzsimmons.com

# CHAPTER 1

For me, Uncle Malachi died at seven-fourteen a.m. on a Tuesday, as I was halfway through my cornflakes. The coroner pegged him as having expired quite a few hours earlier—exactly how this estimate was reached, I didn't want to know—but seven-fourteen was when Chief Brundage called to deliver the bad news. A sophomore soccer player conditioning for fall tryouts had gone for a cross-country run and stumbled across the body, by then a twisted lump lying facedown in the brown detritus of last year's leaves.

That would teach *him* to add variety to his workouts.

I didn't learn about the traumatized tenth grader until Wednesday, when I saw the half-column story in the midweek *Gazette*. Tuesday passed in a haze of visits to institutional rooms that smelled of cheap antiseptic—the police station, the rural clinic, the tri-county morgue. Finally, I found myself home on the couch with a bottle of chardonnay and Mia, who kept the wine flowing until it finally hit me that I was now well and truly alone in the world and broke into sloppy drunk sobs. She peeled me up on Wednesday morning, made double-strength coffee, and ordered me into the shower so that I could face the world with a modicum of presentability. "Eat, Suze," she directed, plopping a plate of cheesy scrambled eggs and toast in front of me, and though I had little appetite, I knew Mia well enough not to argue.

We were old pros at that macabre dance by then, Mia and me. We'd been roommates during senior year of college, when Uncle Malachi called two weeks after Christmas to give me the bad news about Dad. As I'd floundered in my grief, she'd forced me to bathe and eat cheap pizza and stare at something besides the off-white walls of our suite. It was Mia who'd kept her arm around me during the funeral, and it took Mia and Uncle Malachi working together to coax me out of my too-quiet house and back to school to finish the semester. That spring, I'd held Mia's hand while she called her mother and confessed that the reason she'd never brought a nice boy around was that she much preferred nice girls, and that had been almost a death of sorts, too, considering the subsequent silence from home. We'd walked at graduation with only each other to cheer us on—Uncle Malachi never left Cole's Crossing, and Ms. Randolph still wasn't speaking to Mia—but we'd done it together. And then Mia had flown away to New York for an internship with an architectural magazine, and I'd returned to the Crossing to pick up the pieces of my father's life and reassemble them into something I could own.

But once again, it was Mia and me—her smarting from a bad breakup and an ignominious, unemployed end to her internship, me living alone in my childhood house, still sleeping in my old bedroom instead of in Dad's wide brass bed. When Uncle Malachi died, Mia knew the steps of our depressing tango.

On Thursday afternoon, after Chief Brundage called again to report that my uncle had died of a heart attack and not foul play, I met with Uncle Malachi's lawyer, Paul Croaker. I'd been left with no particular instructions pointing me toward his office off Main Street, but I didn't need them. Mr. Croaker was the only attorney for thirty miles, and he'd handled the Crossing's paperwork for the last forty years, just like his father before him. He sat me down in a tan leather chair and offered me a ginger ale, then he settled behind his desk for the reading of the will. The document was handwritten, albeit notarized, and it bore none of the expected flourishes of legalese—but then, nothing about Uncle Malachi had ever been normal. I was given his cabin, his rattling Chevy pickup truck, and his bank account and told to do with them as I wished, and that was that. But when I asked Mr. Croaker about funeral arrangements, he informed me I had no further responsibility there. Uncle Malachi had prepaid for his cremation, and Ms. Quince, my middle-aged next-door neighbor, was to scatter the remains in the lake. He'd turned down the space saved for him in the family plot at Grace Methodist, where the Coles had been buried since the days when old Samuel Cole built a cabin and began affixing his name to landmarks.

"*Cremation?*" I asked Mr. Croaker, not quite believing my ears.

He nodded and considered me over his half-moon reading glasses. "Says he's ready to go traveling, and he plans to reach the sea eventually. That's Malachi for you," he concluded with a little sigh. "Never thought of him as anything but a homebody. Guess he was waiting for the right time to go on an adventure, eh?"

It was well past time, to be frank. Whenever Uncle Malachi had left his cabin, it was usually just to walk in the surrounding woods. I could count on one hand the number of times I'd seen him in town. He'd never stop by our house. Instead, Dad and I had made the trek every time we got together, even if that meant packing up Thanksgiving dinner straight from the oven and driving it down the rain-rutted trail into the trees. He hadn't been agoraphobic, nor misanthropic—he'd always had a kind word for Dad and me, and his pantry had been full of popcorn and cookies from the enterprising scouts who'd pegged him as an easy mark. But as far as I knew, Uncle Malachi had never been as far as the next town, and whatever he'd seen of the sea had come from the old satellite dish that squatted on the cabin roof like a rusting vulture.

In a town as small as the Crossing, everyone knew everyone else's business, and so I spent my grade school years fielding enquiries about my weird uncle, the recluse. He was a minor celebrity, at first the mayor's son, and then the mayor's younger brother. The old-timers remembered Uncle Malachi's granduncle, Pericles Cole, who'd built the cabin and lived out his bachelorhood there, and assumed they were witness to some quirk in the bloodline. If so, they must have imagined that whatever afflicted Uncle Malachi had died with him, the last of the true Coles. I bore the family name, but neither Barnaby nor Malachi Cole had ever married or fathered children, and it was no secret that Uncle Malachi had found me lying in the woods, alone and still filthy from birth, discarded in a patch of clover like a baby bird fallen from a nest. He and I had been close ever since—or as close as two people could be when one of them refused to venture back to civilization—and when I was old enough, Dad had sent me on my mountain bike every Sunday afternoon to deliver Uncle Malachi's weekly groceries. We'd visit while we unpacked, and though my uncle had always seemed tired, his dark eyes sunken and shadowed, he'd ask me about school and my friends, and he'd *listen*, a rare quality in a grownup. Without fail, he'd shoo me on my way well before nightfall, chiding me not to be out after dark, but though he could be gruff in his delivery, there was always love in the sentiment.

But there would be no more trips out to see Uncle Malachi with bags of rice and beans and boxes of the frozen meatloaf dinners he favored. There was only the cabin and sixty-three years' worth of the paraphernalia of life, and the task of sorting through it was mine alone.

I could have put it off. Maybe I should have waited until the grief wasn't so fresh and raw—it wasn't as if I planned to put the cabin on the market anytime soon. But part of me wanted the comfort of the familiar, and so I drove out to the cabin on Friday morning to begin picking through my uncle's belongings.

It wasn't exactly a herculean task—Uncle Malachi's cabin was barely a thousand square feet, a box built of logs and roofed with ribbed steel. The furnishings of the main room were limited to an old brown leather recliner, a TV stand, and a small dining table with four mismatched chairs. To one side was the kitchen, a cramped space dominated by its avocado-colored antique appliances, and a deep storage closet. To the other was the cabin's sole bedroom, where I'd seldom had cause to go. I'd never stayed overnight at the cabin—Uncle Malachi certainly hadn't offered.

By noon, I'd stuffed the contents of the bedroom closet into black lawn bags for charity, which I drove back to town before grabbing lunch at Cole's Cuts. The closest thing to fast food that our town could boast was a sandwich shop, but I'd had an account there since I was a kid, and Mrs. Ludlow insisted on feeding me gratis that week. I took my pastrami on rye to Dad's shop, feeling a twinge of guilt for being so late to put in an appearance, and relieved Annie Plunkett at the cash register. Pulling up a stool, I ate my sandwich and oversaw the quiet shop with its wooden shelves and wire racks of groceries—nothing fancy, just the sort of pantry staples that had kept the town running for generations.

When I thought of Cole's Crossing General Store—and a lot of creativity went into that name, let me just say—I thought of it as Dad's shop, and I always would. True, it was far older than Dad, the modern incarnation of a side project started by our town's founder upon seeing a buck to be made from the people he ferried across the wide lake, but I couldn't walk in without picturing Dad stacking cartons of soda or hand-lettering the specials of the week on the old chalkboard. As long as I'd been alive, Dad had leaned on Annie as his right-hand woman, and she'd convinced him to give her son Dewey a job when I was barely out of kindergarten. The Plunketts had kept the store afloat while I finished college, and naturally, I'd kept them on once I assumed management that summer. I'd run the place for a year by then, still schlepping Uncle Malachi's groceries out to him every weekend. Remembering that I'd made my last such delivery, I lost my appetite and wrapped up my sandwich for a later attempt.

The afternoon was quiet, but that wasn't unusual. With a proper grocery store having moved in twelve miles outside of town, the general store wasn't as crucial as it had been in its heyday, though we still did a steady stream of business in odds and ends: a box of chicken broth forgotten during the weekly shop, a bag of flour for last-minute baking, a pack of paper plates for a picnic, a gallon of milk for a thirsty toddler. I wasn't going to retire at thirty, but thanks to my untimely inheritance, I wasn't hurting.

Before I headed back to Uncle Malachi's cabin that evening, I stopped by Antoinette's, where Mia had snagged a job as a waitress upon her return to town. The restaurant was nothing fancy—you could have anything you liked as long as it could be breaded, fried, and served with gravy—but it did a business, relatively speaking, and Mia stayed on her feet all shift. "I'm going to keep cleaning," I told her once she had a moment to breathe by the Pepsi fountain. "Don't wait up. I'll probably just sleep out there."

"Yeah, *no*," she replied with a scowl. "Does the cabin even lock?"

"I'll be fine."

"You'll be miles from help if redneck cannibals come out of the woods. That's just dumb." Folding her arms, she glanced at the decorative wall clock, then said, "We close at nine, and I'll be out of here by ten. I'll stay with you."

"There's only one bed, and all your crap is at the house," I protested.

She shrugged. "Since when do you mind sharing a bed?

*Rude.*" With a parting elbow in my side, she returned to her tables, and I took off for the cabin.

Driving through the twilit woods, slowing every time I imagined I saw the motion of a deer through the trees, I thought back to my not-so-distant college years, when Mia and I had made our plans to run the world. She would ascend through the editorial ranks of New York's most prestigious publications, while I would strike off for parts unknown, maybe teach in a foreign country and settle down with a handsome man and his charming accent. Dad's death had thrown me into a tailspin, and duty had called me home to the Crossing—there had been a Cole in the general store for two centuries, and I was the last available option. As for Mia, she'd been unable to find another internship that paid in anything more than experience. Broke and brokenhearted, she'd moved in with me, and we nursed our wounded pride with ice cream and white wine while we strategized our next attempt at adulthood.

"You're doing just fine," Uncle Malachi had told me on my last visit to the cabin. "You've got a roof, a business, and a savings account. Things could be so much worse, Susan."

"I still want to take a stab at life outside the Crossing," I'd replied, leaning against the side of my sedan.

He'd smiled wistfully and patted my shoulder. "I want that for you, too, baby girl. We don't always get what we want, but that's my hope for you."

I hadn't changed my mind since our last conversation, but part of adulthood was taking responsibility for the unfortunate duties of life, and that meant that my place was in the Crossing until Uncle Malachi's cabin was cleaned and settled. Parking beneath an old oak in the flat patch of scraggly grass he'd called a driveway, I climbed out of the car, grabbed my leftover sandwich, and headed for the door. I'd left the porch light on, anticipating a late return, which is why I saw the delivery instead of running into it.

I'd stopped Uncle Malachi's mail and switched his utilities into my name earlier in the week, so the fact that there was a long, leather-wrapped bundle leaning against the door took me by surprise. Frowning, I unlocked the door and carried it in, then dropped it onto the kitchen table for an examination under the rustic chandelier. Yes, that *was* leather—tough brown leather, the sort better suited for saddlery than for designer handbags—tied in five places with rawhide thongs. There was no name on the bundle, no guarantee that it was for Uncle Malachi, but who else could have been the intended recipient? There wasn't a neighbor for miles.

Telling myself that someone must have anonymously returned a garden implement, I cut the thongs with the kitchen shears and unrolled the leather wrappings. But there wasn't a rake inside them, nor even a rifle, my second guess.

Lying on the table was a three-foot sword.

I stared at it, wondering why the hell anyone would dump a medieval weapon on Uncle Malachi's doormat. To my untrained eye, it looked like the real deal—it was certainly heavy enough. The scabbard was a deep burgundy leather with decorative stitching of leaves and vines, much suppler than the packaging material had been, and as for the hilt...I took a closer look and whistled softly. For a piece of metal, it was gorgeous, steel etched with an elaborate four-lobed knot pattern. At the center of the design was set a blue-green gem that had to weigh at least ten carats—an aquamarine, I guessed, or maybe some sort of quartz. A similar gem of much larger size was set in the tip of the pommel. A peculiar frisson prickled the hairs on the back of my neck as I studied the sword, as if I had ventured too close to an electrical field.

I couldn't resist. Gripping the hilt, I pulled the sword free of its scabbard, revealing a shining steel blade. The piece had to cost a fortune, I thought, but before I could begin to wonder about its origin, a searing pain stabbed at my palm as if I'd grabbed a hot iron. I yelped and dropped the sword, then ran to the sink and shoved my hand beneath the cold water until the burning feeling had subsided to a twinge. Patting my hand dry, I was shocked to find the hilt's decorative knotwork branded into my flesh, and so I wrapped the wound in a layer of gauze from Uncle Malachi's first-aid kit, hoping the red marks would fade by morning. Arming myself with potholders, I gingerly slid the sword back into its sheath and left it on the table, a problem to be dealt with by daylight.

Though I'd intended to keep working, my hand still throbbed, and the thought of cleaning out my uncle's dresser and footlocker seemed less appealing by the minute. In the end, I decided not to make a bad night worse, popped a couple aspirins, and went to bed, making sure to keep the left side open for Mia.

*Maybe I should leave a note warning her about the sword* was my last thought before sleep took me.

A scratching noise in the leaves outside the cabin pulled me from my uneasy rest. Groaning at the interruption, I looked at my phone for the time—quarter of ten. Whatever was moving beyond the cabin wall wasn't Mia.

As the fog of sleep dissipated, I recalled that I was out in the woods by myself, alone in a house that was roughly the antithesis of impregnable. Sure, the cabin was sturdy in a snowstorm, but something sufficiently large or armed with opposable thumbs and a can-do spirit would have no real trouble getting in. I lay still beneath Uncle Malachi's lighter spring quilt, listening for the sound again and wondering whether I'd latched the windows.

*There*—a scritching somewhere in the trees. It started, then stopped, then resumed once again, uneven bursts of motion over the forest floor. Probably a foraging raccoon, I told myself, or maybe a feral cat. Who knew what Uncle

Malachi had been feeding out there?

I still told myself there was nothing to worry about when the sound moved closer and the footsteps grew heavier. A *big* raccoon, my mind insisted. No need to panic.

But when I heard it bump into my car, logic began to win out over the part of me that just wanted to curl up and ignore the interruption. Something was out there, something large and headed my way, and hiding under the blankets wasn't going to protect me. I needed to take a look. If it was just a deer, fine, I could laugh about it in the morning. If it was something else…well, hopefully, I'd have a few minutes to call the police before it found me.

Creeping through the cabin, imagining the unsettling violin crescendo of a horror movie score, I slunk back into the main room and felt for the wall. Turning on the porch light and opening the door would be a rookie mistake—I wasn't a pretty blonde in a slasher flick—but I needed to see what was lurking in the darkness, and that meant sneaking a peek through a window. I dropped to my knees, crawled the last few feet to a window with a view of my car, and slowly raised my head to look out at the night.

*Something* was out there, all right, and it sure as hell wasn't a damn raccoon. Trash pandas didn't have orange-glowing eyes, and they didn't stand eight feet tall.

I ducked back beneath the windowsill and held my breath as my heart jackhammered against my ribs. When I allowed myself to breathe again, my exhalation came as a whisper of barely coherent profanity, and I scrambled away from the window, still on my hands and knees. My mind whirled, trying to process what I'd seen by the moonlight. Not a bear—it was too thin, and it wasn't lumbering, but more than that, its fingers were claw-like talons at least six inches long. I couldn't tell whether it was furred, feathered, scaled, or just some asshole in a Halloween mask, but I wasn't about to try for a better look. I had to call the police, and then I had to call Mia—

God forbid she be attacked on arrival by whatever was prowling around the place. Unfortunately, my phone was back in the bedroom, which seemed roughly as far away at that moment as northernmost Siberia.

Or perhaps I could stand my ground. Uncle Malachi had been a hunter and kept guns in the cabin, but they were on the other side of the building in the storage closet, locked in their safe and unloaded. As I knew roughly enough about guns to identify the business end, I wouldn't have a prayer of being able to access the safe and load one in the dark, much less aim it with accuracy. Phone it was.

I could do this, I told myself. If I moved slowly and avoided the squeaky spots in the floor, that thing outside would never know I was home. Carefully, ever so carefully, I crawled toward the kitchen table to put space between me and the door. I froze and scrunched my eyes closed in fear as I heard the creature step onto the wooden porch, and I stayed motionless in the dark cabin, praying that it would go away.

But when it started beating on the door, my paralysis broke. I jumped up and looked around in vain for an escape. Finding no safe exit, nor any secure place to hide, I let my mind go on autopilot. I wasn't entirely sure what I was doing when I yanked the sword off the table and tossed the scabbard aside, but I held it in both hands, cocked back like a baseball bat, and glared at the door.

I didn't have to wait more than a few seconds before the door was ripped off its old hinges and tossed aside. The hulking *thing* squeezed through the doorway and loomed over me, its head nearly touching the ceiling, its claws clicking against the wooden floor. It saw me and screeched, a noise something like a mountain lion with notes of angry bear, and I screamed like a little girl with a snake dropped down the back of her shirt. As the creature advanced on me, its footsteps rattling the dishes in the cabinet, I tensed, sucked in a fresh gasp of air, then swung at it with the sword in a desperate attempt to save myself.

I wasn't expecting it to *work*.

The sword went through the fiend like a fork through flan, meeting almost no resistance. My attacker screeched louder as its left arm flopped onto the floor, and I took advantage of its shock and pain to strike again. While my second hit was even more ungainly than the first had been—I simply held the sword in front of me like a pike and ran at my target—it did the trick, and the beast fell. Pierced cleanly through by the blade, it twitched its last spasm at my feet.

It took me five long minutes before I could convince my trembling legs to cross the room and turn on the overhead lights, and then I sincerely wished I hadn't.

The thing was a cryptid of some sort—that was as close as I could get to pinning a name on the creature. It was tall but thin, its muscles visible beneath its purplish flesh. A black fluid—*ichor*, my brain insisted, watching with odd detachment—puddled on the floor beneath its chest wound and oozed from the stump where its arm had been. Briefly, I thought of Grendel, running away into the night and leaving his arm with Beowulf, and I giggled. Even in my daze, I heard how close to hysteria my laughter was creeping and tried to rein it in, but the scene before me wasn't helping the effort.

Though my arms shook, I forced myself to bend closer to the body and continue my examination. In the places where the sword had struck, the flesh was faintly smoking, and an acrid smell like rancid barbeque stung my nostrils. Circles of thick violet fur had burned away at the impact sites. I dropped the dirtied sword and exchanged it for a stiff push broom, which I used to flip the body over. The face that greeted me seemed almost porcine, if pigs came equipped with fangs as well as tusks. It, too, was covered in fur, which rose to a cowlick mohawk in the middle of its head. Its hands were easily twice the size of mine, the fingers impossibly long, the claws wicked. Letting my gaze sweep down the body, I saw that it was naked but for its pelt—and definitely male, its member grotesquely large and half-sheathed.

If *that* was a sasquatch, then I was never setting foot in the woods again.

I was still standing by the opening where the door had been, prodding at the beast with the broom handle and fighting the urge to retch, when the crunch of tires over leaves and the twin white headlight beams of Mia's secondhand Toyota cut through the stillness of the night. She parked and jumped out of her car, then jogged to the door and stopped on the porch, gawking at the thing in her path.

"I can't drag it by myself," I said, hearing myself as if from a distance. "Too heavy. It's skinny, but it's dense."

"The *fuck* is that?" she whispered, kicking one of its clawed feet with the toe of her tennis shoe.

"Hell if I know. It tried to break in, and—"

"*Tried?* It succeeded." She pointed to the thrown door, her blue eyes wide. "Are you okay? What happened?"

I started to babble an answer, which grew faster and less coherent by the second until Mia stepped over the creature's legs and pushed me into the recliner. "Stay," she ordered, and retreated to the kitchen.

I had no intention of disobeying—the chair retained a bit of Uncle Malachi's scent, and as stunned and disturbed as I was that night, I found the smell almost a comfort. Then again, anything was better than the creature's stench.

After a quick search through the cabinets, Mia returned to me with a scratched tumbler half-full of cheap bourbon and shoved it into my hands. "Cheers," she said, clinking her similarly filled jelly jar against my glass, and knocked back the liquor in a long gulp.

I followed suit and coughed at the burn. "Long day?" I joked between wheezes.

"Had better." She shuddered as the last of the alcohol made its way down, then nodded to the corpse. "So what do we do with Gorgeous there? Call the cops?"

"And say what? 'I was attacked by a prowler, but it's not human'?"

"Good point." Mia put her glass down and bent over the thing for a better look, then noticed the sword I'd dropped in the corner. "Where did *that* come from?"

"No clue. It was on the porch when I got home. Something of Uncle Malachi's, I guess."

"You *stabbed* Gorgeous?"

"You sound surprised," I muttered, beginning to feel more like myself as the bourbon calmed my nerves. "I wasn't going to invite him in for a snack."

"Granted, but I've never thought of you as the stabby type."

As she reached for the sword, I remembered my injured hand. "Stop, don't touch it!"

Mia paused and eyed me curiously. "Why not?"

In response, I pushed myself from the chair and joined her by the sword, giving the corpse the widest berth possible. "I held it today when I got home, and look what happened," I said, unwrapping the gauze. The burn still stood out, a livid design against the flesh of my palm, and I pointed from it to the identical markings on the hilt. "See?"

"You grabbed metal that had been sitting in the sun for hours," said Mia, looking at me like my sanity might be slipping. "Of course you got burned. Ever touched a curling iron?"

"This is different." I hurried back to the kitchen and returned with my trusty potholders. Pulling the sword upright, I showed Mia the hilt again and said, "Look more closely."

One of her eyebrows rose. "At what, the gemstone?"

"The design. How is it made?"

Her face scrunched in bemusement. "Do I look like a metalworker to you, Suze?"

"Just…" I floundered, searching my scattered thoughts for the right word, then jabbed a finger at the design. "It's etched into the metal, see?"

"Sure…"

"So then how did *that* get burned onto me, and not the rest of the hilt? That should have been the *last* thing to touch my skin."

Mia puzzled over that briefly, then beckoned for the sword. "Give it here."

"What are you—"

"Remember when we talked about getting matching tats?" She pulled the hilt from my potholders, wrapped her hand around it, and gave it a little test swing. "I don't feel anything."

I took the sword back, and we both looked at her unmarked palm.

"Maybe it's poison ivy or something," she tried. "Like, someone rubbed the oil in the design, and you're having a reaction."

"Does that make *any* sense whatsoever?"

"Well, no, but it's late, and there's some sort of hell-beast blocking the door, so let's not be judgmental, okay?" She cut her eyes to the corpse and grimaced. "Speaking of which, we can't leave it there. We're letting bugs in, if nothing else," she added, pointing to a pair of moths circling the chandelier. "So…put it on the porch?"

"That's a lot of fresh meat to have around, and I don't want to draw bears," I replied. "Um…hang on, let me check the freezer."

Uncle Malachi kept a chest freezer on the premises, where he stored his butchered kills in heavy foil and plastic bags. Fortunately, the freezer was almost empty, and the venison steaks I found in the bottom fit into the regular unit. "Give me a hand," I told Mia. "I'll take the shoulders, you get the feet."

Though the smoking had stopped, the thing still emitted a stomach-turning stench, and we dumped it into the freezer as quickly as we could. With a little pushing and turning, we wedged it into the chest and locked the lid, then surveyed the damage.

"Think you can get the door back on?" I asked Mia. "Toolbox is in the storage closet."

"I'll try. What about you?"

I pointed to the drips and pools of ichor staining the floor. "Thought I'd start with a mop."

# CHAPTER 2

Midnight came and went, and still Mia and I lay close together in Uncle Malachi's bed like children hiding from a thunderstorm. I won't say we huddled—both of us were trying to affect an air of nonchalance, as if monsters regularly crashed in on our Friday evenings—but neither did we scoot far from the middle of the mattress. That night, there may well have been something tentacled or taloned beneath the bed, and I, for one, didn't intend to leave a foot dangling over the side to find out.

We'd debated the wisdom of abandoning the cabin for the relative safety of town, but ultimately, we decided to shelter in place until morning. Fearful of what else might be lurking in the night, neither of us wanted to attempt the dash for our vehicles in the dark, and the thought of running into another monster along the dirt trail back to civilization was enough to make me queasy. After all, Gorgeous had broken down the door, and I could only imagine his buddies peeling open my car like a sardine can.

Somehow, I finally dozed, exhausted from the night and the week. But just as I was slipping into a dream, a heavy scrabbling sound on the roof yanked me awake.

I was imagining it, I told myself, lying still in hopes of silence. Nothing but a nightmare…

The sound returned, heading toward the main room, and a gnawing suspicion in my gut suggested that the thing in the freezer had a friend. I shook Mia awake, shushing her when she groggily complained, then slipped out of bed and grabbed the sword, which I'd left propped in the corner like a club to wield against intruders. When the sound returned a second time, I couldn't deny that it was footsteps, and Mia whisper-swore.

I turned on the chandelier again, just in case whatever was above us was a garden-variety prowler, while Mia headed for the kitchen. Watching from my position behind our poorly repaired door, I saw her open and close the cabinets until she located her prize: a cast-iron skillet. Dad and Uncle Malachi had learned to cook at their mother's side, and like her, neither ever believed in nonstick pans.

"Come on," I whispered, and motioned for Mia to join me at the door. If something tried to break in again, I reasoned, perhaps we could catch it in an ambush. But the thing on the roof had a surprise of its own, and before Mia could cross the room, it skittered down the chimney.

*You're not Santa* was the best my exhausted mind could manage when a creature like a cross between a green, monstrously overgrown wasp and an army ant squeezed itself into the cabin. Its crooked mandibles were as long as my arm, and it snapped them as its hairy black legs scrabbled for purchase on the wooden floor.

Before I could do more than gasp, Mia reared back and swung the skillet like a tennis racket, bringing it down onto the bug's head with a sickening crack. I hoped that would end the intruder—after all, its predecessor had gone down easily, and I hadn't struck with nearly as much force as Mia managed. But the bug only shook its head and turned on its assailant, and Mia scrambled back until she hit the wall, holding the skillet between them and panting. "Little help, here!" she cried.

Remembering the weapon in my hand, I ran up from behind the bug and plunged the sword into its back. The monster screeched in pain, and as it writhed, trying to dislodge the blade, one of its wings knocked me off my feet and sent me sliding into the TV stand. Fortunately, Uncle Malachi had never seen the point of upgrading his ancient television, which weighed a good twenty pounds but merely wobbled with the impact instead of toppling onto my head. By the time I picked myself up, the bug was twitching in its death throes, and Mia and I watched from a safe distance until it curled up and lay still.

"Nice aim," she said, approaching for a better look, then paused and frowned at the corpse. "Uh, Suze? I think it's on fire."

I yanked the sword free from the blackening, smoking wound. "Did that with Gorgeous, too. Maybe there's something about this sword…"

"Gee, you think?" Mia took it from me, squinted at the blade as she twirled it, then wiped it clean of ichor on the cooling body and dropped it on the table. "Okay, let's be logical about this."

"*Logical?*" I echoed with an incredulous laugh. "What logic? We've been attacked by two—count them, *two*—monsters tonight, and who knows where they've come from or what they are, and we are *very* far from town, and—"

"Sit down."

She pointed to the kitchen table with the skillet, and I slumped into a chair, the flood of adrenaline making my hands tremble. While I caught my breath, Mia poured more of Uncle Malachi's bourbon into fresh glasses and joined me. "Let me get this straight," she said as I slugged back a shot. "You came home tonight, and the sword was at the door?"

"Yeah."

"You haven't been taking fencing lessons behind my back, have you?"

"Nope." The bourbon burned, but it gave me something to focus on besides the dead bug. I thought of hosing down the monster with roach spray to be certain it was dead, then bit back my rising giggle. Hysterics wouldn't help the situation.

"Didn't think so," she continued. "So, I clocked that thing with a high-speed skillet, and it was like a love tap.

You took off Gorgeous's arm and stabbed both of those things, and they were left with smoking holes in them and died quickly. Is that about right?"

"More or less," I mumbled.

"Then I guess it *is* the sword. Maybe there's something about it that those things can't stand. Like, you know, werewolves and silver? Fairies and iron?"

I cut my eyes to the bug and the spreading black puddle beneath it. "You think *that's* a fairy?"

Mia made a face. "God, I hope not. And if it were, shouldn't cast iron have left a dent?" She considered the bug as she drank her nerve tonic, then put her empty glass aside and rose from the table. "What do we do with contestant number two? There's no more room in the freezer."

I pushed back my chair and stood on wobbly legs. "We leave it for morning. I'm going to bed."

"You know it's still bleeding out, yeah?"

"I can't clean up after two bodies in one night," I replied, and shuffled off to the bedroom with the sword. "You coming?"

"Well, I'm sure as hell not staying alone in here," said Mia, hurrying after me with the emergency skillet in hand.


We left the chandelier glowing, hoping that the well-lit cabin would serve as a deterrent to prowling monstrosities.

Unfortunately, it seemed to have the opposite effect.

Shortly before dawn, Mia bolted upright when something threw itself against the cabin door, rattling the windows in their frames. "Shit," she hissed, reaching for the skillet on her bedside table. "Get up, Suze, we've got company."

Sword at the ready, I took point as we crept back into the main room. As I peered through the nearest window, I could make out the silhouette of something large and dark beating against the door. Given our handiwork, I guessed that we had perhaps a minute before it broke in.

"What's the code to the gun safe?" Mia whispered.

"Tell you later." I darted past the shaking door, gripped the sword with both hands, and had just taken a steadying breath when the hinges gave way for the second time that night. The beast on the threshold could have been Gorgeous's twin, but I only examined it long enough to be sure it wasn't a confused hiker before I ran it though. Roaring in agony and clutching the hilt, it staggered backward like a hammy actor in his death scene until it toppled off the porch and died in the weeds.

Mia stood with me in the doorway until it stopped twitching, and then I yanked the sword from the smoking corpse. "Get your keys," I said as I cleaned the blade on a patch of monkey grass. "We're getting the hell out of here. I don't know if a secret government lab was just breached or what, but I'm not staying out in the woods to be eaten."

"Guns first," she replied. "In case this *is* the monster apocalypse, I'd like something more effective than cookware."

I'd never cared for guns—Uncle Malachi's safety presentation had backfired when he'd accidentally traumatized me with graphic photos of injuries—but Mia had no such qualms. As I gathered our purses, she packed up Uncle Malachi's shotgun, filled a duffel bag with boxes of ammunition, and belted on his hunter's sidearm. When I emerged, she looked ready for a shootout. "Can you use those?" I asked.

She nodded. "Shotgun, no problem. Now, I've never shot with anything like this bad boy," she said, patting the pistol on her hip, "but the principle's the same as with the one I know." Seeing my confusion, she elaborated, "My mom trained me on a .38. This thing's a .454 Casull."

"That's…bigger?"

"The rounds are. A .38 is a pretty standard sidearm. *This* thing is a bear gun."

"The joys of backcountry living," I muttered,

shouldering my bag. Sword in hand, I stepped out beneath the lightening predawn sky and searched for creatures in the trees. The morning was still, and I made out the shape of my sedan, unharmed where I'd parked it. Mia and I loaded our vehicles, and we'd just begun the awkward dance of turning two cars around in the clearing when something built like a gorilla, with horns like a trophy buck, thundered out of the woods. He spotted us and roared, revealing three-inch fangs strung with saliva, and I screamed as I groped for the sword on the passenger side.

But Mia was in the lead car, and she was quicker. Before the creature could lumber two steps, she'd rolled down her window and taken aim. She waited until the beast was within a yard of her Toyota, then shot it between the eyes.

Given the bug's non-reaction to the iron skillet, I'd worried that perhaps the thing would be impervious to gunfire, somehow armored against projectiles.

I needn't have been concerned. While a blow from a pan could be shrugged off, it was generally difficult to keep going with a quarter of one's head missing. The monster fell dead in the leaves, and Mia leaned out her window to yell at me, "Gun's got a wicked kick, but I think I like this one!"

"It's yours!" I called back. "Drive!"

Not until we reached the paved road did I stop staring in my rearview mirror, expecting to find an army of horrors emerging from the shadows to gallop after us.

We locked the doors of my house *and* threw the deadbolt—an unusual step in a town as small as the Crossing, but Mia and I were taking no chances. Once the windows were secured, the blinds drawn, and a loveseat pushed in front of the fireplace, we sank onto the couch and stared at each other. Mia looked exhausted and grungy. Her tall, stick-thin frame slumped, and her blonde hair fell greasy and snarled over her shoulders. She'd changed into one of her trademark oversized shirts before bed, and it seemed to hang from her like a weighted sack. I could only assume I appeared no better—I was pudgier than Mia, certainly, frizzy brunette to her dirty blonde, and sporting loungewear that was at least in the neighborhood of my correct size, but I was similarly unprepared for polite company.

After a long moment, she mumbled, "We've got to tell someone."

The new mayor—Joel Rogers, who'd been Dad's lieutenant for a decade—was a cheery fellow with great plans to improve the local schools and boost lake tourism. I liked him well enough, but I couldn't see him doing anything more helpful than pacing City Hall. "Chief Brundage?" I asked Mia.

She shook her head. "Even if he called the sheriff and got together a posse to help search the woods, how many people would that be? Four? Five?"

There were, I mused, and not for the first time, certain drawbacks to growing up in a small, rural community. Dad had never had a cross word with the county sheriff, but the reality of the situation was that only two deputies ever patrolled at once, driving in lazy circles around the back roads unless a call went out. The Crossing's whole police force was the chief and his two junior officers, and those few other hamlets in the area with police wouldn't have been able to offer a half-dozen cops among them.

"Then who?" I replied. "We can't just call out the National Guard by ourselves."

Whatever suggestion Mia might have offered was cut short by a rapping on the front door.

We jumped up at the sound and looked at each other. "Gorgeous and friends didn't knock," Mia reminded me sotto voce, though her hand went to the butt of the pistol at her hip.

I forced myself to creep to the door, then turned the

lock, threw back the bolt, and prayed that whatever was on the welcome mat wasn't about to disembowel me before I flung open the door...only to find Ms. Quince waiting with an old-fashioned Tupperware cake box in her arms. "Good morning, Susan," she began, offering me a tight smile as the silver filaments in her neatly coiffed brown hair winked in the morning sun. "May I come in? I brought breakfast."

Though I was in no mood for a social visit, I *was* starving, and Ms. Quince had the grace not to comment on my appearance. Stepping aside, I admitted her to the house, but I locked the door behind her.

My neighbor paused in the foyer, taking in the tactical redecoration Mia and I had done that morning, then put the cake box down and pointed to the loveseat. "Good instinct to block that entrance, but your choice of barricade is ineffective. Much wiser to build a fire if you want to stop fireplace entry."

"It's *May*," Mia replied.

Ms. Quince fixed her with a gray-eyed stare. "My dear, this house has central air conditioning. I should think you could remain both comfortable and secure with the aid of the climate-control system. Here, let me show you."

As her no-nonsense tone washed over us, Mia and I seemed to simultaneously realize that Ms. Quince was unfazed by our precautions—indeed, that she expected them. After sharing another look with Mia, I interrupted my neighbor as she fiddled with the gas jets. "Uh...Ms. Quince? Can I ask you something?"

The flames roared to life, blue where they emerged from the pipes into the fake logs. "You may ask whatever you like," she replied. "Whether I answer is another matter. Now, what would you like to know?"

"What the hell is going on?"

She straightened and pushed the loveseat back into the place where Dad had always kept it, the deep depressions in the rug guiding her work. "The same thing that's been going on here for centuries."

"No, you don't understand," I babbled, "we were out at the cabin last night, and there were these *things*, and—"

"And you were gifted that blade," she interrupted, gesturing toward the sword I'd left lying on the sideboard. "I assure you, child, that I understand. Mia, why don't you get some plates and silverware? Napkins, if you can manage. Susan...you'd best sit."

I perched on the edge of the couch and watched my neighbor bring the cake box to the coffee table. The lifted lid revealed Ms. Quince's blueberry crumb cake, legendary at town picnics and bake sales, but something in the set of her jaw and the way she looked at everything but me dulled my appetite. When Mia returned, armed with Dad's everyday dishes and a roll of paper towels, Ms. Quince doled out our breakfast, took a seat in a blue antique wingback chair, and sighed. "Malachi and I were so hoping this wouldn't happen."

Hearing her mention my uncle reminded me that I wasn't alone in my fresh grief. Though Uncle Malachi and Ms. Quince had never publicly been a couple, rumors had swirled for as long as I could remember. People had hoped—there had *always* been a Cole in the Crossing, and as Dad never showed interest in marriage, Uncle Malachi had been the last, best hope for a true heir. The town had even been willing to overlook the fact that Ardith Quince wasn't native to the area...though when, exactly, she had moved to the Crossing had been forgotten, so seamlessly had she integrated. Ms. Quince was polite, a considerate neighbor, and kind to children, the watchful eyes when I'd played alone in the yard, and I hadn't minded that she was sweet on Uncle Malachi. But nothing ever came of it. The two remained friends, and she drove out into the woods to visit him several mornings every week, but Uncle Malachi never mentioned marriage—at least not within earshot of me.

And now, of course, it was too late.

She seemed composed as she contemplated the untouched cake on her plate, and I suspected that whatever grief she felt wouldn't be shared with us. Ms. Quince seldom discussed herself—she wouldn't even tell her age, deeming the question rude—and matters of the heart were so much more personal. But as much as manners dictated that I should try to offer her comfort, maybe put on coffee and give her photos of Uncle Malachi, the more overwhelming problem of lurking monstrosities made me a poor hostess that morning.

"What *are* those things?" Mia asked around a mouthful of blueberry cake. Blessed and cursed with a fast metabolism, my friend stayed hungry and didn't pass up meals, monsters be damned.

Ms. Quince said nothing for a long, tense moment, then looked up from her plate and finally held my gaze. "Outsiders."

The word made my head buzz, and it took a second to understand why: the sounds my neighbor had made were nothing at all like the ones I'd heard. Mia looked puzzled, but Ms. Quince only watched me with a sad, weary smile.

"Outsiders," she said again—and mercifully, the sound and sense coordinated when she spoke. "But I believe you understood me the first time." Seeing my confusion, she pointed to my bandaged hand. "Burned yourself, did you?"

"I…um…" Exhausted and less sure of my footing by the moment, I found myself stretching my hand toward her as if expecting a kiss on a boo-boo. "The sword was hot."

She gently unwrapped my hand, revealing the previous night's injury. To my surprise, the red brand had faded to pale white lines, a faint tattoo that almost disappeared into the creases of my palm.

"A powerful symbol," she murmured, turning my hand in the shaded room to catch the light slipping past the blinds. "The mark on the sword was imbued with a charm allowing the Watcher to understand all tongues and be understood in turn."

I blinked as I tried to make sense of that. "Sorry...*what?*"

"Don't just listen, watch my lips. Susan, what I'm about to tell you will be difficult to hear, and I don't like it any more than you do. But the sword has chosen the new Watcher, and..." She paused and smiled again as my eyes widened. "It's a strange sensation, but you'll adjust soon enough. If you merely listen instead of trying to read the other speaker's face, your mind won't be so scrambled." Turning to Mia, she added, "That sounded like gibberish, I assume."

Mia nodded, her cheeks stuffed with cake.

"What the hell..." I whispered, staring at my marked hand. Though Ms. Quince's words had made perfect sense to me, her mouth had failed to synchronize with the sounds I thought I was hearing.

"You would call it magic," said Ms. Quince, settling back in her chair. "The term I was taught as a child translates as 'speaking to the Aen.' Slightly more poetic, but 'magic' will do." We goggled at her, and she shrugged. "There's no easy way to have this conversation, girls. Magic exists in worlds beyond the one you know, and Susan...well, my dear, you've been chosen to protect them."

I saw pity in her eyes.


**D**ad had always kept a wipe-off board on the fridge for grocery lists and quick notes. Ms. Quince swiped clean my reminder to buy more peanut butter and held the board against her crooked arm as if she were reading us a picture book. Using the attached purple marker, she drew four circles at the cardinal directions, then inscribed a circle within them and added another just outside their radius, trapping the four circles in a band. "This is the Aen," she said, coloring in the connecting band for contrast.

I found that if I focused intently, I could hear the word she spoke as well as its sense: *breath*.

"Think of it as a river," she continued as she finished her shading. "A poor illustration, but suitable for now. And these four worlds are like islands in the stream. Kopaat, Ildon, Ga'besh, and Honslia," she said, tapping each of the circles in turn. "They have other names, just as there are other words for the Aen, but if one mentions Ildon, anyone born of the four worlds will know of what one speaks."

True, Ms. Quince's lecture sounded like lunacy, but having survived a night at the cabin and discovered the strange sword's alleged gift, I was willing to listen.

"But what's this Aen thingy?" Mia asked.

"An energy flows through it—it's an etheric beltway," Ms. Quince explained. "And many of the peoples of these worlds that are bathed in the Aen can manipulate their environment using its power. Again, you would call this magic."

She paused and gave us both a long look, but I was too tired and strung-out to argue, and Mia seemed to be in the same emotional boat.

"The only way to move between the worlds is through…well, you might call them tunnels," she continued. "That's the best translation I can offer of our word for them. The Common Elvish is something like 'the lightning through stone,' but their terms are usually odd—"

I lifted a finger to stop her. "Wait—*Elvish*?"

"Patience, I'll get there. As I was saying, these tunnels allow travel among the four worlds. They appear at random—you might think of sinkholes. They're useful when they form, and they've allowed the peoples of our worlds to mingle and spread. Fantastic for trade and the sharing of knowledge, but dangerous, too."

"Wars?" asked Mia, halfway through her second piece of cake.

"Not as often as you'd think. We've seldom attacked each other's ancestral territories, and border disputes are usually confined to one world. Well, I mean, there was the War of the True Children about a century ago," she mused, "and *that* was a multi-world disaster, but in general, the danger from the tunnels isn't each other. It's the Outsiders we fear."

"The things at the cabin..." I began.

"Let me guess: they came sniffing around in the dark, and they looked like something out of your nightmares?" Mia and I nodded emphatically, and Ms. Quince sighed. "Creatures from beyond our worlds, beyond the Aen. Tunnels are weak points, and Outsiders find ways to slip through. They're attracted to the Aen—we believe they follow it in search of prey, almost always under cover of darkness."

"But *we're* not part of this Aen thing," I pointed out.

"Technically, no, but this world...well, it is and it isn't affected." Adjusting her grip on the wipe-off board, she added a fifth circle in the center, surrounded by the circle of four, and tapped it with the marker. "You are here. Don't ask me for a more detailed map, girls—our finest scholars have spent lifetimes on the question of our place in the universe, multiverse, whatever it may be, and this is the best they've managed. There are the four worlds of the Aen, the unexplored dangers of the Outside, and your world. It's rather like plopping an island in the middle of an atoll," she added, giving the board an appraising squint. "A barren island, at that. Tunnels have occasionally opened onto this world, but our peoples were reluctant to explore for the longest time. Without the Aen, even the air here feels...*prickly*. Unpleasant until one acclimates. It's been used as a penal world off and on for millennia."

For reasons I couldn't quite state that morning, I bristled at the news. "They don't have the right—"

"I agree, but power is so much more effective than mere right," said Ms. Quince.

"You're a prisoner, then?" Mia interjected.

My neighbor arched a perfectly manicured eyebrow. "Do I *look* like a prisoner to you, Ms. Randolph?"

"Well, no, but you said—"

"I'm an exception. One of my people remains near the Watcher to offer guidance and whatever support we can. I arrived shortly after Malachi inherited the sword, and my exile here is nearly finished. Another of my sisters will be along soon to assist you," she told me. "There would be too many questions if I remained for your lifetime as well as Malachi's."

My head swam as I tried to take in too much at once. Ms. Quince, yet another fixture of my life, was leaving me. She wasn't even human. The monsters of the night before hadn't been the product of a vivid nightmare…

But Mia, at least, seemed to keep it together. "If there's no Aen here, then why do we have a corpse in the cabin freezer?"

Ms. Quince's eyes widened. "I beg your pardon?"

"Couldn't leave it by the door," I mumbled, staring into space.

"Of course not! Use the burn pit out back! If you leave the sword in contact long enough, the body will catch fire—"

"Yeah, well, since no one bothered to deliver instructions with the damn sword, we did the best we could do," Mia snapped. "*You* try waking up to find a giant bug coming down the chimney and see how well you handle it."

"I'm not criticizing," she soothed. "Malachi and Barnaby should have prepared you, Susan. The Watcher has come from your family for generations now, and I warned them that you were a likely candidate, but they convinced themselves you were safe." She muttered a single word under her breath, which my newfound internal translator rendered as a grumpy, "*Men.*"

"You keep saying 'watcher' like that's supposed to

mean something," Mia replied as she cut a third piece of cake.

Ms. Quince waited until Mia had filled her plate, then put the wipe-off board beside her on the couch, her mouth tightening with distaste. "The tunnels I described…very few ever opened onto this world, and you had correspondingly few attacks from Outsiders. We weren't so fortunate. The Aen is like blood in shark-infested water, and as soon as a tunnel opened, the Outsiders would find a way in. We could either force the tunnels closed—terribly taxing in terms of magic, not to mention the loss of a potentially useful connection to another world—or we could continually send soldiers to the tunnel mouths to wait for each wave of invaders. That was the preferred option for a long time, especially near the important tunnels, but Outsiders are notoriously difficult to kill. Defending ourselves was an incredible drain on our fighting forces, in terms of both lives and support. So," she continued with evident reluctance, "about five hundred years ago, our peoples came together and produced a third solution."

The tumblers fell as my frenzied thoughts began to clear. "You sent them *here*."

It might have been my imagination, but I thought I saw her wince at the venom in my voice.

"How could you do that?" Mia demanded, putting her plate aside in her indignation. "There are people here, too, you know—or was all of this a big surprise?" she asked sarcastically, twirling one finger to encompass the shaded room.

Ms. Quince didn't rush to her own defense. "Oh, no, we knew of your existence. Humans have been finding their way to our worlds for ages—several human kingdoms endure today, and many more have fallen to time. No, we knew exactly what we were doing. It was a calculated decision."

"Our lives for yours," I murmured.

She nodded. "We forced open one set of tunnels among our worlds with a common intersection point. You know that old asbestos mine near the cabin with the barbed wire and the warnings signs? Descend to the bottom, walk along, and you'll find the place where the paths off this world cross. We closed every other tunnel, so now all traffic uses your world as a hub."

Mia frowned as she listened. "But if the tunnels are still open onto your worlds, then shouldn't the monsters head your way?"

"We planned for that," said Ms. Quince, who looked less comfortable by the moment. "The tunnels are long, and the weakest point is at their joining place here—we designed it that way so that the Outsiders would take the easy option. And then we planted a source of the Aen here to serve as a beacon to them. The path to the surface of the false mine is quite short, you see, and so that source is the nearest...*attraction* for them." Pointing to the sword on the sideboard, she asked, "May I?"

Warily, I rose and brought it to her, but she didn't remove it from its scabbard. Instead, she held it by its leather sheath and tapped the blue-green gems set in the hilt and pommel. "That, girls, is pure, crystalline Aen, rarer than tanzanite or fine black opals. You have no idea how many gave their lives to forge this weapon. Firebrand, my people call it. In Elvish, it's the Bright Blade. The dwarves know it as Heart's Blood. The humans have various names for it, but Shadowbane is the most common." Her fingertips traced the patterns stitched in the scabbard as if following a labyrinth only they could detect. "Malachi called it the Cole Family Curse."

"Why us?" I asked, watching the gems flash in the light through the blinds.

"That, I'm afraid, is a mystery." She carefully laid the sword on the coffee table, then pivoted on the couch to face me. "The tunnels were constructed long before European settlement of this continent. One of my sisters—not my actual sister, one of my people," she explained, seeing our confusion—"brought the sword here and set it free. It was an attempt to ameliorate what we had done, you see. The Aen crystals in the weapon act as a beacon, but the blade was forged with such workings upon it that it is virtually unstoppable against Outsiders. It burns their flesh better than any fire. And one of those workings allows the sword to choose its wielder—the person best suited to guard the opening to the tunnels. The Watcher."

My stomach twisted. "Uncle Malachi."

"He was the latest. The first Watchers were Native American, and my sisters explained the position as a sacred duty."

"You lied to them," Mia muttered.

"At first, regrettably, yes. Eventually, the Watcher learned the truth, but it made no difference. Once the sword chooses the Watcher, it may as well be a sacred duty. The Watcher guards the Crossing and kills whatever slips through the cracks—he protects this world against the sort of monsters you must have faced last night. And once the sword makes a choice, it is for life."

"*Life*?" I echoed.

Ms. Quince nodded. "The sword's choice cannot be challenged. The weapon belongs to the Watcher until his death—even if it's taken from him, it will find a way to return. You can hide it with ease," she hastened to add before I could interrupt. "Just belt it on and concentrate, and it will be as if nothing is there until it's drawn. Malachi wore it constantly."

I stared at the sword as if it might bite me. Hell, it had branded me once already.

"When Samuel Cole found this place, the Watcher was an old man, sick and dying," she continued. "The sword chose him, and my sister explained what that entailed. He railed against it, but he had no more choice in the matter than any previous Watcher, and so he planted the seeds of this town."

"Cole's Crossing," I murmured. "It's not about the lake…"

"Never was. Anyway, ever since Samuel, the sword has chosen a Cole as the Watcher. Before Malachi, it was his granduncle, Pericles, who lived quite a long time for a human. The sword chose Malachi the day after Pericles's death, when he was about your age," she told me. "He and Barnaby thought you'd be safe from the family curse, but the sword knows what it wants, and it's chosen you."

"But…but I…"

"It's a difficult task, but not without benefits," said Ms. Quince, injecting a note of brightness into her voice. "You have the gift of tongues already. It's possible that you'll develop a bit of minor skill with magic—Malachi did."

"*Huh*?"

"Those crystals," she explained, indicating the sword. "The humans of our worlds are no more naturally gifted in magic than you are, but some use tools to enhance their limited abilities. These tools are forged with crystalline Aen. I was able to teach Malachi a few tricks over the years—nothing remarkable, but for one with no previous ability with magic, he proved a decent student. And there is, in fact, a slight bit of etheric Aen in the Crossing, as it flows through the tunnels. Barely enough to allow me to use any of my gifts, but this *is* a hardship post." She paused, then quietly said, "It's perhaps not my place to speak of such, but of those curious few from our worlds who've settled on yours, most in the last centuries have made their homes in the Crossing because of that trace of Aen. Their bloodlines are diluted now, but I could point to *many* in this town whose heritage is not entirely human. Such news would take *them* by surprise, I'm sure, but I think the Aen has a deep pull on them still. Consider how many of the old families here never leave."

The world around me began to narrow until the glinting hilt seemed to fill my vision, and a rushing noise echoed in my ears like a torrent.

*Never leave.*

Never leave? I had a passport to fill! Adventures to seek out beyond the borders of my hometown! A life to build in…well, in somewhere that wasn't so familiar to me that I could make deliveries in my sleep. Yes, I'd come home, but only for a little while. Putting the store to rights was my duty to Dad, not my lifetime career!

I thought of Uncle Malachi, living alone in the old cabin at the edge of the cave, spending his life killing whatever came out before it could get far. And now that would be me…

"No," I heard myself whisper. "*No.* I don't want it."

Ms. Quince was unruffled by my declaration. "I'm sorry, my dear, but you don't have a choice."

"Says who?" Mia interjected. "What if Suze and I pack up tomorrow and never look back, huh? What are you going to do then?"

"Me? Nothing. But Susan can't leave. To ensure that the pull of the Aen here would always be stronger than the lure at the end of the tunnels, the sword was forged with a…a leash of sorts. The radius is about ten miles. Go beyond that," she told me, "and you'll be struck with debilitating pain."

"How bad?" I asked.

"Malachi told me that he wished he were dead at the time. My predecessor took him to the edge to demonstrate, and it's my job to take you. I have no intention of doing so," she added as Mia and I started to protest. She rose, straightened her blouse, and looked down at us. "The sword has never before chosen a woman. I know this comes as an unpleasant shock, Susan, but I would be remiss in my duty if I failed to remind you that the sword clearly sees something in you, and the sacrifice you make as the Watcher will protect billions of lives, both here and in the worlds of the Aen. It's a noble calling, even if it's not the one you would choose."

My eyes started to fill, but Mia exploded. "*Fuck* your 'noble calling'! You made us your dumping ground, you've cursed Suze, it's not fair, it's not *right*—"

"I never said it was," said Ms. Quince, and softly sighed. "Enjoy the rest of the cake—I seem to have no appetite. I'm off to scatter Malachi's ashes, and then I'll be on my way, I should think. One of my sisters will be here soon to assist you, Susan. Perhaps in a day or two."

I watched in horrified silence as she walked to the door, but as she opened it to the warm morning, she turned back and faintly smiled at me. "You know, there's a funny thing about the leash on the sword. We always demonstrate to the Watcher what happens if he goes beyond its boundary, but we never tell him that the leash only exists on *this* world. Odd little oversight, that. Ah, well. You take care, now, dear. Good luck," she said, and closed the door behind her.

# CHAPTER 3

I tried to tell Mia that she didn't have to come back to the cabin with me. After all, it was entirely possible that Ms. Quince was nuts—even if I did seem to have acquired a familiarity with at least one theretofore unknown language—and both of us were dragging after the long night. But Mia wouldn't let me go alone. "I'm not making you haul corpses by yourself," she said as she packed up the rest of the cake. "Get some grocery bags, will you? There's not much food out there."

I picked through my pantry, not planning for meals so much as survival rations, and loaded the car with emergency flashlights and a smattering of Dad's tools from the garage. As I reached for the sword, however, Mia said, "Leave it."

"You sure?" I frowned, my hand hesitating above the table. "Uncle Malachi doesn't have another bear gun."

"Little experiment," she muttered, then waited by her car while I locked up.

We drove separately back to the cabin—having watched dozens of horror movies on my laptop during our frequent high school sleepovers, we saw the benefit of not relying upon a lone escape vehicle—and Mia took the lead through the woods. When we pulled off the paved road, I reached toward the passenger seat to stop the bags of gear from jostling to the floor, only for my fingers to brush against something unexpected. I glanced to the right and almost drove into a tree before yanking my hand away from the sword and spinning the car back onto the trail.

A few moments later, I parked behind Mia, jumped out, and pointed to my unexpected cargo. "It's in there!" I cried as she unfolded herself from her seat. "I swear I left it on the table, but it's *there*!"

She peeked in my open door, noted the sword propped against the window, and grunted. "Goddamn."

"It followed me!"

"And Ms. Quince might have been telling the truth." She leaned against my car and swept her oily bangs from her face in agitation. "*Shit*."

"So what does this mean, I'm screwed?" I pulled the sword out and grabbed a bungee cord from my trunk, which I used as a makeshift belt. As soon as the hooks locked together, the hilt and scabbard vanished—even I could no longer sense the weapon bumping against me unless I concentrated. "*Look* at this!" I cried, gesturing to the seemingly empty air beside my left leg. "I've got a fucking magical sword! What the hell am I supposed to *do*?"

As my panic began to spike, Mia raised a hand to still me. "First thing is I call Antoinette with an acute case of food poisoning. Then we get rid of the bodies. We can't keep carrion around the house."

"Hang on, wait," I protested as she plucked her phone from her purse. "This isn't your mess. Why don't you stay at the house in town until I figure things out here?"

"Like hell, Suze."

Ignoring my insistence that she return to civilization, Mia left a graphic message on her boss's voicemail concerning the present state of her digestive tract, then shoved the phone back into its pocket and headed for the cabin, stepping around the corpse in the weeds. "Where's this burn pit, anyway?" she called as I hurried after her.

The answer, we discovered, was behind the cabin, as far from the door as one could go. Uncle Malachi had constructed a ring of stones large enough to comfortably encircle a feral hog, and the dirt within was swept almost clean of debris—all but a few drifting leaves and streaks of fine gray ash. It would do, we decided, then cursed my uncle when we realized he hadn't kept a wheelbarrow on the premises.

We donned whatever protective gear we could scrounge together to tackle the corpse out front. Mia called dibs on Uncle Malachi's thick grilling mitts, while I improvised with a pair of kitchen garbage bags tied onto my arms. I looked like a deranged Christmas pageant angel and smelled of artificial lilac, but at least the dripping ichor stayed off my skin. Once we'd added ski masks to our ensembles to help with the stench of death, I grabbed the monster under the arms, Mia hoisted his legs, and we made our ungainly way around the cabin to dispose of our victim.

With a final grunt, we dropped him in the stone ring and stepped back. "Where's the firewood?" Mia asked, her voice muffled through the thick wool.

"Don't think we need it," I replied, then carefully peeled off my right garbage bag, which by then was stained and slick with sweat. Tossing it onto the body—there was no way I was taking it back into the house—I reached for the invisible sword at my side. I hesitated as my fingers found the hilt, but the metal felt...well, *right* in my hand, neither hot nor cold. With a deep breath and a knotting stomach, I pulled the blade free, then plunged it into the monster. The fresh wound began to smoke almost on impact, and within thirty seconds, flames licked over the creature's skin. I held the sword steady until the heat grew too strong to bear, then pulled it free and stood by Mia until the preternatural blaze had reduced the corpse to charred bone and ash.

"Convenient," she said as the wind began to scatter the homemade cremains.

I rolled my stiff shoulders, then coughed when the breeze sent a blast of acrid smoke toward my face. "One down. Headshot, Wasp, or Gorgeous?"

Mia's reply was unintelligible with her ski mask, but I could make a solid guess.

With a fresh plastic arm covering in place, I helped her haul the remaining three monsters into the pit and set them alight. We'd finished our gristly work by noon, and Mia dropped her gore-soaked mitts on the porch as she stomped inside. "I call shower," she said, and disappeared into the bedroom before I could argue with her. She took her sweet time, eventually emerging in a cloud of steam that smelled like Uncle Malachi's drugstore shampoo and clove soap, and once I'd done my part to drain the hot water tank and dried off, I found her unconscious on the bed, wearing the proper pajamas she hadn't bothered to change into the night before and sleeping with her wet hair splayed on her towel-covered pillow. I managed to find a semi-clean pair of leggings and a T-shirt, and I dropped the sword onto the rug beside me as I collapsed onto the mattress and knew no more.

I woke with a start to the sound of movement in the kitchen, the shuffle of feet on the wooden floor and the banging of cabinets, and I scrambled to untangle myself from the blankets before something huge could find and devour me. By the time my feet hit the ground and I squatted to grab the sword and take cover, I recognized Mia's tuneless humming like an idling engine under the percussion, and my heart slowed from its sprinter's pace. I wasn't about to die. Mia was just hungry.

With the immediate rush of danger past, I took stock of the bedroom. The light had shifted through the window—late afternoon, I guessed—and in the golden haze, I saw that our dirty clothes still lay in twin heaps just inside the attached bath. Mia's towel remained where she had dropped it, damp and wrinkled on her pillow. The bungee belt I'd rigged waited for me on the thin rug. Though I felt like an idiot walking around the house with a weapon on, my paranoia from the night before insisted that I take precautions.

When I padded into the main room, I found Mia still rummaging through the cabinets, though not the pantry. Judging by the sad state of the blueberry cake on the counter, she'd eaten her fill before beginning her search. "Looking for something?" I asked, my voice froggy with sleep.

Mia turned and smiled grimly. "Going to rig a warning system. Did Malachi keep any bells out here?"

"Bells?"

"Yeah, like those little Christmas jingle bells. No?"

"Why would he—"

"Eh, never mind. We'll manage." She nodded to the collection of pans, glasses, and mugs she'd amassed on the table. "We string these up nice and taut around the cabin, and when something trips into the line, we hear it—maybe a clanging, maybe something breaks. That way, we have time to get ready before the monsters find us."

"Unless they can fly," I pointed out.

"Try to be positive, Suze. Going to help me before it gets dark?"

Using the twine and fishing line we found in the closet, Mia and I hung up our kitchenware-festooned alarm wire about ten feet from the cabin, making the old place look a little like a ritual murder site from a found-footage movie, then retreated indoors to prepare for the coming night.

By sunset, we were as ready as we could be. Mia had inspected and loaded all of Uncle Malachi's guns, which she left placed strategically around the cabin, banking on our hope that creatures with claws and fangs wouldn't immediately perceive firearms as weapons. I kept the sword strapped on and practiced until I could pull it from its hilt in an almost fluid motion. Though that was a poor substitute for actual competence with the blade, at least I looked less awkward in my fumbling. We couldn't risk turning on the TV and missing the warning jangle outside, so Mia and I settled in with Uncle Malachi's old Scrabble set and made our halfhearted attempt at fun.

It was a three-letter-word sort of night, as my mind was anywhere but on the game. Was this really my future? Me and the quiet cabin in the middle of the woods, far even from the limited excitement of town, cut off entirely from the wider world? My sightseeing list was long and barely struck through—Paris, London, Rome, Tokyo, Reykjavik, and a hundred other entries remained pristine on my mental page, places I'd hoped to see for myself. I wanted to stand on a romantically windswept hill by the North Atlantic, trace the Southern Cross from Sydney, buy a telephoto lens for a safari in the Maasai Mara, trek up to Machu Picchu. I'd be twenty-three in less than a month, and though grief had brought me home, the world was once again beginning to open to me...and just as suddenly, the door had been slammed in my face.

No wonder Uncle Malachi had wanted his ashes scattered on the lake. The thought of continuing his imprisonment must have been unbearable.

*Ten miles.* Ten paltry miles. I doubted I'd even be able to make it to the big grocery store outside the Crossing, much less the California sunset I'd planned to watch from San Francisco someday. I'd never travel again, never meet anyone from outside my hometown...never marry, never have a family...and when Mia left, as she surely would, I'd be on my own.

Was this it? Was this what my life had become? Sleepless nights with a sword by my side, subsisting on deliveries from town and the occasional glimpse of the world beyond the woods?

Or maybe not. Sure, Ms. Quince seemed to be on to something with the sword and its...*unusual*...properties, but maybe the night before had been a horrible fluke. Maybe there was no magical barrier like an invisible dog fence penning me in here. Maybe I wasn't condemned...

A thump on the roof yanked me from my thoughts,

and Mia looked up at the shower of dust descending from the rafters. "Had to be a flier, didn't it?" she muttered, reaching for the bear gun as the footsteps above us headed for the chimney.

"I didn't *want* to be right!" I protested as we took up positions around the fireplace. My palm began to sweat as I tightened my grip on the sword. "What's the plan?"

"Cover me."

Before I could suggest a better plan, something that put at least a table between us and the invader, a furry, mottled gray monstrosity with taloned feet and wings like a bat landed in a crouch on the dusty hearth. It ducked to fit through the opening, and as soon as its wolfish head came into view, Mia calmly fired twice. Once would have been more than sufficient—if the shot hadn't removed a good chunk of the creature's skull, the splinters sent flying as the bullet embedded itself in the stone would have done damage—but neither of us was taking any chances. The thing slumped without a whimper, and as my ears rang from the close-range gunshots, I got a look at the blast of gore left inside the fireplace, a black splotch over the lighter soot stains.

"Oh, God," I mumbled, tasting something sour at the back of my throat.

"Stay with me," Mia snapped, and holstered her weapon. She approached the creature and gave it a strong kick, but it was well and truly dead. Satisfied, she dragged it into the room by its feet, then nodded to the door. "Let's get this one burning. Maybe its buddies will think twice, eh?"

I didn't want to help her carry the corpse outside—hell, I barely wanted to be anywhere but kneeling in front of a clean toilet—but I wrapped my arms in fresh garbage bags and grabbed the monster's shoulders, sending a twinge of pain through my overworked muscles. Soon enough, the thing was alight in the burn pit, and Mia waited until I'd sloughed off the bags to high-five me. "And *that* is how you do it," she began. "All we need now are marshmallows…"

Her voice faded at the sound of breaking glass, and in seconds, we'd drawn our weapons again and were scanning the darkness for movement. The flickering bonfire didn't help when it sent shadows dancing from tree to tree, but at least it illuminated the four pairs of glowing eyes watching us from the woods.

"It was a good try," I muttered. "At least the alarm rope worked." Edging closer to her, I asked, "How many bullets does that gun hold?"

"Five."

"So you've got three left?"

"Yep."

I noted the position of the eyes around us. "There's two monsters at nine and eleven, one at two, and the one at four is coming closer to his buddy. You go left, I go right."

"You sure?" Mia asked.

"Positive," I replied, trying to sound confident, and charged.

As the gun thundered behind me, I ran at the nearer of the monsters, raising my sword and bellowing what I hoped was an intimidating war cry. In retrospect, I probably just sounded crazed and a touch on the hysterical side, and my handling of the weapon was less than graceful. My only saving grace was the fact that it burned so well on contact with the creatures—had I been relying on actual skill, I'd have been ripped to shreds. Disappointingly for a magical sword, it sure as hell didn't enhance my combat abilities.

So pleased was I to have one monster dead that I forgot his approaching comrade, who reminded me of his presence with a screech and a slash of claws against my face. I screamed and ducked, then blindly swung the sword until it hit flesh and stuck. My victim howled in agony, and I yelled back at him, by turns terrified and enraged.

It was Mia who talked me down, who grabbed me by the shoulders and shook me until I stopped making animalistic sounds, who helped me carry the bodies into the fire pit and feed the blaze. With the night aglow, she ushered me back inside, reloaded her gun, then washed my wounds with water and alcohol while I hissed and tried to hold still.

"The good news," she said, dabbing at a deep cut across my cheek, "is that he missed your eye."

My peremptory wince when she reached for the brown bottle again didn't stay her hand. "And the bad?"

Mia soaked a cotton ball and pressed it against the bleeding wound. "You should probably go to a hospital. I'm worried about scarring."

I laughed in spite of my burning face. "*What* hospital? Ten miles, right? That's all I get! We can call Dr. Nichols and tell her I fell on a trowel or something, but if she wants me to go to the ER…"

"Shit," Mia muttered, and finished her painful work in silence.

I won't say I woke at dawn because I never truly went to sleep that night. Nothing else came hunting us in the wee hours, but I was too wired to rest, and neither Mia nor I could focus enough to complete our abandoned Scrabble game. But at first light, I gave up on the pretense of sleep and pushed back the blankets of Uncle Malachi's bed while Mia snorted and rolled over against the glow through the blinds.

*My* bed now.

I made a cup of tea in the old microwave and stared out the window at the burn pit. Nothing but ash remained of our night's work, and even that was beginning to scatter in the spring breeze. Turning from that unpleasant reminder, I bobbed my teabag and gazed around the main room of the cabin: the well-worn furniture, the scuffed wooden floor, the bright white streaks of fresh caulking against the dark window frames, a bandage against the shifting of the settling building.

This was to be my prison, then. These were my cell walls, to decorate in any way I pleased—assuming said decoration could be found in or brought to the Crossing, that is. This rough-hewn cabin was to be my living quarters for the rest of my life, a camp far from the center of town where I would spend my nights guarding against monsters from another world that should never have been our problem. I'd been shackled to a sword that was drawing the creatures in and told to kill them, and I would do so from now until the day I dropped dead.

My hands clenched on my mug until my fingers began to whiten.

Ms. Quince's people and the rest of those bastards, whoever they were, had made our world their dumping ground. *They* slept soundly while ravenous horrors invaded my town. *They* ruined Uncle Malachi's life, just as they were going to ruin mine, and the best they could offer in compensation was a few pitying looks and a blueberry cake from a representative sent to make the best of a "hardship post"?

No.

*No.*

I was still standing by the sink, staring into space with my cooling tea mug, when Mia shuffled in, sleep-mussed and spittle-crusted. "You okay?" she asked.

"Nothing about this is okay."

"True," she replied, opening the fridge, "but at least there isn't a body in the freezer this morning." She pulled out the orange juice and plucked a glass from the cupboard. "Did you get any sleep?"

"Not much."

She grunted as she poured. "Go back to bed. I'll keep an eye out for creeping horrors."

But I shook my head. "I can't do this, Mia."

"I know," she said, her voice gentle. "It sucks, and it's not fair. Maybe when Ms. Quince's replacement gets here, we can figure out some way to make the sword choose a new person."

"I'm not waiting that long."

Mia stiffened, and she left the juice carton uncapped as she hurried across the kitchen toward me. "Let's not be hasty, okay? Suicide is *not* the answer—"

I stopped her advance with a hand to her shoulder. "Who said anything about suicide?"

Her forehead wrinkled into deep furrows. "I...you said..."

"I said I'm not waiting." A quick moment's concentration made the sword strapped over my pajamas visible once more, and I smiled as I patted the scabbard. "Thought I'd take this damn thing back to where it came from. Make it someone else's problem."

"What about the ten-mile limit?"

My smile curled toward a smirk. "You heard Ms. Quince: it only applies on *this* side of the tunnels. And if I go now, before her replacement gets here, then maybe I'll have a chance to get some answers."

Mia took a step away from me, and I watched as a slow grin spread across her face. "Ardith Quince, you sneaky *bitch*."

"I know, right?" I took a sip of my over-brewed tea and dumped the remainder in the sink. "It's worth a shot. Maybe it's my only shot. And once the sword's out of here, the monsters will have no reason to mosey on over, and you can go to work today without fear of disembowelment."

She snorted and returned to her juice. "What're you talking about?"

"Aren't you supposed to be working Sunday lunch?"

"Sure, but that was before you announced this little field trip."

Had I still been holding my mug, I'd have dropped it.

"Wait, no," I said in a rush, "this is a solo mission—"

"Bullshit." She drained her glass and waited while I babbled my protestations, then interrupted with a simple, "I'm going, Suze. End of discussion. If you're planning to spit in Destiny's face, then I'll have your back. That's what friends are for."

"Giving each other rides and maybe a couch to crash on is what friends are for," I retorted. "Loaning twenty bucks and not expecting it repaid, maybe. Plant-sitting. Taking a cursed magical sword back to an unknown, probably hostile world while pursued by a pack of nameless horrors—"

"Is how we're ending this weekend." Mia poured herself a refill and shrugged as I stuttered. "I'll call Antoinette and explain that the food poisoning appears to be norovirus. So, what do we have in the way of camping gear?"

In general, expeditions aren't spur-of-the-moment events. Wise, experienced explorers take time to plan for their basic needs and the likely contingencies before striking out. I'd seen pictures of backcountry hikers with packs half as large as they were carefully stuffed with clothes, food, shelter, and medical supplies. A trip into uncharted territory would require weapons as well, either for defense or to bring down food when the stocks ran low—and if those weapons were firearms, then someone would have to carry the heavy ammunition so as not to render the guns quickly useless.

But I didn't have time to waste on such trivialities as careful preparation. Fearing what might transpire when Ms. Quince's colleague arrived to babysit and fed up from two nights of attacks, I was determined to leave that day, and Mia proved to be a willing enabler.

Neither of us was an outdoors aficionado, and before that morning, my inclination to camp began with a cheap motel and ended with a futon. Uncle Malachi's closets offered little in the way of gear beyond his weapons cache, and as Dad had never seen the appeal in roughing it, either, the only solution was an emergency shopping trip. While I couldn't escape to the sporting goods superstore fifteen miles outside of town, Mia cheerfully borrowed my debit card and set off with the list we'd thrown together over breakfast, promising to return with everything we'd need for a few days in the wilderness.

Around lunchtime, she rumbled back to the cabin, her trunk loaded with white shopping bags. "How are we supposed to carry all of this?" I demanded, staring down at the sea of handles.

"The clerk claimed that everything compresses. Trust me, I found someone who *likes* this crap," she replied, loading bags onto her arms. "I told him we were going to hike the AT for a week this summer. Big mistake—the guy's through-hiked it twice, and he had so many stories that I almost couldn't make it out of the store. Here, help me with these."

While I finished making soup and sandwiches, Mia unpacked her haul and began the tedious process of snipping away tags and plastic ties. I watched as she separated the gear into three piles: one for each of us, and a larger one of communal items. She'd purchased a pair of dark green camping backpacks, the sort that came with all manner of straps and waterproof covers, and attachable sleeping bags that I sincerely hoped would puff up once they were unrolled from their tight casings. A good multi-season waterproof jacket landed beside each of our piles, followed by half a six-pack of thick socks. The middle pile grew larger as she worked: cooking gear, plates and utensils, matches, pocketknives, a small hatchet, clothesline, a water purifier, extra bags, a first-aid kit, a second kit just for snakebites, and a book of camping tips and techniques. As I set the table, she carried the ammunition out of the closet and added it to her pile, along with a cleaning kit for her pistol. "We'll find a way to squish it all in after lunch," she declared, and joined me. "Add a few shirts and pants, and we'll be golden."

I eyed the spread while we ate. "Shampoo?"

"Dry shampoo. I got some little cans, plus baby wipes—and a good bandana can do wonders to hide the mess. We can divvy it all up."

"What about shoes?"

Mia shrugged while she chewed a bite of her sandwich. "The guy said it wouldn't be a great idea to get new shoes for a last-minute trip. I mean, yeah, proper hiking boots would be ideal, but not if you're breaking them in and getting blistered. I've got my winter boots—at least they're waterproof. You?"

"It's either those or decorative cowboy, so not much choice." I looked over the gear, struck by a fresh pang of guilt. "Mia, listen, this is really amazing of you, but—"

"I'm going, and that's final." She brushed the crumbs off her hands and grinned. "Okay, let's get cracking. Did I mention I bought instant coffee and teabags?"

An hour later, our bags were loaded down and strapped tight, and I'd exchanged my trusty phone for one of Uncle Malachi's watches, which wouldn't have to be recharged to be of use. Ignoring the tendrils of fear that seemed to snake through my limbs like icy vines, I texted Annie Plunkett, saying only that I was taking an impromptu trip out of town and to carry on at the store without me. Her response was quick, an admonition to have a nice time and reassurance that the store would still be standing when I returned.

I wished I had her confidence.

With my affairs squared away for at least a few days, I locked the cabin door, double-checked my car, then hid the keys under a flowerpot and shifted the unfamiliar weight of my pack, which I suspected was going to be a pain before long. "Ready?" I asked Mia.

"Ready." If she shared my anxiety, she hid it well. "Asbestos mine?"

I nodded and led the way.

I'd long wondered why the path to the mine was so well trodden, seeing as the place was obviously a no-go. Under ordinary circumstances, if one tells a group of teenagers that something is off limits and fenced for their protection, they'll find a way to get in and turn it into a hangout, just to thumb their noses at the world. But this wasn't a slightly unstable cave or a too-deep swimming hole, or even a condemned building—this was an asbestos mine, and even though it was old and a small-scale operation, my generation had grown up with too many informercials about lawsuits for mesothelioma patients. Our parents had warned us away from the place, saying there was no telling what might be fouling the air down in the darkness, and even though many of my classmates eventually took up smoking, no one wanted to risk exploring the mine. Getting lung cancer in exchange for social cachet was one thing, but there was nothing to be gained by sticking one's head in a hole and sucking up crystalline fibers.

Now that I knew the asbestos warnings were nothing but a ruse—and I knew what came up from the "mine"—I understood why the path between the fenced-off site and Uncle Malachi's cabin was so clear. The creatures homing in on the crystals in the sword had kept the way open, a constant stream of unwanted hikers stomping a trail through the woods. I couldn't say I was altogether thrilled to have *that* mystery solved, but at least the trail was easy.

A twenty-minute walk took us to the edge of the ten-foot fence surrounding the ersatz mine. Between the barbed wire atop it and the faded red warning placards hung at regular intervals along the fence's length, the place was as friendly and welcoming as a plague ward.

Mia *tsk*ed as she adjusted her pack on her shoulders.

"Should have closed off the top. Caged the whole place in. That way, Malachi could just have come out here and shot whatever got trapped...oh." She made a face as I pointed to a gaping hole in the fence, the sort large enough to give a bear passage. "No point, huh?"

"Probably would have raised too many questions. I can't imagine how they passed this place off as a mine," I said, heading for the hole. "I mean, even if they fabricated the records, how would *no one* in the Crossing know about this mine before it mysteriously closed?"

"What do you mean?"

"Commercial mining isn't two guys with pickaxes—it's a big operation. So suddenly, this cave in the woods is labeled a dangerous former mine and fenced off, and no one finds it odd that not a single soul in town has ever been employed out there?" I wriggled through the hole, broken fence wires scraping along my bag. "No one bothered to ask questions?"

"Maybe they didn't have to," Mia replied, following me through.

"Come again?"

She tightened her ponytail with a sharp yank. "You heard Ms. Quince—she's not the only inhuman living in the Crossing. The mine's been fenced off since the seventies, and maybe enough people in power back then were...you know, *foreign* enough to understand the importance of keeping their mouths shut."

"Mm." I looked toward the open hole in the ground, a pit mouth roughly twenty feet in diameter, and decided to worry about my town's long tradition of covering shit up another day. "Ready?"

"Close enough."

Having never ventured within the fence, I had no idea what the cave might be like, and I fought against my worrying visions of amateur rappelling. To my surprise, the hole wasn't the vertical shaft I'd feared, but rather a gentle slope into the darkness...and if my eyes weren't deceiving me…

"Stairs," Mia muttered. "The bastards cut *stairs* in. Easy exit."

"Assholes," I concurred. "Shall we?"

I'd never been the steadiest on my feet, and the heavy backpack was doing a number on my center of gravity. Still, I thought that if someone was going to tumble headfirst into the cave, it should be me, and so I took the lead, wishing for a handrail. Just in case something was lurking below, waiting for nightfall, I pulled the sword free and held it in front of me like a pike. The stairs turned to the right, spiraling deeper into the earth, and I stared ahead, hoping my eyes would adjust to the dimming light. I was just reaching for the flashlight clipped to my pack when I noticed the soft green luminescence of the blade, an eldritch torch that brightened as the sun vanished behind us.

"And it glows in the dark," Mia puffed behind me. "Does it sing, too? Purify water? Turn stuff into gold?"

"Give away our position to anything lying in wait?" I countered.

"It didn't do that last night. Maybe you're controlling it."

I paused on a wider step and concentrated, and the light disappeared as quickly as if I'd flipped a switch. "Yep."

"Well, I don't hear any growling down there, so get the light back on, will you? I'd rather not fall and die before we get out of this damn cave."

The sword responded to my unspoken command, and we made our winding way to the bottom.

Once free of the staircase, we proceeded down a tunnel whose ceiling rose perhaps fifteen feet above us—an easy walk for anything coming up to hunt. An arched opening at the far end marked the exit, and I stopped on the threshold, surprised by the wind that rushed past the arch. The next room was massive—our high school gym could have fit comfortably within the stone walls—and I could just make out two squared-off branching tunnels in front of us, at roughly the ten and two positions. Stepping into the room, I saw another pair of tunnels cutting away to my left and right, the openings forming an X shape with the path to the surface rising from between two of the arms. The wind seemed to blow from all directions in swirling gusts, moaning down the tunnels and reverberating in the main chamber.

With Mia on my heels, I walked the circumference of the room until I reached the first branching tunnel. By the light of the sword, I could just make out glyphs carved into the rock at eye level, strange characters that my mind somehow interpreted as a word. "Ildon," I told Mia, raising my voice to be heard over the wind.

"You can read that?"

"Thank the pointy glowstick."

The other three tunnels were similarly marked: Kopaat, Ga'besh, and Honslia. Completing our circuit, I pulled Mia back into the exit tunnel, where at least we could talk without shouting. "Which way do we go? Do you remember Ms. Quince saying anything useful?"

But Mia just shrugged. "I've got nothing. You?"

"No, and the sword didn't do anything special in front of any of the tunnels. Guess we choose one and hope, eh?"

"Your call, o fearless leader."

"That's a *terrible* idea," I retorted, but when I returned to the Ildon tunnel and stepped through, Mia followed me.

After half an hour in the tunnel, I noticed odd streaks like multicolored lightning that flashed along the walls and faded before I could pinpoint their source, always heading toward the distant exit.

After an hour, the backpack's padded straps began to dig into my shoulders.

After two hours, Mia and I called a halt. We sat against the wall in the darkness while brilliant colors flickered across the stone around us and squinted into the distance, straining to see the tunnel's end.

Finally, as we neared the three-hour mark, we agreed that the faint glow ahead of us was daylight. Not for another hour did we reach it, by then dragging our feet and weary of our burdens, but I'd never been so happy to step out into the gloaming.

Mia dropped her pack and cracked her spine as we surveyed our surroundings. "So…this is Ildon?"

I took in the jagged, barren gray peaks rising around our position like the teeth of an ancient god. The sun was setting behind us, casting long shadows over the stony landscape. The place seemed uninhabited, the kind of terrain fit only for mountain goats and birds of prey, but I could make out a steep path down from the tunnel mouth, a black circle carved into a hillside, heading toward a small green valley below. With no lights of habitation around us, I assumed we'd need a place to make camp for the evening, and the valley seemed safe enough.

But what struck me more than the empty mountains was the *sense* of the place, as if I stood beside a great sea with a monstrous storm roaring inland from just over the horizon. The air seemed to crackle against my skin, a stream of potential flowing around me with a current I couldn't track.

"Do you feel that?" I asked Mia.

She nodded. "Like I'm about to get shocked?"

"Yeah. Think it's the Aen?"

"Either that or a lightning storm." She spotted the valley and jutted her chin toward its little meadow. "Want to get down there before we lose the daylight?"

My legs ached, but Mia was wise. We made our way to the valley, sliding on the trail's loose gravel, then brushed ourselves off and unpacked. Working together, we soon had a tent up and our sleeping bags unrolled, but there was no fresh water, nor was there wood for a fire. Disappointed, we settled in with a dinner of granola bars and sips from our water bottles, and then Mia pointed to a spot away from the door of our tent and announced, "Bathroom's over there. Ever used a squatting toilet?"

"No," I said, massaging my sore legs.

"Neither have I." With a sigh, she picked herself off the ground, dug a pack of travel toilet paper from her bag, and headed for the designated area. "This should be *delightful.* Don't wait up."

# CHAPTER 4

The howling yanked me from sleep.

Fumbling beside my sleeping bag, I found the sword, which glowed to life at my will before I remembered it would be the only light for miles around and extinguished it. Carefully, I unzipped my bedding and knelt in the tent, listening for footsteps or wingbeats, then opened the door flap and peered into the darkness.

Mia stirred behind me and mumbled as she sat up. "Whazzit?"

"Shh. Hear that?" I whispered.

We waited in silence, straining to detect motion, until the howl echoed across the mountains again—mercifully, moving away. Neither of us moved until the sound had receded into the distance, and then I sighed with relief and turned back from the door. "One or two of them?" I asked Mia.

Our tent was suddenly lit with the white glow of her flashlight. "Just one, I think," she said, crawling out of her bag. "Maybe it's looking for a friend."

"Or hunting." I glanced down at the sword in my hand, which remained inert.

Mia followed me out of the tent and stretched. "Wonder why it didn't come for us."

"It tracks the Aen, remember? Back at the weak point where the tunnels join, I guess the sword's the biggest source around. But here, in the middle of the Aen..."

"The sword's a drop in the bucket," she finished. The flashlight turned her grin into a harsh carnival mask of angular shadows. "Looks like it's open season again over here."

A pang of guilt gripped at my insides as I considered the implications. "They're not prepared—"

"Then that's their own damn fault," Mia snapped. "If they're smart, they have a backup plan in case of sword failure, and since we're allegedly dealing with people who know something about magic..." She shrugged. "Come on, it's not like the Outsiders are unstoppable killers. Tough, sure, but they don't work well without their heads."

She had a point, but my mind continued to conjure up charming vignettes of destruction: the quintessential unaware couple on Lover's Lane, a guy out for a stroll, a child waking up to the sound of scratching on the roof...

The flashlight beam hit me in the eyes, and I suppose my face betrayed me, as Mia crouched by the tent and squeezed my shoulder. "You were drafted into someone else's war, remember. *We* were all put in danger because *they* had a problem. If an Outsider attacks someone here, it's not your fault."

Though Mia had a point, my guts continued to clench as I tried to return to sleep, one hand on the sword's hilt as if it were a deadly teddy bear, my defense against the too-real monsters in the closet.

**M**orning dawned bright and brisk, cool enough to necessitate a jacket, but only for the first hour of our trek down the mountain. In short order, Mia and I were sweating, even with the descent, and after a little experimentation, we fashioned our outer layer into padding between our packs and our tender shoulders. My legs, unaccustomed to exertion worse than a bike ride out to the cabin, complained as loudly as my back did with the weight of my supplies. A night on the ground had done me no favors.

At least there was a trail. I'd never been mountaineering—hell, I'd never done more than a low ropes course during a class field trip—and so I was grateful for a path sufficiently traversable that I didn't have to resort to crab-walking down the mountain or scooting on my butt. That didn't mean the hike was *easy*, of course. Enough gravel slid under our feet to make the going slow and our steps cautious, as neither of us wanted to take a tumble down the slope. When we stopped on a boulder for lunch, we were still high above the narrow valley floor, but the path led us ever downward, and we agreed that the muffled rushing noise we heard had to be running water obscured by the tree cover.

Night came much more quickly when surrounded by peaks than when standing atop them, and though the sky remained blue when we finally hit level ground, the shadows were long and spreading. Still, our spirits rose when we saw that we'd been correct about the water: a cold stream perhaps ten feet across ran out of the mountains, the center of a belt of bushes and trees. Even the ground was softer and carpeted with grass and moss. While Mia pitched a tent and built a fire with deadwood and one of our new fire starters—the clerk at the sporting goods store hadn't let her leave without a demonstration, thank goodness—I went to work with the water purifier, topping up our drinking bottles before filling a pot for dinner. Mia coaxed her scavenged wood to blaze, and by the time I was organized for the evening, she had poured enough dehydrated legumes and potatoes into the pot for a halfway decent stew. It wasn't going to win any culinary awards, not with our limited supplies, but after a day on our feet, we ate every bite and were glad for it.

Bathing in the stream was out of the question—it couldn't have been more than sixty degrees, I guessed, and neither of us had yet reached the point of grime-induced desperation—but I appreciated being able to sponge off my face and arms and soak my feet before bed. Mia had the bright idea of rinsing out the shirts and underthings we'd worn for the last two days, and we strung a line with carabiners between nearby trees to let them dry overnight, well away from the drifting smoke of the campfire. Fed, semi-washed, and exhausted, we collapsed in our tent and slept deeply—and after three interrupted nights, I was beyond grateful to wake rested with the sun, even if I was a little stiff from the ground and the trail. Camping, I decided, was never going to be my favorite form of recreation.

Since we still had wood, and as neither of us seemed particularly eager to be on our way, we stoked the campfire again and boiled water for our breakfast, a pouch of what claimed to be freeze-dried biscuits and gravy. The result wasn't Antoinette's breakfast special—not by a *long* stretch—but it was more than palatable, and it promised to stick around better than the previous morning's granola bars had. Satiated, we packed, refilled our bottles, and started our plodding way along the bank.

The valley narrowed at times as it made its sinuous way through the mountains, but it remained passable, and the tree cover was a relief after the exposed hiking of the previous day. Mia and I spoke little—my ears were tuned for the running footsteps or wingbeats of a hungry Outsider, and I suspect hers were as well—but the morning passed without incident, and we made good time.

I was poised to suggest a stop for lunch when I noticed what appeared to be the scrubby end of a trail emerge from the valley grass. "Hey, Mia? Look at this."

She followed my finger from the overgrown depression toward the distant end of the valley. "It's a road. Or it was, once. Doesn't look like there's much traffic through here."

"First sign of civilization since we came through," I pointed out. "At least we're going the right way."

"Assuming whatever's on the other end of the road is friendly," Mia replied, pulling a bar from her backpack. "Let's hope they've got some kind of sacred rule against attacking visitors."

We ate quickly and pushed on, following the trail as it grew more defined. Within an hour of hiking, the pathway was clear of encroaching grass in the middle; within two, it was a defined brown rut through the valley, and Mia and I tramped along it together when it expanded to the width of a car. By then, the stream had likewise spread and picked up speed, fed by the mountain runoff and perhaps springs hidden in the hills, and while it wasn't yet a proper river, it was sufficiently deep for a kayak. The terrain, which had begun to gently slope downward in the early morning, had steepened its pitch, and soon, I realized that the sound of the water was changing. By midafternoon, Mia and I stood on the edge of the valley, where the stream plunged over a four-story precipice into a turquoise lake below.

"I'm suddenly glad we don't have a boat," said Mia, peering over the lip of the land. "That's not the kind of rapids I ever want to try."

Scanning the panorama below us, I spotted a staircase carved into the rock—one with a metal handrail, no less— which ended in a more manicured version of the road we'd been walking. I followed its path along the lakeshore, then noticed a crossroads on the far side…and if I wasn't mistaken…

"See that?" I asked Mia, pointing to the little building set beside the crossing. "Smoke."

She squinted into the distance, then nodded. "Fireplace, maybe, but it's not cold enough…"

"Cooking fire?"

"You think?" she replied, adding a disdainful snort. "These people are supposed to be magical, right?"

"So maybe the tech is lacking. I mean, you haven't seen any planes or anything overhead, have you?"

She conceded with a grimace. "What you're suggesting, then, is that even if we find civilization, it could be a dirt-floor hovel with Ye Olde Outhouse?"

"Maybe it'll be a *magical* outhouse."

Mia sighed and adjusted her backpack. "As long as it flushes. Let's go."


**O**ur descent was uneventful—I won't say painless, as my legs complained when confronted with the long staircase—but we didn't go unnoticed. Halfway down, I looked toward the crossroads again and saw movement outside the building. Two figures, I thought, and the occasional flash from that direction suggested the glint of sunlight on glass. We were being observed.

My hand went to the sword hanging invisibly at my hip and patted it for reassurance. "Hey, Mia?" I said, trying to sound unconcerned.

"Yeah?" she replied, two steps ahead of me.

"Got your gun handy?"

She paused and glanced over her shoulder. "Noticed that, too, huh? Think they're going to be hostile?"

"Just in case."

I helped with her gear as she strapped the pistol's holster around her slim waist and tightened the belt as far as it would go. Uncle Malachi had never been a large man, but Mia's frame hovered on the cusp of emaciation, and the belt rode low over her bony hips. Growing up, as my own body had filled out with new and unexciting fat deposits, I'd been jealous of Mia's physique, but she'd brushed me off. "There's nothing back here," she'd groused, patting her flat backside. "Try sitting in a plastic chair for an hour with no padding. And why are you complaining? The football team's got more chest than me."

Still, though Mia was thin, what meat she had on her was sinewy, and she shouldered her pack with barely a grunt as we continued the descent.

By the time we reached the bottom, I almost expected to see someone from the presumed dwelling running out to intercept us, but our watchers seemed content to wait for our approach. Mia and I plodded on, rounding the sparkling lake, until finally, the little building came into clearer view.

And it *was* a little building, perhaps no taller than six or seven feet, with a barely peaked roof of slate shingles. The walls, too, were made of rock, albeit something in a paler sandstone color, and the smoke did indeed rise from a chimney, not an outdoor burn pit. There was nothing like a car in view, but neither were there any horses—just the low building with round windows, in which our observers awaited our approach.

We'd barely come within hailing distance when the wooden door opened and two figures emerged.

My first thought had been children—they were proportionally sized to the building, maybe only three to four feet tall—but they were broader than children, stocky and presumably muscular, and shaped like adults. Their bare arms certainly gave that impression. Moreover, each of the two wore a full brown beard that fell to mid-chest, and no child I'd ever seen had sported such luxurious facial hair. One man, I saw as we neared, had been content to brush his beard, while the other had framed his with a pair of thick braids. Both wore black vests—leather, I assumed—and nondescript dark trousers over boots, but what really grabbed my attention were the short swords in their right hands, which seemed very much like the real deal.

Mia and I stopped a few yards away from the building and watched our wary welcoming committee. "Suze?" she murmured.

"Yeah?"

"Could be wrong, but I think those are dwarves. Like, honest-to-God...*dwarves*," she said, her voice rising as if she couldn't quite believe the words she was producing.

"What would give you that idea?"

My attempt at levity went unacknowledged, but then it

was mostly reflex, my mouth moving while my mind tried to come up with a solution that left us unscathed. Something in the men's solid stance told me that if it came down to my swordsmanship against theirs, I'd be left in ribbons.

Before I could work out the logistics of retreat, the one with the more natural beard broke the standoff. "Names and passage papers, if you please," he said, his deep, no-nonsense voice clarifying once and for all that we weren't squaring off against a pair of children who split their time between the gym and the cosplay convention circuit. "We weren't expecting anyone from Kopaat until after the harvest," he added, taking no pains to disguise the suspicion in his tone.

I glanced at Mia, who looked at me blankly and shrugged. "Did you understand that?" she asked.

"More or less." I cleared my throat and stepped forward, showing the two my empty hands. "We're not from, uh…Kopaat."

The evident leader of the two frowned. "One of the Ga'besh settlements, then?"

"No." I tried to stand a little straighter, as height was about the only advantage I had at that moment. "We're from the Crossing."

He turned to his companion, whose face mirrored the first dwarf's confusion. "What crossing? Where? State your business."

"*The* Crossing," I replied, focusing on the sense of his questions instead of their sound. "I'm, uh…I'm the Watcher." With that, I reached for my invisible sword and drew it, and the blade and empty sheath appeared as if from midair. The dwarves retreated a pace, wide-eyed and gaping, and I rotated the sword to give them a good look. "We don't want any trouble," I insisted. "I just want to be rid of this damn thing."

"Heart's Blood," the second dwarf whispered. "That…that *cannot* be…"

"I wish. So if y'all could point us toward someone who might be able to get this curse off me, we'll be on our way."

By then, the first dwarf appeared to have recovered his footing. "The sword can't be here!" he protested. "If it's not at the Crossing, then Outsiders..." He whispered something that sounded suspiciously like a prayer. "You must return. Go back the way you came before those creatures follow you here!"

"No."

"You *must*—"

"I'm not going anywhere," I said, tightening my fingers around the hilt in case the sentries got any desperate ideas. "We've spent two days hiking to this point, we're tired, we're *sore*, and we're not leaving until I get some answers, starting with who made this sword and how I can make it no longer my problem. Now, are you going to help us, or do we need to force our way past?"

The dwarves looked at each other, then seemed to reach a decision. "If there's a problem with Heart's Blood," said the more senior of the two, "then the under-king may be able to assist you. His Excellency's father ruled when the sword was forged, but perhaps he can provide the answers you seek."

"What's going on?" Mia whispered.

"Something about a king," I whispered back, then turned to the dwarves again. "Is he close?"

The second dwarf chuckled nervously. "*Nothing* is close to us, Watcher. But there's a carriage at Tightbend. If we start now—"

"No," said the first, shaking his head, and cut his eyes to the setting sun. "Not in the dark, not with the possibility of Outsiders about." His mouth tightened in disapproval, but he sighed and motioned us toward the building. "You'd best join us for the night. At least there's shelter within the walls."

"They seem to like to come down my chimney," I

replied, sheathing the sword. "Nice little surprise to wake up to." The dwarves looked aghast at the idea, and I turned back to Mia. "We're camping here. Let's get the purifier going while we still have light."

The dwarves' outpost was more impressive than it looked from the outside, as the visible part of the building was only its top story. An office with twin lantern-topped desks occupied half the ground floor, with the rest devoted to a kitchen behind a red curtain. The staircase led to two levels of basement rooms: storage directly belowground, including a cache of armor and weapons suitable for ten, and beneath that, half a dozen bedrooms. Mia cringed when our hosts directed us to the privy out back, but as they couldn't understand her, she was free to complain all she liked as long as she did so through a polite smile.

That we could communicate at all was strictly thanks to the sword. The dwarves—Owir, the senior sentry, and his younger partner, Dewin—had no such translator, and so while I could understand them and make them understand me in turn, they and Mia could only gesticulate at each other. When I asked why the dwarves didn't have any sort of magic linguistic assistance, they laughed as if I'd suggested running down the street to buy a Maserati. "Forging a piece with that sort of spell is skilled work," Owir explained as he examined the sword, cradling it like a precious relic. "Work such as that merits considerable payment. Personally, I prefer warm food and boots that don't let the water in. Ambassadors and merchants who traverse the tunnels tend to have at least one among them who can translate," he added, "but translators don't come with this post."

"It'd be nice if they did," said Dewin, who was checking the pot on the fire for signs of boiling. "Convenient."

"And if a piece were broken, would you like to pay for

it from your wages?" Owir replied, smirking as a grimace flashed across Dewin's face. "*Think*, boy."

Having already taken two spare bedrooms, Mia and I tried not to further burden our hosts, and we offered to make dinner from our freeze-dried rations. Dewin, who seemed to be in charge of the kitchen, cautiously stepped aside and let us rehydrate a couple bags of beef stew, but he regarded the result with uncertainty. "Is this a traditional food among your people?" he asked, peering into a bag at the nondescript mess and wrinkling his nose.

When I relayed the question to Mia, she laughed aloud, and I shook my head at Dewin. "This is camping food. Easy to pack and cook, but that's most of the appeal."

"I see," he replied, then reclosed the bag and offered a wan, polite smile. "Perhaps a first course, then. I'll prepare the rest of the meal."

He wasn't kidding. What the dwarves lacked in interior plumbing they made up for with the hearty evening spread: cured meat, served warm and smothered in a fresh, savory gravy; potato-like vegetables roasted to golden-brown and seasoned with an herb akin to rosemary; a pair of fish fresh from the lake, pan-seared and flaking off the bones; a salad of wild greens with a tangy vinaigrette; softball-sized rolls fresh from the oven; and a tart filled with slices of a fruit somewhere between an apple and a pear in texture and sweeter than either. Feeling rather ashamed of our culinary offering, Mia and I squeezed around the too-low table, tucked in with compliments to the chef, and apologized for crashing their dinner. But the dwarves seemed perplexed by our contrition. "Night's fallen, and you're travelers in the Barrens," said Owir, cutting off another piece of fish with the communal knife. "Why *wouldn't* we extend hospitality?"

"If they'd been elves…" Dewin muttered between bites of bread.

His partner made a face. "A closer call, perhaps."

"We thought you might be, at first," Dewin confided to

us. "From a distance, before you came clear in the glass. She's certainly built like one," he added, gesturing to Mia with his roll.

I repeated his remarks for Mia, who frowned. "What's wrong with elves?" she asked.

When I made the translation, Owir took the lead. "Conceited, obnoxious twits, if you ask me, and that's at their best. Practically godless. I doubt they'd deign to enter this building, even if they were being chased by Outsiders."

"Not after the war, anyway," said Dewin.

I shared this with Mia, who considered it while she forced herself to down a few bites of our rehydrated stew. "It's surprising that they still have such hard feelings," she told me. "Ms. Quince mentioned a war, but wasn't it a while back?"

I asked the dwarves, who nodded emphatically. "The War of the True Children," said Owir. "The truce was signed only ninety-seven years ago."

"I'd just joined the Under-King's Guard," Dewin added, mumbling around a mouthful of food.

"And you're still green, boy," Owir teased, shoving Dewin's shoulder. "But you see, the war is rather fresh," he explained. "We fought on four fronts in Ildon alone, and they attacked us on the other worlds as well. Horrible time. I lost two brothers and a sister in combat."

"I'm sorry," I murmured.

He reached over to pat my wrist. "Nothing *you* did. Now, tell us what's wrong with Heart's Blood. That's a legendary piece of forging—I can't imagine what would break it."

I glanced across the room, where the sword lay sheathed on a counter. "It's fine, I guess. Seems to be working. I just don't want any part of it."

The dwarves seemed taken aback. "But...but it's a sacred duty," Dewin protested.

"Says who?"

He stammered briefly, then managed, "Well, I mean...surely the High King intends for you to fulfill this duty..."

"Funny," I replied, resting my chin on my fist, "but I haven't heard a voice from the heavens ordering me to do this. There's no holy text on the subject. My uncle died last week, and the sword decided to ruin my life next." I squinted at the befuddled dwarves, then asked, "Do you understand how this works? Your monsters get confused and invade our world, and whoever holds the sword gets to fight them for the rest of her life."

"Perhaps it's not *sacred*, as such," Owir began, "but it's a noble duty—"

"How long are you stationed here?"

His head cocked at the non sequitur. "Here?"

"In the Barrens."

"Three months. We rotate to share the hardship."

"But you get to go home, right? Go see your friends and family in other places?"

"Oh, assuredly," he replied with a little laugh. "Why do you ask?"

I smiled, but in truth, I felt like punching a wall. "Because once that sword gets hold of you, it traps you near the tunnel entrance. I can't even go..."—I paused, trying to convert the units I knew into something comprehensible to my companions—"that is, I can't walk more than two or three hours away from the tunnel. *Ever.* Not on our world, at least. What I'm trying to say is that the sword's holding me prisoner. If I don't get rid of it, I'm going to be living alone in a cabin, waiting for monsters to attack, until the day I die."

The rest of the meal was a quiet affair, though Mia went back for thirds, and neither of the dwarves managed to look me in the eye until after the plates were cleared and cleaned.

After dinner, down in my guest room, Owir knocked and carried in a small basin of water as I rummaged through my pack for my toothbrush. "There is no bath, exactly," he said, nestling the metal basin into a depression in a stone countertop, a piece of built-in furniture proportioned for the dwarves and comically short for me. "The lake suffices for us, but perhaps that should be a matter for daylight." He retreated toward the door, then hesitated on the threshold. "Is there anything else you and Mia require? A warm drink, more blankets? I fear you may need to tuck your knees on the bed…"

"We're fine, thank you," I said, smiling as I unzipped my sleeping bag into a duvet. "This is, uh…quite cozy. Much nicer than a tent."

But he lingered, shifting his weight from foot to foot as he watched me go about my preparations. I'd just set aside my can of dry shampoo, which was grossly unmatched against the state of my scalp after three days without a shower, when Owir murmured, "I did not realize the task was for life."

I stopped rummaging long enough to nod at him. "That's what my uncle's handler said when she explained it to me."

"Handler?"

Something was lost in the translation, and I tried again. "Her name's Ardith Quince. She said she's from one of your worlds, and her people send someone to babysit the Watcher."

"*Ah*. She's of the maladetas?"

"I really couldn't say. She looks human, but I guess that's no guarantee, huh?"

"I've had no dealings with them," he replied, "but that sounds accurate. Unless a maladeta reveals herself, the only way to tell the difference between you would be to lock you in a room for a hundred years and see which was still breathing at the end." He chuckled weakly. "Terrible joke. Guards are full of them. Do you know how to tell the difference between a human and an elf?"

"Wait another hundred years?" I guessed.

"No need. Lock them in a room together, and the elf will drive the poor bastard to suicide before long." He cleared his throat, then muttered, "There's another one about differentiating between your people and mine, but it involves a dark room and a subject best not discussed in front of ladies, so…"

I grinned to myself as his face reddened above his beard. "Wait until they're finished servicing each other, then listen for one to complain about his knees?"

Owir's flush darkened. "More or less," he admitted. "You, um—"

"I'm not a child," I said, sinking to the corner of my bed, then tossed my bandana onto the counter to pick a comb through my greasy snarls.

"You'll forgive me, but it's difficult to tell with your people. If I may ask?"

"Sure. I'm almost twenty-three."

His mouth hung slack for a moment, and then he whistled softly. "That's *all*?"

"I'm grown," I protested. "I mean, I'm young for an adult, but I'm definitely grown."

"And Heart's Blood…" His voice faded as he cut his eyes to the sword, which I'd left propped against the nightstand. "It chose *you*."

I winced as the comb caught a bad tangle. "Unfortunately."

"But you're barely more than a babe!" He struggled briefly, then managed, "Your uncle died recently, you said. Does your family know you're here?"

"No one to inform," I replied, continuing my futile effort to make my hair presentable. "My father died about a year and a half ago, and Uncle Malachi was the last of the family."

Owir seemed to grow more distressed by the minute. "No mother?"

"None."

"I…am sorry for your loss," he said, and rubbed the

back of his neck. "Truly, though, your family should be proud of you. Your sacrifice is a noble one—"

"Not really *my* sacrifice, is it?" Putting the comb aside, I shrugged and stared back at him until he glanced away. "I don't have any say in it. Neither did my uncle, or his granduncle, or any of the Watchers before them. All of you just directed your problem our way and trapped one of us into dealing with it. More than a little shitty, if you understand me."

It wasn't easy to read Owir's face, half-covered as it was by hair, but the guilt in his expression was unmistakable.

"You know," he said after a moment of uncomfortable silence, "when my father joined the guards, my grandmother used to pray to the High Queen that he would be given a posting at the under-king's side. Better odds of living, see. Even with the threat of assassination, it was far safer for him to guard the royal family than to be sent to the tunnels and wait for Outsiders. The men who received that duty had double pay, and it was often sent to their widows and children. When the Crossing was built and the monsters ceased to hunt our families…"

He paused, but I held my tongue.

"This posting is the last vestige of the old system," he continued. "We never need do more than check traveling papers, but I suppose we're the first line of defense, should anything escape from the tunnels. All two of us," he added with a weak chuckle. "Almost ceremonial, I suppose. We do have weapons, should one find us—"

"Have you ever seen an Outsider?" I interrupted.

The dwarf shook his head. "I've heard stories."

Picking up the silvered mirror from the countertop, I examined my face, noting the deep red line running from the corner of my left eye in a diagonal almost to the corner of my mouth. Mia had doctored it as well as she could with antibacterial cream and butterfly bandages, but the wound was too jagged to heal cleanly. Without plastic surgery or pancake makeup, I'd be marked for the rest of my days.

"One of them gave me this the night before we left home," I told Owir, brushing a fingertip over the procession of dirty white plastic flaps. "My second night of Watcher duty. The closest I'd come before now to even *holding* a sword is the toy I used in a costume in a school play, so I suppose I should be grateful that the injury's not worse. I mean, at this rate, I'm going to die alone anyway, so what's a prominent facial scar in the grand scheme of things?"

He stared back at me, seemingly searching in vain for an appropriate response, then cleared his throat and offered a curt nod. "I'll leave you to rest," he said, and hurried away with as much speed as his dignity would afford him.


I thought I'd have a pleasant night's sleep, seeing as I was both far from sunlight and atop an actual mattress, but my optimism was sorely misplaced.

Rough hands shook me awake, and I floundered in the unfamiliar dark until I smacked a face with my flailing. Feeling coarse hair brush against my arm, I remembered where I was and mumbled an apology to the dwarf I'd attacked. "Owir?"

"Dewin," said the junior guard, though he sounded little like the confident man of the night before. His voice had acquired a higher pitch and a slightly breathless quality, and his words spilled forth in double time. "Something's outside. Something *big*. It's trying to find a way in. If you could come...just in case..."

I uncurled and grabbed the sword, which had been sharing the too-short mattress with me. A thought was all it took to summon the blade's weird glow, casting Dewin in a sickly green light. Wide-eyed, he retreated a pace, but he beckoned for me to hurry and join him.

At least I'd slept in leggings and a T-shirt. Ignoring my boots—my swollen feet would complain enough when I finally shoved them on again—I followed Dewin into the hall, then banged on Mia's door until she made her bleary appearance. "Whassat?" she slurred through a yawn.

Before I could answer, we heard a muffled cry from above us, then a slam and the sound of running footsteps on the ceiling. "Gorgeous and friends, maybe," I replied.

"God*dammit*," she whispered, and returned to her room only long enough to grab her loaded gun. "Lead on."

If Dewin didn't understand why Mia's preferred weapon was a short club, he didn't bother to make enquiries. He ushered us toward the staircase, but as he reached for the door, it flung open wide, throwing him into the wall. Owir dashed through and slammed the door closed, only noticing his moaning colleague after ten seconds of heaving breaths. "Dewin, lad," he said between gasps, "are you all right?"

"How many?" I asked.

The look on the older dwarf's face spoke of terror. "I...I don't know. One broke down the door, it's trying to fit into the staircase..."

"How fire-proof is this building?"

"Why should *that* matter?"

"Because I'd rather not burn alive." Turning to Mia, I said, "You clear the stairs, I'll take point once we're up to the surface."

"Right." She gave her pistol a final check, then waved for Owir to step aside.

His beard flew with the force of his vehement head shaking once he understood what she was asking. "You can't! If it clears the upper door—"

"Just stand back," I told him, and pried him aside. Sword at the ready, I nodded to Mia and opened the door to the stairwell. The sound of scrabbling feet intensified without the wood in the way, and we held our position until something darker than the windowless room approached at the top of our staircase. By the light of the sword, I could just make out a creature like a giant beetle with fangs before Mia shot twice and it fell over, dead.

She and I started up, the panicking dwarves a few stairs behind us.

The good news, we discovered, was that only one of the Outsiders had made it into the building—the storage rooms and the main floor were messy but unoccupied. The bad was that the bug's three buddies hadn't made it in yet because they were slightly too huge to fit through the dwarf-sized door, and the one that had tried was stuck at the shoulders and snapping at us. Mia dispatched him with a single shot, and we pushed him back out the way he'd come before I used the sword to set him alight. While he burned, his friends tried their luck, but I stood just inside the door and waited to skewer each through the mouth. The Outsiders were tenacious, at least, if not particularly bright, and they soon joined the bonfire.

After Mia and I finished dragging the corpses away from the building, I wiped the grime off my hands, stepped over the puddle of ichor by the door, and looked down at the two dwarves, who waited across the threshold with their weapons drawn. "Well," I said, "now you've seen Outsiders."

Dewin, still stunned, clutched his sword too tightly, but Owir had begun to recover from his fright. "How did you do that?" he demanded.

"Do what?"

"*That!*" he repeated, jabbing his blade toward the flames. "My sword barely nicked that creature, but yours…"

"Perks of a magic weapon, I guess." I sank onto a low chair as Mia ducked back inside. "Nice shooting," I told her.

She grunted. "The recoil's still a beast, but I'm getting used to it." Cutting her eyes to our hosts, she muttered, "They okay?"

"And that thing," Owir continued, pointing to Mia's gun. "What manner of weapon—"

"Uses controlled explosions to shoot larger than average metal projectiles toward a target," I explained. "The Outsiders may be armored, but a gun that size can do some damage."

"As long as we don't run out of bullets," said Mia.

The dwarves didn't understand her commentary, of course, but then there were more pressing issues facing them than the intricacies of bilingual conversation. "Will there be others?" Dewin asked.

Take away the beard, I thought, and he would have seemed all of about ten that night.

"Can't say," I admitted. "But since this is the first point of habitation after the tunnel, I wouldn't be surprised if you get another round of visitors."

"Tightbend," Owir murmured. "They're unaware..." He stood, once again in control of himself if haunted by the charred corpses outside. "Back to bed, all of you. We leave at dawn." When Dewin made no move to uncurl himself from his corner, Owir tugged him to his feet and shoved him toward the staircase. "That's an order, lad," he said with a touch of gruff tenderness. "I've got the watch."

# CHAPTER 5

While dwarves have much to commend them as a people, creativity in place naming isn't among their strong suits.

Tightbend was a fishing settlement wrapping around both banks of…well, a tight bend in the Blue River, which arose from the Blue Lake, the local name for the body of water along which the trail to the tunnel ran. Dewin had given us almost a tour guide's running monologue while we made the two-hour walk to Tightbend, though I suspected his loquacity had more to do with forgetting the events of the previous night than with a desire to impress us with the scenery. Nonetheless, he did a fine job of it, interspersing commentary about the flora and the rock formations with tidbits of dwarven history, and I had my work cut out for me keeping up with the translation for Mia, who hiked in silence. Owir said little beyond the occasional grunt, but as he'd been awake all night, I couldn't fault him for letting Dewin provide the entertainment.

Our destination was, to be charitable, quaint. Tightbend was a hamlet with aspirations of being a town someday, though judging by the suspicious looks the few locals gave Mia and me, I doubted it would ever be a hotbed of cultural fusion. Most of the townsfolk looked and were dressed much like Owir and Dewin: simple tunics beneath plain leather vests, dark trousers, and sensible shoes. Their primary source of adornment seemed to be their full beards, which they wore to a man: naturally hued or dyed at the ends in a sort of ombre, loose and brushed or festooned with beaded braids, even one gray-bearded old man who had coaxed his into a complicated arrangement like a French braid clasped with worked silver. The dwarves peered at us on the cobblestone street, watched in silence from the small harbor, and sneaked looks from the low windows of shops and a building that exuded the familiar stench of a well-loved college bar.

I was remarking to myself on the apparent absence of women in town when I noticed a dwarf with elaborate side beard braids step out of a bakery, give us an appraising once-over, then disappear inside with a swish of floor-skimming skirt. Startled, I hesitated, then murmured to Owir, "Would you be offended if I ask a culturally insensitive question?"

To my surprise, he chuckled softly and smirked up at me. "Beards, yes?"

"Was it obvious?"

"That's always the first question from you people."

"*My* people?" I echoed. "You get a big crowd from the Crossing, do you?"

"Humans," he clarified. The word in his tongue was guttural and brief, the sort of term that lends itself to annoyed muttering. "You keep too much to your own kind, and when you finally take a look around, you know nothing."

"That's…probably fair."

He patted my elbow. "I don't hold it against you, lass. The humans here could be educated if they cared to be. Don't suppose you've had the opportunity, eh? Not coming from *that* place."

"I mean, I only learned there was a way off my world four days ago, so…"

His laughter that time was warmer, though he kept his voice down as we headed for a three-story stone building on the lone hill in town, a mound rising perhaps twenty feet above the river. "To answer your question, then, yes, our women are bearded. The better question is why yours aren't. It's bizarre—your elders walk about looking like wrinkled children, and the thought of *bedding* a beardless partner…" He grimaced and shook his head. "The High Queen has a special hell for those who lure children between the blankets."

As I glanced around, I concentrated and began to pick out the women among our observers—more delicate faces, a slight rise beneath the vest, the occasional skirt. We paused as a pack of children ran across the road, boys and girls together, all streaked with grime and waving wooden swords at each other. Dewin yelled encouragement to the pursuing half of their game, and they ran off toward the river in a flurry of braids.

"No school today?" I asked.

Owir shook his head. "Not around here. This is the end of the redbelly running season," he said, cocking his head toward the harbor. "You have fish where you come from, yes?"

I thought of snippets of nature documentaries showing streams choked with salmon eager to spawn. "They're going back to the lake to breed?"

"Precisely. The run will end in a week or two, and the fish will regain their strength in the lake before they mate and die. The eggs grow over the winter, and the yearlings head downriver to the sea once the ice breaks. You should have been here a month ago—the river clogs with fish, and the big ones leap over each other in their haste to find the lake."

Considering his description, I was surprised to see only a few small boats out on the water that morning. "I take it there's a limit to how many you can catch."

"Oh, most certainly," Dewin chimed in. "My aunts have a smokehouse closer to the capital, and every year, they complain of the same struggle to buy loads. A hold full of redbellies…" He whistled softly. "Half a year's wages or more for me, I'd reckon. It's hard to imagine the money that flows around the smokehouses this time of year."

"It's the river, you see," said Owir, catching Mia by the elbow before she could step into a pile of cooling dung. "He's particular about the run. Wants things kept fair, so if he thinks a boat's taking too many, he'll capsize it."

"And good luck getting to shore if the river's peeved with you," Dewin added. "Happened to a cousin once. The river let him go because he was just the bait cutter— he wasn't more than a lad. But the captain and the mate never surfaced." Drawing closer to me to avoid another fresh deposit from a passing animal, he said, "The Blue's a powerful river and the basis of quite a few fortunes, but he's not to be trifled with."

I frowned as I listened to their explanation, trying to work out why my translation seemed imperfect. "He?" I asked. "Your rivers are, uh...male? I'm not critiquing," I hastily continued, "we tend to use female pronouns on our ships and such. Just trying not to say the wrong thing."

Owir's squint spoke of bemusement. "Of course they're male. Are your elementals not?"

"Would someone like to tell me what's going on?" Mia interrupted.

"Hang on," I said, flustered, and pulled her and the dwarves out of the middle of the road. "Mia, I'll translate in a second. Guys, what the hell is an elemental?"

Dewin looked up at me like I was a few eggs short of a dozen, but Owir muttered, "*Ah*. Of course. The Crossing is outside the Aen, isn't it? That's the whole blasted point of the thing."

"Yes..." I allowed.

"Elementals, well..." Briefly, he struggled, then said, "I'm no expert, to be sure, but this is what I recall from my schoolmistress. They're born at the border of our worlds and the Aen, though no one's entirely sure how. Maybe the maladetas have considered it, but we don't have answers. Anyway, they're incorporeal entities—spirits, I suppose—and they lay claim to bits of land as they go along. Every major lake and river has an elemental, and the seas have several. Numerous earth elementals live in the mountains around the capital. Far to the east, some of the mountains are volcanoes, and that's the only place I'd know to find fire elementals. And the airs, of course. They go as they please, but if a gale comes up, you're sure to find at least one flitting about."

I gave Mia a hasty synopsis of Owir's lesson, and her eyebrows rose. "So what happens if you pee in a river around here?" she asked.

The dwarves laughed at my mumbled translation. "Usually nothing," said Owir, "unless you've angered him in some way. Now, let's be on our way," he said, and set off without waiting for follow-up questions. "I'll tell you whatever you want to know once we're on the road to Heartfast."

For a man with short legs, Owir set a brisk pace, and we didn't dally. Soon, he'd marched us up the hill to the stone building—"The mayor's office," he'd offered as we walked along the front path—and gave two sharp raps at the green door. It opened a moment later to a dwarf who'd forked his blond beard and tied the ends with red thread. "Sorry to arrive unannounced," said Owir, stepping back a polite pace. "It's urgent. Is the mayor available?"

The man disappeared briefly, then returned and opened the door wider. "She'll see you in her study," he said, and frowned at Mia and me. "I thought we weren't expecting anyone from Kopaat—"

"They're not from Kopaat. Come, lasses," said Owir as he hurried down the hall and up the staircase.

The mayor's office resembled the guards' building only in its stone walls and low ceilings—perfectly fine for dwarves, but short enough that I could have grazed my fingertips along the colorful plaster medallions, had I so desired. Mia and I had to duck as we ascended to the second floor, then dodge the iron chandelier hanging in the middle of the corridor. Owir led the way to the far end of the hall, but as he was raising his hand to knock, the door swung open to reveal a gray-haired dwarf in a long blue dress, her beard plaited with silver strings that twinkled in the light. "Guards," she said, nodding to him and Dewin. "May the High King offer his protection to you both."

"And the High Queen to you," Owir replied. "We're sorry to intrude, but—"

"Something about an emergency?"

"Your carriage. Is it in good repair?"

She glanced from him to Mia and me. "I'm unaccustomed to loaning my carriage to humans who can't be bothered to make their own travel arrangements. Was no one sent to meet them?"

Owir turned to me and murmured, "Show her."

He didn't need to explain. I gripped my sword and pulled, willing it back to visibility, then presented the hilt to the mayor.

She gasped as she examined it. "Is that...that can't be..."

"Heart's Blood," said Owir. "I've seen what it can do with my own eyes. We were attacked last night," he added as Dewin vigorously nodded. "That's the Watcher's sword, and the lass there is the Watcher."

The mayor lifted her dark eyes to mine, uncertainty wrinkling her brow. "She's but a *babe*."

"I know," Owir replied. "And she'd like a word with His Excellency. I'd see her there quickly." As the mayor began to protest, he said, "As long as that sword is here, Outsiders will follow. The lasses killed four last night. Let us *hurry* her to Heartfast, and were I you, I'd order a curfew and the doors barred."

"And chimneys," I said. "They've come down mine."

The old woman's face drained of color. "Be on your way, then," she said. "It's in the shed. And may the High King grant you all speed."

**"A** carriage ride. Just what I've always wanted," groused Mia as we followed the guards to the stone outbuilding behind the mayor's office. "Wooden wheels on cobblestones, I guess. Bets as to whether they've discovered rubber?"

"Be nice," I muttered.

"What? They can't understand me."

I sighed, envisioning a long journey in a bumpy coach, like a haunted hayride from hell. "Would you rather walk? Who knows how far away this place is?"

She stepped oddly on a paving stone, almost twisted her ankle, and swore. "What's it called again?"

"Heartfast," I replied, then offered a rough translation of the Dwarfish—which, until I had a better term for it, was the name I'd settled on for their language. "Look, I didn't sleep on the ground last night, and the guys can *cook*. Things could be worse."

She gave me a look of deep incredulity. "Remember what *else* we did last night?"

"We could have fought them from the tent."

After a moment's consideration, she reluctantly allowed, "True. But if you hadn't been cursed with that fucking sword in the first place—"

"Watch your step," Dewin interrupted as Owir opened the shed door. "I see nails on the ground. Perhaps someone's been doing maintenance."

I told Mia, who flashed a weary smile and shrugged. "Could have been more poop. Speaking of which, where's the stable? Don't carriages usually come with horses?"

As my eyes adjusted to the dim light of the shed, I could make out a black box the size of a stretch limo and similarly pocked with windows. It rested on two pairs of sturdy legs, and Owir opened a door in the side and pulled down a short entry step, which was polite of him but completely unnecessary for half our party. "Up you go, lasses," he said, standing back from the door. "Make yourselves comfortable. We've a ways to travel."

Mia and I climbed inside to find three rows of benches, split down the middle for an aisle, and an empty space at the rear for cargo. We chucked our gear into the back and took two of the dwarf-height benches, tucking our knees as well as we could, while Owir and Dewin slid onto the front bench. I was about to ask where we might find horses when Owir pressed his hand against a panel in the sloping front wall of the vehicle. The panel began to glow yellow, and he turned to Dewin with a grin. "A fine carriage this is. Take it slow until you have a feel for it. I'll set us on our way." With that, he gripped a lever in the wall, and I heard a loud clanging noise from beneath us.

"What was that?" I called to the front.

"Nothing to worry about," said Dewin, smiling at us over the back of his bench. "Legs going up, that's all."

"Legs…" I echoed, then looked out the window to find that the carriage was hovering over the shed floor. "Um…how…"

"An excellent piece of forge work. And once Owir does the tricky bit…"

The senior guard maneuvered another lever until the carriage floated backward out of the shed, the ride smoother than any flight I'd ever taken. He reversed almost to the mayor's rear door, then turned the carriage toward the distant mountains and pushed the lever to the wall.

Mia and I were thrust back with the force of the sudden acceleration, and Dewin looked slightly sheepish. "Sorry, should have warned you," he said. "Owir doesn't waste time in transit."

I pressed my nose to the window—not glass, but rather a sheet of quartz, thin but strong—and marveled at the speed of the passing landscape. "How long is the trip?" I asked.

"We'll be there by nightfall if the High King favors us," Owir replied, and slipped into the aisle. "All yours, lad," he told Dewin. "Try not to wake me."

I wasn't sure what I was expecting, but Heartfast came as a shock.

Dewin had slowed the carriage as we approached and merged into traffic, which flowed along at a steady pace toward a sentry port in the black stone wall around the city. Only once the clouds parted and a glimmer of waning light hit the wall did I realize that its face wasn't purely utilitarian. The expanse, probably thirty feet high and miles long, glittered like a nightclub disco ball, and even Mia, who'd suffered through an unexpected bout of travel queasiness that afternoon, murmured, "*Whoa.*"

Owir, who'd awakened once we slowed, caught the object of our attention and smiled with faint pride. "A beauty, isn't she? Korin Blackfoot, who was under-king when my grandfather's grandfather was a boy, had the wall made taller for security, then had it adorned as a show of piety. The Great Temple is in Heartfast, you see, and he wanted anyone coming to worship to have a proper sense of the grandeur of the place even before they reach its doors. Took half the treasury, and sixty-two artisans lost their lives on the wall project, but the result speaks for itself, does it not?"

"Impressive," I replied, trying to count the precious stones by their flashes in the sunlight. "And no one, uh…takes souvenirs?"

He stiffened, then looked at me as if I'd asked about local policies on cannibalizing babies. "Certainly not! Those belong to the High King and the High Queen— taking a pickaxe to the wall would be gross sacrilege." His bushy eyebrows drew together as he gave Mia and me a longer look. "You would desecrate a temple?"

"No," I hastily assured him, "I just…I mean, that's a *lot* of money in the wall. No one's ever tried? I would think that'd be tempting."

"For an elf, perhaps," he countered, somewhat mollified by my denial. "Heathens, all of them. *We* respect our gods."

I gave Mia the synopsis as we paused for sentry inspection, and then the city opened up before us: low stone buildings at the periphery, gradually rising in size and ornamentation toward the twin peaks to our left and right.

"The palace," said Owir, pointing to the great edifice on the left hill. A quick count netted more than a dozen turrets, all of them decorated with stalagmite-like stone spurs and pennants flying a blue banner with a white diamond in the center. "And the Great Temple," he said, indicating the even larger complex on the right hill, the walls of which put the city wall to shame in terms of embedded riches. Even the little I could see of the path to the top of the hill sparkled.

Behind both hills, rising to an impressive height, was a solitary peak topped with the final vestiges of the winter snowpack. "Blackhorn Mountain?" I asked.

Owir nodded. "Clever lass. Our forefathers' first stronghold in this country, and once they tunneled deep enough, they found gems to finance the foundations of Heartfast. No one lives in there now, but in time of war, it's a good place for a last stand." He reclaimed the empty seat in the front bench and straightened his vest. "Take us in, Dewin. Let me do the talking."

Dewin deftly maneuvered the carriage up the palace hill and pulled it to a stop between a pair of guard shacks, the one break in the relatively short and undecorated wall around the building. As four guards trooped out, two with swords already drawn, Owir slid his window back into the carriage's casing and raised an empty hand to the dwarves. "The High King's protection to you all," he said. "I seek an audience with His Excellency. It's a delicate matter concerning national security."

The other guards' beards might have obscured their mouths, but their eyes made plain their skepticism. "You have an appointment…"

"Owir," he offered with professional calm. "And no. I would not impose upon His Excellency were this not so—"

"He's entertaining some of the old families tonight," another guard interrupted, sounding bored. "Make an appointment. Or do the wise thing and take whatever 'important' problem you might have to your commanding officer. I'm sure you'll find with all due speed that it's not so urgent."

The guards shared a chuckle at that, but Owir remained unflustered. "My message is for His Excellency alone, not my commander. If you would be so kind as to relay to his secretary—"

"Forget it," the first guard snapped. "Don't be stupid, lad. You're not worth his time."

"Screw this," I muttered, then flung open the carriage door, leaned out, and waved to the startled guards. "Hey, assholes! I'm the damn Watcher, and I want to see your damn king *now*."

If my profanity was insufficient on its own to sway them, making the sword appear in my hand proved to be a convincing move. I hopped down from the vehicle, sword out and glinting in the light of the setting sun, then advanced on the guards, who bunched up and took a few hasty steps in retreat. "You boys want to escort me," I said with as much attitude as I could muster, "or should I see myself inside?"

Their leader, suddenly no longer so cocksure, gaped at my weapon. "Is...is that—"

"Heart's *fucking* Blood," I snapped. "Yeah. Very shiny. Very sharp. King, *now*."

Trading panicked glances with his comrades, he cleared his throat, then squeaked, "If you...um...if you would be so kind as to return to your carriage, my lady, I'll see that you're announced."


**P**rotocol has never been my strong suit, and trying to absorb enough to avoid an inter-world incident in the space of a five-minute march taxed my abilities.

"Under-king, not king," Owir muttered, keeping pace at my side in the middle of a column of eight guards. As we'd left our camping gear in the carriage, I was moving more quickly than I had in days, and he half-jogged to keep up. "There is no king but the High King. Calling the under-king by that title is blasphemy."

"Bad enough to get me burned at the stake?"

The dwarf seemed equally bemused and horrified by the notion. "No, *no*, but if you'd like to avoid antagonizing the room…"

"I'm not really in a friend-making mood."

"I understand," he said, giving my wrist a squeeze, "but His Excellency is dining with some of the most powerful families of Blackhorn Mountain. You'll gain nothing by insulting them, lass."

I glanced down, remembered that the midlevel soldier beside me had just driven up to the palace and asked for a sit-down chat with a king on my behalf, and forced back my indignation. "I'll try to behave, all right? Make an effort not to do anything that'll get you two branded as heretics."

He chuckled softly and looked over his shoulder at Dewin and Mia. "The gods are merciful to the ignorant. His Excellency should be as well, but perhaps you could allow me to explain our purpose here before you start waving that sword around, hmm?"

A moment later, our column came to a halt outside a pair of iron-banded wooden doors—eight feet tall, I guessed, impressive by dwarf standards—and our escort's leader barked at us to wait. The wardens on the doors opened one to him, giving me a glimpse into a long, banner-strung hall filled with laden tables and lit with gleaming candelabra. At the far end, facing the doors, a man sat at a smaller table elevated by a short dais. His chair back rose well above his head and terminated in a series of what I took to be stylized mountain peaks, judging by their jagged shadow on the stone wall. Of the man himself, I could make out few details beyond dark hair, but I tracked the motion of the guard as he threaded his way through the boisterous dining crowd and up to the head table. The man beckoned him closer with a curt, two-fingered wave, and the guard bent to his ear to relay his message. Stiffening in his chair, the man turned from the guard to peer out at our party in the corridor, and rose. As the diners gradually noticed his movement and stood in turn, he motioned them back into their seats. "My friends, enjoy yourselves," he said, his sonorous voice echoing around the hall. "A matter requires my attention for a brief moment. I'll return before the toasting—and toast we *shall*."

A rowdy cheer met that declaration, and he grinned as he stepped down and marched up the center aisle. The guards around us nudged us back, and as soon as the man and the messenger were clear of the doors, the wardens shut it fast behind him.

Our entourage took a knee, and even Mia, unsure as she was without the benefit of translation, dipped her head. But I held my ground and stared down at him, and his politician's smile rapidly fell away.

"*You* are the Watcher?" he asked, disbelief coloring his inflection.

"For now," I replied. "I take it you're the under-king."

"Your Excellency," Owir cut in, "we apologize for the interruption, but—"

He held up a hand, and Owir fell silent. "What does the Watcher require?" he asked, never dropping my gaze.

His eyes were the golden-brown of old honey and set deep in his craggy face, framed by thick eyebrows and the discolored bags of troubled nights. His hair bore more silver than I'd first thought, especially around the temples, and he accented the braids of his beard with artificial threads to match. Unlike the vests his guards sported, he wore a red tunic, belted around his trim waist, over dark trousers and well-polished black boots. But most striking, the under-king was taller than any dwarf I'd seen, close to five feet. If a dwarven basketball league existed, he'd have had a sneaker deal.

I'd never planned to have a royal audience in trail-grungy leggings and a sweat-stained T-shirt, a magic sword affixed over my hips with a bungee cord, but there we were, all the same. "I think we should talk about this somewhere that isn't a public hallway, don't you?" I said.

The under-king nodded and politely gestured toward a stairwell to my left. "My study, perhaps?"

"Sure, that'll do." As the guards around us rose, I added, "Susan Cole."

I could barely make out his faint smile through his beard. "Rokund."

"That's it?"

The smile crinkled the corners of his eyes. "Third of my line, the Elf-Bane, if you'd prefer to be formal about it, lass."

"Fair enough." I nodded to my waiting companion and said, "Mia Randolph. Where I go, she goes."

"Please," he replied, spreading his hands, and started for the staircase.

"And I'm sorry if you miss some of the drinking," I said, following after him.

I couldn't be sure, but I thought I detected a soft chuckle. "You haven't been hosted by many dwarves, have you?"

"Just Owir and Dewin here."

Rokund glanced back at the pair, who seemed to shrink into the rest of our escort. "As they're on duty, I'm sure the libations were not as plentiful as they might otherwise have been. Trust me," he said, mounting the first step, "if I miss a round or two, I'll not regret it."

# CHAPTER 6

The under-king might have been entertaining guests, but he was a well-bred dwarf, and the fact that we were gate-crashers didn't mean we were to go hungry. While his guards took up posts inside and out of his well-appointed study, a cozy chamber decorated with warm wooden furnishings and wall hangings in blues and greens, he sent a servant to the kitchen with orders to bring up a little of everything that was going out to the main tables, then pointed Mia and me toward a small door in the wall. "I understand you've come from Tightbend, and at speed. Perhaps you'd like to take a moment and freshen up," he offered.

Sure, I was eager to be rid of the sword—the brazen façade I'd adopted that evening was little more than a disguise for my nerves, and I was finally glimpsing a chance at relief, now that we'd been given an audience— but Dewin had seen no point in pit stops that day, and I was too grateful to be shown anything resembling a restroom to turn it down. Willing by then to settle for a chamber pot and a prayer, I was thrilled to find a stone contraption in a familiar configuration, separated from a wash basin behind a gilded wooden screen. A moment's study with Mia revealed a half-hidden button in the wall in lieu of a flush handle, and I'd never been so happy to see a basket of coarse paper napkins. There was no watery finish to the affair—depressing the button simply made the bowl clean again, as whatever had been placed in it vanished— but the sink ran hot and cold, and it felt wonderful to get a bit of the road grime off my hands, arms, and face.

Dewin and Owir had apparently been shown to a similar facility, as they returned shortly after we emerged. "I apologize, and I do hope that wasn't confusing," Rokund told us, indicating the empty couch and chairs. "First-time visitors have been left perplexed by some of the forging in this place, and one tends to forget."

"Oh, no, that's fine," I replied, overlooking for the moment the issue of the possibly magical toilet. "Uh...maybe I got the wrong impression, but I didn't think indoor plumbing was popular around here."

His brows drew together as he considered that—I could only imagine how my response had translated. "Plumbing?" he repeated.

I heard the English word and gathered that there was no good equivalent in the local language. "You know, brings water inside, carries waste away?" His expression didn't change, so I tried again. "Pipes, you know? In the walls?"

Still, he regarded me blankly.

"How do you have hot water in there?" I asked, cocking my thumb toward the restroom.

"*Ah*," he said with a hint of pride. "That's a fine piece of forging. A central basin in the bowels of the palace fills with water, and when the handles are turned, the water appears where it needs to be. Waste is then reduced to dust outside the city, the water is cleaned, and the basin refills. Took three teams of forgers a full year to work through the details—we had water randomly appearing throughout the place for *months*—but they managed it in the end." He laughed to himself as we took our seats. "Imagine waking in the middle of the night to a cascade of cold water in the face, pouring from thin air. But I believe the inconveniences were worth the end result. You've seen something similar, now?" he asked with a curious frown. "Your world is outside the Aen, is it not? How is your forging accomplished without it?"

The mention of home reminded me that I hadn't hiked through the wilds of Ildon for a polite chat about utilities. "Maybe we can discuss that later. I need your help."

Rokund's head dipped in acknowledgement. "I'd assumed you weren't on a pleasure tour. What do you—" He paused at a knock, then waited while the servant wheeled in a cart loaded with dishes of roasts and vegetables and a reddish-brown bread that smelled amazing. "Please help yourselves," said the under-king once the servant had left us. "All of you."

Mia, Owir, and Dewin didn't have to be told twice, but my stomach was too knotted for food. "Here's the situation," I said, and stood from the couch to unhook my belt. A thought brought the sword back into view, and I glanced at Rokund in time to see his eyes widen. "This thing attached itself to me a few days after my uncle died. It's been attaching itself to members of my family for *generations*. And I've been informed that because I've been *selected* by this damn thing, I'm supposed to sit outside your precious Crossing and fight your monsters for you until I drop dead." I tossed the sword onto the rug and folded my arms. "Didn't sign up for this, bub."

He stared at the sheathed weapon. "Is that truly Heart's Blood?"

"You tell me."

Cautiously, he rose and came around the table to retrieve the sword from the floor. A moment's study of the ornate hilt was all he needed for the confirmation he sought. "High King show us his mercy," he whispered, and extended the sword to me. When I refused to take it from him, he settled for propping it against an empty chair. "I haven't seen that since I was a lad of five," he told me, returning to his seat. "My father showed me before the maladetas took it. A *beautiful* piece of forging—it has no like."

"It's yours," I said, resuming my perch on the edge of the couch cushion as Mia, only able to follow half the conversation, settled for filling her growling stomach. "I don't want it, so take it back."

The under-king paused, and his face began shifting toward a grimace. "Lass, I'm afraid—"

"Take it. *Please*," I said, my shell cracking as my words sped up. "I don't want this, it's awful, I'm a prisoner in my uncle's old cabin, Mia and I killed *four* of them the first night, and I can't do this—"

"Lass—"

"It's not fair!" I cried, willing my eyes to stop pricking. "What did I ever do to you, huh? What did we ever do?"

Absently, he licked his lips, the gesture speaking more of unease than appetite. "I'm sorry," he murmured. "I didn't make the Crossing—that was my father's decision. Anchoring it to your world seems...cruel," he admitted. "I understand the rationale, now, but the collateral damage—"

"You are *looking* at the collateral damage."

He no longer held my stare.

"Please," I tried again, "sir...Your Excellency...you've got to help me."

"And what would you have me do?" he mumbled, studying the plate of roast as if the answers were hidden between two of the perfectly pink slices.

"Take the sword back. Close off the tunnel between the Crossing and our world, and leave us out of this mess."

"I can't. Yes, your situation is unfortunate," he said, speaking over my protestation, "but if we closed your world off from the Crossing, there would be nothing keeping the Outsiders away from ours. I must think of my people before all others—please try to understand that."

He had the decency to sound apologetic, but that wasn't going to help me. "So make more swords like that one," I said. "Put a few people outside the tunnel exits and arm them. You've already got guys like them doing stints out past Tightbend," I continued, nodding to Dewin and Owir. "Make it a short-term assignment with bonus pay, and I'm sure you'd be able to find someone to go kill monsters for you for a month or two at a time."

Rokund had poured himself a draught of a red liquid from the pitcher on the table while I laid out my plan, and he took a swig before answering me. "We did that in my father's day," he said, his lips suddenly stained crimson, "and his father's before him, and so many fathers going back. I can't give you an accurate count of the dead tunnel guards offhand, but I would think ten thousand would be a low estimate."

"But you didn't have swords like that one, did you? Make more! Make a hundred of them, raise your own Outsider-slaying unit..." My voice died as the under-king mirthlessly laughed. "What's so funny?"

He put his goblet on the table and regarded me over the dinner spread. "Has anyone told you why that sword is called Heart's Blood, lass?"

I shook my head.

"There are other names for it, I suppose. Prettier names, names suggesting its power. But the ones who use those names didn't lose many people in the sword's creation. Dwarves *died* to forge it. The best forgers of their time." Cutting his eyes to the restroom door, he said, "You liked that, yes? Interior water? It was complicated, but the worst that happened in that forging was unexpected wetness and a few headaches for the forgers. Making the sword, trapping that many energies in the metal itself, working with so much concentrated Aen..." Seeing my confusion, he said, "What humans call forging is only half the job. *True* forging isn't merely working metal—it requires one metalsmith to shape the item and one speaker to give the item its desired effect, to make the Aen work through it."

I sensed that something was lost in the translation that resulted in *speaker*, but I let it go for the moment.

"It's a tandem process, you see," Rokund continued. "Forgers usually specialize, and they form teams. Twenty of the finest such teams worked on Heart's Blood— dwarves from Blackhorn Mountain and Deepwood, certainly, but also from some of the kingdoms of Kopaat and Honslia. Our best and most talented. Of the forty of them, only one lived to see the sword's completion, and she took her own life in sorrow less than a year later."

"How—"

"Working with the Aen is a delicate process, complicated at the best of times," he explained. "The energies involved in the forging of that weapon were enormously difficult to manage, even for gifted forgers. They knew the endeavor would likely be suicidal, but such was our desperation to rid this world of Outsiders. They sacrificed themselves for the good of our people and *all* the peoples of the four worlds." Rokund took up his goblet again and slowly drank while I digested that information. "So you see," he said softly, "we cannot make a hundred swords like Heart's Blood. The cost in lives would be enormous, even if we had enough forgers sufficiently skilled for the task—and anyone less than a master would be assured a painful death. Do you understand?"

"Take it," I replied. "Bring all the dwarves back here, put your soldiers at the tunnel entrance, and give someone the sword. You can defend this world—"

"And leave the other three vulnerable? No. Heart's Blood was a collective effort—I have no right to protect this world to the detriment of the others."

"So you put mine in danger instead."

The flicker of guilt in his expression wasn't a product of my imagination, nor was his subtle wince. "Your world is uniquely positioned," he protested. "Thanks to the Crossing's configuration—"

"You dragged us into your war! *We* didn't build your damn Crossing!" I snapped, staring him down as he squirmed. "Look, there are humans living somewhere around here, yeah? They could pass in our world. Or the...the maladetas, right? That's what you call them?"

He nodded.

"They look like us—one of them was my neighbor, and I never knew it until she told me. So why don't you give the sword to one of them? Maybe a year at a time?" I suggested, the words *hardship post* echoing in my mind. "There's the cabin near the tunnel opening, it wouldn't be too onerous if it were only for a year, and with extra pay..."

My rambling petered out as he silently held my gaze. When he spoke again, I heard pity in his deep voice. "Perhaps that could have been done. When the sword was being forged and the Aen harnessed within it, perhaps that could have been the arrangement, sharing the burden among those who could have most easily lived among your people. But my father and the others would have seen the risk in that—leaving the sword untethered to anyone, a weapon to be bickered about and fought over. Imagine if someone had done as you suggested and posted the sword's wielder at the tunnel to only one world, leaving the other three defenseless. So there was wisdom, you see, in choosing a Watcher without a particular loyalty to any of our worlds and binding the sword to him." He raised a hand as I began to counter that. "But I don't suppose the sword's architects considered the cost to the unknown person who would bear it."

"Gee, you think?" I muttered.

My disregard for protocol seemed to leave Owir and Dewin increasingly uncomfortable, but the under-king never batted an eye. "I feel very badly about your situation, lass," he told me after a long pause for a contemplative drink. "I do, believe me. My youngest daughter is probably close to your age..." He frowned, considering Mia and me. "Fifty, I would wager?"

"Twenty-three, Your Excellency," Owir murmured.

"Nearly," I added as Rokund's dark eyes widened.

His reply came almost too softly for me to hear, but I

did catch *High Queen* and *mercy* in his rapid whisper.

"Look," I tried, "you can't or won't take it away from me, I get it. But isn't there someone else who could? Who else was involved in making it?"

Rokund began to count off on his fingers. "My father oversaw its forging as the representative of our race. The elves worked their own magic upon it to strengthen its power against Outsiders, which was done in tandem with the forging. Their power is greatest over living things, you understand—it's innate, but it's more specialized than ours. Whatever else one may say about them, and I can think of a few choice terms, they are incredible healers. I suppose the converse is true as well, considering the task for which that sword was designed."

"Where would I find them?"

His lip rose as if his drink had suddenly turned bitter. "You would want to seek out the Twins in the Greenwood of Honslia. They call their lands Nokan'ti."

"Which would be…where?"

With obvious reluctance, he replied, "The Honslian tunnel opens into the Greenwood, but the forest stretches to the horizon in all directions. Precisely where within it the Twins have established themselves is unknown to me—their last fortification was destroyed during the war, and for some reason, I've not been invited to see their new home," he added with a quick smirk.

Turning to Mia—who, unable to participate in the conversation, had settled for the consolation prize of a good meal—I said, "He can't help me, but he said that some elves in Honslia were involved in making the sword, too."

"Fuck," she muttered through a bite of meat. "Guess we know what plan B is, then."

"Who else?" I asked Rokund.

He tapped another finger. "As for the humans, I know that the Aen crystals in the sword came from the Darili crown…Daril, one of the kingdoms of Kopaat," he elaborated, seeing my confusion. "The richest of them all. Humans learned the knack of finding solid Aen from the maladetas, and they alone go to the trouble these days. The mines are deep and often unstable, and I would think that there's not a single crystal untainted by blood spilled to find it. But the Fulquirs were a wealthy family long before they came to the throne. Few others would have the resources to fund the mining of crystals like those," he said, gesturing to the sword. "Erianthe wasn't involved in the forging, of course—that's their present queen, Erianthe of Daril—but if any records concerning Heart's Blood lie in human hands, they would be in hers. And it was the humans who designed the spell locking the sword to the Watcher, I believe. But if I were you, I would speak with the Twins first. If they talk, Erianthe listens."

I passed this in turn to Mia, then asked, "What about the maladetas?"

A fourth finger extended. "They, like us, gave their lives for the sword. I cannot say what, precisely, the maladetas did—their secrets are their own, and only a foolish man attempts to force them to speak. That they assisted in the forging, I have no doubt, but *which* maladetas made the sword is unknown to me. Still, they have a settlement in Kopaat, fairly near the Darili border, so if you should go to that world, you might seek them out."

"One of them is supposed to find me soon enough," I said with a sigh. "My neighbor's replacement."

The under-king perked at that. "Perhaps you could await her arrival, then. Return to your home, and when the maladeta comes, ask her your questions."

My eyebrow rose. "Draw all the monsters back to our world, you mean."

His silence spoke volumes.

"That's Ildon, Honslia, and Kopaat," I continued. "What about Ga'besh?"

Dewir snorted, and Rokund, glancing his way, nodded

agreement. "The tekorish homeland, and they are less than useless," said the under-king. "One dwarven trading post, a few elvish outposts, and some human cities—Cirivant first among them, I would think. The mines are productive if the hurricanes don't wash you away."

"Back up," I said, cutting him off. "Tekorish?"

"The tekoraet," Owir grumbled. "Parasites."

"Precisely," said Rokund. "Parasites, pirates, and prize-hunters, that's the sum of Ga'besh. Nothing that need concern you tonight, lass." With that, he rose, gesturing for us to keep our seats. "And now, I fear I have other guests under my roof to entertain. The four of you should eat your fill and take your rest. I'll send an escort here shortly to show you to your rooms. We can speak more of this in the morning," he added, then nodded to me and hurried out, his guards falling in behind him.

When the office door closed, I looked at Mia and the dwarves, then shrugged and picked up a roll. "Got a better idea?"

"It would be unwise to reject His Excellency's hospitality," said Owir, refilling his plate with a heaping serving of a fragrant concoction that bore a resemblance to pale purple risotto.

I passed on the under-king's offer to Mia, who concurred with Owir. "Give him a chance to think it over," she added, topping up her goblet. "Maybe a night of guilt will make him more helpful."

I took the pitcher from her and sampled the drink, a fruity concoction with a strong note of spirits and a color like blood in the flickering light of Rokund's lanterns. "Sure," I mumbled, and drank deeply. "Maybe."

For the second night in a row, I was shaken awake, but at least the culprit that time had more sense than Dewin and stepped back before my flailing arms could make contact. As I sat up in bed, I noticed a form standing a few feet away, holding a small lantern with all but a single shutter closed. The window of my guest room, which had offered a view of the darkened capital before I crashed, remained night-black, and I feared the worst.

"What's going on?" I asked, groping on the rug for the sheathed sword.

"You're leaving," said an unfamiliar voice—young, female, and low enough to border on contralto. "Now. Get dressed."

The edge in her tone discouraged argument, and groggy as I was, I didn't resist. By the time I'd worked my boots onto my swollen feet, a servant had shown Mia into my room, and I saw the source of my rude wakeup call in the light from the illuminated corridor: a woman perhaps four feet tall, sporting a hooded brown cloak over her matching tunic and pants, her dark blonde beard braided into an unadorned plait. She'd folded her arms over her broad chest and planted her boots shoulder-width apart, an unmovable pillar of dwarf with a lantern between her feet.

"Uh…good morning?" I tried, wincing as I stood.

"Nothing good about it," she said. "There's twenty-seven dead in Wideplain."

"Huh?"

"A fishing village beyond Tightbend," said Owir, hurrying into the room with Dewin on his heels. "Three Outsiders attacked two nights ago, and word has just reached here. The survivors were only able to kill one of those beasts, so every available guard's being sent to patrol the Barrens and the districts nearby." Seeing the woman, he bowed low. "Princess. The carriage we borrowed is ready. I'll see them back—"

"My father has requested that I handle this personally," she interjected. "But thank you. Join the search party. Take whatever arms and armor you like from storage."

Dewin executed a hasty bow and scurried on, but Owir paused at the door to give us a last look. "I'm sorry, lass," he said, and then he was gone, another pair of scurrying boots as the palace awoke around us.

The woman—the *princess*, rather, my sleep-addled brain noted—waved for Mia and me to follow her. "We've a long journey ahead," she said as we fell into line, staying near a wall to avoid the traffic. "You're going home, Watcher."

"It's Susan."

"You're still going home, whatever you call yourself. Father has ordered you back to the Crossing."

"Hold on a second," I protested, grabbing her shoulder to stop her march. "He can order us out of this kingdom, but that's *all* he can do. I've got elves and more to find."

She had Rokund's golden-brown eyes, I noticed, and the look they were giving me was impatient. "The Under-King of Blackhorn Mountain has ordered you home. You intend to defy him?"

"Might," I said, and reached for the hilt at my hip.

But before my fingertips could do more than graze the leather, the princess had knocked me to the ground. As my head bounced off the thick red hallway runner and the unforgiving stone beneath, I gasped for breath, only to find the dwarf kneeling atop me, a dagger in her fist. "Would you like to rethink that answer?" she enquired.

A sharp object aimed at the pulse point in my neck did wonders for my compliance. "Maybe?"

She grunted and stood, watching with disdain while Mia helped me to my feet. Once I was upright and ambulatory, if a little wobbly, she announced, "This way," and started off without a backward glance.

"Good morning to you, too, crazy bitch," Mia muttered, wrapping a steadying arm around my shoulders. "You okay, Suze? What the hell was that about?"

I explained our predicament while the princess led the way back into the palace's carriage shed, where at least two dozen vehicles of a variety of sizes and degrees of ornamentation appeared in the light of her lantern. She opened our borrowed conveyance and motioned us inside with a curt toss of her head. Tired and bruising, I slumped in my seat from the day before, watching out the window as the princess skillfully guided the carriage into the air and out over the palace compound.

The ride was quiet until we were well clear of the torchlit bejeweled city wall, and then our pilot, barely turning to look over her shoulder, said, "Anjikora."

I frowned and looked at the sword, wondering if the translating bit of it had been broken in my fall. "Sorry, what was that?" I called toward the front.

"My name. Anjikora." She paused, then added, "Sorry about your head."

Prodding the back of my skull with two fingertips, I said, "Seems to be intact. At least I didn't bleed all over Daddy's rug."

"No, really, I'm sorry. Keeping up appearances...wait a moment, let me put this down..." She guided the carriage into a fallow field and tapped a button on the console panel, at which point all the windows turned opaque, blocking out the night. Sliding out of the front bench, she pressed another button in the ceiling, and the interior roof emitted a pale white glow. "Let me see the damage," she said, heading for our seats.

Unwilling to antagonize her further, I turned and felt a gentle touch on my scalp. "You'll have a knot, I'm afraid," said Anjikora—and to my surprise, she sounded penitent. "Any nausea? Dizziness?"

"Not yet..."

"Good." She stepped back while I straightened on the bench, twisting to maneuver my knees in the dwarf-sized vehicle. "I wish you hadn't done that," she chided.

"Likewise," I muttered.

"Necessary, I assure you. And I'm not crazy," she said, glancing at Mia. "Whatever else you called me didn't come through, but I'm of sound mind."

Mia looked at me for an explanation, and I quietly said, "I think she's got a translator."

"Correct. A one-way translator, I'm afraid—it only helps me understand what's being said." The princess reached under her tunic and pulled free an intricate golden pendant set with a milky white gem—a moonstone, I thought. "See? And here." Digging in a pocket, she extracted a similar necklace and offered it to Mia. "Father said she was at something of a disadvantage," she explained to me, dropping the translator into Mia's lap. "I apologize, there are two-way translators in storage, but no one will miss this one."

After a moment's hesitation, Mia slipped the necklace on, and Anjikora offered her a lopsided grin. "Does that sound better?"

Mia chuckled. "*Whoa.* How, uh…"

"Forging is a useful skill…as is combat," she added, giving me a meaningful look. "You know nothing, do you? About swords, I mean," she amended as I bristled.

"I know which is the stabby bit. Killed a few Outsiders," I replied.

The princess rolled her eyes and sat on the bench in front of me. "You can't have had much training. Father said you were a babe half my age."

"Does learning on the job count?" said Mia. "If so, then…what, six days of training? Seven?"

Anjikora's eyebrows rose, and when she saw that Mia wasn't kidding, I heard her mutter to the High Queen. "*Humans,*" she said with a sigh. "Why you fail to educate your women at arms is beyond all comprehension."

"Hey, now, hardly anyone in our corner of the world knows how to fight with a sword," Mia protested. "It's archaic."

She barely had time to take a breath before the princess's dagger was at her throat. "But effective," Anjikora replied, returning to her chair as Mia slid away toward the window. "Well, if you've had no training, then at least we have a starting point, and I'll have no bad habits to untrain."

"Sorry…*what*?" I asked, distantly noting that she sounded far too peppy about the prospect of swordplay for my comfort.

Her mouth curled toward the place midway between a smile and smirk. "I heard about your predicament last night. The guards talk if one asks nicely. Hearing what they had to say, I confronted Father after his banquet for the full truth, and he confirmed every word I'd heard. I had no idea how the Watcher was selected," she insisted. "All I knew was that he was always human. Or, uh…she?"

"First," I said, lifting a finger in mock celebration.

Her expression grew wryer. "Well, then, congratulations. But honestly, I thought someone from Daril or such might be the Watcher, not an uninterested party."

"What," said Mia, "you didn't know about this sweet little system your grandpa helped rig?"

"It's unjust, is what it is," she replied. "And I told my father as much. He sympathizes—believe me, he does," she stressed, looking me in the eye—"but his obligation is to our people, just as any ruler would owe his first duty to his subjects."

Mia cocked her head. "And you?"

Anjikora turned to her, the perfect picture of innocence. "Ah, I am but the under-king's seventh daughter, barely a presence in court society, occupied as I currently am with my martial education. If I were to be absent for a time, well, I can't suppose that anyone would notice at first."

A feeling curiously like hope began to stir in my chest. "You mean…"

"Father agrees that the system that has entrapped you is unfair. I informed him that I intended to offer you assistance, and he told me to do so without causing a scene. A public display of dominance will perhaps convince anyone who hears of it that I couldn't *possibly* have accompanied you back to the Crossing and that I must have gone off on a foolish solo mission to hunt down the roving Outsiders."

"You're coming back with us?" I asked, not quite believing what I'd heard.

The princess snorted. "I intend to keep you alive long enough to seek out the others involved in Heart's Blood's creation and see whether they can free you." Glancing back at Mia, she said, "The two guards who brought you to us reported that you were something like the Watcher's bodyguard. Accurate?"

"Best friend, not bodyguard," said Mia.

"She's a good shot," I offered.

"Yeah, but that's a bonus. I'm here because Suze has been screwed over."

Anjikora considered that for a moment—parsing whatever the translator had offered, I assumed—then nodded. "A loyal companion, then. Commendable, if not entirely helpful."

"I'm not *helpless*," Mia retorted.

"And you will be even less so once I've worked with you." She stood and stifled a yawn, then headed for the controls once more. "Forgive me, it's early. Does this home of yours have an extra bed, perchance?"

"There's a recliner," I said. "Big chair that leans back and comes with a footrest. Smells a little funky, but it's comfortable."

"It's a shitty cabin in the woods," added Mia. "Your Highness is going to be roughing it."

The princess shrugged. "I've had worse. Incidentally, 'Anji' will suffice." With a few taps, the lights dimmed, the windows unclouded, and the carriage was airborne once more. "Join me in the front," she called over her shoulder.

Having seen the bags under Mia's eyes, I took the seat beside the princess, giving Mia space to sprawl behind us. "You realize we don't know how to fly one of these things, right?" I said.

"Of course. Your job is to keep me conscious in case I

try to sleep." She stretched, cracked her back, then rotated her neck until it popped. "Tell me about yourselves."

And so we did, in the interest of collegiality and not dying a fiery death by vehicular crash. We talked until the sun rose, telling Anji about the less than thrilling wonders of Cole's Crossing, and then Mia, whose yawns had steadily increased in frequency and duration over the course of our ride, took a closer look at her translator in the early pink light. "This is really gorgeous," she said, turning the pendant back and forth to make the crystal flash.

I had to agree—the piece was almost the twin of Anji's, a braided circle around a perfectly faceted gem, the gold decorated with the tiniest of carved flowers and accented with hints of silver.

"This must have cost a small fortune, huh?" Mia asked. "Owir and Dewin were talking about how expensive translators are, and this one's so pretty. You, uh...you might want to rethink entrusting me with this," she added, weakly chuckling.

"I'm not concerned," said Anji.

"Access to the royal treasure room has its perks, right?"

"Granted, but *that* hardly constitutes treasure," the princess replied. "An early forging project of mine. As I said, no one will miss it."

Mia perked up behind us. "Wait—*you* made this?"

"A practice effort, I assure you. I've been studying both halves of the forging process—"

"It's *beautiful!*" Mia gushed. "Oh, my God, you can't loan me this! What if I break your necklace?"

Anji's shoulders tensed. "Truly, it's of no consequence."

"It really is lovely," I assured her. "And I thought forging was a two-person job—one to make the thing, one to add the magic."

"Ordinarily, yes," she said, "but with proper practice, one can learn elements of both. Translators are useful, so

I've been experimenting."

"Hell, I'd wear it even if it didn't work," said Mia. "You've got a real talent, Anji. I'm a *terrible* artist."

"It's a poor thing," she said stiffly. "Look there, to the left—do you see the smokehouse? They work day and night during the redbelly run."

I didn't fight her awkward change of topic, and as for Mia, within an hour of sunrise, her snoring was a constant sonic accompaniment to Anji's and my conversation. I looked back to find my friend's head awkwardly propped against the window, her mouth agape, and laughed to myself.

"What's amusing?" asked Anji.

"Mia looks like a landed fish," I replied, shifting position on the bench. "And I'm sorry if we embarrassed you earlier. Didn't mean to make you uncomfortable about your translators."

She kept silent for a brief moment, one hand gently tugging her braided beard, then murmured, "Are you religious, Susan?"

"Kind of," I admitted. "Go to church on major holidays, try to be a decent person, stuff like that. You?"

"Yes. You've heard of the High King and High Queen, I trust."

"Bits and pieces…"

She leaned back in her seat and closed her eyes—a somewhat terrifying thing to do in a flying vehicle, even one more or less on autopilot, though I tried not to panic. "They are the creators of this world and all worlds. Perhaps yours, too."

"That would be *highly* debatable in my hometown."

"Understood. To us, though…" She paused, her face working ever so slightly as she thought. "Their creations are perfect. Everything we do is a poor copy of that, an attempt that can never reach that degree of perfection. For example, though there is no one in Blackhorn Mountain more powerful than my father, he is the *under*-king.

Claiming kingship would be tantamount to claiming equality with the High King, and that's pure blasphemy. Do you understand?"

"I think so..."

Anji hesitated again before continuing. "The same principle applies to the things we make. Our creations are inferior copies, rubbish beside that perfection. So, even if one appreciates a fine meal or a well-made weapon...or a piece of forgework..."

"One doesn't gush over it," I finished, catching her drift.

She nodded. "It's not exactly blasphemy, but...you see..."

"We didn't know—"

"Of course not," she hastily replied, opening her eyes. "How could you have been expected to know? And, um...thank you," she mumbled. "Your praise is unwarranted, but I'm pleased that you find my work satisfactory."

Even with her beard, I could pick out the flush rising into her cheeks. "Most satisfactory," I said. "Or as satisfactory as it can be without getting you in trouble with your gods."

She chuckled and adjusted our heading against the wind. "We should reach the tunnel by nightfall. What was your plan?"

"Will you be upset with me if I say I don't exactly have a fleshed-out *plan* yet?"

"That's what I thought. Have you any ideas about a potential plan, then?"

"Go find some elves?"

A soft groan met that suggestion.

"Come on," I prodded, "they can't be all bad. You're biased."

"And you'll see why," she replied. "But here, now— would you like to learn to fly a carriage?"

"Are you offering?"

Anji cut her eyes to me and smirked. "Since I'd like to sleep at some point before I drop of exhaustion, that was really more of an order. Pay attention."

# CHAPTER 7

By the time we limped out of the cave and into the cabin that night, I was ready to drop, and Mia didn't look much better. Anji held up better than we did, or else she had an excellent stiff upper lip. She swore only when she tripped over a root in the darkness and went sprawling on her face, and though she was scratched and carried leaf litter in her beard when we reached the cabin, she didn't complain about the rustic setting. As Mia sloughed off her pack in the corner and I turned on the lights, Anji shifted her lighter wilderness pack and considered the sudden illumination from Uncle Malachi's beloved chandelier. "Are those...horns?" she asked, squinting at its bulb-tipped arms.

"Deer antlers," I replied, dropping my bag beside Mia's. "Put your stuff down wherever you'd like. See that brown chair?"

She followed my finger. "That would be the famous recliner?"

"The cracks in the leather give it character," Mia offered, heading for the kitchen. "And I'm starving."

Anji shook off her pack and followed her. "I'm no master, but I can make food that's, um...*edible*, if you want assistance."

"Save it for the camp cooking," Mia replied, pulling a sun-faded menu off the refrigerator. "I'm going to Little Italy. Who wants what on their pizza?"

We explained the concept of the dish to Anji, who seemed relieved to have avoided kitchen duties, and she and I watched from the porch as Mia's taillights faded into the trees. "The restaurant is in the next town over," I explained, locking the door as we returned to the house. "The drive's not bad, but it's farther than I can go with the damn sword attached to me, so…" I shrugged and pulled a couple of beers from the fridge. Uncle Malachi's taste in alcohol was always shitty, but after the week I'd had, I wasn't about to turn my nose up at his last six-pack. "They deliver, but I didn't feel like paying for them to make the trip all the way out here. Any time you ask delivery guys to turn off the paved road, the expected tip doubles. Here, have one," I said, sliding a can down the counter to Anji.

She followed my lead in popping the top and wrapped her hands around the can. "Cold."

"Sorry, do you prefer yours room temperature?"

"No, no…" She took a sip, grimaced, then forced another down. "There's almost none of the Aen here, correct? The air feels different."

"Pricklier?"

"Perhaps," she said after another thoughtful sip of beer. "Thinner, maybe. Like there's nothing to grab and harness, if that makes sense."

"Sure." She had a point—I'd noticed the change on our return, and in all frankness, I missed the atmospheric feeling of enormous potential that we'd left behind in Ildon.

Anji studied the room, eventually landing on the fridge. "How does that work? The cooling box."

The flashback that accompanied her question left my brain feeling like mush. Our fridge broke when I was fifteen, and Dad had taken it upon himself to repair the compressor—and to teach me how. Never the most mechanically inclined, I remembered parts and tools scattered along his workbench, pieces I couldn't name that somehow, perhaps magically, kept my ice cream sandwiches from turning to soup, but I couldn't have explained the mechanism if my life had depended on it.

"Electricity," I replied, hoping that would suffice. But as she frowned in bemusement, I forced myself to elaborate. "We produce power elsewhere, send it along special lines into our houses, and let it run our appliances. It's not forging, but it does the trick."

Curious, she opened the fridge door, let the blast of cold air rush into her face, then closed it and resumed drinking. "Strange. And not at all a product of the Aen?"

"Nope."

She cocked her can toward the chandelier. "The lights?"

"Same deal."

"Remarkable," she murmured between sips of mediocre beer.

Gross as I felt after my time on the road, I tried to be a decent hostess while we waited for Mia. "Want to get a shower? You can have first crack at the hot water tank."

The princess brightened at the notion of cleanliness, and soon, the tiny bathroom was steamy. She sang to herself as the shower beat down—a song I didn't know, but in a rendition I was fairly confident was off key—and when she emerged in her undershirt and clean trousers, her hair and beard hung loose and water-dark. Before I could show her the wonders of a hairdryer, Mia arrived with dinner, and the three of us sat around Uncle Malachi's little table. We made short work of the pizzas and garlic bread—even Anji was licking her fingers by the end of the meal—and as Mia slipped off to shower, I made up a bed of sorts in the recliner for the princess.

"We're just in the other room if you need anything," I told her as she tested the reclining capabilities. Short as she was, Anji had space to stretch on both ends of the chair. "If you hear any weird scratching, come get us, okay?"

She pulled the thin summer blanket to her chin and snuggled down. "You're not setting a watch?"

"Do *you* want first watch? Besides, when Outsiders come around here, they don't tiptoe."

"Point taken." With a yawn, she rolled onto her side and curled up, and I turned out the lights.

"You know," mumbled Mia when we awoke around midnight to the sound of unearthly howling and an arrhythmic thump against the cabin walls, "we probably should have restrung the alarm wire."

"Need more breakables first," I replied, yanking the sword off the floor. "We did a number on Uncle Malachi's mug collection."

She plucked her gun from the nightstand and slid out of bed. "Fair. If we have to overnight here again, I could make a run to the dollar store—"

The bedroom door flew open, revealing Anji with her knife in one hand and something like an overgrown lighter in the other—a forged piece, I guessed. "Do you hear—"

"Outsiders," I confirmed. "Come on, before they break the door again. And stay behind us, all right?"

Her expression spoke of disbelief. "*Behind* you? Remind me, which of us has actual training?"

"And which of us has a magic sword?" I countered. "You've got our backs."

Though she muttered a prayer for safety and patience to the High Queen, Anji did as I asked, exchanging her light for her short sword and taking up a defensive stance beside the recliner. Meanwhile, Mia and I hurried toward the front, staying clear of the windows, and listened to the movement outside the cabin as we flanked the door.

"Two?" she whispered.

I nodded. "Think so."

"Want me to check?"

"Careful."

Ever so gingerly, she peeked around a window frame and into the night. Without the porch light on, I doubted she'd be able to make out details, but a moment's observation satisfied her. "Two," she whispered, slotting herself back into position. "One's a bug."

"The other?"

"Head kind of looked like a vulture, but there were too many legs."

"Joy." I gripped the sword more tightly as my palms began to sweat. "You ready?"

Mia eased forward, unlatched the lock, and grabbed the doorknob. "On my count," she whispered. "One…two…"

On *three*, she pulled the door open, revealing the vulture-adjacent monstrosity on the porch. Having been snuffling at the ratty welcome mat, it raised its bald head in surprise and opened its nightmarishly large, hooked beak just before I shoved the blade through its neck. Screeching, the creature pulled itself off the sword and staggered back, but the damage was done. It is, after all, difficult to live with a fist-sized hole burned in one's throat, and the Outsider fell down the stairs as it gasped its last breath.

By then, its buddy was scurrying toward the door, mandibles snapping. "Mia?" I said.

She answered with a single shot from the .454, which landed squarely between the thing's multifaceted eyes. Unlike its vulturish partner, it didn't bother with dramatics and simply collapsed where it stood.

I held up one hand, motioning for quiet, and Mia and I stood still and listened to the woods around us. All I could make out were the distant footsteps of a deer through a drift of the last year's fallen leaves, and after a moment, I let out the breath I'd been holding. "I think that's it. Yeah?"

"Yeah." Mia turned and beckoned Anji closer. "Want to see?"

The princess marched across the room, peered into the night, then goggled and took a step back as she noticed the corpses. "What—"

"This is what I'm stuck dealing with for the rest of my

life," I said with forced cheer. "Things like *those* that want to make me a midnight snack. Every night. Yay!"

She stared at the dead Outsiders, then looked at me, her expression a blend of horror and pity. "No. That's...*no*," she said more firmly, "that's not going to happen."

"Oh?"

"I meant what I said. At first light, I'll help you find the damned elves. Unless you want to leave now—"

"*No*," Mia and I chorused.

"Outsiders are more active in the dark, apparently," she explained to Anji. "At least the cabin offers a hiding place."

"Yeah," I muttered, "but for the fact that they're drawn to the sword." After another moment's consideration of the massive corpses, I sighed and closed the door. "Cleanup in the morning. Elves can wait. I'm going back to bed."

Though Anji seemed uncertain of the wisdom of leaving monsters on the porch overnight, she didn't protest. "I'll take the watch," she said. "Not like I'll sleep well after *that*."

"Oh, trust me," Mia chirped, "hang out with us long enough, and you'll get used to it."


Of the three of us, Mia possessed the closest thing to actual skill in the kitchen, a smattering of techniques picked up from her time in New York and enhanced by her chats with Antoinette outside the lunch and dinner rushes. Since she'd returned to the Crossing, I'd gradually come to understand that Mia had learned most of what she knew from her girlfriend in New York, now known only as Raquel the Whore, who had been a year into a culinary program when she and Mia met at a bar. They'd hit it off, and Raquel had proven equally willing to cook for Mia and teach her the basics. Mia had been on the verge of asking

Raquel to move in with her when their leases expired until she'd stopped by Raquel's studio one evening with a bottle of wine and surprised her girlfriend…who, unfortunately, had been in bed with a mutual friend of theirs at the time.

I knew *damn* well not to mention Raquel unless Mia got drunk and brought her up, but I could still silently appreciate what she'd done for us.

"Pancakes," I explained to Anji the next morning as she helped me lug the stabbed Outsider—which, I discovered in the soft, dewy light of dawn, looked much less like a vulture below the neck than like a mutant arachnid from a schlocky horror movie—"are the perfect breakfast food. They're filling, you can put fun stuff in the batter, and you can top them with whatever the hell you like as long as there's sugar somewhere in the mix."

"Sugar?" she puffed, straining under our unwieldy burden.

"It's sweet. Good in syrup form." I shifted my grip on the monstrosity's front legs, which had stiffened into halfway decent handles overnight, and nodded toward the burn pit. "There."

We shoved the body into the cleared ring, and I stabbed it again until it caught fire. Anji watched, appraising the sword's work, then wiped her hands on her pants and rolled her shoulders. "Should we get the other?" she asked.

"May as well take a breather. Mia's going to be busy for a while."

Honestly, my plans for that spring hadn't included warming myself in the cool morning air beside a burning corpse with a dwarven princess at my side, but in the moment, it wasn't altogether *horrible*. At least no one was bleeding, and if we stood upwind of the smoke, the stench of burning flesh wasn't retch-worthy.

As the ashes began to drift, Anji quietly said, "There is a story told among my people of a righteous king."

I glanced her way, but her eyes were trained on the fire.

"Oh?"

Her head bobbed. "There was once a great man—a kind husband, a loving father of many sons and daughters, a mighty warrior. The people around him looked to him for guidance in small matters, then in more important matters, and one day, they decided that he should be their king. That night, the High King appeared before him, declared him a pious and worthy leader, and offered him a great and powerful kingdom."

"Nice of him."

"So it seemed. The High King walked with him through this beautiful city—roads set with the smoothest of stones, a temple more beautiful than the one in Heartfast, a palace fit for the High King himself—and said that it could all be his. But the man was wise, you see, and he asked what the High King would require of him in return for this unmerited blessing. So the High King brought him into the temple plaza and showed the man all of the people he led—the people who would make him a king—and told him to choose one. The man asked what would become of the person he chose, and the High King explained that this person would be a sacrifice, sent into the deepest darkness below the world until the end of time. Every hundred years, the king would choose another to be bound below. But in return, the kingdom would prosper, and his reign would last for generations.

"The man was stunned. You see," she explained, "unlike some of the humans' gods, the High King and High Queen have never demanded blood sacrifices from their children. He protested that he couldn't do that. What about the sacrifice's family, you know? He couldn't possibly rip a husband from his wife, a mother from her babes. The High King reassured him that no one would hold his choice against him—as soon as he made his selection, it would be as if that person had never existed at all in the minds of the people of the kingdom. He or she would be wiped from the record like chalk from a slate, and no one but the king would ever remember so much as his or her name. The king would be loved by his people and protected by the High King, so wasn't that a fair trade?"

"Tempting, I suppose," I replied.

Anji nodded. "For a lesser man, perhaps. But the would-be king was a man of honor, and he refused. 'Thank you, Your Supreme Majesty,' he told the High King, 'but I must decline your offer. The injustice would kill me.'

"Well, the High King seemed surprised by this. 'Don't be foolish,' he told the man. 'What is one life every hundred years to protect all of the other lives of your kingdom? This beautiful, powerful, prosperous kingdom I lay before you? Do you think yourself so wise that you would *reject* my gift?'

"At that, the man said, 'I do not pretend to be anything more than the lowliest fool beside you. But I know my own mind and soul, and I cannot make the sacrifice you would require in trade. If my people will name me their leader, then I will struggle and fight to make our kingdom strong and myself worthy of their trust. If my present weakness offends you, it is my failing.'

"The High King had questioned the man with a storm on his brow. But when the man finished, the High King smiled. 'Indeed,' he said, 'your weakness is your strength. Loyalty I prize, compassion I honor, but justice I treasure. Return to your bed and sleep soundly—you have proven yourself wise and worthy of kingship.'"

Anji folded her arms and cut her eyes toward me. "Legend says he became the first king of Blackhorn Mountain. Rokund I, called either the Blessed or the Just. My ancestor, if you believe the stories." Her gaze landed on the sword, which I'd left visible at my hip. "His is not a name that my father bears lightly."

"Look," I said, "I understand that he's in a difficult position—"

"He hates it. If the stories are true, you see, then the

original Rokund wouldn't have rested until he freed you, regardless of the threat to the kingdom. Even if the just path were one of struggle, he would have taken it."

Considering the position Anji had put herself in, I tried to be generous. "You know, stories say a lot of things that never necessarily happened. We've got our share of them, too."

"But there's truth in them, all the same," she replied, then sighed and pointed to the path back around the cabin. "Shall we dispose of the other?"

Mia's thick, fluffy pancakes didn't disappoint, and by the end of the meal, Anji had joined us in abandoning all propriety to scoop up her leftover syrup and butter with a finger. She and I still stank of sweat, smoke, and burned Outsider, but Mia had insisted that showers could take a backseat to a warm short stack, and I couldn't argue with that logic.

Once satiated, Anji turned to the problem of strategy—more specifically, our lack thereof. "The elves are probably your best option," she mused as I topped up our coffee. "That's not to say I'm thrilled at the prospect of going anywhere near those degenerates, but I don't see a better choice this morning."

"Elven magic is that good?" Mia asked.

"It's powerful," Anji conceded after a moment's waffling. "Good or bad is a matter of use. But if what I know of it is accurate, then they should be able to help."

"They can destroy the sword?"

She took a sip of coffee, grimaced, and reached for the cooled syrup in the ancient plastic measuring cup, one of Uncle Malachi's few microwave-safe containers remaining after our alarm wire experimentation. "Probably not. Forging done well is difficult to undo. But consider what the elves did to create the sword—they made it lethal to Outsiders, correct?"

Mia and I shrugged.

"Right. Sorry," Anji muttered, stirring syrup into her drink. "We forged it—we made the sword itself, and we forged it with the spells that made it a translator and gave it invisibility and a glow. The elves made it deadly against the monsters, since their talents lean toward matters of life."

"That *kind* of seems antithetical," Mia pointed out.

"Life and death are two sides of a coin. Elves can heal and kill with equal facility—their magic focuses the Aen to affect the life force. Now, generally, their religion forbids the use of magic to kill—one of its few redeeming aspects," she added with a snort—"but in times of crisis, let's just say they're not as pious as they could be."

"The war?" I asked, returning to the table.

She nodded. "Not every battle, and not every elf, but it happened. At least their priests protested." After a long, slow sip, she said, "Father and the others who lived through the war have much to say on the subject of elves. I was born after the peace was brokered, so I believe my view on them is somewhat less biased."

"Oh?"

Seeing my disbelief, she grinned. "Some of the old guards insist there's no such thing as a decent elf. I'm willing to be convinced."

Mia, who was sucking leftover syrup off her fingertip, frowned in thought. "Okay, so say the elves cooperate and undo what they did to the sword. That just takes away a helpful bit—it'll be less effective but still attached to Suze."

"Correct," said Anji, "but you're forgetting that the elves have *influence.*"

"Can't forget what you don't know," she hinted.

The princess's head bobbed. "True. It's all to do with humans, see. Not you," she hastily added as our foreheads furrowed. "Those of your kind who live within the four worlds. They lack inherent magical talent—some of us born within the Aen have it, but since humans originated outside…*here*, I suppose," she said, glancing around at the walls of the cabin, "they aren't naturally sensitive. But many can learn. They're not talented like the elves, and they can't forge like we do—and they're nowhere close to the maladetas, no matter what they look like—but they can master minor curses, small charms, and such. Their spells are markedly stronger if they are close to crystalline Aen, however, so most human practitioners of exceptional ability own at least one crystal."

I cut my eyes to the sword, which I'd left propped by the window during breakfast. The blue-green gems in the hilt glittered in the morning light.

"Just holding a crystal can help," Anji continued, "but to make them truly effective, they need to be incorporated into a forged piece—Heart's Blood, for instance, but pieces of jewelry are far more common. Rings, pendants, bracelets…even the crown of Daril has a few worked into the metal."

"So…you forge for them?" I guessed.

"Heh. *No*." She smirked as my eyebrows rose in query. "Elves are restricted in their use of harmful magic by their religion, at least most of the time. Maladetas are far stronger, sometimes even stronger than elementals, but when they use magic for destructive purposes, it causes them physical pain. That's why the maladetas who worked on Heart's Blood died, you see—creating such a powerful weapon, one designed to take life quickly and effectively, cost the makers their lives in turn. That, plus their own ethical code, prevents them from conquering us all. But humans? The only limits on their power are ability and access to amplification tools. We would be foolish to forge weapons of our own destruction. The guilds prohibit forgers from taking any jobs involving Aen crystals for that reason."

"Then who—"

"Freelancer forgers. Mercenaries who care more about

gold than they do their own people," she said with distaste. "Forging outside of guild oversight is forbidden by law, but there are those willing to risk punishment in the pursuit of wealth. And believe me, any dwarf who accepts an Aen-work commission for a human has contracted for a small fortune. They hide in Ga'besh, mostly. Faithless," she muttered. "Anyway, some of the larger human kingdoms took offense during the war when we refused to forge weapons for them, and they allied themselves with the elves. Those alliances are weaker now than they were even in my childhood, but if the Twins call for the sword's destruction, then Daril may be convinced to acquiesce— and *that* is what you need."

Mia's brow puckered. "I thought you said humans aren't good at magic."

"The adepts of Daril are among the best of your race," said Anji. "They contributed to the sword's creation by building the blood lock tying it to the Watcher. I don't know who tied the Watcher to the Crossing," she added apologetically, "but if we could make Daril agree to unlock the sword…"

"Then someone else could take it," I finished, a burst of hope fluttering within me. "Another human, a maladeta—"

"*Anyone*," said Anji. "You could make a tekori guard the Crossing—that would probably be the first time one of them did anything useful. But in any case, Susan, you'd be free."

I felt myself smile in earnest. "What if we cut out the middleman and went straight to this Daril? You don't seem especially keen about dealing with elves, so—"

Anji grimaced at the suggestion. "Humans are…complicated. No offense intended to present company, but dealing with them can be a nightmare. As little as I want to seek out the Twins, I think our odds are better if the elves intercede on our behalf."

Mia rose to pour herself the dregs of the coffee.

"You're not worried that some elf is going to hold a war grudge?"

"Oh, I fully anticipate that. But if we come to them, state our business, and convince them that we've traveled to them on my father's orders, I think they'll at least grant us an audience. It's worth a try." Downing the rest of her drink in a quick gulp, she pushed back from the table and pointed her mug toward the sword. "Mia, the meal was appreciated, but Susan and I have work to do before we depart."

The hopeful little butterfly bumping around my ribs turned into a rock and plummeted. "You mean—"

"Your form is *atrocious*. Get the sword and meet me outside—and Mia, where is yours?"

My friend snickered at the suggestion. "Guns or nothing here. I don't fight with sharp objects."

Anji grunted, then pulled a long knife from the block on the counter and extended it to her handle-first. "You do now, and you're next on my list."

"What about the elves?" Mia protested. "You said you'd take us to them."

"And I will," she said, heading for her weapons. "But I'd rather not take you there as corpses, lass."


Collapsing in bed that evening, I prayed to any god within earshot that the Outsiders would give us the night off.

Anji was *good*, and scarily so. What she lacked in height and reach, she more than made up for in speed and stamina, and she ignored my gripes and pleas for a rest while she put me through her crash course in swordsmanship. I couldn't touch her as a fighter, and within about two minutes of skirmishing in our makeshift practice field behind the cabin, we both knew it. By the fifth time she knocked me off my feet and held the point of a blade to my throat, I was frustrated; by the tenth, I'd grown discouraged and more than a little winded, but she didn't let up. Only after I'd hit the ground a couple dozen times did Anji let me take a water break, and as I plopped into the grass and gulped from my bottle, she crouched beside me and gave me a careful once-over—red face, sweaty hair, streaks of dirt, damp shirt, and all.

"You're out of shape," she said as I belched. "There's little we can do to rectify that today, but a few seasons of steady practice and exercise would harden you. I think you'd be impressed with yourself after a year's work."

I put my fingers to the hollow below my jaw and felt my pulse still pounding like I'd been doing sprints. "I used to work out in college. Uh...a year ago, and a few years before that," I explained as her thick brows drew together. "Like, I got on a treadmill a few times a week. A running machine."

"Why did you stop? And did you not strength train?"

"Didn't have a treadmill here, running outside is a pain, and no," I admitted. "Look, I've never exactly been *svelte*—"

"This can be corrected, but only with time," she replied. "For now, we'll work on your form." She paused while I drained my drink, then said, "You're not terrible, you know."

I tried to laugh but ended up coughing my disbelief as I inhaled water. "Come again?" I wheezed once the fit subsided.

"I've seen worse beginners. Considering that you've had no instruction, you're intuiting nicely. A good sign."

"The bruises you've given me would suggest otherwise."

Anji chuckled. "My father's guards put a sword in my hand when I was eight. I'm still in training, mind you, but it would be fair to say that I've got the advantage between us. Here, now, on your feet."

Wincing, I let her help me upright and stumbled as my sore muscles protested. The ground was a safe place, but *hitting* the ground was another matter.

By lunchtime, the purpling bruises across my arms and torso made me look a bit like a mutant Dalmatian, and I gingerly sponged off in the bathroom as Anji took her first crack at Mia. I'd assumed that my friend would be the better athlete, but when I ventured back outside, I found her a tomato-faced mess, puffing and glaring daggers at our unbothered tutor. With an enraged yell, Mia hoisted Anji's sword—mine refused to stay in her hands long enough for practice—and charged at the dwarf, who executed a rapid pivot and sent Mia sprawling. "Running at me like an angry troll isn't effective," Anji chided. "You're allowing your emotions to rule you. Channel your anger into the strength of your sword arm instead of letting it guide your hand." Spotting me, Anji smiled and cracked her back. "Washed off the blood, then?"

"She's all yours, Suze," Mia muttered as she pushed herself to her feet.

"Perhaps food first," Anji suggested, an idea that met with no resistance.

After sandwiches, when we could no longer come up with reasons to linger at the table, Mia and I volunteered to do the dishes, which either of us could have extended to a half-hour process with a bit of creativity. But Anji was neither stupid nor blind, and she snorted as Mia collected the plates. "I worked with you all morning," she said. "It's my turn as the student."

I dropped the griddle pan in the sink and regarded her bemusedly. "What do you mean?"

"Your weapon," she said, pointing to Mia. "The...gun, was it? I would learn its use, if you would teach me."

I took full advantage of the unexpected reprieve, flopped into bed with a dose of aspirin, and drifted off to sleep to the sound of gunfire outside the cabin. But my nap ended all too soon, as Mia shook me awake barely an hour after she and Anji went out to shoot. "She's good," Mia reported as I groaned myself into a sitting position. "Better than a fair shot. I mean, she's had archery lessons, but once she adjusted to the recoil, her aim improved. I'm running back to the house to get my .38—the grip should fit her hands a little better."

"Sounds good," I mumbled. "I'll tag along and make sure nothing's spoiled in the fridge—"

Mia interrupted my offer with a wicked laugh. "Oh, no, you don't. The honor of your presence is requested in the yard. Round two, babe."

I'd have thrown a pillow at her head had my arms not ached so badly.

By nightfall, I was ready to swallow a few bites and hit the sack, and Anji didn't intervene. So weary was I that I didn't stir until I heard gunfire coming from the main room, followed by an inhuman roar of pain. Mia's side of the mattress was empty, and I staggered out of the bedroom, sword in hand, to find her and Anji kneeling at the windows, lining up shots like bandits in an old Western. "How many?" I demanded.

"Three now," said Anji, and then Mia fired again. "Ah—two. Very nice."

"You've got to hit the head," said Mia. "The .38 doesn't pack as much of a punch, but if you can keep them distracted…"

Anji fired twice more, then paused to reload the revolver by the glow of a flashlight while Mia finished off the target. "One would think these things would be made to hold more than five bullets," the dwarf groused. "In the heat of battle—"

"That's not a combat weapon. You can get an automatic sidearm with a considerable magazine, but I don't have one here, and Malachi didn't exactly leave us an arsenal." She shot the last Outsider between the eyes— well, between two of its eyes—and grunted at the night. "I'll get more ammo in the morning. Going back to bed."

She plodded past me, gun in hand, and I watched as Anji made a last scan of the dark trees. "Thanks," I said, standing there like a fool with the naked sword in my fist.

"I, uh…I'm sorry, I didn't hear a thing—"

"Nothing to worry about. Though I do see where this could become rather tiring," she replied, and climbed back into the recliner. "I'm a light sleeper when on duty. Never fear—if more come, I'll rouse you." Pausing, she looked over the wide armrest and noticed her blankets on the floor. "Um…perhaps you'd be so kind…"

I passed her the bedding and waited while she burrowed down. "Did you want to do more training in the morning, or—"

"I think we should focus on getting rid of Heart's Blood and avoiding further nights like this, don't you?" she said through a yawn.

"Honslia?"

"Honslia," she agreed, and rolled over. "Try to sleep, Susan."

I did as she ordered, but my ears strained to hear every sound that night around the quiet cabin, and when dawn broke, I was a wreck. The beeping of Mia's alarm clock finally heralded six, and the mattress shifted beside me as she sat up, groaning. "Drugs?" she rasped.

"Nothing stronger than ibuprofen. I searched the bathroom yesterday."

"Fuck." She stood and limped in that direction. "Go back to bed. I've got errands to run, and the corpses outside will keep."

The part of me that believed in fair play and teamwork tried to protest, but the part of me that had been hoping for unconsciousness for the last few hours was far louder that morning. "'Kay," I mumbled, and knew no more.

# CHAPTER 8

When I dragged myself from bed, Mia had returned from her morning foraging, and the kitchen table was covered with yellow plastic bags. Taking a closer look, I noticed the blue Dirk's logo on the nearest and frowned. "Thought they didn't open until ten."

"They don't. You have to plug that into the wall, Anji," she added over her shoulder as the dwarf attempted to puzzle out the coffeemaker. "Socket's to your left. Help me unpack, Suze."

Digging through the bags, I found meal replacement bars, fruit snacks, half a dozen collapsible water bottles, and several boxes of ammunition for the pistols. "You're bringing both?" I asked.

"Since my proficiency with a sword is, in technical terms, *shit* right now, yes. Shouldn't be that much heavier, especially if Anji can carry some of the food."

"And my share of the bullets," she offered, standing on tiptoe to pull a mug from the cabinet. "Where did you find all of those provisions, anyway?"

Mia gathered up the bags and balled them into a crinkly wad. "Dirk's Hunt Camp. It's a family operation—their selection isn't as good as what you'd see at the big stores out of town—but they're also a lot less likely to ask annoying questions about what I need with this much ammo."

"Duffy?" I asked with a knowing grin.

"Useful little twerp," she replied, and rolled her eyes. Catching Anji's puzzlement, she explained, "Duffy

Shoemaker is Dirk's son, and he's had the hots for me since we were, oh, ten or so. Will *not* take no for an answer. So when I called him up this morning and told him I needed to do a little shopping for a trip"—she began to pout, and her eyes grew large and sad—"and I *just* hadn't had time to buy what I needed, and I would only take a few minutes...well, he had to come to my rescue."

Anji's eyebrows rose. "You used him?"

"He got what he wanted out of the deal. Nice little sale for Daddy, and I didn't protest when he found an excuse to grab my ass in a dark corner of the grocery section. Cretin," she muttered. "Duffy knows I don't go for guys. I've made that *abundantly* clear. But he's convinced himself that he's going to be the one to show me what I've been missing, so as long as he's there to annoy me, I may as well make him useful."

I wasn't sure how the princess's eyebrows could inch higher than they already were, but they drew quite near to her hairline at that. "You...um..."

Mia leaned against the table and folded her arms. "I don't sleep with men. Is that going to be a problem?"

To my relief, Anji merely shrugged. "No. No, that's..." she began, then paused, seemingly hunting for her words, before concluding, "My apologies. That surprised me."

"We're not *all* butch," Mia replied with a smirk.

"Of course not. I'm just unaccustomed to hearing it spoken of so openly." Turning back to the coffeemaker, she scanned the buttons, then pressed the largest and was rewarded with a red light and the first stirrings of the brew cycle.

Mia and I traded glances, and she opened the sugar cannister and began doctoring her mug in anticipation. "If it makes you feel any better," she told Anji, "it's not something I talk about much around here. New York was different—my ex and I seldom got a second glance. The Crossing...well." She snorted and put the sugar away. "My mom has barely spoken to me in more than a year. I think we've talked twice, and both of those time, I was the one to call. She's more or less giving me the silent treatment until I see the error of my ways and bring home a boyfriend." Pulling the creamer from the fridge, she added, "But that's not surprising. This town is provincial on a good day. Slim pickings for a lady like me, and odds are good that the nice old biddies who don't tell me to my face that I'm going to Hell are still thinking it, but it's home. What are you going to do?"

"A conundrum, I suppose," said Anji. "But at least there are places in this world where…*such*…may be spoken of. My people, regarding this matter, are quite like yours here."

Mia watched with a curious expression as Anji rummaged in the fridge for the pancake syrup, then administered a healthy squirt into her coffee mug. "I don't mean to ask too personal a question, but—"

"Please don't," Anji interrupted, her shoulders suddenly stiff.

"Sure, sure. Forget I said anything," Mia soothed, and slipped past her to finish unpacking. "Hey, Suze, are we schlepping corpses before or after breakfast?"

We didn't dawdle. The three of us lugged the night's kills into the burn pit for disposal, then made do with Uncle Malachi's dusty pantry supplies for a quick breakfast: canned peaches and Pop-Tarts of unknown vintage. If Anji wasn't impressed by the spread on offer, she didn't complain. By the time Mia had washed the coffee pot, the princess was dressed and packed for the trip, having loaded her bag with as much of the new stash as she could carry. Mia and I scrambled to hit the road, not bothering with showers. As I struggled to fit my share of the Dirk's goods into my pack—which, frustratingly, insisted upon following the basic precepts of physics instead of zipping—I hit upon an ingenious solution. Last time, Mia and I had each packed a tent, but we'd ended up sharing. One was more than sufficient, and so I dumped my tent beside the bed, shoved my load into the tent's strap-on carrying bag, and joined the others. I won't say any of us was excited for the hike ahead, but at least we'd resigned ourselves to a day on foot.

Familiarity hastened our steps. Soon, we'd crossed through the fence into the alleged asbestos mine and descended to the windy tunnels. Recalling that Ildon had been to my right, I instead turned left and soon found the opening to the Honslia arm, indistinguishable from the others but for the name carved into the rock wall. If I stood at the entrance, facing the strange inter-world breeze, I could *just* make out the queer sensation of the distant Aen flowing from the land at the other end.

"Ready?" I asked my companions.

In the sword's light, I barely caught Anji's grimace, but she soldiered on beside me.

The Honslia tunnel was indeed just like its Ildon-bound mate: a long stone passageway occasionally lit by colorful streaks that danced along the walls and vanished. I suggested a break after two hours—if nothing else, it gave us a chance to sample some of the chocolate-cherry granola Mia had snagged at Dirk's, which wasn't too shabby—and Mia tried to console our glum dwarf. "Maybe the elves won't be so bad," she said, digging another handful of granola from the rapidly lightening pouch. "This could be a case of propaganda on both sides."

Anji picked crumbs from her tangled beard. "Come again?"

"You two fought a nasty, prolonged war. It's not surprising that you still don't like each other. Maybe they have awful things to say about you, too."

"Undoubtedly," she muttered.

"But that's propaganda, see? Your people treated us pretty well," she concluded with a note of satisfaction at an argument won.

"Yes," said Anji, unfazed by Mia's logic, and popped a dried cherry in her mouth. "Because you're not elves."

Mia huffed, and I took the opportunity to steal the granola bag. "Maybe we could pass you off as a muscular, hirsute human child," I said to Anji.

She chuckled at that. "Of course…one with a distinctly Blackhornish accent. I can see no problem with that plan."

"Just wondering, but how good *is* your…Elvish?"

"Which one?" she replied, stretching her legs as she leaned her back against the wall. "I'm told there are structural differences between the dialects. But, say, Common Elvish? Without a translator, I think I can manage 'hello,' 'goodbye,' and 'may the High King have mercy on your soul.'"

"Well, that's awfully neighborly of you."

"My tutors haven't subjected me to the elven tongues yet. Not exactly a priority." Digging in her pack, she produced a small brush and a leather thong and began to braid her beard. "I've had enough to learn with the human languages, and if you want fun, try Upper Dwarfish—it's so archaic, it's nearly incomprehensible without study." Catching our blank looks, she explained, "There are differences in spoken Dwarfish—Lower Dwarfish, to be linguistically precise—among the kingdoms. Upper Dwarfish was the common tongue thousands of years ago, but it's complex. Used in the temples and in coronations and such, and that's all. And since I'm neither a priest nor anywhere close to the eldest of my father's children, I know just enough of it to follow along in ceremonial matters, and not a syllable more."

Finishing her braid, she gave it a tug, then tucked her brush back into its pocket. "Human languages are easier, though they're almost completely different from each other. New Kopaati is prevalent, but their Ildonese settlements have another tongue, there are *several* in Honslia, and then there's Common in Ga'Besh, the bastard child of Upper Kopaati and Common Elvish."

"Sounds like a party," said Mia.

"A nightmarish decade of education," Anji agreed. "And I'm still not anywhere near fluent in those languages. Hence the translator." Beckoning for the granola bag, she added, "I suppose the only ones of us in the four worlds to learn your tongue are the maladetas, if one of them is sent to assist the Watcher. Or perhaps they use translators, I can't say. Adding another human language to the pile wouldn't be my idea of fun."

Mia snorted. "Just one? If I remember my Intro Linguistics seminar, we've got well over six thousand."

Anji froze, granola halfway to her mouth, and goggled. "Six thousand?"

"I mean, there are a few big ones—"

"*Thousand?*"

"We're a complicated bunch," I said.

"Not the word I would use," she replied, but passed Mia the granola and gathered her things. "We should keep moving. In case of Outsiders, I'd rather not try to outrun them in here."


**M**y first glimpse of Honslia was of the Greenwood, a twilit forest, the ground little but shadows and the sky overhead reduced to filaments of pale gold thread winding through the canopy. The trees growing around the tunnel entrance, itself a tree-covered hillock, seemed to have begun with the blueprint familiar to me but ended with improvisation. Using the sword as a flashlight, I made out trunks so thick that my arms couldn't have linked around them, which seemed rather like overgrown palms, judging by their rough bark. Starting about ten feet off the ground, their branches grew in almost perfect rings like spokes from a hub, the pattern repeating at regular intervals. The leaves were wide and flat, varying from bluish-green to nearly black—or so I thought, extrapolating from the little light available.

"We weren't in the tunnel *that* long," said Mia, frowning at the sky. "Why—"

"Design flaw," Anji interrupted. "Those who built the tunnels should have coordinated so that day and night were the same at each end. As you can see…"

"We're not going to make much progress," I finished.

She started to speak, then paused at the distant rumble of thunder. "No. But at least we should put distance between us and the tunnel mouth." Gesturing toward what might have been a path through the alien forest, she said, "Susan, light the sword and take point. I'll bring up the rear."

"No chance that you know where the elves keep their capital, huh?" I said.

"Look at it this way," Anji replied, falling in behind Mia. "We'll all learn together."

The thunder rolled again—nearer that time—and I kept my eyes on the litter of the uneven forest floor. "Fantastic," I replied with undue enthusiasm, earning a swat on the back of the head for my pains.

We pressed onward as the sky darkened—whether from nightfall or the approaching clouds, I couldn't say— but we were no closer to discovering civilization when the first raindrops hissed through the canopy and plopped onto us. Looking around, I spotted a natural clearing just off the makeshift trail and pointed it out to the others. "Let's camp before we get drenched, okay?"

"Fine by me," said Mia. "Want a hand with the tent?"

"You have the tent. I left mine back at the cabin so I could carry more food."

Her eyes widened in the sword's light, and she swung her pack off one shoulder to show me the place where her tent should have been: a tent bag stuffed with boxes of ammunition. "You really didn't bring one?" she asked plaintively.

"No." Another cold raindrop landed on my nose. "*Fuck.*"

We turned to Anji, who had already begun to unpack her tent—a pop-up structure that would comfortably sleep one adult dwarf. "We can squeeze…" she offered.

"Not that much," said Mia. "Shit. Well, enjoy being the smart one, Anji," she added, and dropped her pack. "Maybe we can make a lean-to or something out of branches."

"Do *you* know how to make a lean-to?" I asked.

"Hell, no, but I'm desperate enough to *try*."

Five increasingly cold and wet minutes later, we'd assembled a pile of dead branches and were attempting to make them stick together. Unfortunately, the branches wanted no part of our plan, and the only flat leaves we could find were brittle and decaying. The lean-to effort was soon abandoned in favor of sitting with our backs to a tree, huddled in our jackets as the rain began to pour. Before we could spend too long contemplating our fresh misery, Anji crawled out of her tent and demanded our bags. "Best that we keep *something* dry," she explained, then joined us in the rain, squeezing between us for warmth.

"Anji," I tried, "you don't need to—"

"None of us showered today. This is fine."

"But—"

"This is *fine*," she insisted, but groaned as the thunderstorm's fury fell upon us.

I tucked my head against my sodden jeans, silently cursing my stupidity…when suddenly, the rain slacked off, as if someone above me had turned a tap. Startled, I raised my dripping head, then illuminated the sword for a better look.

The rain was still falling like a car wash, but an invisible umbrella seemed to have manifested over me. "What the hell?" I muttered, peering at the force field.

Anji and Mia noticed and crowded closer. "Try to widen it," said Mia, nearly squishing Anji in her rush to shelter.

I started to say that I hadn't made it, then realized how

silly that sounded when I was holding a *magical sword* aloft. Concentrating, I envisioned the umbrella widening until its radius extended several yards in all directions, and my companions sighed with the reprieve. "So," I said as Anji stood to wring out her hair, "which of you do I thank for *this* bonus feature?"

"No idea," she replied. "I didn't know that Heart's Blood came with water-repelling powers, but I can't say I'm opposed to it."

Lightning flashed overhead, and the trees around us shook with the thunder.

"Think this goes away if I fall asleep?" I asked.

Anji bent forward to squeeze the rainwater from her beard braid. "Hard to say, but give it a try. If the repellant stops, believe me, I *will* wake you."


Though I didn't think I could get to sleep with the time change and the soaking, I managed to drift off eventually, as I woke to find the patches of sky lighter, a dark gray instead of pure black. The rain continued, but at least my umbrella endured. Lying still, I listened to the soothing percussion of the drizzle in the canopy and tried to doze again, but then I overheard Mia and Anji talking quietly nearby.

"We were going to get away, Suze and me," Mia was telling the princess. "Go make a better life for ourselves in a place that didn't know us. Didn't exactly pan out."

Anji seemed hesitant in her reply. "You and Susan…are you, um…"

"Hmm? Oh—*oh*, no, not that," she interjected, catching Anji's drift. "No, we're not a couple. She's my best friend, but not in *that* way."

"I'm sorry, I—"

"It's okay. Really, I don't mind talking about it. Not exactly my deep, dark secret." She sighed and shifted in the wet leaves, her windbreaker crinkling. "It's just…people can be really shitty, you know? In small towns, especially."

Anji cleared her throat. "Because of your..."

"Sexuality? Yeah, but that was a later development. The *nice* people have been keeping their distance ever since I was born, so really, the only person I lost in coming out was my mother."

"What could they have held against a child?"

Mia laughed softly. "Against Mom—I got it by association." She paused for the space of a long breath, then said, "My mom was raised to be a nice girl, see, but when she was off at school, some of her girlfriends organized a trip to Vegas one spring. Las Vegas—it's a party town," she clarified. "Casinos, shows, restaurants, booze, all the fun stuff. 'Sin City,' they call it. Anyway, Mom and her friends got a little crazy one night and went to a male strip club."

"A what?"

"Strip club. Good-looking guys get on stage, prance around to music, and take their clothes off."

"I...I'm sorry, *what?*" Anji sputtered.

"Female strippers are far more common," Mia replied, unflustered. "But back to the spring break trip. Mom had *way* too much fun that night, and somehow, she ended up in a dressing room with one of the strippers—'exotic dancers,' if you like. Sounds classier. They had sex, Mom's friends finally noticed she was missing and dragged her back to the hotel, and she woke up the next morning without so much as a clue as to what his name was. By the time the summer rolled around and she realized she was pregnant, she was too embarrassed to call the club and try to find out who the father might be. So my grandparents pulled her out of school and hid her in their house—they were too religious to get her an abortion, so they were trying to keep the pregnancy a secret—but once Mom delivered, she decided to keep me. Moved out, got a job in the Crossing, and raised me on her own. Her parents disowned her, and I can count the number of times that I went to their house on one hand, but Mom kept a roof over our heads and food on the table. Still, it's no fun growing up in a town where all the kids in your class know your mom got knocked up by a dude who dances in his underwear for a living."

"At least you have a mother," said Anji. "I never knew mine."

Mia's tone softened. "I'm sorry. Did she…"

"Complications at my birth. I lived, she and my twin brother did not. Father has been an excellent parent," she hastened to add, "but still…you would wonder, wouldn't you? What was she like, what would she have thought of me…"

"I get it," said Mia. "You know, my dad's probably still out there. Mom never looked for him, and I don't know where I'd begin to find him, much less whether he'd *want* to be found, but…" She chuckled. "Ironic, isn't it? He must have been a *fine* specimen, and how do I end up? Flat stick. Where's the justice in that?"

They sat quietly for a moment, and then Anji said, "I suppose Susan's family wasn't opposed to you, then?"

"No. The Coles were good people, and I'll fight anyone who says otherwise. Suze's dad never looked at me like I might be contagious, and since he was the mayor…you know, he could have been a jerk, but he wasn't. The Cole family *founded* that town. But Barnaby and Malachi were as down-to-earth as they come. Malachi was stuck being the Watcher, but Barnaby ran a grocery store *and* kept City Hall intact, and if you knew some of the people on the town council, you'd understand what a feat that was." Mia let loose a groaning yawn. "His death is the only reason Suze came home. She'd been thinking about getting a job in the City, but once he died, she went back to clean up the mess, and she never got away again. And now the damn sword's trapped her."

"No mother?" asked Anji.

Mia hesitated, and in that space, I considered rolling

over and "waking" to stop her answer before it could come forth. But as I lay there, weighing my options, she lowered her voice and said, "Her mom's not in the picture. Don't bring it up around her, okay?"

The princess sounded perplexed. "She died?"

"We don't know. Probably not."

I held my breath, still debating whether I could interrupt them without revealing that I'd been eavesdropping for the last few minutes.

Mia's voice dropped until it was barely above a whisper. "Malachi found her in the woods when she was a baby. There's no telling who her parents are. Let's just say that we had more in common than not growing up."

"I see," Anji murmured.

"And that's another reason why it's so unfair that Suze got stuck with the sword. Apparently, it's been passed down through the Cole family for generations. She's adopted, and her dad and uncle thought that might save her from the curse, but no such luck. It *sucks*."

"Sucks what?"

"Just sucks," Mia muttered. "Suze deserves a break. Her birth parents dump her, her dad dies, her uncle dies, she gets the Watcher gig…she's earned some good luck, hasn't she? Fate can't keep shitting on her forever."

"She has a good friend," said Anji. "That's something."

I was surprised to hear the frustration in Mia's tone. "It's not enough. We're going to break the curse, and then I'm going to get us both the hell out of the Crossing, and we're going to find a place where people are *happy* that we're alive."

The leaves rustled again as Anji stretched out. "Focus on the step in front of you, lass. That's what my father's always told me. And for tonight…or this morning?"

"It's not morning until I see sunlight."

"For tonight, then. We have food, we have shelter, and we haven't had to kill anything."

"*Yet*." I heard her rap her knuckles against a convenient

trunk.

"This is a motivational talk," Anji chided. "Play along and take the watch, won't you?"

By the time I fell asleep again, Anji was snoring behind me, and the rain had slowed to a trickle in the trees.


The clouds must have passed overnight ahead of a cold front, as I woke shivering on the damp ground just before Mia nudged me to take the final watch. While she curled up and tried to nap, I crawled into Anji's little tent to retrieve our breakfast—if we'd traded shelter for food, then we were damn well going to enjoy it—and set about boiling water. The available flammable material being far too soggy for me to get a fire going, I dug into the bottom of my bag and found the chemical cooking system Mia had purchased on a lark. A roll of silicone flattened out into a shallow rectangular box big enough to hold a heating packet, and after a few minutes, the box had warmed sufficiently to boil water. Anji awoke to the smell of oatmeal and tea, and she smiled gratefully as I dished out her portion.

Deciding against mentioning to Anji or Mia that I'd overheard them the night before—really, what was to be gained by adding family drama to a slog through the endless woods?—I cleaned up and concentrated on the tasks ahead. Rokund had said to seek out the Twins, whoever they were. I'd go to them, make my case, and show them how unjust it was that I'd been tapped for a job with life tenure that I'd never wanted. They'd understand, and then they'd go to their human buddies in Daril, and maybe *then* Rokund would get on board, but in any case, the sword would become someone else's problem. And then Mia and I could go home, stick around just long enough to pack properly, and get the hell out of the Crossing. I'd sell the store to the Plunketts—Annie didn't need me around supervising, anyway—and we'd take the cash and start over somewhere far away from the familiar whispers and pitying looks.

Heck, maybe we could go to Vegas and start tracking down Mia's dad. Lord knew I owed her after *this*.

I owed Mia for so much.

The first time someone teased me about being a foundling, I was five, a kindergartener in a green jumper and frilly socks on her first day of school, and a girl twice my age had come up to me on the playground and demanded to know if it was true that my mother threw me away. I hadn't known how to answer that, being still at an age where the Easter Bunny is definitely plausible, and so I'd shrugged and mumbled something noncommittal. But as she'd continued to badger me, a skinny blonde girl had marched over and tugged my arm, pulling me a step behind her, then looked up at the older kid and announced, "You're being mean. Go away, or I'll tell."

Kindergarteners aren't known for their powers of intimidation, but Mia had mastered the steely look in her tender years, and my interrogator had backed off and left us to play. Once she was out of earshot, Mia had said, "You looked scared. Are you okay?" I'd nodded, we'd run off to the swing set together, and that was how I'd found my best friend.

But that still hadn't answered the question the girl had asked me, which had fermented in the back of my mind all day until Dad picked me up. He'd barely buckled me in when I asked, "Where's my mommy?"

Poor Dad. To his credit, he'd done his best on the fly with an inquisitive, trepidatious little kid: he told me that no two families are just alike, that he and Uncle Malachi loved me to pieces, and that my mommy knew how much he wanted to be a daddy and gave me to him. And that had been enough, at least for a year or two. Soon, though, I learned to recognize the quiet comments and glances when the people murmuring about me didn't think I was looking, and I began to understand that the story Dad had told me had missing pieces.

Maybe there's no good way to break it to a kid that her parents thought so little of her that they left her in the woods to die alone, naked and crying and still attached to her placenta. I had been full-term and healthy, just a little bug-bitten—there was no reason why I shouldn't have been surrendered for adoption if my mother didn't want me. If she'd needed anonymity, our fire department had a drop box available for surrendered children, the first of its kind in the county: all you had to do was put a baby in, close the drawer, and ring the buzzer, and a firefighter would take it from there, no questions asked. But my parents hadn't given a damn. They hadn't given me so much as a blanket, much less a name or an excuse for their absence. Hell, they hadn't even cared enough to kill me quickly instead of dumping me like a bag of trash and letting nature take its course.

My mother hadn't *given* Dad anything. He and my uncle had plucked up something unwanted like flea market scavengers driving down the street on garbage day. That they loved me, I had no doubt—I couldn't have asked for a better family. Still, it does a number on you to realize that the only reason you're not Baby Doe in a tiny grave at the corner of the Grace Methodist lot is because the town hermit just happened to be out wandering and stumbled across you before you could die of exposure.

When I was ten, Dad sent me to talk to a child therapist twenty miles away, once a week for a year, and that helped as I tried to process the world and my place in it. Being abandoned wasn't my fault, she'd stressed. Some people just weren't cut out to be parents, and we'd never know what their situation was. But I had a father who'd chosen me to be his, and didn't that count for a lot?

Sure, it did. I adored my dad, and not just because he let Mia sleep over whenever we wanted. But the therapist's reassurance didn't stop the whispers around town, nor did it offer insight into my unanswered questions, chief among them being *What did I do wrong?* My therapist could tell me every week that it wasn't my fault, but my heart never quite accepted it.

As I passed from pudgy childhood into oddly curved adolescence, I used to stare at myself in my bathroom mirror while the old shower heated, trying to divine through the growing steam the people who had created me, as if I might be able to pick their features out of mine and produce anything more than ghosts. I was of average height, compared to the Cole men's defensive-line statures, and whereas my dad and uncle had muscle, my body delighted in acquiring new spots of fat. Both of them had straight brown hair and dark eyes, while I'd ended up with unruly chestnut waves and eyes the color of summer pond algae—and now, I mused as we tromped through the Greenwood, I'd soon have a *fantastic* scar to make my face just that tiny bit more exotic. One more thing for the good folks of Cole's Crossing to whisper about: little Susan, who moved out to Malachi's cabin without explanation and somehow sliced herself right open. Short of quickly acquiring professional-level skill with stage makeup or buying a load of headscarves, I didn't know how I'd be able to hide my new fun feature.

Then again, if monsters ate my face in the middle of the night, I wouldn't be around to have to deal with keeping my story straight.

We'd only been on the road—figurative speaking, as there was barely a trail through the forest—for about an hour when the trees began to shift around us. Suddenly, the wide spot we'd found started to rapidly narrow, and saplings from ten yards away rushed to plug the escape routes. By the time we realized what was happening, we were surrounded by trees, a living cage with a top made of curved, interwoven branches.

"What the ever-loving *fuck*?" Mia cried, pushing on the

nearest tree, which once again seemed firmly rooted. "How...how did that..."

"High Queen have mercy on a fool," I heard Anji whisper, and turned to see the dwarf rubbing her forehead. "The path was too clear..."

"What's going on?" I demanded. "What *is* this?"

She looked up at me and huffed in agitation—with the situation or with herself, I couldn't tell. "Elven security. They have great power over living things, so building a trap made of trees is hardly impossible for them."

"So...we're close to their fortress or whatever, then?"

She shrugged. "Let us pray. This could be an old trap, and if so..." Anji pointedly cut her eyes to Mia, who continued her fruitless attempt to pry the unyielding trees apart. "At least you two brought extra rations. Might be more useful than a tent after all."

"*Or*," I countered, drawing my sword, "I could see about making some firewood and getting us out of here."

But Anji stayed me before I could begin my awkward close-quarters hacking. "Not yet. In a few days, if no one's checked the trap, then perhaps, but we don't want to be seen as a threat."

"They *caged* us," Mia snapped, red-faced with exertion and scowling at the wooden bars. "I think we're entitled—"

"*No.* If we try to dismantle their security systems, they'll perceive it as hostility," Anji insisted. "Stay calm, put your weapons away, and be patient. I should have expected the trap, and I'm sorry to have missed it, but as long as no one's hurt and we have food and water, we're in no danger. Let's not do something rash. Not if you want the Twins' favor."

And so, on the advice of the one person in our party who had anything resembling an education in protocol, we settled down to wait in our shaded prison. Midmorning, we popped open another chemical pack and made more tea, an attempt to mitigate the cold damp, and tried to get comfortable. *That* was a feat easier said than managed. While I could stand without brushing my head against the top, our enclosure was perhaps only four feet wide and long. Sitting was possible, but stretching out, not so much. We couldn't even pace, hampered as we were by our sloughed-off packs...and given the close quarters, Mia *strongly* cautioned against continued beverages, as the person responsible for the trap hadn't thought to build in a latrine. Maybe male captives could have aimed through the living bars, but no one in our party was quite so agile in that department. Still, I was anxious enough to reach for the granola and mindlessly eat my feelings, while Mia, a bottomless pit at the best of times, joined me when her stomach began to growl.

Around noon, I was ready to drink again, latrine or no, when I heard the faint sound of jingling. The others noticed, too, and we stood silently by the bars as we strained to pick sense out of the continual susurrus of the wind in the forest. With every second, the tuneless jingling grew louder, and beneath it, I thought I heard heavy, distant footsteps.

"Traveling musicians or something?" Mia whispered. "Rescue by bard?"

"Unlikely," Anji muttered, then took a deep breath and began shouting for help.

Following her lead, Mia and I joined in, then paused when she signaled for a break. The jingling was definitely nearer that time, and by then, I could just make out the rumble of voices. "They're coming," I said, gripping a pair of saplings.

Anji nodded, her expression grim, and hailed them again.

Persistence paid off. Within a few moments, we had our first glimpse of our potential rescuers: eight figures in hooded brown cloaks riding astride large...*things*.

The creatures were quadrupedal like horses, but quite a bit bigger than the ones I knew from the farms around the

Crossing. Sleek, with long legs and thick gray and brown coats, they could have eaten an apple off my head with ease. Instead of hooves, they had three-toed paws, while their faces were stubby—for horses, at least—and ended in wide mouths. When the nearest lifted its top lip, I caught a flash of distinctly non-equine teeth, a mixture of flat edges and worrying points. Their ears flopped to either side like a donkey's, albeit half the size, and atop their foreheads, each bore a pair of short, backward-curving horns. Adding to the bewildering mixture were their harnesses and reins, pale strips of leather decorated with tiny silver bells, which gave the slightly terrifying beasts a merry jingle when they moved.

"The hell?" Mia whispered.

"Chiquiws," Anji whispered back. "Native to Honslia, sturdy and omnivorous. We use them, too—"

"*Those?*"

"I mean, a smaller breed."

As Anji reassured Mia that we weren't about to be eaten, I studied the chiquiws' riders. Their cloaks kept their features indistinct as they emerged from the trees, but I caught glimpses of dark leather boots, slim-cut brown or green pants, and the odd flash of rings when a hand crossed through a stray sunbeam. Eight on three was hardly a reassuring scenario, but though my sweating fingers itched to grab the sword at my hip, I stood still and tried not to seem threatening.

All things considered, this wasn't a difficult look for me to accomplish.

As the riders drew near and came to a halt, their leader threw back his hood, revealing a face that would have worked nicely with the bedroom décor of any number of lovelorn teenage girls. His was a look begging for headshots: clear, lightly tanned skin, square jaw, cleft chin, straight nose, and dark blue eyes that, even peering at me, gave me a little rush of giddiness. His hair was auburn and slightly wavy, worn loose over his shoulders. Really, he might have stepped straight out of one of my more textbook fantasies were it not for his ears, the long tips of which poked through his perfect mane and went on for a good two inches. That he was an elf, I had no doubt; the ears were anything but subtle.

While I tried not to drool and even Mia gave appreciative consideration to the aesthetics of the immediate scenery, Anji took the lead. "Greetings," she said, keeping her hands exposed and her tone friendly. "I am Anjikora of Blackhorn Mountain, seeking only an audience with the Twins. Could we trouble you for an escort to your lord and lady?"

The elf's face remained a blank, and a few of his companions began to mumble and snicker behind him.

Anji groaned. "Useless garbage translator. He can't understand me...let me see if I can remember enough Common Elvish to keep us from—"

"Uh, hi," I interrupted, giving the elf a little wave. He turned, hitting me with the full force of his—well, frankly, gorgeous—stare, and I offered what my libido *deeply* hoped was an attractive smile. "Is this translating correctly?"

A perfect eyebrow arched. "It is translating, yes," he replied, his smooth bass doing nothing to stop my flooding hormones. "I would not say *correctly*. No piece of forging"—he gave the word the same inflection one might reserve for *trash*—"can cover the deficiencies in an unlearned tongue."

"Sorry, come again?"

"Your accent is appalling." He dismounted, and the chiquiw gave its jangling harness a shake as he marched toward our cage. "Two humans and a *dwarf*? State your business, girl."

I tried to repeat Anji's message, hoping for the best. "This is Anjikora," I told him, nodding to the princess. "From Blackhorn Mountain. She has a message from her father for the, uh...the Twins?"

The elf's eyes narrowed. "Does she, now?"

# CHAPTER 9

Even with my limited hiking experience, I knew that walks through the woods were generally more enjoyable when one's hands weren't bound and leashed to a chiquiw. Trees I could handle, wet mulch was tolerable, but keeping pace just to the left of a massive beast's pristine back end in case it decided to further muddy the forest floor was no fun, especially when said attempted splash-zone aversion continued for hours.

The elves' leader hadn't deigned to dirty his beautiful fingers with us. With a whispered word, the nearest vines had flown from their trees and wrapped themselves around our wrists in tight figure eights. We'd protested the maltreatment, but the elves were unmoved. After Anji and I were relieved of our bags and blades—Mia's gun didn't seem to register as a weapon with our captors—a pair of underlings took hold of Mia's and my vines and tugged us into motion behind their chiquiws. The leader seemed to take special joy in yanking Anji along, periodically nudging his mount to walk a hair faster just to force her into a run.

As much as I wanted to fight back, or at least to tell the elves where they could go stick their camera-ready heads, Anji continued to warn us against it. Unintelligible to the elves, none of whom seemed to be in possession of a translator, she kept her tone low and calm—or as calm as she could, seeing as she was rarely marched along at anything slower than a jog. "Don't antagonize them," she stressed. "This will be over soon. Their commander will have more sense."

"You don't think they're taking us to the Twins?" Mia asked.

"I find that—"

Anji grunted and face-planted into a patch of thin grass, victim of a hidden root across the trail. Her rider continued without slowing, dragging her along on her belly for a solid minute as she struggled to right herself. When he stopped his chiquiw, he and the others had a good laugh as I awkwardly helped Anji back to her feet. By then, her front was filthy with muck, and her beard looked as wet and matted as if she'd soaked it in a sludgy pond, complete with odd twigs jutting from her ruined braid. "I'm fine," she said before I could speak. "And remember, they understand you. Let them have their fun."

Jaw clenching at the laughter around us, I asked, "Are you hurt?"

"Not enough for you to ruin this by throwing a fit. Keep walking."

At least my sword seemed to be on board with Anji's game plan. The elf to whose chiquiw I'd been tethered was also carrying my bag and the blade, which he'd lashed to his mount with more vines. I'd feared that the sword would free itself and manifest at my side again, which would have been a *fine* thing to try to explain to our captors, but to my relief, it behaved itself and remained where it had been tied.

By the time we arrived at the elves' camp, the limited sunlight was quickly waning, and the three of us on foot were tired and dirty. As a few of the riders hefted our bags, their leader untied us from the mounts and led us toward a massive tree, the trunk of which opened at our approach to reveal a sort of wooden elevator—or the Aen-powered Honslian equivalent, I supposed. Tugging us aboard like a dog walker with a pack of Pomeranians, he sent the elevator toward the canopy. When the next opening in the trunk appeared, a long wooden hall stretched before us, pocked with pointed windows and broad skylights. A treehouse fort, I realized, albeit one large enough to feed and sleep several dozen men. The planks of the walls and floor appeared to be ordinary lumber, but as I was marched past the windows, I saw that each had a shutter made of thickly entwined living leaves and branches—convenient, as those skylights would have made the previous night's rain particularly unpleasant.

The leader led us up an aisle between two long tables toward the head table, where an older elf sat alone before a stack of maps and loose papers. While he was gray-haired and his face bore the topography of age, he retained the unnatural beauty of his underlings, which I'd have appreciated far better had my heels not been blistering. His eyes, bright blue and hooded, gave Mia and me a quick inspection, then lingered on Anji—who by then, after several falls, looked as if she'd spent the last month hiding in a swamp. Glancing back at the band's leader, who wore the smug smile of a teacher's pet who knows he's about to receive extra credit, the older elf said, "Explain."

"Caught in a trap near the tunnel, sir. Two humans and a dwarf—"

"I'm not *blind*, boy," his commander snapped. "Their business?"

Gesturing toward me, he said, "That one claimed the dwarf's from Blackhorn Mountain, seeking an audience."

No translation is ever perfect—some linguistic nuances simply lack equivalents in other languages. The sword's translations to that point seemed to make sense, though I couldn't help but notice that the word for *dwarf* in the elves' tongue occasionally came through to me as *broken*. Charming as that little factoid was, I kept my thoughts to myself.

The commander peered at us again, his eyebrows furrowing. "You," he barked, pointing to Anji. "Who are you, and what do you want?"

Anji sighed, muttered under her breath, and haltingly replied, "I speak not. Speak Susan."

I cut my eyes to her and whispered, "That's it for your Common Elvish, huh?"

"Languages are not my strength," she replied in her usual tongue. "Try not to get us killed, won't you?"

I cleared my throat and waited until the commander shifted his gaze. "Hi. I'm not from around here, so if I mess up whatever protocol you're expecting, don't take it personally."

"But you speak properly," he pointed out.

"Thanks to a translator. Hers only goes one way," I said, nodding to Anji, "or she'd be telling you this with all the fancy flourishes, I'm sure. Anyway, that's Princess Anjikora of Blackhorn Mountain. She's not here spying— she's trying to help me. And we'd like to talk to the Twins, please."

He stared at me, blinked twice, then burst into a belly laugh that left him almost doubled over onto the table. When his spasms had slowed to a deep chuckle, he wiped a tear from his cheek and smirked. "I've heard quite a few ridiculous excuses in my time, girl, but that—*that* may be the most audacious yet. You would have me believe that this is…what, one of Rokund's brats?" he continued, waving dismissively at Anji—who, to be fair, had seen cleaner days. "Do you take me for a fool?"

"I'm serious—"

"As am I. Why would a dwarven princess be wandering the Greenwood with…well, whoever you two are? You're her escort, then?" he said, his voice thick with sarcasm. "Sent from Daril to smooth her passage? And your friend there, she's…the princess's bodyguard? A particularly tall dwarf?"

A few of the other elves laughed at his taunting, and he flashed them a satisfied smile.

As the underlings added their own japes to the mix, I stood there in silence with Mia and Anji, taking the abuse and trying not to get flustered. The vines around my wrists had begun to chafe hours before, and I gently twisted my hands, trying to ease the pain. It would be nice, I mused, ignoring the mirth around me, if they'd take the ropes off. Where were we going to go? Out a window to splat onto the forest floor? If I just had the sword, I thought, maybe I could pull it far enough from its scabbard to give me a sharp edge against which to rub the damn vines...

I yelped when the sword, which our captors had dropped on the floor with our bags, sailed through the air, cut through my bonds with a clean stroke, and hovered in front of me, glowing for good measure. While the elves' amusement turned to alarm, I grabbed the hilt, then reached over my shoulder and beckoned. A few seconds later, the scabbard hit my palm, still attached to its makeshift bungee belt, which I hooked around my waist. I shoved the sword into its scabbard, smirked in turn at the wide-eyed commander, and made the whole kit vanish with a thought as I planted my hands on my hips.

Sure, I didn't want to be tethered to that particular magical sword, but I had to admit that the darn thing had its uses.

The room fell silent but for the rustling of fabric as the elves all around us reached for the weapons they were wearing, waiting for a signal from their commander. But he continued to gape, glancing back and forth between my face and the place the sword had been, and finally whispered, "That...that's not possible."

"Oh? Whatever do you mean?" I asked, laying on the sarcasm just as thickly as he had. I may have lacked actual martial skill, but there was something about the scabbard bumping against my leg that gave me a boost of undeserved confidence.

"The sword." He pulled himself together, coughed, and pointed to the invisible weapon. "Show me."

I obliged, then angled myself toward him to show off the crystals in the hilt. "Recognize it?"

"Bright Blade," he murmured. "I haven't seen it in centuries, not since its creation—"

My heart leapt at that. "You helped?"

"*Me?* No, I merely guarded the ones who did. But...if that's Bright Blade, then..."

I smiled under his troubled gaze. "Then I would be the Watcher, correct. And as I said, the princess is generously assisting me. We'd like a word with the Twins. *Now.*"

The commander sputtered, then managed, "But...but if you are *here*, who's guarding the Crossing?"

"No one," I said sweetly. "And since I'm not going back until I see the Twins, I suggest that you send some of these *brave* gentlemen, who so fiercely subdued three women in a cage"—a few of our captors cringed at that— "to patrol near the tunnel mouth. We didn't see any Outsiders last night, but then again, it was raining pretty hard. Looks like the clouds have cleared," I said, giving the nearest skylight an exaggerated glance. "Might be a good night for hunting. Hard to say, really. I don't get much time to study the Outsiders before they try to rip my face off, but maybe your team here will have better luck. I mean, if they were strong enough to tie us up and march us through the woods when we were offering no resistance, then surely they can defend this world from the horrors that hunt me nearly *every goddamned night.*"

The leader of the scouting band actually took a step back when I glared at him, which left me feeling all kinds of warm and tingly. True, he was gorgeous, but after the day I'd had, I was *this* close to attempting to punch his pretty nose in.

His commander, at least, had a spine. "If that's what you require, Watcher, then I will escort you to Their Serene Majesties. But the ride is long, and—"

"And we don't need to be traveling by night. Trust me on this." After a brief, silent conference with my companions, I told him, "What I need at the moment is a bath, as do my associates here. Maybe some salve for the cuts and bruises your men gave us today. A proper bed. And we'll start off at first light."

He nodded, then pointed to an elf loitering nearby and barked, "You heard her. Prepare guest chambers. And as for you idiots," he continued, turning to the scouting party, "don't you have somewhere to be?"

Their leader blanched. "Sir...with all due respect, you can't be serious."

"*Oh?*" he snapped, the word barbed and full of warning.

But his underling wasn't deterred. "We've been riding all day, our shift has ended, and—"

"The tunnel is undefended. All available men are to ride out tonight in case of incursions."

"But...*Outsiders*, sir?" he protested. "We've never fought those! I was a babe when Bright Blade was created, and...and they weren't yet born!" he added, sweeping one hand toward a vehemently nodding clump of his men. "We have no experience—"

"The Watcher defends against them," said the commander over his babbling. "And you subdued the Watcher. I should think you'd enjoy the sport."


About fifteen minutes later, I observed their departure from the window beside my steaming soaking tub, none of them riding at anything more than a trot. Anji and Mia reclined in the tubs next to mine, groaning with the pleasure of hot water on tired muscles. Communal bathing wasn't my idea of a party, but the candlelit room was dim, and besides, with the amount of grime we'd sloughed off in the bath, the water was practically opaque. Anji, who could almost swim in her deep tub, leaned against the side and carefully combed the tangles out of her hair and mud-matted beard, while Mia submerged every few minutes, her location marked only by the stream of bubbles that popped at the scummy surface.

Once the last of the chiquiws had disappeared beyond the tree fort's artificial exterior spotlights—Aen-made,

Anji had explained—I turned back to the matter of cleanliness and poured out a generous palmful of woodsy-smelling liquid from a bottle on the shelf beside the tub. I couldn't make out the label in the dark room, but the goop lathered, and that was good enough for me.

"You did well," said Anji as I covered my head in suds. "Nice improvisation. I didn't know that you could move the sword by will alone."

"I didn't," I replied, then held my breath and slipped under the water.

When I rose and wiped the moisture from my eyes, I found Anji facing me, her elbows hooked over the side of her tub to hold her in place. "What do you mean, you didn't?" she asked.

I pulled a chunk of hair in front of my nose, took a deep sniff, and reached for the cleanser again. "I didn't just *think* it into my hands. I was thinking that I might be able to cut through the vines if it were closer, but it surprised me as much as anyone when the sword went flying."

"The thing's got a mind of its own," said Mia, who had likewise decided that the mystery shampoo was better than nothing. "I mean, it chooses the next Watcher, right? It's...I don't know, a smart sword or something."

"Not that smart if it picked me," I muttered.

Anji gave the matter a moment's contemplation as she soaked. "Perhaps. There *is* an intelligence to Heart's Blood, but I have no idea how that was accomplished. It's not a forging technique. Nice work, there," she added, nodding to the sword, which I'd left propped in the corner of the bathroom.

Remembering what the sword had done for us the previous night in the rain, I decided to experiment and focused on the water around me. A column slowly rose from the bath, forming a sphere of dirty water, which I dumped over myself to rinse my hair. Mia laughed as I pushed my sodden hair from my face, and even Anji chuckled. "If you've finished playing, we should eat and rest," Anji said, straining to reach a towel with her short arms. Mia handed her one, and Anji stood and wrapped herself in a fluid motion, exposing nothing but arms and calves. Climbing out of the tub with her comb, she padded to the mirror across the room, hair dripping before and behind her.

Mia and I soon followed suit, and I dug clean clothes from my bag, knowing full well that little could be done to style my unruly hair in the morning. I hadn't intended to make a habit of dropping in on heads of state while looking like a trail-weary mess, but at least people tended to focus less on my appearance once they noticed the weapon I was wearing.

"You don't think they'll feed us?" Mia asked Anji as she bent over to wrap her hair into a towel turban.

"You've seen elven hospitality thus far, have you not?" Anji retorted. "Do you have a stew or some such in your food stores? I think I could eat a whole pot tonight."

"Not sure who we'd ask, anyway," I said as I joined them at the mirror, trying not to look at the healing gash down my cheek. "Don't know about you two, but I've yet to catch a single name from them."

Anji began plaiting a thin braid in the middle of her chin. "You haven't, and you won't. We don't rate introduction."

Mia frowned and stopped picking at a vine scab on her wrist. "Huh?"

"It's an elf thing. Not in all of their settlements," she amended, "but my understanding is that Nokan'ti is fairly traditional. Here," she said, catching our bemusement in the mirror. "The kingdom in the Greenwood."

"See, you're looking at us like you expect us to understand the geopolitical intricacies of this place," said Mia, "and while I hate to be the bearer of bad news…"

"My apologies." Anji worked in silence until she finished her braid, then tied it off and began another to its left. "As I was saying, the lack of introductions is an elf thing. Knowing an elf's name means having a degree of familiarity with him—it's like you're at least his equal. For example, I guarantee that the commander here knows every one of his men's names, but I doubt there's reciprocity."

"He didn't use them today, if he did," I pointed out.

"No, because we were standing there, we had translators, and giving us their names would have been degrading his men. We don't rate introduction, *especially* not me. You heard what they call us, didn't you?"

"I wasn't going to bring it up, but yeah."

The princess snorted and started a third braid. "According to my tutors, elves have an obnoxiously high opinion of themselves as compared to every other intelligent race. If we overhear a single name in the Greenwood, I'll be *shocked*." She paused, then gave me a sly look in the glass. "Must be disappointing. You'll never know the name of that stupid boy you were drooling over today."

"I wasn't *drooling*," I protested, though I could feel my face flaming at the lie.

"Totally drooling," Mia chimed in. "Jaw on the ground, tongue hanging out. I've seen ten-year-olds with more finesse."

"How do you *possibly* find that attractive?" asked Anji as she finished her braiding. "Too tall, no beard, the weird ears…"

"He was pretty! Objectively pretty!"

Anji and Mia shared a look of pity, and then Mia clucked her tongue and headed for her bag to start dinner.

Horses are a fine thing in principle. The ones I encountered growing up were sweet, if a little skittish, with big, dark eyes and twitching tails. I was never a horse girl—even if I'd shown an interest, Dad wouldn't have had the time to shuttle me to lessons and competitions, nor the inclination to pay stable fees—but I'd seen them on our drives through the farmland around town, and I had nothing against them.

Their weird Honslian cousins, on the other hand, could prance straight off to Hell.

I wasn't a well-balanced person on the best of days. My ideal position involved having both feet on the ground if I couldn't have both legs on the couch. My attempts at roller skating, all made under duress at classmates' birthday parties at the dilapidated rink, had ended in bruises. I lasted five minutes on ice skates before deciding that I preferred not being black and blue. Biking I could manage, but I might still have training wheels had my peers not shamed me into removing them in the third grade. In short, I preferred to be in control of where my body was going and at what speed, and I wanted a sure way of throwing on the brakes.

The female chiquiw to which I found myself clinging that morning for our ride to the Twins seemed docile enough, but she was *tall*, and glancing over her side only served to remind me of how unpleasant the forest floor would be if I reached it headfirst. The elves used saddles, fortunately, and the stablemaster had put my reins in my hand—as if *that* would make a difference to my riding skills—but there was nothing to hold on to. The saddle was smooth and lacking in any sort of handle, tugging at the reins confused the chiquiw, I couldn't reach the thing's horns, and I quickly learned the hard way that digging in with my knees only made her go faster. But the elves were watching and silently judging, exchanging smirks whenever I thought I was about to fall and gasped, and so I tried to comport myself with relative dignity as I prayed that I wouldn't slide off.

Like me, Mia had never had the benefit of riding lessons, but she was the far more graceful and coordinated of us—she'd even managed to master the basics of skateboarding without breaking her legs. Within the first hour, she'd relaxed into the ride and was quietly offering me pointers while I pretended to be one with the saddle. Beside us, Anji rode with stoic resignation atop a massive chiquiw, the largest in our pack. Too short to properly straddle the broad-backed beast, much less reach the stirrups, she kept her legs stuck out to either side, which seemed awfully uncomfortable. The stablemaster might as well have put a grade schooler atop a Clydesdale. But she didn't complain, though we all knew damn well why she'd been given that particular mount.

The first hour or two weren't terrible, once I got past my entirely rational fear of imminent death. But by midmorning, I *ached*. Unaccustomed to spending time in the saddle, my rear warned of retribution, while my inner thighs complained about the extended stretch. Mia, who had almost no posterior padding, grew quiet as the discomfort set in, and finally, I broke down and asked the elves' commander how much longer we had to ride. He considered the angle of sunlight and the woods around us, then said, "We'll be there before dinner."

"How long before dinner?"

"I can't say, but it'll be longer if you make us stop to work out the muscle kinks, Watcher."

By then, I was growing weary of the elven smirks, even on such handsome faces, but I bit my tongue and rode on, hoping the commander's estimate had been generous. With the trail having widened sufficiently for us to ride two abreast, Anji nudged her chiquiw up beside mine. "This is what I was expecting," she said, her tone as blasé as if she were commenting on the weather during a long elevator ride. "The condescension is integral to their culture, or so my tutors say. Father just calls them a pack of heathens."

That word, at least through my sword's translator, carried strong overtones of *assholes*.

"Look around," Anji continued, leaning forward to give her chiquiw's neck a pat. "Did any of them react to me?"

Trying to be discreet, I glanced at our escorts, but no one seemed to have caught Anji's drift. "No," I murmured.

"Good. And don't say anything more than that—they understand you, not me, remember. By the way, you'll be more comfortable if you don't keep your legs so tense. Move with the chiquiw, not against it."

I considered her perched atop her giant gelding. "Didn't know you rode."

"Our chiquiws are smaller, for obvious reason, but yes, I was taught." She paused, giving the elves her own critical appraisal, then continued in the same neutral voice. "It's their religion, you must understand."

"Uh-huh."

"What about it?" asked Mia, riding up behind us. "'Be nice to strangers, be forever damned'?"

"Not exactly. Let me think of how to explain this…" She raked her teeth over her upper lip as she considered the matter, then said, "We come from the same world originally. Both of our races arose in Ildon, and we've spread. But Ildon is the spiritual home for elves and dwarves alike, you see—"

"So we're in Honslia because…?" Mia prompted.

"*Because*," Anji replied with a flicker of impatience, "over time, the elven settlements in Honslia have grown more prominent, and we destroyed the best they had left in Ildon during the war."

"What the hell happened, anyway? How'd you get into a multi-world war?"

Silently listening to a discourse on the political history of the four worlds wasn't the most exciting way I could have been spending the day, but it was a distraction from the ache in my legs.

Anji dug in her bag for a bottle of water and took a long swig. "Again, it goes to their religion. Our priests teach that the High King and High Queen created our races at the same time as two expressions of Their life-giving power and artistry. While we have our differences, we are as one in the eyes of the Divine, imperfect as creators ourselves but perfect in the sense that we are Their creations."

"Fair enough," said Mia.

"Well, *their* priests teach that their gods—they recognize male and female, but they consider them twin siblings, oddly—created elves alone. They say that dwarves began as nothing more than the misshapen forms with which their gods experimented in designing the elves, and since they were left with a little spark of life, they survived, even though they were castoffs. Rubbish. So elves call themselves the True Children, and they have any number of less than complimentary names for us—often, 'the Broken.'"

"Classy," I muttered.

"It gets better," said Anji. "Because they are their gods' true children and perfect creations, it follows that their needs and interests are paramount, and if the rest of us protest, it's blasphemy." She chuckled softly. "Except the maladetas, I assume. Elves can boast as they like, but there are few foolish enough to provoke *them*."

"So," Mia prodded, "the war…"

"Nothing I'm sorry to have missed, I'll say that much," the princess replied. "But I'll give you the brief version. There was an old elven kingdom in Ildon called Fioul, deep in the south. We have two continents," she clarified, "northern and southern. Our first settlements were in the north, while the elves arose in the south, and they still consider much of the forested land there sacred. Anyway, Fioul was ancient but had lost prominence, particularly to Nokan'ti, and its territory had contracted as its population diminished. There was a dwarven kingdom called Deepwood on its border. Deepwood grew and flourished as Fioul shrank, and eventually, some of its frontier towns began expanding into formerly elven territory."

Mia whistled. "Think I see where this is going."

"The boiling pot was hotter than you imagine. There's a strain of extremism in the elves' religion. I'm not suggesting that we're better on that count," she hastened to add, "but our extremists tend to be of the self-flagellating, 'retire to a cave and never emerge' sort. Theirs see an affront to any elven interest as a declaration of holy war. Anyway, Fioul being a settlement with a deep religious tradition, it tended to…well, if not cultivate, at least tolerate that sort of thought. To make this brief, a band of elves, allegedly spurred on and blessed by their priest, attacked the offending settlements in the night, burned them to the ground, and slaughtered the townspeople in their beds. The survivors sent word to their king for help, the Two of Fioul refused to admit fault—"

"Two?" I interrupted.

"Again, it goes to their religion. As their gods are siblings, every elven settlement is ruled by a pair of siblings, male and female. They aren't each other's consort," she said, then paused and considered that statement. "Not most of the time, at least. Elves are degenerates, but even they seem to frown upon incest. But a male–female pair of twins are seen as a particular blessing from their gods, which may go a ways toward explaining why everyone began looking to Nokan'ti around the time of the Twins' ascension. Clear?"

I nodded, paranoid of the listening ears around me.

"As I was saying, Fioul refused to apologize or punish the murderers, so Deepwood retaliated by setting fire to one of their sacred groves or some such. *That* constituted holy war in the eyes of even moderate elves, and so the fight was on. They each called their allies, and the war spread. Wherever there was a dwarven settlement, there was sure to be an elven band of soldiers on the way, and the converse was just as true." Anji's chiquiw snorted, and she patted his neck again. "The whole thing was stupid.

Deepwood should have kept to its lands, and Fioul should have brought the killers to justice. Instead, we had a fifteen-year war on tens of fronts. Two of my brothers and my eldest sister died in the fighting, and I never met them. Finally, the maladetas stepped in and spoke reason, and a peace was brokered in the Meali Republic—it's a human settlement in Kopaat, and they stayed neutral throughout the conflict," Anji explained. "So everyone went home more or less dissatisfied, the priests on both sides claimed that their people had the divine victory, and today, Fioul and Deepwood are no more than rubble, both being quickly overgrown by that damned forest. And *that*, lasses, is the War of the True Children."

"You don't sound overly enthusiastic," Mia remarked.

"And why should I be? Lives lost, soldiers maimed, homes and farms burned, all for nothing." She drank again, draining her water bottle, and tucked it back into her bag. "The High King and High Queen created us both," she said quietly. "I don't pretend to know Their will, but I don't think They'd want us to destroy each other. Elves may be heretics, but in a way, they're our siblings. Obnoxious, estranged siblings, perhaps, but one cannot choose one's family." She paused for the space of a long breath, then added, "And seeing as that sentiment would be considered heretical in many corners of the Great Temple, I'd appreciate it if you didn't attribute it to me."

"I heard nothing," said Mia as I nodded in turn. "So, uh…about these twins…"

Anji grimaced. "Signatories to the Peace of Meali, as was my father. That's how he learned their names—everyone involved signed their marks in full. But I'll not speak them here, not in this company. They dislike me enough already without me offending their rulers. Besides, it's easier to think of them as a unit. They only act officially in tandem—though as both have spawned children, I sincerely hope they do *some* things without the other present."

While I was unable to ask the question that leapt to mind, Mia seemed to have the same query. "They're married, then? Do they have, like, official consorts or something?"

"You're asking me for the intimate details of a pair of rulers with whom my father has no diplomatic relationship, understand," said Anji, "so give this the weight it's due. We believe that each has a consort—Father says they traveled with apparent spouses to the peace talks, just as Mother accompanied him. But elves…" She made a face. "To be polite about it, monogamy isn't a particular virtue among them. They marry, just as we do, but it's understood that they'll take other partners from time to time. Deviants, the lot of them."

Mia snickered behind us. "Don't get any ideas, Suze."

"*Please* don't," Anji added. "At least not while I'm around to witness it. The interesting thing is that when they choose their next rulers, they place no particular weight on whether the children are born of the marriage—or even of the same parents. If either of the siblings has twins, they will inherit, but otherwise, preference seems to go to the woman's children…and if they happen to be half siblings, the elves don't mind. Nothing like flaunting their indiscretions, is there?"

"You know," said Mia, whose voice had suddenly gained a slight edge, "I think I remember telling you that my parents weren't married."

Anji looked over her shoulder and shook her head. "I mean no insult to you. Your partnering is a matter between you and your gods. But I know what *ours* say on the subject, and for the elves to ignore it as blatantly as they do…'True Children,' indeed," she muttered.

She and Mia fell silent, and I sighed and continued in my quest to not tumble from the poor mare to which I was clinging. Anji had given me plenty to think about, but one fact was clear: even if the handsome men riding around us were open to flings, "slightly overweight with unruly hair and a certain camper's funk" was unlikely to be their type, with or without a magic sword thrown into the bargain.

Feeling surer than ever that I was going to die alone, I tried to ignore my protesting muscles and hoped dinnertime would come quickly.

# CHAPTER 10

I had a treehouse growing up, a little fort of two-by-fours with a castoff piece of corrugated tin for the roof. Dad built it five feet off the ground in the backyard pecan tree, and it had everything a kid could need: a rope ladder for access through a trapdoor, a window for a view, and walls that kept out the worst of the elements. True, the place was uninsulated and leaked like a sieve, but I'd loved it until the tree came down in an ice storm—and by then, I'd grown to prefer the comforts of climate control and my bed.

The Twins' citadel—our escort had declined to give me its name, though Anji whispered that it was probably called Caritulo after its previous incarnation—was like an ocean liner next to the tub toy my treehouse had been. It wasn't supported by a mere tree, but rather by seeming acres of forest, a roof of boards and supporting branches some thirty feet off the ground that stretched as far as I could see. The underside of the citadel was lit with Aen-powered lamps and more conventional torches—whatever skill the elves possessed, I supposed it included fireproofing—and separated from the woods around it by a living fence of chain-linked limbs and vines. Through the arched gate, I could make out lights in an apparent stable and pick the contours of a street from the shadows.

The commander stopped our pack a little ways from the gate, then dismounted and approached the armed guard on foot. "Locking down early today?" he asked, casting a pointed glance at the fading sky—which, I finally noticed, was a curious shade of bluish turquoise. "We've time yet until nightfall."

"Orders," the guard replied. "You've not heard?"

"Heard what?"

The guard beckoned him close and whispered in his ear, and the commander stiffened. He whispered back to the guard, and then both turned and stared at me. Trying not to squirm under their gaze, I offered a weak wave, which wasn't reciprocated.

After another few moments of inaudible conversation, the guard allowed us to pass through the city gate into its underbelly. The lights I'd seen were indeed from a stable, and I gratefully made my ungainly dismount from my patient mare. Wincing as I tried not to walk with a bowlegged stride, I shouldered my backpack and followed the commander through the warren of streets.

If the rushing elves noticed us, they seemed too busy to care. Men passed wearing swords, carrying bows and packed quivers, and rolling heavy barrels. Noticing a leak from one of the latter, Anji murmured, "Pitch."

"Seems like a bad idea to keep so much around in a *forest*," I replied, watching another barrel follow its leaky fellow.

"Not if you want to create a fire ring. The Greenwood isn't as sacred to them as the forest back in Ildon. Looks like they wouldn't mind sacrificing a few trees."

I thought about the unprotected tunnel and the rainy night we'd spent huddled together. Sure, we hadn't seen any Outsiders yet in Honslia, but if something had slipped through…

There was no *if* about it, I realized. The elves were on high alert. Why else would they be preparing to burn their land unless it was to ward against nightmares lumbering out of the forest?

Queasy, I followed the commander down one turning street after another—the city planners seemed to have taken inspiration from a hedge in designing the layout—

until finally, we came to a thick trunk flanked by half a dozen guards, who stepped forward to block our way. "Their Serene Majesties are seeing no one," the nearest guard told him, then paused to give us a closer look. His beautiful face wrinkled in disgust. "Is *that* what I think it is?"

"Unfortunately," said the commander. "But allow me to send a message, at least."

The guard shrugged. "Your head, not mine. Do you need paper?"

"No." He pulled a folded stack from a bag he wore beneath his brown cloak, extracted a sheet, and held it close to his face. As he whispered, I could see words appearing on the page by the light of the torches around us. Satisfied, the commander folded it into quarters and handed it to the guard, who opened the trunk to reveal another elevator and sped upward.

We didn't have to wait long, and when we retuned, his eyes were saucer-round. "You're expected," was all he said, and stood aside to let us pass.

The commander nodded and ushered us onto the elevator, and I tried to calm the butterflies drunkenly careening around my stomach as we rose. A cutout window in the inner door revealed the main arboreal level, but we continued to rise…quite a bit higher than I expected, I realized, trying to calculate the floors we must have climbed. When the elevator stopped, the door opened to reveal a stunning hall spread before us, a cathedral-like room of soaring arches and leafy walls. Night had descended below, but there, in the top of the canopy, the last rays of daylight fell golden and pink through the windows and onto the sumptuous woven carpet, an intricately patterned rug of greens, blues, and browns. Where dwarves decorated with jewels and stone, elves preferred trees and the more earthen end of the palette, but the result was no less rich.

Positioned at the far end of the room—perhaps a

football field away—atop a dais were a pair of wooden thrones. From the elevator, I couldn't make out the details of their occupants beyond dark hair and white clothing, but as the commander marched us through the tense double line of guards toward the thrones, the blurs resolved into faces—and they looked none too pleased to see us.

Had I not known that the Twins were a fraternal pair, I'd have thought them identical: pale faces with large, dark eyes; straight, waist-length mahogany hair through which the points of their ears protruded; thin, disapproving mouths; and white, gold-trimmed robes over their thin, androgynous forms. Coming closer still, I spotted the threads of silver in their hair and the faint lines of age in their faces, but both were possessed of an almost ethereal beauty—the kind that, I supposed, would give even a supermodel a moment's self-doubt.

I glanced at Anji, unsure of how to play this, but she gave me a slight nod before cocking her head toward the thrones, an invitation to take the lead.

"You don't think they can understand you?" I whispered.

"Oh, I'm certain they can," she replied. "See their rings? My people forged those—two-way translators, some of our finest work. When the tunnels were being anchored, we gave Fioul the rings, and they agreed to put the opening in the north. More convenient for trade, you see."

"And monsters."

The princess grimaced. "Talk for us. They're probably furious that I'm here."

Her plan didn't thrill me, but at least my nerves at the impending royal audience distracted me from my aching legs and backside.

The commander stopped a respectful distance from the thrones, then went to one knee, bowing his forehead to the level of his kneecap. Mia, Anji, and I remained awkwardly standing behind us, no one eager to make the first move, but we didn't have to wait long before the Twins took charge of the situation.

"Rise," said the king.

Surely, I mused, his baritone would set him apart from his sister—and I wasn't disappointed.

The queen's voice was on the lower end of the soprano register, but it marked a clear departure from his, the first easy difference I'd detected between the two rulers. "Take your rest," she said. "A room will be prepared for you tonight. You ride in the morning."

The commander's head dipped almost to the rug that time, and then he stood, brushed past us without a word, and headed for the elevator.

He hadn't made it halfway across the throne room when the Twins' façade of serenity cracked. "*You* are the Watcher?" the king demanded, pointing a long finger toward my chest.

I nodded and patted the sword hanging at my hip. "Unfortunately. I've come here to ask—"

"How *dare* you," he snapped, the color flaring in his sculped cheeks.

As I fumbled for a response, Anji saw my struggle and smoothly intervened. "The intrusion is my fault," she told the Twins. "I offered to escort her here. Perhaps we should have gone to the maladetas for diplomatic assistance before crossing into Nokan'ti, but—"

He cut her off with a curt wave and continued to glower at me. "If we wished to hear the blathering of the Broken, we would have requested it. As for you, *Watcher*, who do you think you are? Leaving your post, abandoning your sacred duty—"

His anger had startled me at first, but his righteous indignation, combined with my fatigue, made me laugh aloud in disbelief—which, judging by the Twins' shocked expressions, wasn't the reaction they'd anticipated. "Sacred to whom?" I retorted. "To *you*? If it's such a sacred responsibility, then choose someone of your own damn religion to do it!"

They stared, stunned and silently gaping, and it occurred to me that perhaps Their Serene Majesties were unaccustomed to blasphemous backtalk. Still, I didn't waste the opportunity.

"You helped make this thing," I said, pointing to the scabbard at my side. "I'm here to ask you to unmake it, or at least give it to someone else. You—*all* of you on this side of the Crossing—you have no right to do what you've done to my world. To *me*," I said, feeling my face grow as red as the king's. "How dare you make us fight your monsters for you? Imprison me and my uncle and all the Watchers before us just so you can sleep better at night? Who do you think *you* are?"

"Fourteen of our people are dead," said the queen in a low voice, the ice to her brother's fire. "Slain by three creatures that must have come through the tunnel. Outsiders." She nearly spat the word. "Five men. Three women. Six children. An uncounted number of chiquiws. Half their town was burned before the defenders killed those fiends. And *every drop* of their blood is on your foolish head. The Divine have ordained—"

"Spare me. This little arrangement you cooked up was a group effort, not some god-devised plan to screw me over."

The Twins cut their eyes to Anji, who remained unflustered. "I saw no point in *lying* to the lass," she said, folding her arms across her broad chest. "And I've come from Blackhorn Mountain with my father's blessing. The position in which our peoples have placed the Watcher is unjust. The...*arrangement*, as she put it, is tantamount to life imprisonment for a human who had no part in the sword's creation and receives no benefit from the pact that made it. She did not ask for this," Anji continued, sweeping one hand toward me. "I've seen the conditions in which the Watcher is forced to live. Those things hunt her nearly every night! Do you see the mark on her face? That was from an Outsider. And she's only had the job...how long?" she asked me.

"About ten days."

"*Ten days*," she repeated. "Can you imagine—"

"Be quiet," the king muttered.

But Anji wasn't finished. "She's a babe, unskilled at arms, and in her own world, she's trapped at the edge of the Crossing. She'll be hunted by Outsiders until the day she dies. It's not right."

"I said, *be quiet*!" His face, already red, was edging toward the unhealthy color mine turned whenever I was forced to do sprints. "Her dereliction of duty has killed our people—and if that is not sufficiently alarming for Rokund, then he would do well to remember that his lands are equally at risk."

"He knows," said Anji. "We've suffered casualties already."

"Then why—"

"Because we cannot fairly thrive in a system that functions only if we torture an innocent bystander. Surely you know that the gods love justice."

"Do not presume to lecture us about the Divine," snapped the queen. "You...*you*..." Perhaps lacking a vocabulary sufficient to express her derision, she settled for flipping one hand dismissively at Anji. "I would sooner hear theological musings from the stables."

"Look," I interrupted, "I'm not going to stand here and argue religion with you, but I think we can all agree that the Watcher system is unfair. You send us your monsters, you get the benefit of your precious Crossing, and I'm forced to live as your unpaid army of one. I didn't agree to this, and I'm sure the same could be said for all of my predecessors. Help me," I begged. "If you can't free me from the sword, then help me find the people who can—"

"*Free* you?" said the queen, arching a sculpted brow.

"This thing has ruined my life," I said, jiggling the sword in its scabbard. "If you could just—"

"It has given your life purpose," the king cut in over my plea. "Human lives are so fleeting, often too brief to be anything more than meaningless. Now, you've been given the opportunity to be useful. To protect your betters. Bright Blade is a blessing to you, girl, not a curse."

I stared back at him, momentarily struck dumb, then caught Mia's aghast expression and realized I hadn't misheard him. "*Excuse* me?"

"Excuse you for what?"

"For—shit, forget it, translator issue," I said. "What you just said is ridiculous. Who are you to tell me who my betters are?"

The Twins regarded me as if I were feebleminded. "We are the True," the king slowly replied, perhaps making sure I had time to catch his meaning. "The perfect creation of the Divine. You are not. But for you, a life spent in service to our needs—and the needs of the four worlds," he allowed—"will be a life with purpose. That is the best life that a lesser being like yourself can hope for."

My patience, frayed already, ripped apart behind the force of my mounting anger, and my fists clenched as I marched toward the thrones. "You've got a lot of nerve, you sick old bastard," I said, climbing the dais as the Twins' guards rushed closer. "And if you think for one minute that I'm going to waste my life protecting your pasty ass, then you're as stupid as you are arrogant. So why don't you do us all a favor and free me from this goddamn sword before I shove it so far up your—"

As focused as I'd been on the king, who had stiffened in alarm at my approach, I'd neglected to keep an eye on his sister. With a word and a curt gesture, she sent me flying backward across the room, straight into a supporting tree trunk. My head hit the unyielding wood, and the blackness cut short my unpleasant audience.

When I opened my eyes again, it was to dim, flickering

torchlight and a throbbing headache. I barely had time to moan before Mia was kneeling beside me, shining a little flashlight with the glow of a thousand suns in my face. "Stay down," she ordered as I whined in protest. "Follow the light. You've been out for a while."

I gave in and tracked the beam as it moved around my head, and Mia, satisfied with my performance, allowed me to sit up. "What happened?" I mumbled.

"You threatened the Twins, and now we're enjoying their hospitality for the night," said Anji, who sat nearby with a bag of granola. "I can't say it's the tactic I would have chosen, but you did make an impression."

"And your thick skull probably made an impression in that pole, too," Mia quipped, passing me a bottle of water. "Nice going, Suze."

By then, my smarting eyes had begun to adjust to the shadows of the room, and I could make out its contours: more of the wooden walls I'd come to expect, but there was no window onto the forest, nor any furniture beyond an unmistakable bucket in the corner, and the only door lacked a handle on our side. "Damn it," I groaned. "Are we in elf jail?"

"Uh-huh," said Mia. "The royal assholes told us we'll be escorted back to the tunnel tomorrow, and if you don't return to the Crossing and the monster-slaying, they'll send guards to kill you and let the sword choose someone else."

I glanced at Anji, who nodded and picked a raisin out of her beard. "A rough recitation, but a fairly accurate synopsis."

Letting that sink in, I gave our cell a more careful study, then prodded my sore head and took a sip of water. "Anji, you remember when we suggested that your people's anti-elf sentiment might just be a case of negative propaganda?"

"I do."

"I was wrong, and I'm sorry."

"Likewise," said Mia, crouching beside the princess.

"Share?" Anji angled the granola bag toward her, and Mia helped herself to a large handful. "They didn't offer dinner, but at least they left us with our gear. We might as well roll out the sleeping bags before it gets any colder in here tonight."

At a loss for a better plan, I made my bed beside Mia's, and the three of us snuggled close. I lay still and stared at the ceiling, trying to pick out individual branches in the darkness, when suddenly, I heard Mia's whisper in my ear: "Unzip and get under the covers."

Curious, I burrowed and tugged down the zipper just enough to find myself facing Mia, who had also pulled her bag over her head like a scared kid at a slumber party. "What?" I whispered.

"I want to try something. Wait."

A moment later, Anji moved her bag so that she was lying head to head with me, and she joined our hidden huddle. "What's this about a plan?" she asked Mia, her voice barely audible over the creaking of the trees in the night wind.

"There's only one guard on us, right?" Mia replied. "The ginger."

"As far as I can tell," Anji whispered back. "But unless you intend to break down the door, I don't think it matters how many men they've left to watch us."

"So let's get the door open. I thought I'd try the Duffy approach."

I couldn't see Anji, but the tone of her voice was sufficient to convey her disapproval. "You would *seduce* him?"

"No, no—just lead him on," Mia assured her. "Give him the idea that he might get lucky and see where that takes us."

"That is—"

"Underhanded but effective. I'll give it a go and see if we can't work something out. I mean, unless you have a better idea…"

"No," Anji reluctantly admitted, "but why *you*? What if—"

Mia grunted. "Process of elimination. No offense intended, but I think it'd be the rare elf who lusted after you, and Suze, you know I love you, but you're so damn *awkward* with boys."

The truth stung, but I couldn't argue with it.

"I can fake my way through this," Mia continued. "I've had practice. So cross your fingers and pray to whatever deities you trust that our guard likes blondes," she concluded, then shimmied out of her sleeping bag, gave her hair a stylish mussing, and sashayed toward the door with its barred window.

"This is going to be a disaster," Anji muttered as she sat up to watch.

Had I been observing from the princess's perspective, I'd have concurred. Logic dictated no other outcome— Mia was pretty enough but not a ravishing beauty, and though the only female elf I'd observed to that point was the queen, she seemed just as lovely as her male counterparts. But I'd seen Mia in action. Her superpower was scoring free drinks in bars, and she and I had seldom paid for our nights out in college. It wasn't how she dressed (almost always in a shirt two sizes too large) or how she flaunted her assets (difficult to do in a bralette from the juniors department), but there was something unmistakably intriguing about Mia when she turned on the charm, and slightly tipsy guys couldn't resist her half-lidded eyes and weird lip-nibbling routine. I was a believer, but only because I'd enjoyed too many free vodka tonics to doubt.

Mia wrapped her fingers around the bars in the door's window and peeked into the corridor. "Hi, there," she said, her voice dropping into her practiced husky register, and I struggled not to snicker. "Did they leave you all alone here tonight?"

At least our guard, unlike the patrol commander, was

wearing a translator. "I…uh…" He paused, then managed to squeak, "Yes?"

"Aw, that's too bad," Mia purred. "Must be so *boring* just standing out there."

I'd expected a little pushback from the guard—we were incarcerated, after all, not pulling up stools on Ladies' Night—but to my surprise, he reacted almost immediately. "Yes," he said, drawing closer to the window, "it's quite boring."

"Mm." Even watching Mia's back, I could envision the lip nibble. "Maybe we could keep each other company, then."

"Yes," he murmured.

"Entertain each other?"

He nodded.

"You know," Mia continued, "it's so cold in this room. Drafty. And we don't have enough blankets."

"No?"

"No," she said, putting on a pout. "Just…huddling for warmth. Body heat's the best thing on a cold night, don't you agree? You know…skin to skin?" She reached for the top buttons of the old plaid shirt she'd thrown on the night before—which might have fit an actual lumberjack properly—hesitated, then slowly undid them.

It wasn't as if Mia had an ample chest spring-loaded under the flannel, but whatever flash of clavicle she was giving the guard seemed to be doing the trick—*too* well. His stare remained fixed on her, but his jaw hung slack, the sort of expression one might find upon the face of a thirteen-year-old boy who's just been invited backstage at a burlesque show.

"Would you like to come in and join us?" Mia asked, crooking one finger through the bars. "It's just us girls, and we won't bite." Her finger caught the guard beneath the chin and gently pulled him closer to her. "*Hard.*"

He whispered a word under his breath, and with a quiet *snick*, the door unlatched. Mia stepped back, giving it room to swing inward, and turned to Anji and me with a flip of her hair. Out of the guard's sight, her expression shifted in an instant to bemused wonder, and she sidled close to us and muttered, "Whatever you're making the sword do, keep it up."

"I'm not doing anything," I began, but Mia had already turned her attention back to the guard, who wandered into the cell like a man entranced, the short blade at his side forgotten.

"I'm Mia," she murmured, tracing the line of his jaw with two fingers before brushing his long hair back over his shoulder. "What's your name, gorgeous?"

"F-Fanakel."

"Mm," she replied with a smile. "I like that. I like *you*, Fanakel." One finger landed atop his lips, as if she were shushing him, then slowly trailed down and away. "Would you like to play with me? I know some *wonderful* games."

Even having witnessed the spectacle of Mia's routine on hopeful college boys, I could barely believe what I was seeing, and Anji's eyes nearly bulged from her head. The nodding guard had fixated on her like he was in the presence of Venus, naked and floating ashore, and I knew I wasn't imagining the slight sheen of drool threatening to escape his open mouth.

"Who gave the sword hypnotic powers?" I whispered to Anji.

"No one," she replied in kind. "I've never heard anything about *this* sort of ability…"

"I mean, first the umbrella, and now this. Maybe this thing's got some bonus tricks."

"Perhaps."

She sounded unconvinced, but before I could respond, Mia upped the ante. "It's so uncomfortable in here, isn't it, Fanakel?" she said, running her hands over his shoulders and upper arms. "Won't you take us somewhere better? Wouldn't you like that?"

"Yes," he mumbled, nodding again.

Mia leaned so close that she could have licked his pointed ear, had she been feeling particularly frisky. "It should be a secret place. Somewhere outside the city. If anyone sees us, they might try to take me away from you."

His pale green eyes hardened at the notion, and he reached out to grip her waist. "I won't let that happen."

"I know," she murmured, and planted a soft kiss on his cheek. "My *brave* Fanakel. Surely you know a way out of here…don't you? For me?"

The answer to that was a resounding *yes*. Mia gasped as he hoisted her into his arms like a groom with his brand-new bride, and I barely had time to grab our gear and sling *both* of our bags onto my back before he carried her out of the cell and down the corridor. Anji helped me as she could, repacking the sleeping bags as we jogged after them.

The Twins were overly confident in their security situation, as we passed not a soul before we reached an elevator—judging by the scratches all over the interior, a cargo hoist. Fanakel hurried us to the bottom, then slipped out of the hollow trunk and made a beeline for a dark alley in the city's ground-level labyrinth. Anji and I struggled to keep up—the elf was a man on a mission—but after a few turns, five tense minutes hiding behind a stack of barrels, and a close call with a pair of inebriates staggering out of a seeming tavern, we reached the living fence. Fanakel muttered briefly, and the vines and branches gave way, parting in a hole barely big enough for two. He ducked and carried Mia through the opening, and we hurried behind them before the fence could mend itself.

A few yards into the shelter of the trees, Fanakel's sure steps began to slow, then stop. "It's okay," Mia soothed, patting his youthful face. "Put me down, and I'll take you *exactly* where we need to go. Can you trust me?"

He didn't hesitate to set her back on her feet, and he watched with a dreamy, dopey gaze as she wrapped her hand around his wrist. "Suze, give me my bag, won't you?" she said, the request made ridiculous by her seduction voice, but I didn't dare to laugh as I handed it over. Once we were properly loaded, she gave Fanakel's arm a gentle tug and started off through the woods.

"Where are we going?" I whispered to Anji.

The princess shrugged. "I don't know the Greenwood, especially not at night. And if there are indeed Outsiders prowling..."

"We need shelter. Something defensible."

"Agreed, but where?" She glanced over her shoulder at the lights of the tree fortress we'd escaped, then patted the knife at her hip. "Perhaps we should unpack the guns before we go any farther."

But Mia, apparently, wasn't one to risk losing her momentum. On we stumbled through the forest, guided only by the occasional flicker of moonlight through the canopy—we didn't dare to use our flashlights, and I sure as hell wasn't going to let the sword glow. After about half an hour's walk, however, we caught a break. The trees thinned, then gave way to the gentle slope of the muddy beach abutting a large body of water.

I frowned at the sparkling chop. "Is that..."

"A lake," said Anji. "Not the Great Sea, but the Greenwood is pocked with lakes and rivers. Is that an island, do you suppose?" she asked, squinting at a dark shape perhaps two hundred yards from shore. "I don't know anything about the local elementals..."

Fanakel said nothing, and Mia tried her luck. "Is that an island?" she asked, linking her arm around his. "A *private* island?"

"Yes," he murmured dreamily. "Wild. Kingkiller."

She turned to me. "Well, *that's* reassuring, but it looks like our best option right now. Think the sword's up to the task?"

"What task?" I asked.

"Can you get us across?"

"Like..."

"Red Sea–style."

I shrugged but pulled the sword free of its scabbard. "Worth a shot," I muttered, then held the blade over the water, tried to remember what it felt like when the invisible force field blocked the rain, and imagined that force extending through the lake instead of over my head. After a few seconds' concentration, the water directly ahead of me began to recede, parting into a narrow pathway, and I quietly tried not to freak out.

Anji took a test step onto the lakebed and sank to her ankle. "This will be *disgusting*," she warned, pulling her boot free. "Can the sword make a boat, do you suppose?"

"Never tried," I said, watching the path carve its way toward the island through the night-dark lake. "But since this seems to be working…"

She sighed, hitched up her bag, and plowed into the muck. After observing her struggle for a moment, Mia stroked Fanakel's arm and murmured, "You're so big and strong. Don't you think you should carry me?"


There was no structure on the island, but there *was* a clearing just past the beach, guarded from prying eyes on the mainland by a row of trees and some dense bushes, and that was good enough for us. Anji and I dropped our gear, Fanakel gently put Mia back on solid ground, and the three of us set about making camp while our elven accomplice stood by, staring into space like he'd been hit upside the head.

"So…what do we do with your new boyfriend?" I whispered to Mia.

"Just keep the sword working," she assured me, and sashayed back to her beau. "Poor baby," she said, kissing his cheek once more. "You're so tired, aren't you?"

Fanakel nodded, his shoulders slumping as if bending beneath the weight of the suggestion.

"Take a little nap," Mia coaxed, gently drawing him down to the scrub grass. "I'll be right here when you wake in the morning, okay?"

"Yes," he mumbled, then stretched out, closed his eyes, and was soon snoring.

Mia disentangled herself from his arms, stepped over his mud-caked boots, and beckoned me down to the beach, where Anji was busily washing the foul-smelling grunge from her boots and trousers. The lake mud stank of decay, and I was eager to do my own cleanup with the Fanakel problem momentarily tabled. Mia followed me to the water's edge, and as I tugged off my filthy boots, she rebuttoned her shirt, then hugged herself. "Well, that was...*different*," she muttered.

"Your finest work yet," I replied, dunking my boots into the lake. Assuming we survived to see winter again, I decided that I'd treat myself to a new pair—snow they could handle, but the stains they'd accrued over the last two weeks were another matter entirely. "How'd you do it?"

"I'm telling you, it's the sword. I didn't do anything new—it's not like I picked up hypnosis in New York." She sighed and sank onto a rock while I worked. "God, I feel gross."

"To be fair, they're the ones who locked us up."

"Yeah, but that come-hither routine...ugh," she grunted, then fake-retched. "Scoring freebie drinks from drunk guys always made me feel a little guilty, but *that*...shit, I want a bath. Is the lake cold?"

Knee-deep in the unpleasantly cool water, I splashed her, and she recoiled. "Maybe later," she said. "Don't suppose you could use the sword to heat water, could you?"

"Don't know," I said as I scrubbed at the stinking mud, hoping the boots' claim to waterproofness wasn't just a marketing ploy. "Think I'm too tired tonight after our prison break and"—I gestured at our island hideout with one dripping boot—"everything."

"I hear you. How's the head?"

"Throbbing, but I'll live. My legs are going to be miserable in the morning."

"Same. I just hurt all over, you know? Anji, hanging in there?"

The dwarf paused to parse that question, then got the gist of it and nodded. "I've felt worse. Incidentally, do you two know if Outsiders can swim?"

"Couldn't say one way or another," I replied, eying the trees at the lake's far shore. "We should post a watch, shouldn't we?"

By then, my eyes had adjusted to the darkness well enough to make out the incredulous look Anji shot me. "*That* was never in doubt. My question is whether we should be most concerned about being eaten by Outsiders, attacked by a boatload of elves, or killed in our sleep by Mia's new friend when he wakes and realizes that love is dead."

"Come on, you don't think you could take him?" I asked, smirking.

Anji snorted, then sloshed out of the lake. "Never said *that*, lass, but my odds would be better if I were anticipating the attack. And just for that, one of you can take the first shift."

Mia and I watched her make her dripping way toward our primitive campsite, and I sighed and returned to the task of de-sludging my gear. "You know, this is going to take a while. Get some rest—you win MVP for the evening."

She stood with a soft groan. "My mother would be so proud. Wake me in case of aquatic horrors."

# CHAPTER 11

If the Outsiders could indeed swim, I was none the wiser come dawn. Though I'd never been an early riser by choice, I had to admit that the morning was pleasant as I sat wrapped in my unzipped sleeping bag, listening to the first-light birdsong and the lapping of the breeze-stirred water against the shore. The sun was barely above the horizon when Anji joined me, saw that I'd stayed up all night, and volunteered to make tea. Soon, she returned with steaming mugs, courtesy of a chemical heater, and we soaked in the serenity of the new day.

And then the damn elf woke up.

He moaned as he stirred, having barely moved since crashing the night before, and slowly raised himself from the ground, squinting at his surroundings. Bits of dead leaves clung to his tangled red hair, and a dark, damp patch had spread across his brown tunic from his night in the grass. He smacked his lips as if trying to get a bad taste out of his mouth, then suddenly seemed to realize he wasn't in his own bed and leapt to his feet. A few seconds' frantic search led him to Anji and me, and while her hand went to her dagger, I stood and tried to motion him down. "You're all right," I began, keeping my voice low. "It's okay, Fanakel, no need to panic."

He jerked as if I'd slapped him. "How…what…"

"Name," Anji muttered beside me.

"*Shit*," I hissed, then returned my focus to the frightened elf. "Sorry, sorry," I said in a rush. "You told us your name last night, and I just forgot about the cultural hang-up because I've only been in Honslia for, like, two and a half days, so…sorry. No offense. Calm down, we're not going to hurt you."

But my attempt at reassurance was less than successful. "Who are you?" he demanded, reaching for his sword. "What have you done? Where—"

"She's the Watcher," Anji interrupted, "and you were meant to be guarding us last night. Remember?"

Fanakel frowned, and then a look of terror swept across his face. "No…oh, no, no, *no*, this isn't happening…"

"You helped us escape," she continued, and I didn't think I was imagining the note of smugness in her voice. "Right through the fence. You, um…you seemed rather fond of our companion…"

I cut my eyes to the Mia-sized lump of sleeping bag behind me. "You carried her here, in fact. That's why your shoes are filthy. Sunk in the lakebed."

He looked down at his mud-caked boots. "I did *what*? To whom? *Where are we?*" he asked, then glanced out at the lake. The little color in his face drained away. "The Kingkiller? You dragged me into the damned *Kingkiller*?"

An uneasy shiver ran up my back at the word. While dwarven place names had translated, their elvish counterparts had sounded like gobbledygook to me up until that point. I supposed they'd been pulled from an older language, hypothesizing that I'd only hear the translated sense if the speaker understood what he was actually saying. But *that* word, to my deep disquietude, came through without a hitch.

Just in case, I felt for my own sword and tried to keep him calm. "My friend Mia—and be quiet, she's still sleeping. She, uh, came on to you last night, and you were great about getting us out of that cell, and we found this lake, and I kind of got us out here, and…look, you're safe," I assured him as his panic escalated. "We don't want to hurt you—I just need someone to help me get rid of this sword, and the Twins were being *real* assholes about it."

At least he was too distraught to be offended that I'd insulted his sovereigns. "No," he whispered, rubbing his temples. "No, this can't…I'm dreaming, this is a nightmare…"

Anji tugged at my sleeve until I bent within whispering range, then asked, "Do you suppose it would help if I slapped him a few times? You know, just to disabuse him of the notion."

"Tempting, but better not," I replied, watching the elf pace and mutter to himself. "Let's give him a minute, see if he calms down, maybe offer him breakfast. Yeah?"

She sighed. "If you insist—"

"The *fuck*?" Mia's groggy voice interrupted, but as I turned around to fill her in, I stopped in my tracks and gaped.

There was indeed a person where Mia had been lying, now sitting up with her sleeping bag pushed to the waist. Said person was female, like Mia, and seemed to be wearing Mia's clothing, but she *wasn't* Mia…

No, I realized as the stranger goggled at her ample chest, which had popped two of Mia's flannel shirt's buttons and was testing the tensile strength of the undershirt beneath—she looked like Mia after extensive plastic surgery.

The Mia-adjacent woman was *stunning*. Whereas Mia's hair had leaned toward the dirty end of the blonde spectrum and always hung straight and flat, no matter how much product she used, the stranger's hair was nearly platinum, thick, and lightly wavy as it cascaded over her shoulders. I might have thought it an expensive wig, had I seen her on the street. Her eyes resembled Mia's, though they seemed larger and of a deeper blue, with a fringe of dark lashes that would have made a mascara model weep with envy. Mia's pasty, breakout-prone skin had been swapped for a dewy porcelain complexion, flawless even after her night on the ground. Her lips were redder, too, and as plump as if she'd bought fillers.

And then there was the slight matter of her body. As the woman hastily sloughed off the sleeping bag and stood, I saw that whatever artist had sculped her face hadn't skimped on the rest of her. Mia had always been stick-skinny and flat, to her chagrin, stuck between boyish and waifish. Beyond *this* woman's substantial bosom, her waist curved into an hourglass, then flared into what I could only describe as a perfectly heart-shaped rear. I had no idea how Mia's leggings were still intact.

"Holy shit," I whispered.

Unfamiliar as the woman appeared, she still had Mia's voice, and she was poking at her modified frame as if wondering how everything had been attached. "What the hell?" she said, peeking down into the built-in bra of her undershirt—which, for once in her life, seemed unfit for its task. "What did you *do* to me, Suze?"

"Nothing!" I protested. "I haven't touched you! You slept all night, and—"

"And *what*? Went through freaking puberty again? Oh, my God," she marveled, looking over her shoulder at her backside, "where did *that* come from?"

"I swear I didn't do it," I insisted as she gave her rump a test shake, perhaps waiting to see whether it would fall off. "If this is the sword, it's got a mind of its own, and—"

Anji cleared her throat to interrupt my babbling. "It's not the sword."

"Then what?" Mia demanded, pointing to her chest. "This ain't a bee sting!"

"Try to be calm." Turning back to the muttering elf, she snapped, "Pull yourself together, lad! One crisis at a time, if you please!"

He stopped in his tracks, presumably to rebuke her, then noticed Mia in her too-tight clothing and gasped.

"*Sit*," Anji ordered, drawing her dagger for good measure, and the elf had sense enough to cooperate. With him shocked into silence, she focused on Mia, though not without a mumbled, "High Queen have mercy."

"*What* is going on?" Mia asked, trying to self-consciously fold her arms over her breasts. Stymied by physics, she settled for crossing them beneath the bulge under her shirt.

Anji raised a hand for patience. "You said your mother is fairly ordinary, yes? An average human?"

Mia frowned. "Yeah…"

"And your father—he was some sort of titillating dancer?"

"*Yeah*," she repeated, an edge of defensiveness creeping into her voice. "What about it?"

"Well…I could be mistaken, but in light of what we witnessed last night and…now"—she gestured at Mia's augmented form—"I suspect that you father was a tekori."

"Tekori?" Fanakel yelped. "That thing is—"

Anji whipped around and pointed her dagger at him until he shut up. "It's only a hypothesis," she said to Mia, "but it seems to fit the facts. I believe you are half tekori."

Mia's gorgeous face wrinkled with confusion. "I'm sorry…*what*?"

"You don't know," Anji muttered, giving her beard an agitated tug. "How to explain…"

Vaguely, I recalled hearing the term during our meeting with Rokund, and my guts clenched. While the dwarves had brushed aside my questions then, the impression they'd left at the time was far from positive.

"Tekoraet are native to Ga'besh," said Anji. "Not quite as long-lived as dwarves—or elves," she added, gesturing to Fanakel with her dagger—"but five hundred years isn't unheard of."

Mia's eyebrows shot up. "Five hundred?"

"That's my understanding. Our dealings with them are minimal, so…" She shrugged. "This is the best I can offer, Mia."

"Parasites," said Fanakel, glaring at my suddenly

voluptuous friend. "Nothing but—"

I couldn't see the look that Anji shot him when she turned around, but he backed off in a hurry.

"They resemble humans," she resumed as Mia nibbled her lip. "Our history actually speaks of a war in the distant past that began as a misunderstanding—humans had just begun appearing in Ildon, and the dwarves they encountered mistook them for a tekorish band and attacked. Human scholars suggest that an easy way to tell the difference on sight is that tekoraet are almost universally beautiful, but...I mean, beauty is a highly subjective thing."

"What about elves?" I interjected. "You saw them—"

"And you people seem to find them attractive, too, for whatever reason," said Anji, "but the *look* is different." Tossing her head toward Fanakel, who remained in a wary crouch behind her, she said, "They skew tall and thin, seemingly delicate, always pale and lacking hair but on top of their heads. And the ridiculous ears are a giveaway."

"*Hey*," Fanakel snapped.

The princess smirked briefly, then sobered. "Tekoraet are shorter, more like humans. The males are often more visibly muscled than male elves, while the females..." She gave Mia a meaningful glance.

"But *overnight?*" said Mia. "How'd I get a pinup figure in my sleep?"

"Oh, that's not all you got," I muttered, and passed her the hand mirror from our emergency fire-starter kit.

Her jaw dropped as she examined her modified face and ran a hand through her bouncy tresses. "What the hell?" she finally repeated. "How...but what..."

"And why did Fanakel call them parasites?" I asked, glancing over in time to see the elf wince at the use of his name.

Anji sighed and rubbed the back of her neck. "Because...well, to be blunt, they are."

"I don't understand," said Mia, then gave me back the

mirror and hugged herself again, more tightly than she had the first time.

From the expression on Anji's face, she might as well have been delivering a diagnosis with survival measured in weeks. "Tekoraet eat like anyone else, but they don't subsist merely on food. To be properly...*fed*," she said with distaste, "they siphon off the life force of others."

Mia's eyes widened. "Like...blood?"

"No. They can induce intense lust in other people. Tekorish males affect females, and their females affect males—"

"What if one of them is genderfluid?" I interrupted.

"I don't know," Anji replied testily, "and that's not important this morning. As I was saying, they induce lust, and they feed off of it. It leaves the victim in a stupor, highly suggestible. Ordinarily, these feedings aren't fatal, especially if the victim is young, but—and again, this is what I learned from my tutors, not an actual tekori," she stressed—"for a tekori to be truly fit and healthy, he or she needs to, um...to take that lust to its physical end every so often."

"Sex," Mia mumbled.

The princess nodded. "The reports of death by tekori usually involve fatal copulation."

"But...but that doesn't make sense." Mia scowled at the lake as she puzzled through Anji's offering. "Raquel and I were as intimate as anyone, and I never hurt her."

"Because Raquel is female, is she not?" said Anji. "Tekoraet have power over the *opposite* sex."

Horror dawned on Mia's face, and she retreated a few paces from Anji, holding up her hands as if to keep the dwarf at bay. "No. *No.* You *cannot* be serious."

"We all saw the effect you had on Fanakel last night—"

"So what are you saying, I have to screw him or die?"

At that, the elf finally remembered how his feet worked. "Stay away from me," he ordered as he recovered his footing. "I'm warning you, I *will* kill you if you come closer."

"I don't want to come closer!" Mia protested. "You're not my type! I…"

She turned away, trembling, and I wrapped her sleeping bag around her shoulders. "It's going to be okay," I murmured as I hugged her. "Whatever's going on, it'll be okay. We'll figure this out."

"Suze, I—"

"We'll get to the bottom of this," I said, though I wasn't even reassuring myself, and held on until her shaking subsided.

By the time Mia released me, Anji had moved closer and looked up at her wet eyes with pity. "I can't prove any of this, you know," she said. "It's only a theory. But tekorish children look much like human children until they reach maturity, and perhaps, since you grew up in a place outside of the Aen, you've never fed properly, and so your body has been stunted all of these years. Here, now, with *him* on hand as an easy meal…"

"Instant puberty," I finished.

"That's my conclusion. Are you hungry, Mia?"

I was puzzled by the non sequitur, then shocked when my friend, usually hungry enough to eat steaks still on the hoof, shook her head. "No," she said, bemused. "Not really. I mean, if you've made breakfast, I'll eat something, but—"

"But you don't need it," said Anji, "because you fed well last night."

Mia stared down at the princess in silence, then pulled the sleeping bag around her, hiding the unfamiliar body beneath it. "So," she mumbled, "you really think I'm some sort of…what, incubus?"

"Succubus," I babbled, desperate to find words that would improve the situation. "They're the female ones. Incubi are male, and—"

"Not helping, Suze."

Anji hesitated, then patted Mia's arm through the puffy

bag. "This isn't a terrible thing for you. A longer life than you'd expected—"

"Except you think I'm a sex demon."

"You're not a *demon*," I said.

She turned to me, her eyes on the brink of overflowing again. "But what if I am? What if I hurt you?"

At that, Anji heaved a sigh. "Have you been listening to me? Tekorish females only have an effect on males. Whatever power you possess, Susan and I are immune. Which brings to mind another matter..." Turning to Fanakel, she said, "It was my understanding that elves are unaffected by tekorish attacks. They're meant to be safe against mental manipulation—that's why they have real settlements on Ga'besh, while we only have a trading post. So, assuming that elves can defend against tekoraet...what are *you*?"

Twin spots of color rose in his fair cheeks, but his expression spoke more of embarrassment than anger. He was a dog cringing into a corner, not one baring its teeth for a fight.

Anji's stance softened as Fanakel's demeanor shifted. "Half, eh, lad?" she asked more kindly. "What's the rest, human?"

He flinched in silent acknowledgement.

"Bad luck for your commander—no one knew they were leaving a susceptible man with a tekori woman," she continued. "The Twins can't fairly blame you for our escape."

"Easy for you to say," he muttered, and glared at the far shore through the trees. "How am I supposed to show my face again? Unless I bring the tekori's head with me..."

I clutched my sword's hilt, and the calm water lapping at the edge of the island instantly turned to a violent, white-capped chop.

Fanakel tensed and retreated a few steps inland, and Anji cautioned, "I wouldn't say that so loudly. Or even think it, really. Touch Mia, and if the Watcher doesn't kill you, I will. Oh," she added in an almost conversational tone, "and should you attempt to swim back to shore and alert the Twins, you'd never make it. The Watcher has power over water."

"Never mind that, it's the *Kingkiller*. Of course I'd drown in the crossing."

She frowned. "Unfriendly elemental?"

"Exceedingly."

"Well, he gave us no trouble last night," she replied with a shrug. "The sword made a path for us, and he never protested."

Fanakel looked puzzled at her explanation. "That's not one of Bright Blade's abilities."

"*You* helped in its making?"

"No, but my father did. He and his sister coordinated those among the True who made the sword deadly against Outsiders."

Her eyes narrowed as he spoke. "Your father and—"

"The Twins, yes," he snapped, his shoulders hunching like a shield. "My father is the king. Got me on a serving girl. Are you satisfied, or is there more of my shame you wish to dredge up this morning?"

She stared him down for a long moment, then sighed and folded her arms. "We should at least level our footing. I am Anjikora of Blackhorn Mountain. Rokund's youngest."

"Good for you," he muttered, then stalked off to the shore.


Of the three of us, the last person I'd have expected to be anywhere close to stable that day was Mia. She sat with Anji and me as we scrounged up a halfway decent breakfast behind the sheltering trees, sipping tea and keeping her sleeping bag wrapped around her like a security blanket, and said little. I didn't know how to console her—I couldn't imagine what was going through her mind—and while Anji was unusually gentle, her attempts to distract Mia with conversation fizzled. Mia barely touched her oatmeal, even though maple and brown sugar had always been her favorite, and when Anji and I finished eating, she rose and excused herself.

I watched as she headed for the shore, still trailing her sleeping bag, and followed at a distance in case Fanakel got any bright ideas.

The guard—well, the prince, rather—had plopped behind a large boulder, which, combined with the thick brush, would have hidden him from searchers on the mainland. Mia approached slowly, waiting for him to notice her, then stopped when he did and said, "I'm not going to hurt you, I promise. I just wanted to apologize."

Though he regarded her warily, he didn't try to run as she joined him in his hiding place.

"I'm *not* sorry for busting out of prison," she began, settling into the weeds beside him. "The Twins had no reason to lock us up."

"Oh? I was told that the Watcher attacked my father."

"Suze lost her temper, but she didn't *attack* him. And if you were in her position, you'd be a little testy, too."

"Who, the Watcher?"

"*Yeah.* That stupid sword attached itself to her, so now she's a monster magnet, and no one over here will help her get rid of it."

"Because that is her job."

"It's not! How'd you like it if someone put a magic sword in your hand and told you that you'd be stuck fighting Outsiders every night for the rest of your life?"

"I wouldn't," he admitted after a long pause, "but—"

"But nothing. It's *wrong.* You guys and the dwarves and everyone else involved with that sword have no right to do what you did, and so I'm here to help Suze get free. If your father won't do the decent thing, then fuck him, we'll try elsewhere. But he could have just said no. Locking us up was unnecessary."

She paused to adjust her makeshift cloak, grunting as the slippery material refused to stay in position. "All of that said, what I did to you last night was shitty. I didn't mean to get in your head like that, or...or leech off of you, or whatever it is I did. I used to flirt with guys to get free drinks," she explained, "but it was never like that. I was desperate and thought I might be able to distract you long enough to steal the keys or something, but actually having you carry me out of there..."

He groaned at the notion.

"Honest to God, I thought it was the sword, and we had a good thing going—"

"You thought the sword had mind-control abilities?" he asked incredulously.

"Why not? It glows in the dark, sets Outsiders on fire, translates everything for Suze...hell, it flew through the air and cut her loose the other day when she thought about it. Mind control didn't seem outside the realm of possibility...but maybe I was mistaken," she muttered, brushing her newly thickened hair out of her face. "Like I said, I'm not sorry to have broken out of that cell, but I didn't know I was feeding off of you in the process, and for that, I apologize. And, uh...well, for psychically roofie-ing you."

"For *what?*"

"Yeah, that was expecting too much of the translator. For mind-controlling you. I got carried away, and if someone had done that to me, I'd be furious, so...I'm sorry."

He said nothing for a moment, then sighed. "You thought you were unjustly imprisoned, and you escaped. In your position, I suppose I would have done much the same."

"Doesn't make it right," said Mia.

"Many things in life are not."

"Maybe, but I try not to add to that pile too often." When he offered no response, she said, "Once we're on our way, go back and tell them that Anji or Suze knocked you out, and we kept you as a hostage. That's plausible—no one needs to know that I got in your head. I mean, whatever the deal is with your parents, I'm not going to spread anything around. Secret's safe here."

I thought I saw a small, strained smile flicker and vanish. "Thank you."

"Least I can do." She adjusted her sleeping bag again and stared into the distance. "In case you were worried, we didn't do anything, uh...*physical*...last night. You and me, I mean. You carried me out here, and then I told you to take a nap, and that was all."

"Reassuring, I suppose," said Fanakel, then mirthlessly laughed to himself. "Not handsome enough for you, then?"

"You're cute," she replied with a shrug. "I just don't go for men. It's nothing personal."

He turned to her, squinting in befuddlement. "But...if you're a tekori—"

"Yeah, please don't remind me," she said, and shuddered. "If Anji's right, I've got *problems*. See, it could be worse," she added, nudging him in the side. "You woke up in the body you fell asleep in. That's one up on me."

The intended consolation had no effect, however. "You jest, but a new face would be welcome right now. I can't show this one again in Nokan'ti, maybe not in all of Honslia."

"I told you, just pretend that we beat you unconscious—"

"Father has his ways of seeing through lies. The truth would come out quickly, and with it, all my shame."

He looked so despondent that I felt sorry for him until I recalled the bruise his father had given me the evening before, which served to sour my feelings toward elves in general.

"It's not your fault," said Mia. "Whoever left you to guard us didn't know what I can do. Heck, *I* didn't know what I can do."

"You don't understand," he said, pulling his knees to his chest. "All my life, I've tried so hard to be worthy of being called True, and now that's gone."

"Huh?"

"The dwarf was correct—elves' minds can't be controlled. So if I'm sitting here with you, covered in *that*"—he gestured to his muck-stained legs and feet—"then obviously, I'm not True."

"Half, right?"

"Still a lesser being," he said morosely. "And there's nothing I can do about it." As he folded his arms atop his knees and started to rest his chin in the hollow, he suddenly twitched and pulled his head away. "Oh, no," he muttered, giving his cheeks a pat on either side. "*No*, I don't need this today…"

"Need what?" Mia asked.

Fanakel tilted his head away from her, exposing his jaw and neck. "Notice anything?"

She leaned closer and studied him for a few seconds, then sat back and tightened her wrappings. "You've got great pores, but…no?"

"Did you not see the stubble?"

"Yeah, so? I thought shaving was a daily thing for guys."

"*Humans* can grow beards," he replied. "Dwarves, certainly—the one with you is proof of that. But not elves. And *this* little reminder returns every morning to torment me," he concluded, rubbing one hand over his reddish fuzz. "You wouldn't have a razor, would you?"

"No—we've been camping, and shaving has been way down my list of priorities. Sorry."

"Worth a try," he mumbled.

They sat in awkward silence for a few long seconds, and then Mia said, "So…you're a prince, eh?"

He nodded.

"What's that like?"

"I wish I knew." Seeing her frown, he said, "Father recognized me. That doesn't mean he's ever considered me an equal to his other children."

"I'm sorry."

"It's to be expected. He knows I'm not True. My mother's coloration was the least of my deficiencies," he said, waving a hand over his face. "Rare for an elf, but not unheard of. But once *this* began"—he ran a finger down his jaw with disgust—"there was no denying it. I was fifteen, and Father put a blade in my hand and told me to fix the problem. Never mind that I have his other children's ability with magic. I was tutored, just as they were, and I never proved lacking. But…"

"Still not enough?" she guessed.

"Never." He scowled into space. "All of his sons and his sister's sons have done a stint in the palace guards. No matter which of us takes the throne someday, he'll have an appreciation for the service they render."

"Sure…"

"The others served no more than ten years. A few barely served five before they were posted as ambassadors or put onto councils or sent to the Schools for an extended education with the masters. And then there's me. Father gave me to the guards at twenty-five, and that was seventy-four years ago."

Mia whistled softly.

"I've hoped for years that he would reassign me," he continued, hugging his knees. "Put me on an unimportant council, marry me off to a minor princess, *anything* but continued servitude. But this is all he thinks I'm worth," he said miserably. "And he's correct—"

"Okay, *first*," she interrupted, "there's nothing wrong with a job in security. I've got cousins in the police and the Navy, and no one looks down on them."

"Their father isn't the king of Nokan'ti, is he?"

"No, but that doesn't make the work any less valuable. And second, if your father's a jerk who doesn't appreciate you, why not get out of town for a while? Let him remember that you should have a little consideration."

"Were it only that we had disagreed, I'd consider that wise," he replied. "But absence won't make me True."

Mia rolled her eyes at his self-pity. "You know," she said dryly, "there's really no shame in being human."

He looked at her as if she'd offered him a tinfoil hat to ward off alien radio signals.

"I'm serious! What's so freaking great about elves, anyway? I mean, I'm not saying the rest of us are perfect, but at least the dwarves fed us and gave us beds without dragging us through the woods—*literally* dragging. Ever been tied behind a chiquiw and told to keep up?"

"That...seems excessive," he allowed.

"And Anji's father—he's conflicted about doing away with the Watcher gig and opening his people up to attacks, but at least he knows it's wrong. That's why he sent Anji with us. If your father can't see the injustice in the Watcher setup, then *he's* the one with the problem."

Fanakel struggled briefly, then managed, "Asking a lesser being to serve the needs of the True—"

"What *lesser* being? Again, what the hell makes elves so special?"

"They are the True Children of the Divine—"

"Says you. I don't believe a word of it."

He leaned away from her like a man expecting a bolt from the heavens. "You would blaspheme—"

"Put aside your religion for a moment. What makes your life worth any more than mine? Than Anji's? Suze's? Maybe it's longer, maybe you can do some nifty tricks with the Aen, but that doesn't give you inherently greater *worth*." She shook her head as he searched for a response. "You grew up in a culture that thinks itself superior to everything and everyone else, I understand that. But who's to say you're right?"

"The priests—"

"Not them. Who here can objectively stand back, look

at all of the lives in the universe, and say, 'Yes, *those* are the most important'?"

Though he frowned, no answer was immediately forthcoming.

"Look, I'm not trying to drag you into a philosophy discussion before you've even had breakfast," said Mia. "All I'm suggesting is that being human isn't the worst thing that could happen to you...and you'd probably look good with a beard. Maybe not one as full as Anji's, but something close-cropped, neatly groomed..."

"I thought you didn't like men," he replied.

"Doesn't mean I can't appreciate the aesthetics." She lowered her voice far enough that I had to strain to hear. "Want to show your father that you're the better man? Help us."

"Help you do what, escape? I thought I had."

"You know the Greenwood, right? Help us get back to the tunnel. We've got to find Daril."

"You've got to cross the lake first," he retorted. "And you think you'll have a better reception in *Daril*, of all places?"

"I don't know, but we've got to try." Standing, she brushed herself off and adjusted her sleeping bag. "Think it over. If you want to get out of here for a few days, maybe make it look like we abducted you, that's fine."

"Or I could return to the city and tell Father your plans."

"You could."

They stared each other down, and then Fanakel cocked his head. "You're not trying to force me?"

"I'm asking you to do the right thing," she replied, and headed back to our camp.

# CHAPTER 12

Half an hour later, we'd cleaned the little mess we'd made and packed. Mia had exchanged her precariously buttoned flannel for a formerly oversized T-shirt and spent a few minutes fiddling with the straps of her bag until it fit her new form. "This is a pain in the ass," she grumbled as I helped her load up. "Assuming we find a way out of Honslia, I'm going to have to throw out half my closet. And what's Antoinette going to say when I show up for work looking like this? If she hasn't fired me by now," she added with a sigh.

"She's forgiving," I said. "Let's get you home, see what you can still wear, and then you go back to work. There's no need for you to keep slogging along with me."

"Uh, *no*. I said I would help you, and that's what I'm going to do."

"That was before we ended up in elf jail and you...um..."

"Went full succubus?"

I moved closer to her and said, "If this place has an effect on you, I don't want you going through weird changes on my account. My life's a wreck already—one of us should get to enjoy something like normalcy."

"There's nothing normal about lust-hypnosis superpowers," Mia countered, "and if I sashay into Antoinette's, she's going to think my norovirus excuse was cover for a plastic surgery bonanza. And can you imagine what Mom would say if she saw me?"

"She might not recognize you on the street."

"But if she does and she demands an explanation, what am I supposed to tell her? 'Hey, funny story, the dude who knocked you up in Vegas probably wasn't human'? I can see that going over *so* well, can't you? And what about Ms. Quince's replacement? You think she's arrived yet?"

That thought made my guts twist. Everyone we'd met beyond the Crossing seemed to view the maladetas with healthy respect, if not a little trepidation. Maybe Ms. Quince had gone rogue after her time in town, and her replacement would do everything in her power to keep me tethered to my unwanted fate. I didn't know what they were capable of, especially given the low Aen concentration in our world, but I didn't want to risk my freedom on the new babysitter's whims. More worryingly, in light of what we'd learned concerning local sentiment toward tekoraet, could Mia risk being alone with her?

Mia gripped my hands and squeezed. "I'm not leaving you to fend for yourself, okay?"

"If something happens to you—"

"Something already has, and honestly, if *this* is the worst your magical mystery tour is going to throw at me, I can cope. Just promise you'll help finance my new wardrobe, and we'll call it square."

"Mia—"

"*Suze.*" Releasing me, she stepped back a pace and grinned. "Besides, the next stop is Daril, right? I think we know how to deal with humans."

I pivoted slightly, showing off the sword's bejeweled hilt. "Humans with magic crystal thingies?"

"Sure. Remember the time that Shawna Brewer and Justin Flynn tried crystal meth and ended up naked on the roof of the high school?"

"That's a *little* different."

"Maybe," she admitted, chuckling. "We'll muddle through. Come on, let's find Anji and get off this island before…"

She paused at the sound of footsteps in the leaves, and

then Fanakel emerged, still looking glum but more resolute. "Hi," she said, offering a quick wave. "Made up your mind?"

"There is nothing for me if I go home now," he replied. "You have need of a fourth?"

"You want to come with us?" I asked, surprised.

The elf shrugged. "Not particularly, no. But I don't want the humiliation waiting for me once Father learns of this, and..." He nodded to Mia. "You're the first person who's ever deemed me worthy of an apology—"

"*Seriously?*" she interrupted.

"Had you any familiarity with the True, you wouldn't be so shocked. But...thank you. And I admit that I'm intrigued by this quest of yours, so—"

"Less talking, more leaving," Anji cut in, marching up with her loaded bag. "Susan, can you get us back across? And you," she added, turning to Fanakel, "where around this lake would a search party be least likely to lurk?"

"You won't find one close by," he replied. "No one goes near the Kingkiller unless he seeks a quick end to his life. But you said the sword created a path?"

I cast an uneasy glance at the placid lake. "It did last night."

"Try it again, then. Perhaps it holds him at bay."

I didn't want to walk out the way we'd walked in—that shore was too close to the elven capital for my taste, and there was no sense in making things easier for our pursuers. Instead, I led our new foursome across the island to the far side, where we found another gritty, grass-pocked beach and a wide expanse of water between us and the mainland. With a silent prayer to anything listening, I extended the sword over the lake and concentrated.

Instead of splitting and retreating, however, the water in front of me began to build up from both sides, massing and twisting until I realized I was staring at a head and torso. True, it was at least ten feet tall, but it seemed to be built on the standard one-head-two-arms plan, and I could discern the outlines of spaces for eyes and a mouth. Shocked as I was, all I could think at the moment was that reaching out to touch the thing's swirling surface would be exceedingly unwise.

"Elemental," muttered Anji, tugging at my arm until I bent to within whisper range. "Be polite."

The best I could manage for the first few seconds after the thing coalesced was stunned silence, but since I was the one with the magic sword trying to screw with the lake, I figured I should say *something.* "Um…hello," I squeaked, cleared my throat, and tried again. "Can we, uh…can we cross, please?"

The elemental's reply came as a deep, sonorous voice, but its mouth area didn't move—rather, I realized with surprise, I was hearing it in my head. *Who are you?*

I looked to Anji for help, but she nodded, urging me on. "Just talk," she whispered. "He'll understand."

Facing off against the sculpted water and fighting the urge to run for higher ground, I said, "I'm Susan. The Watcher. Um…if I've done something to upset you—"

*What were you fleeing last night?*

"The Twins locked us up. Well, *us,*" I amended, pointing to Mia and Anji. "Fanakel over there was accidentally sucked into this mess."

He gave the elf brief consideration, then returned his focus to me. *You broke their laws?*

"Honestly, I'm not sure. I'm looking for someone who can free me from being the Watcher. This thing attached itself to me," I explained, pulling the sword's hilt just free enough of its scabbard to show the elemental a glint of blade, "and now I'm being stalked by Outsiders—"

*There are five in the Greenwood.*

"Because I'm not back at the Crossing as the designated Outsider target. Look, we're not trying to cause trouble—we were just searching for a hideout last night. If I've offended by bringing everyone to the island—"

*As you were fleeing the butchers of Nokan'ti, you have not offended. But if you wish to avoid them, you should not leave now. Wait until sunset. Where are you bound?*

Relief swept over me like a warm shower on a frigid morning. "The tunnel."

*If you travel on foot, this is two days' journey. But I see a path. Follow the stream,* he said, as one watery arm gestured toward a narrow outflow at the other shore. *That will guide you to your destination.* With that, he shrank until we were almost of a height, then cocked his head. *How did you manage to cross to the island?*

"Magic sword."

*Curious. Remain here and rest. You will travel by night, and I will escort you as far as I may.*

"Thank you, uh…"

Though I was new to telepathy—and honestly, overwhelmed to be chatting with a being made of water—I thought I detected the faintest trace of amusement in his reply. *I am called Kingkiller.*

"Nickname?" I guessed.

He mulled over the question for a moment before replying. *I am myself. The elves use certain sounds in reference to me.*

Hoping I wasn't about to step in it, I ventured, "Just curious, but…any idea why they use those *particular* sounds?"

"Because he drowned one of our kings," Fanakel interrupted.

The elemental grew again until he towered over the prince. *An evil creature. Will you defend him now, here?*

Before Fanakel could speak, Mia gripped his shoulder and said, "That seems like a remarkably bad idea, okay, bud?"

"But—"

"Remember, we're trying to live."

Though he huffed, he gritted his teeth and said nothing.

*Indeed, you would defend him,* said the elemental, a

statement that seemed almost a query and tinged with disgust. *Why?*

Mia's fingers had to hurt Fanakel as they dug into him, but he replied, "His bride was stolen and slaughtered, and so was he, without cause—"

*Slaughtered? The only slaughter was at your precious king's hand.*

"You stole—"

*I did nothing of the sort. He was cruel, and she wished to escape him. Seeing her bloodied and begging on the shore, I carried her here, and my dearest friend sheltered her.*

The elf's brow furrowed. "Friend?"

*Another of my kind. She inhabited that island.*

The thought was colored with anger, but I knew I wasn't imagining the current of sorrow running through it as well.

*She and I came here together. Lived together. Watched as your invading ancestors drove away the ogrim and bent the trees to your will. We tolerated you. But then the woman ran here in the dark of night, bleeding and sobbing for help. One of your men wished to take her to mate. She wanted nothing of him, and he had attacked her when she refused him. Her arm was broken, as I recall,* he added. *Bent oddly. She cradled it.*

"You hid her," said Anji.

The elemental's head dipped and rose. *We took pity. I carried her to the island, and my friend made a hollow for her in the soil and covered the place with branches. But the man followed her footsteps to the shore and realized where she had gone. He came with a host of men, and when I tried to stop them from crossing, a few of them attacked me together. Distracted me,* he said bitterly. *The evil man reached the island and soon found the woman he claimed. My friend tried everything in her power to stop him, but this island is small, and she had little to work with. And when she failed, he and some of his men struck her dead.*

He loomed over Fanakel, who had the sense to stay quiet. *When I heard her death cry, rage fueled my revenge. Yes, I killed them all. Dragged them to the lakebed until their final breaths escaped them. You would condemn me for this?*

Fanakel's throat bobbed as he swallowed hard. "I...heard it told somewhat differently."

*I am not surprised.* He shrank again, as if resignation had smothered the fire of his anger. *The island was dead for many years. Another came, and she gave it life once more. We speak little. She is young, and I am not who I was before the butchers slaughtered my friend. But I will allow you to leave,* he told Fanakel, *as you did not come of your own volition. This once. Return, and I will show you no mercy.*

The elemental disappeared into the lake before any of us could utter another word, and I glanced at the weird blue-green sky. "Guess we're not going anywhere until tonight," I said, and pointed back at the trees. "So, who wants to try to make a deck of playing cards?"

Freed from the oppressively thick canopy of the Greenwood, I sat on the island's shore at dusk and watched the sunset. It wasn't anything spectacular until I turned around and saw the full moon rising...and behind it, a twin.

"Honslia has two moons?" I asked Anji, who'd joined me with the granola.

She seemed unexcited by this discovery. "Ga'besh has three, or so I've been taught. I've never been."

"Because of..."

Looking over her shoulder, she confirmed that both Mia and Fanakel were still asleep in our makeshift hideout, albeit a good twenty feet away from each other. "We have minimal dealings with that world," she said quietly. "The threat posed by the tekoraet can't be ignored."

"Do they, like...hunt everyone else?"

"*Hunt* is a strong word." She leaned back on her elbows and considered the reddening sun as it sank. "Some enter into arrangements—they feed and shelter one person or many, as the tekori can afford, using them as a food source when needed. Like expensive livestock, I suppose. My tutor said that the children born to parents in such arrangements often remain in the system all their lives, passed among the tekoraet until they run dry."

"That's horrifying."

"It gets worse—at least those people choose to be used as food. Some tekoraet lure and abduct their victims, either killing them in one feeding or holding them against their will. The prominent tekoraet denounce the practice, but they don't exactly *prevent* it, you see."

"And you're defenseless," I said.

"Without specialized pieces of forging that cost a small fortune, yes. Father wears one wherever he goes in case of attack. The crown of Daril is another such piece—generally enhancing to its human wearer, but also protective of mental clarity." She checked on the others again, then said, "I can't believe I'm saying this, but I worry for Fanakel's safety if he remains with us."

Miffed, I jumped to defend my best friend's honor. "You saw Mia today—she feels terrible about what happened."

"I don't doubt it, lass. But imagine you've been living on nothing but this all your life," said Anji, shaking the granola bag. "Suddenly, you're presented with a feast—the finest meats, the ripest vegetables, the choicest ales—and allowed to eat your fill. Having tasted that once, would you resign yourself to granola for the rest of your days?"

"If it meant you had to drain someone of his life force to eat well…"

"I'm not suggesting that it would be an easy choice for Mia. Whatever else she may be, she seems honorable. But should her hunger grow too strong, perhaps need will overcome personal ethics."

I thought about Mia at dinner in college, matching football players plate for plate and never gaining a pound while I restricted myself to salads with low-fat dressing on the side. Had she been able to shovel her food in more quickly, she'd have been a legend on the competitive eating circuit, a black hole for anything not nailed to a plate. I knew she'd been hungry during our excursion—her gurgling stomach gave her away even as she insisted she was fine—and now that the Aen, the gods, or dumb luck had triggered the tekori inside her, I wondered if she'd be able to avoid looking at Fanakel like a handsome, ambulatory steak.

"So what are you suggesting?" I asked Anji.

The princess continued to watch the sunset. "I'm not. Merely observing and pointing out possibilities. Though I'm curious why her father abandoned Ga'besh for a world beyond the Aen."

"Maybe he was forced out."

"Perhaps. Or it could have been a balance issue—too many males in one area, not enough females to feed upon to keep everyone satisfied. If he were from a poorer family and couldn't afford to pay for his meals' upkeep, then perhaps he left in search of easier prey. A population that wouldn't know to fear him." She hesitated, then asked, "This 'exotic dancing'—does it truly spark lust in the audience?"

"I mean, I've never seen a show, but I'd think so. They tend to cast good-looking people."

"He dances, then, and he feeds on the room's lust. An easy meal, one no one would notice…"

"And if he takes someone back to his room on occasion, it wouldn't be unusual," I finished. "Probably not a bad life for a tekori."

I fell silent, and Anji gave me a careful study before scooting closer. "It's not your fault. You can't help what she is any more than she can."

"If I hadn't brought her along—"

"She might still have discovered that power someday." Giving my shoulder a pat, she said, "One crisis at a time, eh? We sneak out of Honslia, return to the cabin, you two can pack tents this time, and then we'll take on Daril. And *that* will require some walking," she added with a grimace. "The Kopaati tunnel opens onto on the same continent as Daril, but that's about all that can be said for it. I made the journey when I was ten, but we used carriages, and it was still a full day's flight. On foot..."

"What I'm hearing is that we'd better restock the granola."

"At least."

*Perhaps there is a shorter way.*

We turned to the lake as the water began to rise into a humanoid form once more. "Do you know a shortcut?" I asked.

*Across the land? No. I could not tell you where this Daril lies. But have you considered asking for assistance in the journey?*

Anji frowned. "From whom? There's no settlement of note within half a day's walk of the tunnel."

*One of my brethren*, the elemental replied. *Those who ride the air. Draw his attention, make your case, and ask him to carry you. It should cost him little effort.*

"That's not a terrible suggestion," she said, "but finding an air elemental would be difficult, and holding him in one place long enough to make the request would be nearly impossible."

*Not for her.* One watery arm rose and pointed to me. *Summon the rain. If you can build a storm, you will attract my brethren. I should think they would find you sufficiently intriguing to listen to your proposition.*

"And what will they want in turn?" I asked.

*Nothing*, he responded bemusedly. *What could you possibly offer?*

"Then why would they help us?"

The silence stretched between us for a long moment before I heard his voice again: *The ones who built the sword you wear like to speak of the sacrifices they made to create it. Theirs were not the only sacrifices.*

Anji's disquiet deepened. "What do you mean? Was there an elemental who helped in the forging?"

*I witnessed nothing, and all that I know has been carried to me by those who cross between the worlds. But it is said that one of us was involved in the process. Not by choice.*

"I don't follow."

*It is said that the maladetas used their cunning to capture one of my brethren. His death gave the sword its power.*

I looked down at the hilt, halfway expecting to see it bloodied, but the only reddish stain upon it was the glint of the dying sunlight on steel.

*Tell them who you are and what you seek,* said the elemental. *They will listen. And now, you should leave the island. The forest is quiet, and I sense elves nowhere near the stream.*

Troubled but reluctant to overstay our welcome, I rose and roused the others, and the four of us gathered on the shore. Clutching the sword, I split the water again after a moment's concentration, and we squelched across the muck, trampling water weeds and stepping over decaying logs. Mia paused every few yards to pick up a hapless fish and fling it into the wall of water on either side of us. When we reached the mainland, the lake collapsed again, the evidence of our passage marked only by diminishing waves. We stayed on the beach for a few minutes, just long enough to wash the worst of the grime off our boots and legs before it dried, then followed the stream into the trees.

As we walked single file along its bed, using the glow of the sword as a torch, the elemental kept us company. He chatted about the contours of the land and warned us of downed trees in our path, and once, he gave us sufficient notice to duck behind a deadfall and extinguish the sword before a pack of searching elves wandered through. They should have found us—had there been daylight, I'm sure we would have been an easy target—but their chiquiws seemed to be dragging, and I supposed the elves had been out all day. Exhaustion made them careless, and to my great relief, Fanakel wasn't afflicted by a sudden bout of second thoughts.

I don't know how long or how far we walked that

night. Beneath the canopy, the sky was nothing more than the occasional glint of a black darker than the leaves below it, and time had little meaning. I'm almost positive that I dozed on my feet at one point, as I found myself on my hands and knees with no memory of tripping over a thick root. The only indications that the hours were indeed passing were the growing protestation in my stomach, the creeping weariness in my legs, and finally, the faint shift in the sky from black to darkest navy.

I was about to suggest that we think about making camp for the day when the elemental's voice cut through my mental fog: *Outsider ahead. Approaching. It smells you. Take up your arms.*

"Oh, *great*," Fanakel muttered, pulling his short sword free of its scabbard. "Fighting without a proper war weapon—"

"I've killed with this," Anji interrupted, tossing her dagger from hand to hand. "As long as you're whining about the size of your blade, try to stay out of my way, won't you?"

Duly chastised, he scowled at Mia as she rummaged through her pack. "You could just wear your weapon like a sensible person."

"And risk having your daddy confiscate it?" she replied, pulling her pistol free. "Suze, light."

I held my sword close while she inspected the loaded cylinder. With a satisfied grunt, she then buckled on an ancient denim fanny pack—I had no idea why Uncle Malachi would have purchased such a thing, much less why he hadn't discarded it in the early years of the twenty-first century—and checked the zipper. The bag drooped at her waist, loaded as it was with ammunition, but at least it was close at hand for reloading.

*Nearing. Moving more quickly.*

We positioned ourselves in the widest clearing we could find, me in the center, Anji and Mia flanking, and Fanakel standing awkwardly by. For a moment, I heard little but the burbling of the stream, the sound of our breathing, and my heartbeat in my ears...but then, as I strained, I could just make out the sound of rapid footfalls in the rustling leaves.

"Incoming," I muttered.

The natural reaction when something that sounds like a runaway horse is stampeding through a dark forest straight toward you isn't to hold your position, but somehow, the three of us managed while Fanakel edged a few steps further to the side. Suddenly, a shape blacker than the surrounding trees broke through into our clearing, bellowing like a mad bull. I let the sword glow and held on to the hilt like it was a baseball bat, and as the Outsider charged at me, Mia opened fire. Two shots went high, but one hit the thing in its open mouth, and it screamed in pain. As it threw back its head and roared, Anji took a running leap onto its back and plunged her dagger into its neck at the base of the spine, then held on like a rodeo cowboy as the creature bucked and spun. It threw her after only a few seconds, but the distraction was all I needed to close in. Before it knew what had hit it, I'd hacked its head almost off its shoulders, and it collapsed in a smoking, bleeding heap as I gasped for breath. While Mia ran across the clearing to check on Anji, I stabbed the corpse until it burst into flame, then turned until I spied Fanakel, who was watching with a bloodless face and shaking sword arm. "Going to help us, or what?"

"Th-*that*—"

"Outsider. If you could clear anything flammable so that we don't start a forest fire, that'd be grand."

He pulled himself together long enough to bend the nearest trees away from the blaze, and I used the sword to beckon enough water from the stream to soak the ground. As Mia helped Anji limp in our direction, I pulled her dagger out of the body and passed it to her. "Nice riding. Where are you hurt?"

"Knocked the breath from me," she replied, settling

onto a log, "and I might have turned an ankle in the fall, but nothing feels broken." She considered the burning corpse, then sighed and gestured for her bag. "We might as well eat. This should do for a campfire, don't you think?"

"Aside from the smell," said Mia, wrinkling her nose. "But yeah, I think we can heat water with this. Hey, Fanakel, are you all right? Sit down if you need to."

The elf seemed to be on the verge of fainting, and he stared at the three of us as Mia unpacked her pot, Anji sorted through the food packets, and I tended the fire. "You're all *mad*," he whispered.

"Resigned," Mia replied, heading past him toward the stream. "Hey, uh…Kingkiller? Mind if I fill up?"

*Help yourself.* The elemental rose above the stream, albeit in a smaller form. *I sense none of the others nearby. Eat and take your rest—I will alert you should anything change.*

**W**ithin an hour, the sky was beginning to truly lighten, and the corpse was burning low. With the dishes washed and the trash packed, Anji and Mia had crawled into their sleeping bags, camouflaging them with leaves and branches in case of marauding elves. I sat upwind and watched the flames lap at the logs that Fanakel had tossed on when the body lost its structure. Ash and smoke drifted toward the stream, and though I knew the prudent thing to do would be to extinguish the evidence, I lingered at the fireside, enjoying the warmth in the cool night.

Lost in thought, I jerked when I caught motion from the corner of my eye, then recognized Fanakel crouching beside me. "Sorry, startled," I said with a weak chuckle. "Are you not going to sleep?"

"I'm not tired."

The dark circles under his eyes suggested otherwise, and while the tremor in his limbs had subsided, he seemed coiled as a compressed spring.

"You get used to them," I said, nodding to the remains of the Outsider. "My first night was rough, too. But you can either freak out or stay alive, so…" I shrugged and patted the sword. "This is life right now. Once I'm home, the monsters should stay out of Honslia because they'll all be drawn to me. The tunnel up to the Crossing is much shorter than the tunnels to your worlds," I explained, "and so the sword is the nearest significant source of Aen. It attracts them. And unless I can find someone to rid me of this lovely little curse, you're looking at the rest of my life."

Fanakel made no reply until a log crackled and split in a burst of orange sparks. "That thing was horrifying."

"Eh, not the ugliest I've seen."

He rubbed his stubble in agitation. "I don't want them running wild in Nokan'ti, but…"

"But it's not entirely fair to force a stranger to fight your battles for you?" I ventured, pulling the sword out as a poker to tend the fire. "Maybe my life doesn't mean anything to you. If I live to be your age, I'll be damn lucky, and I won't look nearly as pretty."

The elf snorted, and I glanced his way in time to catch his brief grin.

"That said, it's the only life I get, and there's so much more I want to do with the time I have than kill those things. You don't want them in Nokan'ti, and I get that, but *I* don't want them in my hometown, either, and they wouldn't be coming for us if you assholes hadn't decided we were all disposable." I paused, then added, "It's also worth noting that of the four of here, this human stabbed it, the human-tekori shot it, the dwarf freaking *rode* it, and the illustrious True Child stood back and practically wet himself."

He didn't deny it.

"I'm turning in," I said, remotely pulling a ball of water from the stream and dumping it onto the dying fire. "Suggest you do the same."

The day was quiet, and I woke in the late afternoon to the smell of grilling fish. Curious, I sat up and followed my nose to find Fanakel cooking atop a surface of hot rocks. The fire had been rebuilt—with wood that time, for an aromatic change of pace—and he'd wrapped his food in packets made of folded leaves. As I approached, he looked up from his work and smiled grimly. "A little longer, I should think, unless you prefer your meat raw."

That took me aback. "You made enough to share?"

"*Someone* was generous," he replied, cutting his eyes toward the stream, "and besides, if I'd cooked only for myself, the dwarf would probably punch me."

"She's fast, I'll give her that." Squatting beside him, I watched as the fragrant steam rose from the cooking packets. "Nice of you, thanks. It smells great."

"The longer one remains in the guards and the more patrol trips one is assigned outside of the city, the better one's cooking becomes."

"You and Mia should compare notes—she puts the rest of us to shame in the kitchen."

"Does she?" He glanced at the half-hidden lumps of the rest of our party, then peeked into one of the wrapped bundles and nodded. "Almost finished. Do you have plates?"

By the time Anji and Mia dug themselves out of their nests, there was nothing left of my portion but scales and sprigs of charred herbs. I had no idea what I'd eaten, but the fish seemed to have notes of lemon and licorice, which, if odd, wasn't a horrible combination. Mia tucked in, once more her usual ravenous self, and even Anji deemed it passable after giving it a few cautious test sniffs.

Too soon, we were on our way through the dark woods, all of us armed and wary of Outsiders. The night remained peaceful, however, and as a cold wind picked up in the wee hours, the elemental called a halt. *This is where we part*, he said, his form barely more than a bubble in the shallow stream. *Follow the path north. The tunnel lies ahead.*

We thanked him profusely and prepared to make our departure, but then he said, *Susan, I would speak to you privately.*

I looked at the others, silently querying, and Anji answered first. "We'll walk ahead and scout. Come when you're ready, lass."

"But—" Mia began.

"Give them a moment," the princess insisted, grabbing Mia's wrist and tugging her along. "You too, elf. No dawdling. I intend to sleep beneath a roof tonight like a civilized woman."

When the sound of their footsteps tromping through the undergrowth had faded, I sat beside the stream, and the elemental pulled himself up to eye level. *My kind sense energies better than most*, he began. *I knew immediately that it was Mia who controlled Fanakel when you arrived at my shore. Had it been a function of the sword, I would have felt the energetic pull from that source, not from her.*

"You think she's definitely tekorish, then?"

*Without question, but that is not the reason I asked you to linger.* He hesitated, then said, *What I have witnessed from you in these days—parting the lake, moving water...*

I chuckled. "*That's* all the sword's doing."

But he remained somber. *No, it is not.*

"Huh?"

*The sword was not the source of those energies. You were.*

Blinking hard was the best I could manage for a moment, but I finally said, "That's...not possible. Without the sword, I'm as average as they come."

*Some humans exhibit an ability to manipulate the Aen*, he replied. *Even without external assistance. But I have sensed such adepts in my time. You feel different. Your parents, were they gifted?*

"I...I don't know," I mumbled. "I don't know anything about them. They abandoned me."

*Beyond the Aen?* When I nodded, I felt from him the psychic equivalent of a satisfied grunt, as if he'd solved a puzzle. *You saw what exposure has done to Mia. Perhaps your own gifts are manifesting now that you have experienced the Aen. What those gifts might be, or where they might originate, is beyond my knowing.* He paused, and I felt as though the watery impressions of his eyes were staring straight through me. *Abandoned, you said?*

"They left me in the woods to die," I replied, my head swimming. "Not even a note. No apology, no nothing." Holding his strange gaze, I asked, "Do you think…I mean, if I can, like, do magic…do you think they came from this side of the Crossing?"

*That is certainly possible, but I could not tell you.* An arm emerged from his amorphous body, and its hand squeezed my shoulder with a surprisingly firm grip. *Go to Kopaat. Summon the rain, then make your way to Daril. It is said that all the greatest human adepts in the four worlds pass through that kingdom. Perhaps someone there can guide you, if not free you from your burden.* With that, he released me, leaving not so much as a drop of water soaking into my shirt, and sank into the stream. *Hurry on your way, now, before the morning patrols find you.*

"Thank you," I whispered, then picked up my bag and jogged off to catch up with the others.

# CHAPTER 13

The last thing any of us wanted after the long night's hike through the Greenwood was another march through the tunnel, but short of stealing chiquiws, we had no other choice. Anji voiced no complaint, and even Fanakel seemed resigned to the walk ahead. Personally, I was too absorbed with what the elemental had told me to focus on much more than putting one foot in front of the next.

Magical talent.

*Me?*

When I was a little kid, aware of my past but still young enough to indulge in fantasy, I occasionally concocted romanticized stories about my missing parents. Maybe they were a prince and princess, very much in love, and an evil witch had stolen me from them and left me in the woods. They surely missed me, and they spared no expense to find me. Someday, we'd meet again, and off I'd go to their fabulous castle far away, where I'd have a huge pink suite and a shelf loaded with the sparkliest of tiaras. Naturally, Dad and Uncle Malachi would come, too. We'd all be a family, and we'd live happily ever after.

Then I grew older and took note of just how few tiny kingdoms were located anywhere near Cole's Crossing, or even in North America. If I'd been stolen from royalty, I reasoned, there would have been an international manhunt, and Dad didn't seem like the sort of person to kidnap the heir to a throne and make her stack twelve-packs of soda to form a shape that might have been our high school's jaguar mascot, if you squinted and the room was almost dark.

By the time that Uncle Malachi was surreptitiously teaching me to drive his pickup truck, I'd resigned myself to the far less exciting truth of my origins: I was probably someone's accident, maybe the result of a broken condom or of a careless drug-fueled night, and my mother hadn't had any good options. Maybe she was a teenager from another town—another county, even—who'd dumped me because she was afraid of what would happen when her parents found out that she hadn't just been putting on weight. Maybe she was a young woman trapped in an abusive relationship whose husband had decided he didn't want another mouth to feed. Maybe she was a prostitute, unable to keep a child around and too ashamed to ask her family for help. Or maybe she was a junkie who'd delivered me while she was high, and by the time she came around, she couldn't recall what had happened. True, my system had been clean when Dad got me to the county hospital, but I still held out hope that *something* had caused my mother to abandon me against her will. Fear, substance abuse—anything to show that she was a good person in a bad situation who loved me and missed me. Should I ever find a way to meet her, I wanted her to be overjoyed and apologetic, not upset that I'd narrowly avoided death.

But Kingkiller—or whatever he called himself—had set fire to my accepted narrative. Yes, I'd been thrown out at birth...but in *Cole's Crossing*. And not even in town, but rather somewhere between Uncle Malachi's cabin and the entrance to the Crossing itself.

Maybe my biological parents weren't from town or even the county. Maybe they weren't from Earth at all.

Suppose, then, that they were magically gifted humans. Why would they have abandoned me? Was there something wrong with me? With them? My imagination ran wild as we plodded through the lightning-streaked tunnel. Maybe theirs was a forbidden romance, and they'd had to hide the evidence. Maybe I *had* been stolen by an evil witch after all—I mean, Ms. Quince's people seemed close enough to fit the bill. Maybe my heartbroken parents *had* spent a fortune trying to find me, unaware of just how far I'd been taken.

A scenario coalesced in my thoughts like a rainbow after a storm. Once I was free of the sword—and surely someone would help, someone in this Daril place had to take pity on me—then I could see just how far this power of mine would go. Someone would recognize my talent and train me. I'd become a great adept, or whatever term they used, and then someday, once my fame had spread, I'd spot a pair of faces that looked like mine in a crowd. We'd lock eyes, and we'd *know*, then and there, that we were family. My parents would weep and hold me and explain what had happened, and how they'd heard about me and made the long journey to see me for themselves, just in case I might be their missing baby. They would bless Dad and Uncle Malachi's memories while they claimed me as their dearly loved daughter, and...well, the curtain in my mental theater went down at that point, but what followed would be less important than the triumph of that beautiful moment, when everything would be *right* for once.

I hadn't shared the elemental's message with the rest of our foursome—as Anji had said, one crisis at a time—but I was about to ask her and Fanakel for more information about human adepts when a low growl rumbled through the tunnel up ahead.

"High Queen have mercy," said Anji, drawing her dagger. "It's coming this way."

The tunnels were roughly the antithesis of a good place to fight an Outsider head-on, but we'd come too far to make it back to Honslia and the safety of the trees. The stone walls offered no hiding places, and once the monster zeroed in on the Aen crystals in my sword, it would have no trouble tracking us. In short, we had no alternative but to fight.

"Get behind us," Mia told Fanakel as she quickly reloaded her gun.

He huffed at the order. "I can—"

"You can stay out of the way. Ready, girls?"

My sword shone in the black tunnel, and I tried not to focus on the echoes of the approaching creature's pounding feet, which made it seem as though a herd of Outsiders was running our way. All too soon, however, the sword's light picked a moving shape out of the shadows, a ten-foot-tall monstrosity with three pairs of legs and a beak like a giant squid's. It screeched and galloped toward us, its ropelike tail stretching behind it into the darkness, and I took a steadying breath.

On my exhalation, Mia was shooting, five rapid shots that struck the thing's head and chest. It flailed backward, knocked from its feet by the impact, and kicked at the air. "Mine," I told Anji, pushing her back with one arm, and ran toward the Outsider before it could right itself. Three fast cuts lopped off its clawed feet, which twitched on the ground as I buried the sword up to the hilt in the beast's chest. Within seconds, the thing was out of its misery, and I pulled the sword free before we could find ourselves with a fire blocking the tunnel. "Help me move it," I said, wiping my sword clean against its leathery hide. The others jumped to my assistance—even Fanakel, who muttered a continual stream of pleas unto the Divine as he kicked the severed feet against the wall.

Mia considered the corpse, then looked into the darkness ahead and cleared her throat. "I could do with a snack, but…you know, maybe we should put a little distance between us and our new buddy first."

"How are you *possibly* hungry?" Fanakel asked.

The green cast to his face was the result of the sword's glow, but still, I surmised that it wasn't far from the truth. "It's the rare day she's not," I said, and pushed him down the tunnel. "And since her meal options right now are trail rations and you, try not to look tasty."

Mia shot me a warning glare behind his back, and I shrugged. There was no sense, I thought, in letting the elf get too comfortable.

When I finally unlocked the cabin door, we were ready to drop. Sunrise was still a ways away—as well as Mia and I could estimate, Honslia was about six hours ahead of the Crossing—but I could have slept with the sun shining full in my face. We shuffled in and dumped our bags in the corner, and while Mia arranged her guns and ammunition within easy reach in the kitchen in case of nocturnal visitors, Anji sloughed off her filthy boots with a sigh of relief. "Have you a wash basin here, lass?" she asked me, pointing to her muck-stained pants. "I don't need anything fancy, but if I could rinse these…"

"Come with me," said Mia, beckoning her into the bedroom. "We'll do you one better."

Five minutes later, Anji lurked self-consciously by the folding doors of the utilities closet while I chucked the load from our Honslia trip into the washer. Mia's green plaid boxer shorts were tight around Anji's waist and hung almost to her knees. The black Antoinette's tank top fit the dwarf relatively well, though it was far too long. She rubbed her bare arms self-consciously as the thick blonde hair on her limbs rose with her goosebumps, and the moment Fanakel glanced in our direction, she snapped, "What are *you* looking at?"

Fanakel, who'd borrowed a pair of Uncle Malachi's ratty sweatpants and a holey T-shirt from the dresser I'd yet to sort through, shook his head and held up his palms to keep her at bay. "Nothing. There's a *noise*."

"That would be the washing machine," I explained, closing the closet doors. "Come with me for a minute."

While Anji hopped into the recliner and swaddled herself in blankets, I led Fanakel to the tiny bathroom and pulled a spare Bic from my uncle's stash. "It's not a fancy five-blade model, but it's new," I told him, then rooted beneath the sink until I found a can of shaving foam. "Knock yourself out."

He frowned at the idiom, then seemed to realize what I was trying to communicate through our mutual fog of exhaustion. "Thank you. Will it give offense if I wait until morning? I fear that if I shave now, I'll probably cut my neck open."

"Just don't say anything about my legs or my armpits," I replied, slipping past him, "and we'll call it even. Are you taking the watch?"

He looked to the bed, where Mia was already softly snoring, and sighed. "It seems that way, doesn't it?"

"I'll make it easier for you."

Fanakel followed me into the kitchen, where I brewed a pot of coffee and showed him the sugar and creamer. "Wake me once the sun's up," I told him as he gave his hot mug a test sip. "But if you hear anything big and deadly before then, just yell."

"Understood." He sipped again, then looked around the room at the old appliances and the scuffed wooden cabinets.

"I've got a nicer place in town," I said before he could ask. "But since the sword attracts Outsiders, I can't stay there. It would put everyone else in danger. My great-granduncle built this place out in the woods between town and the tunnels once he became the Watcher, and my uncle inherited the gig and the cabin from him. Mine, now. It, uh…it's seen better days."

The washer bumped and knocked as it went off-balance, and I threw open the door to readjust the wet load. Once I started the machine again, I found Fanakel watching me with an inscrutable expression. "Coffee all right?"

"Fine," he murmured, then hesitated before adding, "I'm sorry for you."

"Uh…thanks."

"This hovel is barely adequate accommodation."

"It's got a roof and walls. More than we've had for the last couple of nights," I replied, and turned for bed. "Try to make yourself comfortable. I'm afraid all the good furniture's been claimed."

It wasn't Fanakel who woke me the next morning, but rather Mia, who groaned and pushed herself out of bed shortly after sunrise. "I'll take the first shower," I mumbled into my pillow. "You can sleep."

"Daylight's burning, and I'm starving." She threw on her bathrobe over her ill-fitting pajamas and shuffled out of the room.

I heard her mutter a greeting to Fanakel, and I'd almost drifted off again when she returned with her bag and began to dress. "Where're you going?" I asked, forcing myself to roll over far enough to see her.

"Walmart." She tried on a shirt, considered her reflection, then struggled out of it. "Need clothes and more granola."

My brain, though not yet fully firing, realized that the appropriate thing to do would be to offer assistance. "I'll come—"

"It's a good twenty miles away. You can't."

The reminder of my reality was a sufficient blow to drag me back to consciousness. "*Shit.* I'm sorry, if you want to take my debit card—"

"I've got it under control," she assured me, patting my blanket-covered foot. "Just need to go try things before anyone I know gets out and recognizes me. *Ugh.*" She rolled her beautiful eyes and wrinkled her nose when she glanced toward the mirror again. "Bra shopping—just how I wanted to spend a morning. Would it have been too much to ask for my body to *not* take this zero-to-sixty approach?"

"You look nice," I offered, which was a gross

understatement. Even dirty from our days in the woods, Mia practically radiated sex appeal.

"I mean, I guess it could be worse. Something hideous could have—" she began, but the rest of her thought died as she turned back to me.

I smiled tightly and ran my fingertips down the side of my cheek, tracing the raised line of the healing scar and hoping it hadn't become infected during our campout. "Could you pick up some more lotion, if you think of it?"

Her face fell. "Suze, I'm sorry. I shouldn't complain—"

"It's your body, you're entitled. Drive safely, okay?"

We hugged, and Mia padded out into the morning. I heard the muffled rumble of her Corolla cranking as I headed for the bathroom to examine the damage.

I looked like absolute shit. Three hours of sleep wasn't enough to make up for the previous day's hike, and my hair had devolved into an unholy amalgamation of oil slicks and frizzes...and a bit of foliage, I noted picking leaf debris out of my tangles. A painful pimple was doing its best to break free in the crease at the side of my nose, while a few of its less obnoxious friends had made their appearance across my forehead. The bruise-colored bags beneath my eyes were an especially nice touch. But all of that paled beside the scar, which stuck out in the harsh bathroom light as a thick, angry red rope against my skin. The tissue puckered at its edges, and I ineffectively tried to smooth it flat with an exploring finger.

Sure, in the grand scheme of things, it was nothing. I'd been tied to a sword that attracted monsters, wandered through the wildernesses of two worlds in the last two weeks, and broken out of jail. And I was no great beauty to begin with, so it wasn't as if I were a disfigured actress suddenly out of a career. But that was still my face in the mirror, and part of me wanted to cry every time I looked too closely.

So I forced myself to turn away and get in the shower. If I was going to be up at the crack of dawn, at least I could help myself to the hot water before the tank ran cold.

Mia returned to breakfast, courtesy of Fanakel, who might not have recognized most items in Uncle Malachi's sad kitchen but knew how to handle eggs. She'd exchanged her tank top for a proper sports bra and a baggy T-shirt, which, while they didn't hide her curves, didn't call additional attention to them. The leggings beneath were new as well, better fitting than her old pair, and I saw several similar pieces of clothing sticking out of the plastic bags she dropped inside the door.

Anji gave her an appraising glance and motioned her toward the table. "There's plenty left to eat," she said, braiding her wet beard between sips of coffee. "The eggs were becoming untrustworthy, so the elf cooked them all."

Mia nodded her thanks to the chef and plopped into the free seat with a groan.

"Busy already?" I asked. "It's just...wait, is it Wednesday?"

"Thursday," she corrected, "and no, but people are *gross*. I had *two* creepers following me around the store, and even some of the staff stared. Didn't make any attempt to be subtle about it, either. Hello, if I'm in the intimates section, I don't need help from *you*, Produce Man."

"Did you have to use force?" Anji asked, braiding momentarily forgotten. "Had you wanted backup, I would have come with you—"

"And they'd have stared at you, too, for another set of reasons. But thanks." She accepted the coffee I handed her and wrapped her hands around the mug. "No, I didn't have to fight anyone off. Hid out and walked quickly. I mean, I really wanted to tell a few of them to go fuck themselves, but I was worried that they might actually *do* it, so..." She sipped, then frowned at the taste. "Coffee's good. What—"

"Fanakel discovered the spice drawer. That's half a bottle of vanilla extract in the pot," I explained.

"Imitation, I hope, but...yeah, not bad," she told him, earning a faint smile in response. "Shower's open?"

I sopped up the last of my yolks with a piece of stale sandwich bread. "All yours. And I took the liberty of returning Antoinette's call."

"She called me?"

"Wanted to know how the norovirus was going. It's been eleven days, and she was worried that you'd been hospitalized or something."

Mia made a face. "What'd you tell her?"

"That right as you were getting over it, your cousin in Louisiana had her baby early. Baby's in the NICU, mom's in the hospital, and mom's wife is home alone with their two-year-old. I told Antoinette not to mention it to your mother, since she doesn't approve of the marriage—"

"Plausible," Mia muttered.

"—but that you'd hurried down to help out, and you're so sorry about being incommunicado, but they live way out in the sticks, and your cousin has been in intensive care..." I finished my egg mopping and ate the evidence. "Anyway, you're off the hook. Antoinette told me to tell you to take your time and do whatever needs to be done—family comes first, and your job is waiting for you."

Staring into her mug, Mia said, "That's...really decent of her."

"Antionette's good people."

"And thanks for the cover-up, but it's still not going to explain the new look." She hugged herself as if she could compress the unwanted growth. "Maybe I could get a binder..."

"Maybe we should worry about Daril first, lass," Anji interjected. "Eat and wash, then come outside. You and I need to work with the elf and the bow."

I frowned. "What bow?"

"I think he's not a great asset in close combat," she

replied before Fanakel could protest, "and I can't fix that by myself in such short order. But I found that in your uncle's armory." She pointed to the camo-print compound bow leaning against the wall beside the front door. "That *is* a bow, is it not? I'm not an expert shot, but I know the general technique. Considering that bow's size, however, I could use an assistant. You told me you can shoot, didn't you?" she asked Mia.

"I said I'd done it once or twice," said Mia, giving the bow a wary stare. "Wouldn't say I'm *proficient.*"

"But I trust that you can bend it, and that will suffice. Rinse off and join us."

For the rest of the morning, I repacked my bag and Mia's—including tents—while the three of them shot arrows into the trees around the cabin. I appreciated the idea of giving Fanakel something to do beyond standing back and soiling himself, but I didn't see how the bow would be much use. Even the shotgun would be little more than an annoyance to an Outsider. Buckshot might hurt, especially at close range, but then again, these were creatures that I'd seen shrug off multiple hits from a handgun. What was an arrow going to do that a .38 couldn't?

When they came in around lunchtime, Anji seemed moderately satisfied. "He's not a terrible shot," she said, nodding to Fanakel, who winced as he massaged his shoulder. "A few months' work, and I think I could make him respectable."

"It's a specialty skill," he insisted, sinking into a kitchen chair. "Only the guards with particular aptitude are trained for bows. I'm *quite* competent with a blade—"

"Are we going to see that someday?" she retorted.

His face flushed. "A proper blade. The one I have with me is hardly a weapon of war."

"It's not the length of the sword, but how you wield it." Pulling her dagger free of her belt, she tossed it into the air and caught it by the handle as effortlessly as if she were playing with a tennis ball. "Stop making excuses. If the lasses can keep themselves together, then you should be able to manage yourself. Now," she said, turning to me, "might there be an extra pack for the lad, here?"

While Mia prepared sandwich fixings, I dug an old army surplus duffel bag out of the storage closet—still functional, even if it smelled of mildew—and presented it to Fanakel with an apologetic wince. "It's not waterproof, and you'll have to sling it over one shoulder..."

He inspected my offering, unzipped it, and offered a tight smile. "It is what it is. What shall I carry?"

In short order, I'd unloaded a chunk of the food and ammunition from Mia's bag and added my tent to the pile. He packed it in tightly, stuffed a few of Uncle Malachi's newer T-shirts and sweatpants into the empty space, and retrieved his clothing from the dryer. Strapping on his sword belt, he slung the bag over one shoulder, then crossed my uncle's quiver and bow over the other. "Not ideal," he remarked, adjusting the straps as he paced across the main room, "but I'll manage."

"Good," Anji called from the kitchen, where she was piling her sandwich high with pieces of the questionable lettuce from the back of the fridge. "Put that down and eat. I want to be on the trail before nightfall."

He did as he was told, and within the hour, we were suited up and heading out. Fanakel looked over his shoulder at the cabin as we departed, and I thought I heard him mutter, "Pitiful."

I said nothing about it. Considering what we'd seen of his people back in the Greenwood, Fanakel was practically a saint.

"The Kopaati tunnel opens onto the continent of Echoril," said Anji as we traversed the dark passageway between the worlds. "It's the largest and wealthiest of the five, so the placement makes sense in that respect—"

"Echoril, Antinil, and Duvila," Fanakel offered. "And the polar lands, but I forget their names. There's little of consequence in the far north and south."

She quirked a thick eyebrow. "Genutil has a mine producing Aen crystals and a decent dwarf presence. You consider that nothing of consequence?"

"When did you last hear of the True seeking *crystals*?" he replied with disdain.

"All I'm suggesting is that it's a feature of consequence, at least to the Kopaati settlements. Look beyond your own interests if you want to understand another culture."

"You conduct all your diplomacy at dagger-point, do you?"

"We don't make a practice of throwing our visitors straight into prison, if that's what you were asking."

Mia shifted her backpack and huffed. "*Y'all*. Seriously. Hate each other on your own time, eh?"

The elf and dwarf mumbled something that might have been a halfhearted apology, had one strained to hear it.

"As I was saying," Anji continued, "the tunnel placement makes sense because it opens onto Echoril, but the problem is that Daril and the Meali Republic argued over *where* in Echoril it should be. They eventually split the distance between them, but that leaves the tunnel opening into the wilderness."

"Much like yours," I countered. "Mia and I walked for two days before we got out of the mountains."

"Yes, but you can make the journey from Heartfast to the tunnel by carriage in a matter of hours, and from Tightbend, you're barely up before you're down. On foot, it should take us at least five days to reach the border of Daril's lands, and from there to Deoni—"

"The capital," Fanakel offered.

"Right," said Anji with a curt nod. "Deoni will be days more. Perhaps we can hire a carriage or chiquiws along the way."

I thought of what Kingkiller had told me back in

Honslia. "Unless we can convince some air elementals to give us a lift."

"I'm not thrilled with that idea," Anji replied.

Fanakel snorted. "Not afraid of heights, are you?"

"No," she snapped, "I'm afraid of entrusting our safety to beings we don't fully understand and can't control. Personally, I'd rather not be dropped if an elemental grows tired of ferrying us."

"You're small enough, he'd probably forget he was carrying you."

"But if he didn't, *I don't bounce.* Maybe you're hardheaded enough to survive a fall, but do we want to test that?"

"Oh, my God, you two, don't make me turn this car around," Mia muttered beside me, then briefly caught my hand as I snickered.

If Anji overheard, she didn't let on. "Assuming we don't find elementals to assist us, we'll need to walk northeast until we reach the Falova. We can follow that straight to Deoni, and I believe the river road has public accommodations within Daril's borders. Perhaps within Ti'cal's as well."

"Ti'cal?" I asked.

"Another human kingdom. Looking at a map, you have Daril bordering the northern sea and extending southward, with most of its towns raised along the Falova or one of its tributaries. South of Daril is Ti'cal, which is landlocked. They're a natural ally of Daril because that kingdom is so much larger, and Ti'cal needs the port access."

"And then there's the *tiny* matter of the Falova," said Fanakel.

"Right. The river is dead," she explained to Mia and me. "No fish, hardly any aquatic vegetation. There's been starvation in Ti'cal in the last years, or so I've heard."

"Daril has supported them, but it's not sustainable," Fanakel added. "Father has spoken of the potential for an uprising in Ti'cal—the queen's in a difficult position if her people can't eat. No food in the river, and then the flooding goes unchecked...I'm no expert, but I'd be surprised if that dynasty sits the throne for another five years."

Perhaps rightly sensing that Mia and I were lost, Anji backed up. "The land around the Falova grows more arid the farther south one goes. Much of the interior of the continent is barely more than desert. Ti'cal has always been in a precarious position, but the river was enough to sustain it. And then, not too long ago, the river died."

My sword gave off enough light that I could see Mia frown. "Someone poisoned it?" she asked.

"No. The elemental died."

"No one knows how," said Fanakel. "They're difficult to kill, and I've never heard of one dying of, say, old age. But *something* happened to the Falova, and there's as yet been no water elemental come to take the old one's place. It's a crisis, but it's not as if Daril can just find another elemental wandering about. They're so infrequently born, and the odds of one coming to rest in the Falova are slim."

Mia cleared her throat. "Speaking of rest..."

No one complained as we made our temporary camp along the tunnel wall and passed around snacks. "Thanks for lightening the load," Mia said to Fanakel between handfuls of trail mix. "My shoulders appreciate it."

"Considering that I've been eating your food, it seemed fair," he replied. "Will we have enough to reach Deoni, do you suppose?"

Anji considered our packs, her mouth twisting into a dissatisfied moue. "If we're judicious. I should think the more pressing issue will be water."

She had a point. I'd filled every bottle the three of us had and stuck a couple of old thermoses in Fanakel's duffel, but that would only give us a few quarts. If the land was as rough as he and Anji were suggesting, we'd be in for a long, thirsty hike.

That is, unless Kingkiller was right about me. If I had

some sort of gift…if I could summon the rain…

Still, I limited myself to a small mouthful of water to clear the salt of the peanuts I'd eaten and packed the rest away. The elemental might have had faith in my abilities, but he was alone on that count.


Judging by the position of the sun, the tunnel exit on Kopaat seemed to be about three hours behind home, which meant we were in for a long, miserable afternoon.

"There is a reason," said Fanakel, surveying the hilly wasteland stretching to the wavering horizon, "that one does not make the journey to Daril on foot. *Especially* not in the dry season."

*Dry* was an understatement. The land was parched and dusty, and the only vegetation not shriveled beyond recognition was a brownish-green vine that grew in clumps consisting mostly of thorns. Without anything resembling a tree in sight, I could imagine the sort of dust storms that would roll across the land, were there a decent wind. That afternoon, we had barely a breeze, and that did little more than blow the occasional puff of grit into our faces. I looked up at the cloudless blue sky, into Kopaat's brilliant yellow-white sun, and tried to ignore the sweat already trickling down my neck and seeping from my armpits.

"How far was it to Daril, again?" Mia asked, shading her eyes with her hand.

"Days," Anji muttered. "Best be moving."

But no one seemed eager to take the first steps. The terrain would have been challenging on a cool, overcast day: an undulating, trackless expanse stretching as far as the eye could see. Factor in midsummer warmth and a merciless sun, and the prospect of setting off in the direction we hoped Daril lay was less appealing than a root canal without anesthetic.

"We'll never make it," said Mia.

Before Anji could argue, Fanakel jumped in. "She's

right. We're not carrying enough water for one day, let alone the full trip. Not in these conditions."

The princess scowled. "If we're careful with the water—"

"It's suicide." Kicking a clod of dirt, Fanakel watched it skitter down the gravel-pocked hill and explode in a dry ravine. "Daril and Meali knew what they were doing. Imagine trying to march an army across this place—it's easy to see why the war only came to Kopaat in the rainy season."

Anji leaned against the tunnel mouth with her arms folded, but the look in her eyes spoke of resignation. "So what, then? We give up? Send Susan back to that cabin for the rest of her days?"

"We could try Ga'besh—"

"Who there would know more than the adepts of Daril? It's our best chance."

"It's *my* best chance," I cut in before their argument could ramp up. "There's no reason for all of you to risk crossing a desert on my behalf. Go home, I'll take it from here."

"Don't be stupid, lass," Anji retorted with a grunt. "I'll not leave you to die alone."

Mia nodded, and even Fanakel, though he looked exceedingly unhappy about our situation, didn't retreat into the tunnel.

"But we can't stay here," Anji continued. "There's no way of knowing how many Outsiders have come through since you took the sword to Honslia, and wherever we rest needs to be defensible." Pointing to a hilltop a disappointingly far distance away, she said, "That's the highest land around. I suggest we aim ourselves there, make camp, and decide our next move in the morning."

Her plan made as much sense as anything the rest of us could come up with on the spot, and so we marched off across the waste, trying not to twist our ankles on the loose gravel as we navigated the hills. Within an hour, I was parched and aching for my water bottle, and Mia had tied her shirt up over her navel, letting the sweat on her stomach and the small of her back dry. Anji walked grimly onward, surefooted enough in her boots to be unbothered by the rough going, but Fanakel turned an alarming shade of red, nearly matching his hair, which hung in tangled clumps over his shoulders. It was Mia who finally took pity, calling a halt to give him a ponytail holder, then showing him how to tie one of the spare T-shirts around his head in a makeshift wrap. True, he looked ridiculous, but at least the back of his neck wasn't burning.

When we reached Anji's designated campsite, I could hold out no longer and downed a full water bottle before bothering with the tents. The others did likewise—given the vista, what was the point in rationing? Even from that height, there was no sign of vegetation nearby, let alone habitation, nor the slightest glint of water. I saw no Outsiders lurking in the twilight, but that was cold comfort. Wherever Daril was, the trek would be too far.

"All we can do tonight is make camp," said Anji, turning back from the dispiriting view. "Mia, do you have more of those heating packs?"

While Mia and Fanakel pulled together a decent dinner, Anji and I put up the pair of tents and tried to make them comfortable. No one had much to say as we ate or took turns slipping off down the hill to heed the call of nature, and as the last light faded, the only good course of action was to turn in. "I'll take the watch," I told the others. "Least I can do for dragging you all out here."

Considering our shared exhaustion, I wasn't surprised that my offer received no pushback. Anji and Mia claimed one of the tents, leaving Fanakel to sprawl alone in the other while I sat out under the alien stars. With nightfall, the air rapidly began to cool, and soon, I'd resorted to wrapping up in my sleeping bag for warmth. I leaned back against a small outcropping, its rocky surface pitted by eons of blowing grit, and searched the sky for answers.

What were my choices?

Hike back to the tunnels and return to my fate in Cole's Crossing? No—*no*, I refused to accept that.

Return to Ildon and beg Rokund for help again? Or maybe there was someone else in that world who could save me, someone beyond Blackhorn Mountain. I had no idea how large the kingdom was, but surely it had a neighbor. Anji would know...and that was a question for the morning, I thought, hearing her snores through the tent fabric.

Honslia would be a poor choice. Perhaps Fanakel could guide us out of the Greenwood and past Nokan'ti's borders, but having experienced an elven reception once, I wasn't inclined to see how much worse they could be.

Or there was Ga'besh. Fanakel and Anji seemed reluctant, and if the place really was swarming with tekoraet, I could appreciate that. But there were dwarven forgers in Ga'besh, forgers who'd said to hell with the guilds and struck out on their own. Maybe they could unmake the sword...but for what price? Even if I cleaned out Dad's bank account, a fat cashier's check would be nothing more than paper in that world. Maybe the Aen crystals in the hilt would be payment enough—a "break the sword, and you keep the materials" sort of deal. But I didn't suppose that these would be the sort of craftsmen to advertise their services, and I could well imagine what Anji would say about the idea. That she wanted to help me, I had no doubt, but I couldn't risk pushing her past her limits and losing her. Fanakel we'd more or less shanghaied, but Anji had volunteered for this mess, and I didn't want to force her into a situation that grated against her ethics or her religion.

And if her High Queen was out there, I thought, watching the distant stars twinkle, I could use a minor miracle. We weren't going to reach Daril on our own steam, that much was clear. Having seen no sign of a fellow traveler all day, I feared that our chances of hitchhiking were slim to none.

Unless.

*Summon the rain*, Kingkiller had said, but how? There wasn't so much as a pond in sight, nothing I could draw upon beyond what was in our water bottles, and I'd face a mutiny at *best* if I tapped those. But the night was still, I wasn't going to sleep, and I had hours until dawn. I had to try. Clutching the sword with both hands—I didn't care if I needed it or not—I closed my eyes and waited, hoping inspiration would strike.

I almost thought I was imagining it a few minutes later when I began to sense the slight moisture in the air, dancing at the periphery of my consciousness. It was faint and insubstantial as a flash of glitter in a spotlight, but...yes. That was water. I knew it was water. Something within me cried out in recognition.

I felt it swirling on the desiccating breeze like a puff of powdery snow blown from a rooftop. There *was* water in the desert, but so little, not even enough to moisten my dry lips. But if I focused...if I called it to me, droplet by droplet...

Maybe I couldn't make a gully-washer out of the meager atmospheric moisture, but I could try for a single cloud.

# CHAPTER 14

I heard a tent unzip, then Mia's familiar morning voice croak, "What the…"

"Not now," I muttered through gritted teeth. I was a conduit, the lightning rod in the electrical storm, and holding my focus took almost everything from me beyond the slight mental power necessary to remind my lungs to inflate and my heart to pump. My hands had long ceased to complain of their cramping, locked as they were around the sword's hilt, or else I'd run out of attention to devote to my body's aches. The sleeping bag had fallen away at some point during the night, leaving my hunched shoulders bared to the elements but for a thin T-shirt, and I was vaguely cognizant that I was shivering, but that didn't matter.

Nothing mattered.

The rain was coming, and it was *beautiful*.

Or at least, it was beautiful behind my eyes, in the place that was seeing the infinitesimally small droplets and the solitary molecules swirling toward the vortex above my head. What this might have looked like through mundane sight remained a mystery, as I couldn't add the load of light and color to my overworked mind.

Inhale. Exhale. Summon the rain. This was all I could manage.

"Suze. *Suze*," Mia demanded, her words like jackhammers against my crystalline focus. "Talk to me. Suze?" She snapped her fingers in front of my face, and I flinched as I struggled to hold on.

"What's happened?" came Anji's voice, accompanied by the crinkling of the tent floor. "Is she...oh. Oh, my. High Queen be praised, is that..."

"Suze," Mia tried again, speaking more slowly, "there's, like, a thunderhead directly above you. Goes halfway to the freaking horizon. *What is going*—hey!" she yelped.

"Leave her be," said Anji. "Come, we'll eat. Let her work."

"But she—"

"Is calling for help."

"You said you didn't want to mess with elementals!"

"That was before I realized just how far it is to Deoni. Would you rather walk, lass?"

Mia huffed. "No, but Suze—"

"Probably doesn't need any distractions," Anji chided. She paused at the sound of more unzipping, then said, "The Watcher is indisposed, don't bother...High King have mercy, your *face*!"

"What of it?" I heard Fanakel mumble on the edge of my consciousness as I redoubled my efforts.

"It's *scarlet*!"

"Ooh." Mia sucked in her breath in a pained hiss. "You, my friend, are *sunburned*. Yikes."

"Small wonder, pale as they are," said Anji. "And living under that canopy at all times...are you in pain?"

From the sound of it, Fanakel was crawling out of his tent. "I...oh, *damn it*, that—"

"That's going to blister," Mia interrupted. "I don't have any lidocaine on me, but my lotion's gentle. We'll keep it moisturized. You, uh...you're not going to want to shave today."

If Fanakel tried to argue with her, I paid it no mind. I opened myself to the sky, seeking water in the farthest places I could reach, and whispered it closer.


I felt the sun setting more as a waning sense of heat than

of a change in the light. By then, the sky was black with water-laden clouds—or so I assumed, having not so much as cracked my eyes open all day. But I could feel the water circulating above me, rising into vapor with the warmth of day and condensing in the high atmosphere. My will kept it corralled, a swelling lake on the verge of overflowing.

And shortly after nightfall, overflow it did.

I blinked as the first raindrops splashed onto my upturned face, then remembered to divert them from me so as not to grow soaked. My companions had no such protection, but then they didn't seem to want it. As I sat cross-legged in the dirt, the lone dry patch on the hilltop, they emerged from their tents and stared at the sky with wonder. Soon, their hair and clothes were drenched, but they reveled in the shower—especially Fanakel, whose sunburn I finally saw by the sword's light. From the neck up, he looked like a miserable tomato, and I could well imagine how much pain he had to be in. As for me, having been drifting somewhere outside of myself for most of the day, being fully aware of my body once again felt like being tethered to a fleshy anchor with a pulse. My stomach growled, my tongue was dry, and I'd cramped in half a dozen places, but rain was falling in sheets, lightning flickered across the distant sky, and a wind had kicked up, carrying the scent of petrichor across the wasteland. Of all my physical complaints, one was easy to remedy: I opened my protective shield just enough to allow a stream to flow through into my cupped hands, and I slaked my thirst, dribbling onto my shirt and leggings as I slurped the rainwater down. I splashed it in my face, rinsing the dust away, and drank in the smells and sounds of the storm

When I looked up again, *something* was watching me.

Barely visible, a humanoid form delineated by swirling wind and airborne debris, it hovered a few inches above the ground, observing as I dripped. I hastily wiped my face dry on my shirt and stood, tottering with the wooziness of a day's fast, but I kept my feet and tried to remember my manners. "Hello," I said, nodding to the newcomer. "I'm Susan."

*I am myself.* It—no, *he*, there was a definite sense of masculinity attached to him—cocked his head. *Did you create the rain?*

"I did," I replied. "Trying to signal for help."

*Ah. An effective technique.*

Mentally, I crossed my fingers and hoped for the best. "There's a water elemental in Honslia who suggested I try this. He's sometimes called Kingkiller?"

*Yes, I know of him.*

"He thought that one of your kind might be willing to help us. My friends and I are trying to get to Deoni," I explained, gesturing to the rest of my wet, quiet party. "We don't have the supplies to make it on foot."

The air elemental considered that for a moment. *What is there for you in Deoni?*

"Help, I hope." Carefully, I took hold of the sword's blade and showed him the hilt. "I'm the Watcher, but I'd rather not be."

*You regret the choice?*

"The choice wasn't mine to make. And as long as I'm attached to this sword, I attract Outsiders. They hunt me."

He seemed bemused by my answer. *Why were you chosen?*

"I don't know. My uncle was the Watcher, and he died, and since the sword picks the successor, I found it waiting for me. I'm not a soldier—hell, I'm not even a competent hunter. But this job's for life, and I'm hopeful that there's someone in Deoni who can help free me. Let me have my life back."

I could feel the weight of the elemental's insubstantial eyes on me. *One of my brethren was murdered to create that sword.*

"So I was told. I'm sorry."

The indentations of his eyes narrowed. *You did not kill him.*

"No, I feel bad about what was done to him," I clarified.

His comprehension reached me more as an impression than as a concrete thought. *The sword is cursed, and now it has cursed you in turn. For his sake, I will take you to the humans, though I suspect you will not find what you seek there. Deoni...* He hesitated, then said, *Deoni is a curious place. Are you prepared to depart?*

I looked at our haphazard campsite just as the others began scrambling to stuff its pieces into backpacks. "Could you give us a moment to grab our tents?"

The elemental nodded, and I hoisted up my bag, shaking with the effort. "Here," Mia murmured, steadying me on my feet. "Take it easy, you've had a day."

*You are unwell?*

"Exhausted," I admitted, sitting on an outcropping while the tents came down. "I've never done that before. Make rain, I mean. I didn't sleep last night, and I haven't eaten, and—"

*And flesh has certain limitations?*

I chuckled. "You could say that. It likes regular feeding and rest, for starters."

*Eat, then, if you are uncomfortable. The journey will take us a full night and well into the day.*

Digging into my pack, I grabbed the closest granola bar at hand and ripped it open, but though I was salivating, I tried to be polite. "Want one? We have food to share."

*Eat,* he repeated, the word colored with mirth. *You have encountered few of my kind, I trust.*

"You're the second," I said around a mouthful of oats and chocolate.

*Then know that we do not require such as that to sustain us. The Aen is sufficient.*

I nodded and swallowed, fighting the urge to shove the rest of the bar into my mouth in frantic bites. Awakened, my stomach demanded attention, and I barely had the last of the bar between my teeth before I was unwrapping a second. "Hungry work," I managed as he watched me inhale my meal.

*You need not apologize for attending to yourself. I take no offense.* Stepping closer to me, he added, *You are inexperienced yet. This will grow simpler with time.*

Too busy chewing to respond, I arched an eyebrow in query.

He passed one hand back and forth through the bubble I'd almost forgotten I'd made around me, my shelter from the pounding rain. *This power of yours. I remember when I first knew myself and the worlds within the Aen, how I struggled to do more than drift for a seeming age. Control came with practice, and then one day, everything became so simple. Your power…it awakened recently?*

I thought back over the blur of time since Uncle Malachi's death, trying to pick increments of time out of the chaos. "About six days ago."

*So soon? And you managed that?* He turned his face toward the cloud-covered sky. *A power indeed.*

"I blame the sword."

*Why? It is not the source of the energy pushing the rain away.*

Lowering my voice, I replied, "Because I was perfectly ordinary two weeks ago, and the notion that I might have some unchecked ability independent of the magic sword—which, you know, isn't a phrase I would have ever associated with myself before recent events—it's more than a little terrifying, to be honest with you."

He considered me in silence for a long moment, then said, *You are right to be afraid. Are we prepared to depart?* he asked as my sodden companions joined us, bags loaded and water bottles refilled. *If you can stop the rain, this will be more comfortable for you.*

"I, uh…I'm not sure how," I admitted, "but maybe I could extend the bubble instead…"

"That'll do," Mia interrupted, sidling closer and out of the storm. "So, first, *thank you*," she said to the elemental, "and how does this work?"

I felt his amusement just before a strong gust of wind scooped us off our feet and flung us into the air. A few seconds later, the wind pushed the four of us close together, beneath the shelter of my rain repellant, and we were buoyed aloft on what felt like an inflatable raft, minus the constricting plastic. The elemental landed beside us, the only one on that ride who was anything close to at ease, and took a seat. *Relax, I will not drop you*, he assured us. *The journey will take time. If you sleep, it will do me no harm.*

Easy for him to say—he wasn't the one being carried along at a disconcerting altitude, flying on what seemed to be nothing at all. But the night was too dark for me to see the ground and all of its pointy rocks rushing by beneath us, and with my thirst quenched and my raging stomach pacified, my brain declared that unconsciousness was next on the agenda. I lay down, curled into a damp ball, and knew nothing more until all hell broke loose.

Mia's voice pierced the comforting cocoon of sleep like a javelin. "Suze. Shit, *Suze*, wake up," she ordered, shaking me until I groaned and opened my gummy eyes. "Look over the side."

Vaguely, I realized that we'd stopped moving. The sky was lightening toward dawn—a subtle bluing of the sky, nothing more—and as my rain-blocking barrier did nothing against the wind, I began shivering as soon as I sat up. By the light of the sword, I saw Anji and Fanakel seemingly kneeling on thin air, looking down at the ground, while the elemental sat a few feet away, regarding them with his inscrutable expression.

"What's going on?" I asked, wishing my mouth didn't taste quite so much like sour garbage smelled.

"Down there." She pointed through our invisible cushion, and I followed the line of her finger toward the ground.

About that time, I woke sufficiently to realize that the noise I was hearing wasn't the wind, but rather screams. That I could make out the contours of the village below us was only thanks to the fact that about a third of it was on fire. Roofs blazed, the bobbing lights of torches zipped between buildings, and then a burst of greenish flame ripped through the night as *something* was flung toward an object darker than the land...

No. That wasn't an object. It was moving, and it brushed off the fireball like cigarette ash.

"Outsiders," I muttered.

"Looks like it. I got the elemental to stop, but what do we do?"

I raised my head to find Mia staring at me, waiting for a decision. Panic leapt in my chest—this wasn't my call, I wasn't a leader—but the sword clutched in my fist suggested that this didn't matter at the moment. A village was burning, people were screaming, and odds were good that we'd find a few casualties down there. But if we didn't jump in, who knew what would remain in the morning?

"Can you take us down?" I asked the elemental.

*You wish to join the fight?*

Though I'd yet to fully adjust to the nuances of communication with a being that spoke into my thoughts, even I could tell that he sounded reluctant, which did absolutely nothing for my confidence in the moment. "Not particularly," I replied, "but since I've got the best weapon around against *those* things, I think I have an obligation."

His head bobbed. *Very well, if you are certain...*

The four of us cried out as the air beneath us suddenly grew thin. We didn't fall all the way to the ground—we'd never have survived the impact—but the drop was enough to leave me queasy. "Thank you," I told our chauffeur, staggering to my feet and jumping the last few inches to the reassuring embrace of firm dirt. "We'll, uh...we'll be back."

*I hope so. And you will understand if I await you here.*

I couldn't fault him for that. Dropping our bags at the outskirts of the village, we ran toward the fight: me with the glowing sword, Mia two steps behind me with her pistol in hand and ammo pack at her waist, Anji beside her with her trusty dagger, and Fanakel bringing up the rear, fumbling with his new bow. As people sprinted past us in the other direction—quite a few armed men among them, I noticed—we neared the heart of the battle, where the town's bravest were squaring off against three Outsiders. The creatures rose to a terrifying height by the light of the burning buildings, fifteen-foot monsters with black fur, bared teeth, and paws the size of my head, like angry bears who'd hibernated in a radioactive pond and woken with a hangover.

We stopped at the edge of the chaos, Fanakel still fussing with the bow and Anji drafting a battle plan. "Divide and conquer?" I asked.

She looked at me as if I'd suggested trying the power of hugs and loving affirmations first. "*Absolutely* not. We take one at a time and let the humans harry the others. Leftmost, *go.*"

Marching orders in hand, I tightened my grip on the sword and ran toward the target monstrosity, doing my best to bellow in an intimidating fashion. The men who'd been trying to keep it at bay broke ranks shortly before I ran past, and an arrow sailed over my head and into the creature's thick neck just as I dodged a paw and sank the sword into its chest. It roared in pain, but its agony was short-lived: a second arrow distracted it, I stabbed it a second time in the gut and ripped the hole wider, and then Mia, coming up from behind, administered the coup de grâce by blowing off the top of its head.

Splashed with stinking ichor but too high on adrenaline to care, I turned my sights on the next Outsider—which, by the time I entered stabbing range, looked like it had lost a fight with a porcupine. Fanakel might not have had much practice with Uncle Malachi's toys, but the guy was proving to be a decent archer under pressure. As Anji screamed and leapt onto the monster's back, I took the opening and went for the torso again. The sword opened the thing's guts like tugging a zipper on a pair of too-tight jeans, but I left the blade in place long enough for the Outsider to catch fire. While it bellowed, Anji stabbed it at the base of the skull, then jumped free to give Mia a clear headshot.

With two down, the townsfolk had noticed us and were giving us a *wide* berth. No one tried to assist or intervene as we approached the third Outsider, which had dropped to all fours and was staring at me—understandable, as the glowing sword didn't seem to be standard kit, even among magic-wielding peoples. Before I could consult Anji as to our next move, the monster growled and charged, kicking up clods of dirt as it closed on us. I held the sword steady, hoping the beast might be stupid enough to impale itself, but Mia and Fanakel took a more proactive approach. Within three seconds, the Outsider had an arrow in one eye. Within ten, having stopped to process what had happened to its vision, it had given Mia a chance to run up in its new blind spot, and it was suddenly missing half its skull. The brain beneath had been pulped by the blast, but the creature didn't yet seem to realize that it was dead and continued trying to fix its good eye on me. While the Outsider wobbled, I jumped onto its back and shoved the sword into its side, holding on until the corpse ignited.

And with that, the four of us took a few steps back, panting, and watched as our kills burned. My arms and clothing were filthy, and a careless brush of my hand against my cheek revealed something tacky on my skin— an Outsider's bodily fluid, I realized, not mine, as my face wasn't in any pain. Anji was similarly soiled, and even Mia and Fanakel hadn't fully escaped the spray. Nodding to the rest of the team, I turned around and found a crowd of villagers gaping at us, swords and assorted metal farm implements at the ready. "Hi," I said, wearily raising my shaking arm. "Any chance of a towel?"

But despite the fact that we'd just slayed the monsters

ravaging their town, the locals were anything but welcoming. A burly, scowling man with a pickaxe, who'd apparently been elected spokesvillager by tacit vote of his more cowardly fellows, strode forward, silhouetted against the housefires behind him. "The gods demand truth. Who are you?"

"Susan Cole," I replied, keeping my ichor-streaked sword pointed at the ground and my other hand in plain view. "I'm the Watcher. These are my—"

"The Watcher?" he echoed with surprise.

At least he had heard of the term, I thought, and hastened to smooth over whatever misunderstanding had arisen between our parties. "Yes, from the other side of the Crossing. My companions and I were traveling to Deoni—"

Unfortunately, he knew *too* well what "the Watcher" meant. "You're supposed to be back there!" he cried. "Protecting us!"

"I—"

"*Where were you?*" As the villagers behind him rumbled their agreement, he gestured toward the ruined settlement. "Our homes! Our livelihoods! All of it, gone! And..."

His voice faded as a high-pitched keening arose from the wreckage—one woman's voice, then another and another, a crescendo of grief. The man's expression shifted from fury to fear in an instant, and he staggered back a few steps when a boy who couldn't have been out of his late teens ran toward the defending militia, his red robe flapping.

"Priest," Anji murmured behind me. "The Darili worship many gods. See his pendant?"

She didn't need to be quiet—I couldn't imagine that any of the townspeople were wearing translators, and her one-way piece only made them comprehensible to her. Fanakel's translator went both ways, I'd learned during our long hikes, but he kept his mouth shut.

Still, I saw what she was talking about: a silver

centerpiece to his necklace with wires shaped into an eight-petaled flower, set with a red stone at the center. Not an Aen crystal, then, but perhaps a ruby or garnet.

"They can't afford separate priests for each of their gods in the little towns," she explained in a rush. "He's a catch-all priest. That's what the pendant indicates. Different colors for different gods, but red is for all together."

But it wasn't the appearance of the priest that left the man so shaken, as it turned out—it was the identity of the person wearing the garb. "Kerul," he said, composing himself sufficiently to greet the boy. "Is...is she..."

"Yes, Father." The boy bowed his head briefly, and when he looked up again, I could just make out the sheen of moisture on his cheeks. "The gods have reclaimed her, and I serve now in her stead."

As the man dropped his pickaxe and covered his face, I heard Fanakel offer a whispered gloss to Anji's brief lesson: "Blasphemous as they are, the Darili hold that their priests may arise from only certain bloodlines. Parents train children."

"His wife," I muttered. "*Shit.*"

By the time the man pulled himself together, his rage had returned tenfold. Grabbing his improvised weapon, he snarled, "*You*," and would have run at us had two of his fellows not restrained him.

Confused, the young priest looked to them for an explanation, and one offered, "That's the Watcher right there. The chubby one with the black all over her. She let the monsters in."

"What do we do?" asked the other man restraining the new widower from taking his best swing.

The boy stared us down—I'm sure we made a strange sight, certainly not a pretty one—and his young face hardened. "Take them to the queen. Justice is hers to give, not ours to take."

His father's head snapped toward him, jaw sagging.

"But...your mother...they—"

"We are *bound* by the law," he said, and I recognized from recent use the note of forced confidence in his wavering voice. "The gods have given matters of life and death to the crown, not to us. *You* taught me as much," he added, and his father cringed. "Take their weapons, restrain them, and see them safely to Deoni. This I charge you," he told his armed flock. "And now, I will see to the dead."

"Wait," I called after him as he turned to go. "Please, I...I'm sorry this happened, I'm *so* sorry about your mother, we jumped in as soon as we saw—"

"You let them in," he said, interrupting my babbled apology. His voice was low but firm, all the stronger for the control he must have been working overtime to maintain.

"I never agreed to be the Watcher. It was forced upon me. I just want my life back—"

"And I wanted my mother to bless my wife and children before her return to the realm beyond, but that's not the path the gods have chosen."

"Gods have nothing to do with this," I insisted. "Nokan'ti, Blackhorn Mountain, Daril, some maladetas, whoever it was, they made this," I said, shaking the dirty sword for emphasis, "and now all of your monsters come to *me* and *my* people, and it's not right, it's not *fair*—"

"Fair?" he echoed. "My mother is dead. My home is ash and embers. Half this town will be a ruin before the fire is contained. There is *blood* soaking into the ground as we speak because we were defenseless. Look around you," he said, an edge creeping into his tone as he gestured to the corpses sprawled haphazardly between the fire and the fallen Outsiders.

Though the shadows made the count difficult, I picked out at least a dozen.

"Fathers, sons, brothers," Kerul continued. "Had you done your duty, they would be asleep in their beds."

"It's not my duty! I didn't ask for it!"

"The gods seldom ask our permission," he said, then marched off toward the wailing mourners awaiting him.

Left with the angry, armed mob and cognizant that the only thing separating us from a death match was the tenuous strength of the young priest's authority, I dropped my sword, then slowly unhooked my bungee belt for good measure, letting the scabbard fall beside the blade.

"Suze," Mia hissed, "what are you doing?"

"The wise thing," Anji interjected. Her dagger joined the sword in the dirt, and she added her short sword to the pile.

Fanakel dropped the bow—useless now, as he'd exhausted his quiver in the fight—and his own blade, and with a disapproving huff, Mia put her gun on the ground. I kept my filthy hands visible as I knelt, then linked them behind my head, like I'd seen on TV—the best *I surrender* pose I could come up with short of throwing myself face-first into the mud. The others followed suit, and we watched the crowd, waiting for a reaction.

At least it wasn't long in coming. Within moments, someone had produced a few lengths of rope, and I found myself with my hands securely trussed behind my back. A sharp jerk sent a shot of pain through my shoulders but got me to my feet, but before we could be dragged off to our fate, our former ride intervened.

*Wait*, said the air elemental, manifesting between us and the burning town, a human-sized form of swirling smoke. *I agreed to carry them to Deoni. See to yourselves—I will deliver them to your queen.*

"They're no longer your concern," the priest's father snapped. "Mind your business."

A stiff breeze whipped around us, fanning the flames of a nearby barn to an impressive height. *I am attending to my business. Release them to me.*

But just as soon as hope fluttered to life within my chest, a knife at my throat sent it to a premature grave. "Be on your way," the man said, pressing the sharp edge against the hollow beneath my jaw.

"It's all right," I forced myself to tell the elemental. "Thank you for your help. I'm, uh, not sure if I'm in a position to repay it, but—"

*I will be watching*, he said, growing taller until he loomed over my captor. *They will live to see Deoni.*

The grumbling of the crowd told me too clearly that this hadn't been a guarantee, no matter what their new priest ordered. Still, their leader didn't back down. "You have no right to meddle in—"

*They stopped to assist you. If your concern is justice, then you will have no objection to my continued presence. If, however, you intend to murder unarmed captives once your town is sufficiently behind you on the road, then you will return to discover that the fire took all.* He cocked his head. *Am I making myself sufficiently clear?*

With a loud crackling of timber, the burning barn collapsed into rubble.

"Fine," the man muttered, pulling the knife away from my neck.

*An agreement, then*, said the elemental, and released the smoke he'd trapped as he dematerialized. *I will bring their packs.*

# CHAPTER 15

The Darili road system could have done with a few thousand tons of asphalt to bring it out of its preindustrial bumpiness, but the ruts in the dusty dirt track were the least of my concerns that morning. The four brown chiquiws pulling the open wagon along were easygoing beasts, and they kept our speed just north of a gentle plodding, no matter how often their driver cracked a whip over their bent heads. These were farm animals, built and bred for long days hitched to plows, and while they were at least as fast as trotting horses, they weren't about to be rushed...which meant that we were in for a long, miserable trip.

That day, the best I could hope for were small mercies. Our captors hadn't bothered to blindfold us, which was nice, since I could at least look over the side of the wooden wagon as the rolling land greened toward the river off to my right. Maybe it was a tributary of the Falova, or maybe it was just an irrigation canal—I couldn't say, nor could I ask, given the rag in my mouth. About an hour after sunrise, once the village's fires had been brought under control, the band of men who'd watched over us had been rejoined by their sweaty, sooty comrades, who'd come bearing makeshift gags. A thick, foul-tasting rag wadded behind my teeth, a second one holding my jaws shut like an old toothache patient, and a final tight wrap over my lips and behind my head effectively reduced anything I'd have cared to say to muffled grunts.

But at least they'd let me explain why my sword was

beside me before they took away my speech. "It's attached to the Watcher, and it follows me," I said in a rush before they could draw their own blades. "I can't make it stop."

The young priest's father crouched in front of me, turned the sheathed sword over to inspect it, then dropped it into the dirt and stared me in the eye. "That's Shadowbane, then?"

Remembering the terms Ms. Quince had used, I nodded.

"Try anything, and I'll kill your friends *slowly*," he said, then shoved the gag into my mouth.

Small mercies.

And they hadn't tied our feet together, which was nice. Sure, my arms ached from the hours they'd been pinned behind my back, but the only restraint to my legs was the rope around my right ankle, which had been knotted to a metal eyebolt in the wagon's short side. With my feet relatively free, I could brace myself as we bumped along. Poor Anji wasn't so lucky—the rough benches in the wagon were designed for adult humans, and her legs dangled above the floor like a child's. Unable to stabilize herself with her hands bound, she alternated between falling against the wagon's side and against Mia, who bore the unintentional shoving without protest. Fanakel sat between Mia and me—his ankle, like Mia's, was tied to an eyebolt behind our bench—and bore the ride in silence, his sunburn an angry red beneath the cloudless sky.

The sword had appeared at my feet shortly after we pulled out of town, a constant offer of assistance, but in all of my calculations, one of my companions would wind up dead before I freed myself. Our sullen guards rode behind and before us, all armed and eager for an excuse to strike, and I wasn't about to make the choice easier for them.

But they hadn't killed us yet. Small mercies.

There had been no offer of water—not that I expected one, considering how much they'd expended on dowsing the flames. A lantern, one of our guards had told another while we lay outside the village, waiting for our fate. Someone had come out with the other men at the sound of roaring in the night, then saw what they were up against and fled, dropping and smashing his light in his haste. It had landed in a straw pile outside a barn, *that* had gone up like kindling, and with the wind as high as it had been, the embers had jumped. This was the dry season, the fool should have *known* to be careful, but there was no changing the result. The town was a ruin, fourteen people were dead, five more clung to life, and the queen would give them justice.

I felt like absolute shit.

No, I hadn't asked for the sword. I'd never wanted to be the Watcher. But that didn't mean it wasn't the best weapon ever forged against Outsiders, and someone—the gods, fate, the fucking sword itself—had chosen me for the dubious honor of wielding it. I hadn't stayed at my post, killing the monsters as they came through, and now there were Outsiders roaming the four worlds, a threat the locals hadn't faced in centuries. People were dead in that little Darili town. They'd been dying days ago in Blackhorn Mountain. Odds were good that Outsiders were stalking the Greenwood. Hell, I didn't know what Ga'besh's tunnel situation was like, but I suspected that they'd had their own unfortunate surprises of late.

Because I'd said no. I wanted my life.

How many lives had been lost because I'd clung to mine?

Of course it wasn't fair that the sword had fallen to me. *Life* wasn't fair. It wasn't some stupid fairy tale with a happy ending where right prevails and injustice is punished. But that burden had been entrusted to me, and I'd rejected it, and now the few who'd tried to help me were tied up on the wagon ride from hell, and *people were dead...*

Sometimes, the itching of the thick ichor that had long since dried on my face and arms distracted me from my circling thoughts for a moment.

Like I said, small mercies.

I was staring at the narrow river, picking farmhouses out of the haze, when I heard the elemental's voice: *You seem uncomfortable.*

I twitched, surprised from my reverie, and looked around for the distortion marking his presence.

*I choose not to be seen. Nor do I choose to be overheard by the others on your wagon. You are uncomfortable?*

Unable to speak, I settled for a sharp nod.

*What pains you?*

My limitations made it challenging to answer anything more complex than a yes-or-no question, and I hoped the elemental would understand his error from the look I was shooting at nothing.

*Talk to me, young one. You need not make sounds.*

I tried to convey my dubiousness via eyebrow quirk, and while I couldn't be certain, I thought that his response felt akin to amusement.

*Try*, he urged. *Form your thought and send it forth.*

Having nothing better to do than either humor him or sink deeper into depression, I chose the former and focused on how his words felt in my mind, as if I could solve the puzzle through reverse-engineering. *This?* I thought.

The men in front of me jerked, and Fanakel shoved his knee against mine. I cut my eyes to his and saw the question there.

*Softer*, said the elemental. *Speak to me alone.*

When the guards had settled in again, I barely nodded to Fanakel, then closed my eyes and bent my head forward as if I were nodding off. Without the distraction of sight, I could almost feel the elemental—he was floating beside the wagon, just off to my right—and I tried to think as softly as possible, aiming for him. *Yes?*

*Good. Very good. Again.*

Carefully, trying to replicate what I'd just done, I

thought, *Is this right?*

*Yes.* He seemed subtly pleased. *I thought you might have the knack. Now, you did not answer my question. What pains you?*

*Arms and shoulders, mostly, though I'm afraid this gunk all over me is going to leave a rash. Itches like hell. And now I have to pee, but I don't see this wagon stopping any time soon, do you?*

*I would not wish corporeality on my worst enemy, had I one. But you have my sympathy.*

*Thanks, but I'm pretty sure I deserve this.*

I could almost feel his bemusement. *Why?*

*Because if I'd just sucked it up and stayed back at the Crossing, none of this would have happened.*

*Your capture?*

*Well…yeah, that, but I was thinking more about the deaths.*

*Ah.* He floated along in silence for a moment, then said, *You feel responsible.*

I nodded.

*There is an argument to be made in support of that position. I do not find it entirely convincing, but I suppose that one who has suffered a more recent loss might be persuaded. But your companions—the elf, the dwarf, the tekori—did you bargain for their services, or are they here because they believe your cause to be just?*

*You think Mia is tekorish, too?*

*I know it to be so. The peoples of these worlds leave different signatures upon the Aen. Your Mia—she may not be purely tekorish, but that part of her is strong. And you did not answer my question.*

*Mia's here because she's my best friend,* I replied. *Anji thinks the Watcher setup is unfair. As for Fanakel…it's complicated, it was either go with us or go home to face his dad, and I think he decided we were the less unpleasant of the two alternatives.*

*There is human in him, is there not?*

I nodded again, hoping that Fanakel couldn't overhear. *Half, he says.* I hesitated, then asked, *Anything weird about Anji?*

*Dwarf,* he declared. *Pure dwarf. She is bright with the Aen, but in a dwarven fashion.*

*She forges well*, I offered.

*That does not surprise me. But you, young one...you do.*

My stomach clenched, but I didn't open my eyes. *How so?*

*Forgive me if this seems rude, but what are you?*

Maintaining my façade of sleep was growing more difficult by the moment. *What do you mean?*

*You're not a dwarf, obviously. Not an elf. Not tekorish. Not a maladeta.*

*I'm human.*

*Not wholly.*

The wagon hit a bad rut, throwing me into Fanakel, and he helped nudge me upright once he'd pulled himself off of Mia. I couldn't exactly thank him, but as I gave him a look that I hoped conveyed gratitude, he nudged his knee into mine and dipped his head.

Once I was balanced again, I resumed my feigned napping and waited, focusing until I could sense the elemental beside me. *Sorry about that.*

*Corporeality must be such a burden*, he replied. *And as I was saying, you may be human in part, but there is more to you. Your parents?*

*I don't know anything about them*, I thought, feeling a little queasy between the rocking wagon and the elemental's assessment. *Abandoned. My uncle found me on the other side of the Crossing.*

He mulled that over for a time as the driver begged the unbothered chiquiws to quicken their pace. *Consider the power you manifested yesterday. Your parents may have feared you.*

*I've never done that before—*

*All the more reason to fear. And I am making you uneasy.*

I couldn't exactly lie to him. *A little.*

*Then let us speak of something else.*

Cracking open one eye, I caught the glint of the water flowing in the distance, then closed my eye once more and waited until I was sure that I wasn't broadcasting. *Is that the Falova?*

*A tributary. He has many branches.*

*"Has"?* I asked. *Anji and Fanakel said that the elemental in the river died.*

His reply was immediate and certain. *No. Were he truly dead, one of my brethren would have helped a youngling take his place. That is a fine home for one born to water. He is not dead, but he was ripped from it.*

I frowned and tried to brace myself as we traversed another deep pothole. *How?*

*Whatever magic they used is unknown to me. He speaks of three humans, but more than that, he knows not. They carried him deep into the desert and dropped him into a watering hole—barely an oasis. It has nearly dried every summer, but we who can try to nudge the heaviest clouds in his direction, and he has endured these years. A hardship, certainly, and the dry season carries the constant fear of death.*

*If it dries up...*

*He dies*, the elemental finished. *And he cannot simply summon rain as you did. But no one will claim that river while he lives.*

*But why can't he make it rain? If he's a water elemental—*

*We are limited to what surrounds us. He cannot produce rain, and I, for example, cannot call down a tornado upon this wagon.*

I bit my lip under my gag to keep from chuckling. *Appreciate the thought.*

*You could probably produce enough rain to make the road impassable*, he suggested.

*Do you know how long that last rainstorm took to pull together?*

*No. But the fact that you did so shows why you are to be feared.* When I said nothing, he asked, *Shall I tell you my theory, or would you rather I not?*

I took stock of myself in that moment—sore, bound, gagged, covered in crusty ichor—and decided it couldn't get much worse. *Sure.*

*Very well. I believe your father was one of my brethren. Water-bound.*

*You just said that they can't make rain—*

*True. But our children are...unpredictable,* he replied, a cast of mild distaste coloring the word. *Most of us are born at the edge of the Aen, parentless and fully formed. We travel the four worlds, and those of a more sedentary nature eventually claim their territories—all but my kind,* he explained. *It is possible for us to produce children of a sort, though rare. We combine parts of ourselves, and the resultant offspring is a being independent of us, often possessing attributes of both. I know of one in this world, born of air and fire. He moves as a flaming vortex throughout the vast desert, and he seems content. Unique, but content. He is a pleasant fellow unless one happens to inhabit a flammable dwelling.*

*That's understandable,* I thought.

*Indeed. But he, now, is purely an elemental. We can produce children with others.*

*You don't sound too keen on that.*

*I find it distasteful, personally,* he admitted. *Though if I am not mistaken and that is indeed what you are, I mean no offense. Such is merely my preference, and children cannot choose their parents.*

*Thank you, I think.*

*Truly, it has nothing to do with you. I simply cannot imagine anything that would make me desire to conjoin in the necessary fashion with a corporeal being. But beyond that is the problem that one cannot anticipate what the child will be. Rogue elementals, they are called. The few I have ever encountered were stronger than their elemental parent, often in different ways. One was born of an earth-bound mother and an elven father. She was incorporeal like her mother but unbound, and she could create rock from the dust of the air. Killed by maladetas in a war long ago, as I recall. And there was the daughter born of a maladetan father and a fire-bound mother. Corporeal and female, and her father's people killed her shortly after they learned of her existence.*

*That's awful,* I replied, seeing Ms. Quince in my mind's eye.

*Had she been male, they probably would have allowed her to live,* he told me. *Maladetas' power passes only to their females. They are brilliant with the Aen, but if they use their power for destructive ends, the attempt can kill them. They could not know if the child had those innate barriers in place, and if she did not, they could not risk allowing her to grow into a fire-wielding terror. This is why maladetas do not produce children outside of their own kind,* he continued as I tried to digest that. *A son might be harmless, but a daughter could be greatly talented without the necessary limitations.*

Uncle Malachi's face flashed behind my closed eyes, and the elemental seemed to pick up on it. *Who is he?*

*My uncle. Adopted, I mean. The Watcher before me,* I clarified. *The maladetas send one of their people to keep an eye on the Watcher, and the last one…I always thought that he and she had a thing for each other, but they never got together.*

I could feel when his curiosity flipped to comprehension. *A maladeta and a human? Never. Far too dangerous. Humans are generally dull with the Aen, but for those with power, they have no limitations on them beyond their own scruples. Had the Watcher and the maladeta produced a daughter, she would not have been permitted to live. I suppose that even if they were fond of each other, they did not wish to assume that risk.* He paused, then said, *And that is why you are to be feared. If you are what I believe you to be, then your power exceeds your father's, and it is unchecked. No wonder my brother told you to summon the rain—he must have felt this in you.*

My head was swimming, and I had no reply to that. But as fate had it, one was never demanded of me. Fanakel, it seemed, was prone to carsickness, and with the bumpy journey and the hot sun, his gut finally gave up.

The elemental solidified enough to rip off Fanakel's gag before he could choke, and the poor elf heaved for breath between vomitous spasms. Of course, our captors weren't pleased in the slightest to be sprayed with his stomach contents, and no sooner had Fanakel caught his breath than one of them whipped out a glass bottle half-full of a dark purple liquid and shoved a healthy gulp down the patient's throat. Fanakel barely had time to ask what it was before he pitched forward into his own sick— unconscious, at least.

*Sleeping potion*, the elemental cautioned as my gag was untied.

Briefly, I weighed the benefits of resisting against a reprieve from the growing discomfort of the trip, then accepted my dose and blacked out.

The rest of our trip through the Darili hinterlands could have been accompanied by a brass band and a troupe of cavorting acrobats, for all I knew. Drugged, I slept until we stopped at sunset, the chiquiws having decided that they would go no farther without a feed in a field. Our captors yanked us to our feet, dragged us down to the creek beside our rough camp, and dunked us face-first into the cold water until we woke enough to gasp and drink a few mouthfuls. With a heavily armed guard on us, we were untied long enough to relieve ourselves and rinse off the road grime—and worse, considering the gunk that flowed off me like black mud—and then Fanakel was made to fill a bucket and walk it back and forth to the wagon until the mess he'd made had run off into the ditch. I started to give him a hand—water was one the one thing I could control at that moment—but the elemental cautioned against it. *Hide your power,* he whispered to me. *They fear you as the Watcher, whether or not they show it. Do not heighten that fear.*

Considering our journey that far, my plan was to be as cooperative as possible. Mia, Anji, and I mumbled only a few words to each other during our quick bath, just enough to ask if the others were okay—a stupid enquiry, but old habits die hard. The princess was a perfect stoic, Mia was too weary to fight, and as all of us were sore from the restraints and the awkward positions in which we'd slept, we put up no fuss when the men ordered us back to the rinsed-down wagon. While the boards still smelled of vomit, at least the wagon wasn't moving—and since that was a day for small mercies, I took it. Of course, it was the last mercy we received that night. Before I knew it, my arms were tied behind my back again, my leg was attached to an eye bolt, and I was left to pass a cold, uncomfortable night on the wet wooden floor of the wagon while the men not on guard snored on the benches. My stomach growled, and the little water I drank at the stream had only served to awaken my thirst, but I knew better than to ask for dinner. Plus, the water tasted odd, somewhat metallic and curiously flat.

In the morning, we were led to the stream once again for the necessities and a few hasty mouthfuls to drink before we were returned to our conveyance and presented with the glass bottle. After the miserable hours we'd spent shivering in the darkness, none of us argued when ordered to take our medicine.

The next time I saw daylight, the clouds were pinking with the sunset, and the wagon was bumping over cobblestones instead of ruts. I sat up and looked over the side of the wagon as we crossed a wide bridge. The river below flowed sluggishly, if it all, a stinking, muddy expanse at least half a mile wide. While the land around us was far more verdant than anything we'd yet seen on our ride, the immediate banks of the river browned as they neared the water, as if whatever contagion had befallen the river were spreading upward onto land.

Our destination came into full view as we reached the top of the bridge's arch: a gray stone wall perhaps forty feet high, beyond which rose the towers and turrets of a city. To the left, in the distance, the towers I could see were topped with flags in a wavy blue and green pattern.

*Deoni*, said the elemental as I blinked blearily at my surroundings. *Royal seat of Daril. The gate is manned until nightfall, so the chiquiws are racing the sun. Or, more properly, the drivers of the chiquiws are racing the sun. I doubt that these chiquiws care one way or another where they sleep tonight.*

*Any advice?* I asked.

*Be careful. Your hope lies with Erianthe.*

*The queen, right?*

*Correct. And should she prove unpersuaded by your cause...*

*Sword?* I guessed.

*Flee. Look behind you.*

Turning briefly, I glimpsed the thick forest through which we must have come. *We can hide there?*

*Not for long. A shallow offshoot of the Falova runs through that wood. Follow it north, toward its mouth at the sea. On the edge of Daril's domain, you'll find a maladetan settlement. Should all else fail, seek them out and beg for sanctuary.*

I recognized a goodbye when I heard one. *You're leaving us now?*

*I will see you to the palace*, he replied. *They will not be able to kill you then without the queen's permission.*

*Well, that's certainly reassuring.*

A faint pressure like a squeezing hand wrapped around my right shoulder. *Be brave, young one. Be brave, but be wise.*

My nerves only tensed as I studied the city wall, so instead, I considered the sky as we crossed the river. The sunset's colors had deepened toward neon pink in only a few minutes, but what struck me most was the fact that there were clouds at all. I hadn't seen so many—at least not of my own making—since we'd arrived in Kopaat.

*Rain is coming*, said the elemental.

*From where?*

*The north. Deoni is sufficiently close to the sea to benefit from the storms that roll in. Feel the wind? That was born over the deep water.*

I didn't need to close my eyes that time to pick up on the sensation. The air around me was heavy with moisture, so much so that I almost wanted to lick it, parched as I was after the long ride.

*I should imagine there will be rain by morning*, he mused. *Perhaps it will bring you luck.*


I didn't know what qualified as an official emergency in Deoni. Chief Brundage had felt free to rouse my dad over any little thing, from graffiti at the high school to goats eating the library shrubbery, and Joel Rogers certainly hadn't been shy about calling him with the slightest question. But Dad had been the mayor of a small town, and something told me that getting a queen's immediate attention would require an event of a rather different caliber than, say, a feral cat delivering a litter of kittens in the City Hall men's bathroom.

I'd assumed that we'd be spending the night in whatever passed for the local lockup, which wasn't nearly as upsetting a notion as it should have been. A cell, at least, wouldn't be moving, and while it might be nothing more than a room with straw on the floor, there could be a possibility of a meal, or even just a long drink of clean water. Hell, if we played our cards right, we might convince the jailer to hose us off and let us change into clothes that didn't stink.

You know you've reached a new low when jailhouse mystery stew and a cold shower are something to look forward to, but even those creature comforts were to be denied us that evening.

Ours was the last wagon to reach the guardhouse before the gates were shut, and from the guard's sullen expression, I thought we might not make it through. "Your business?" he asked brusquely, giving the wagon a once-over before he noticed that the four of us were restrained. "And what's the meaning of—"

"My wife's dead and half our town's ashes because of *her*," our captors' leader said, shoving one thick finger in my direction. "I want the queen's justice."

The guard peered at me—I could only imagine what a pathetic sight we made—then scowled at my accuser. "What, the fat one?"

"She's the Watcher," he insisted. "Came here, and the monsters followed. See?" He reached under my bench and produced my sword, showing the guard the ornate crystal-set hilt. "It's *Shadowbane*!"

"We know how it sounds," an older man cut in before the guard could turn us away, "and had I not seen it with my own eyes, I'd have thought us crazy, too. But there were three of them, *horrible* things taller than a house. This lot showed up out of nowhere while the creatures were trying to kill us. She told us herself who she is," he added, nodding in my direction. "And now my eldest son is dead, and a granddaughter besides, and—"

The guard lifted a hand to silence him. "You're not the first to speak of Outsiders in the country in the last days. Get her off the cart."

One of the men untied my ankle, then slung me over his shoulder like a grain sack and deposited me on my knees in front of the guard. I kept my head down, feeling the bite of the uneven stone through my stiff leggings, and focused on the water just below us to still my racing mind. Yes, the river was lifeless and stank like sunbaked pond mud, but it was near, *so* near, and if I reached out, if I called…

A hand caught me under the chin and raised my head until I was facing the guard. That close to him, I could see the bags beneath his dark eyes, the wart on the side of his bulbous nose, and the strands of gray in his otherwise brown stubble. More than that, I saw the green crystal set in the pendant over his maille shirt—a translator, perhaps. "The gods demand truth," he told me with a flash of yellowed teeth, his fingers squeezing my jaw. "Who are you, girl?"

I suppose I could have lied, but at that hour, after our journey, I didn't see the point. "Susan Cole. The Watcher."

His eyes widened at the admission. "You know what the penalty is for desertion, do you?"

"Can't desert what you never agreed to defend."

He grunted and released me. "Either mad or suicidal, that one," he told the men. "Are you certain—"

I'm not sure what came over me then, but after the ride, the drugging, the binding, the gagging, the hunger, and the thirst, I finally snapped. Behind me, my sword leapt from its scabbard and sliced through the ropes pinning my arms. They fell away before my captors could so much as cry out in alarm, and I felt my fingers wrap around the hilt as I pushed myself to my feet. "Did I *stutter*?" I demanded of the startled guard, who backpedaled at the shock of finding me free and armed. "Yes, I'm the Watcher. My companions and I have been *abused* for two days because we stopped to help these ingrates save their shitty town, and I have had *enough*." Wheeling on their leader, who had also taken a few self-protecting steps away from me, I said, "I'm really sorry about your wife. I feel awful about what happened to your people, and believe me, I never wished any harm on you. But you're not the one who's been trapped by a goddamned magic sword, so don't start yapping about duty and blame. Now," I said, turning back to the guard, "I want a bath, I want a hot meal, and I want a bed with *minimal* bugs in it, is that clear? Or do you need further proof that I am who I say I am?"

He didn't. Within seconds of ending my rant, I found myself surrounded by half a dozen of the guard's colleagues, each of whom had a sword as large as mine—and, I reasoned, probably a few more lessons in how to wield one. I considered them for a long, tense moment, then lowered the point of my blade to the cobblestones and said, "I'll come quietly. But I think you could show me the courtesy of a bath before we do anything else."

I was wrong. The guards disarmed me at sword-point, then pulled my companions off the wagon and started to march us into the city.

But I had one more trick up my sleeve. With a thought, the sword again flew from its scabbard a few feet away, *snick*ed through the ropes binding the others, and came to rest in my hand. "Shadowbane likes me," I told the spooked guards as their hands went to their own weapons. "And since *she's* a princess of Blackhorn Mountain and *he's* a prince of Nokan'ti, maybe you boys should show a modicum of fucking respect, hmm?"

The guards looked at Anji and Fanakel, who nodded silently as they rubbed their stiff shoulders. "Did…did you know this?" the first guard asked our captors, who suddenly seemed to want nothing more than to drive their wagon out of town.

"Uh…I mean…that is…" their leader stuttered. "Um…no?"

"They said nothing about that!" another man protested. "Not a word—"

"Because you gagged us and put us to sleep, you moronic rube!" Anji shouted, then looked at the guard in time to see his comprehension register. "You have a proper translator there, lad? Excellent. Give these idiots the abbreviated version. They want *justice* so badly? Believe me, Erianthe will hear *all* about this, and if I don't have satisfaction, then she'll hear from my *father*."

I didn't know how much of that was bluster, but it had the desired effect. The guard mumbled the gist of her outburst to the men, and as they paled, Anji snapped, "They may bring our belongings behind us. I assure you," she said, staring down their leader as the guard offered his hasty translation, "if a single *stitch* of my pack has been torn by your ill-treatment, you'll wish the Outsiders had ripped you apart. And what are *you* waiting for?" she asked the other guards, who still seemed uncertain of whether to try to disarm me again. "I'll not stand here all night. Take us to Erianthe. *Now*."

Anji might not have been the most feminine of princesses, but she had perfected the "angry royal" act. As the guards escorted us into a proper carriage and our terrified captors tripped over themselves in their rush to be rid of our gear, Mia slid into the seat beside Anji and leaned close. "Would you be offended," she murmured, "if I told you that was *hot*?"

"Susan started it," she quietly replied.

"Yeah, but you're better at it."

Anji said nothing further, but as I was facing her, even in the shadowed carriage, I couldn't help but see the faint smile hiding behind her beard.

# CHAPTER 16

The journey through Deoni took about half an hour, as the evening streets seemed clogged with pedestrians who couldn't be bothered to make way. Then again, it was hard to say what, exactly, the holdup might have been. The guards had locked our doors from the outside and covered the windows with curtains before we departed, warning us not to touch them, and so my view of the city was limited to a thin gap in the scarlet fabric. Through it, I caught glimpses of stone buildings, of wooden fruit stands, of lanterns being lit, but little of Deoni itself.

There was little change in elevation that I could feel as we bumped along—the area around the capital was a glorified floodplain, and I suspected that the city wall did as much to keep the river out as it did to deter invaders. After a time, the evening sounds of the city grew dimmer, and we paused while one of the guards spoke to another of his comrades manning an iron gate set into yet another stone wall. The gate rose, and we trundled through, now veering around what seemed to be a tall, fat tower. The carriage rolled over a short bridge, and when I strained through the gap, I could see that we were crossing a dry channel. Perhaps the river had once been diverted through the castle for drinking water, I mused, but it wasn't any longer. The channel ended in bricked-over holes in the walls on both sides, the baked yellow clay like bandages against the gray stone.

As we rumbled over the pavement—which, though uneven, was an engineering marvel after the trip we'd had—Fanakel leaned toward the middle of the carriage and spoke as softly as he could while still being heard over the creaking of the wheels and the slap of chiquiw feet. "Has anyone come up with a plan yet?"

"Tell the truth and hope than Erianthe is more hospitable than your dad?" I replied.

"I mean, as long as we're being honest," said Mia, "I prefer the reception we had in Nokan'ti to the Darili style of hospitality."

"Agreed," Anji muttered. "Tell anyone I said that, elf, and I'll deny it to whatever gods you like."

He chuckled, but the sound spoke more of weariness than amusement. "Right, then. Susan, make your plea. I can try to apply a bit of diplomatic pressure, assuming Father hasn't sent word already, and Anji…"

"We have relations with Daril," she said. "I can apply pressure as well."

"Good," said Fanakel. "Mia, stay silent and let me speak for you."

The inside of the carriage was too dark for me to see their faces by then, but I could well imagine how Mia bristled at that. "*Excuse* me?" she said. "What kind of bullshit—"

"If they learn that you're tekorish, you're as good as dead. Follow my lead if you would prefer to continue living."

"He's right," said Anji. "You think you can play this, lad?"

"I'm counting on it." He grunted as we hit an unexpected bump, then exhaled slowly. "Nothing to fear. All I have in my stomach now is bile."

"You say that, but you're not the one sitting in the splash zone," Mia replied.

"No, but I have vomit stains on these clothes already, so I'm in no mood to make the matter worse. I'm burning this shirt as soon as I have the chance."

"You and me both, man." She paused, then said, "In

case whatever you're planning doesn't work, thanks for trying. And nice shooting back there. I'd have said something a day and a half ago, but, you know…"

His soft laughter that time seemed more genuine. "Likewise."

"And if I don't get another chance," she continued, "again, I'm sorry for getting you into this mess."

"I'm sorry for dragging *all* of you into this," I added. "Don't know how I can make the last three days up to you…like, *ever*…but I'm really grateful to not be alone."

To my surprise, Fanakel nudged me in the side. "You sound like we've failed already, girl. Try to be positive."

"I'm serious," I protested.

"As am I. Pray to your gods, by all means, but trust that they'll send aid." The seat creaked as he leaned back and sighed. "I haven't been here since the wedding. Wonder if she's redecorated. The river certainly smells worse than it did then. It had only been dead a few months when they married."

"You attended?" asked Anji with what sounded like actual curiosity.

"In Father's guard. Housed in the castle, if not seated near the head table. I thought Rokund came for the ceremonies."

"Oh, *he* did, but I was a lass barely on the edge of thirty. Several of my sisters and brothers accompanied him—the ones more likely to inherit and less likely to embarrass the kingdom. Never mind that the joining couple were younger than me. I heard about the feast long after the fact."

"That damned wine," Fanakel muttered. "It's made with the little berries they cultivate near the sea, what—"

"Kirit?"

"*Ugh*, yes. We had barrels of the stuff to entertain us while the dignitaries had their time with the newlyweds. Just the smell is enough to turn my stomach now." I felt him shudder beside me. "I drank far too much kirit on top of a dinner of those Cirivanti meat pies, the ones with the dried fruit, you know—"

"Why anyone would put fruit in a meat pie is a question for the Divine," Anji muttered.

"I know, right?" he exclaimed. "But...let's just say that I made some poor choices that evening, and I never want to see one of those pies again."

"Whose wedding, anyway?" Mia asked.

"Erianthe and Narod of Cirivant," said Anji.

"Quite the affair," Fanakel added. "And politically advantageous for both. Cirivant is the wealthiest of the human countries in Ga'besh—its navy is without peer anywhere in the four worlds. But while wealth is nice, prestige is better, and Daril far surpasses Cirivant on that count."

"Narod is one of the younger sons of the Terol house, if I recall," Anji offered.

"Correct, and far outclassed by Erianthe. But through the marriage, Daril gained an alliance with Cirivant and protection for its trading posts in Ga'besh, while Cirivant gained the assurance that a child of the Terol line would sit the Darili throne someday. A child bearing the Fulquir name, to be sure, but one with blood in Cirivant all the same."

"Ever met the crown prince?" Anji asked him.

Fanakel snorted. "You sound unenthusiastic."

"As would you, had you entertained him. Erianthe, Narod, and Edes visited Father three years ago. The lad's manners impressed no one."

"To be fair, he's yet a boy."

"He's a man by their reckoning. You know how humans are."

"*Mm.* Yes."

I pointedly cleared my throat. "Hey, y'all? Remember us?"

"No offense intended to present company," Anji soothed. "And seeing as this is hardly a state visit, perhaps we'll be spared his delightful conversation."

Mia answered that with a quiet snort. "Dare I ask *how* delightful?"

The princess hesitated, then stiffly said, "There were certain suggestions made to the female domestic staff that they were of an ideal height to perform particular...*functions*...for him. I will leave the details to your imagination. Fortunately, these suggestions came to an end when two of my sisters pulled him aside and threatened to break every bone in his face if he made another chambermaid cry."

With a sudden jolt, the carriage came to a halt, and I spotted the glow of torches through the curtains. The doors were unlocked, and one of our guards opened the pair on my side, though he stepped back as soon as he saw me. "This way. Leave your weapons."

"Can't," I reminded him, and pointed to the sword at my feet. "Remind me, wasn't one of you carrying that?"

He sharply beckoned to another guard, who turned to reveal my sword's empty scabbard still strapped to his back.

"It follows me," I said, shrugging. "So either it can show up unannounced, or you can let me have it now and save us all the surprise."

They didn't like that one bit, but there was little to be gained by arguing with a magic sword. Reluctantly, they handed me the scabbard, and I hooked the bungee cord around my waist, feeling ever so slightly reassured by the weight against my leg. I sheathed the sword, showed the men that I had no other weapons, and moved aside to let Fanakel out. "Satisfied?" I asked them.

The nearest gave me a sour look. "Threaten Her Majesty, and we'll cut you down where you stand."

The carriage had come to rest inside a castle courtyard. Once the four of us had disembarked, we were hustled through a pair of wooden doors twice my height and along a maze of well-guarded corridors until we reached an apparent vestibule, a waiting room set with overstuffed couches—the sort designed for one to perch on the edge and sip tea, not for lounging—and a pale lilac carpeting that had probably never seen such abuse as the gunk we tracked in. Instructing us to wait, our entourage closed the doors through which we'd come, and I heard the shuffling of guards resuming their positions on the other side. I was pleased to see that the angry villagers had been detained outside—better to face the queen without a shouting mob at my back, I thought—but when I caught sight of myself in the gilded mirror hanging above one of the couches, I almost wished for the distraction the mob would have brought.

If one were feeling charitable, I looked like I'd been dragged through a scummy pond, rolled in dirt, and allowed to bake in the sun for a few days. To be fair, this wasn't far from the truth, but the visual evidence made me seem more like a madwoman than the reasonable, sympathetic figure I was trying to portray. My waves had turned into a frizzy brown snarl that might once have been hair but was quickly evolving into a tumbleweed. The quick wash I'd had in the stream had rinsed some of the ichor away, but several of the patches had proven more resilient, and I sported black streaks down my face like I'd been interrupted in an application of camouflage paint. The rest of my exposed skin was pink with the sunburn I'd felt coming on, and the long, puckered red scar on my face added the cherry to the shit sundae of my appearance. The mirror only showed me the wreckage from the chest up, but I knew already that my clothes were ruined, stained and stinking from the trip. Never had I so missed Uncle Malachi's temperamental washing machine.

My companions had fared little better. Sure, Mia still looked like a knockout, albeit one who'd come off a hard night of mud wrestling only to be shortchanged with the shower and left too long in a tanning bed. Anji, who had greater hair coverage than any of us, seemed to have fared the best on the sunburn front, but the apples of her cheeks had gone well beyond a healthy pink, and the neat braids of her beard had given way to matted snarls—were I in her filthy boots, I'd have considered shaving it all off and starting over just to avoid the painful detangling. And then there was Fanakel, whose red, inflamed skin had already begun to peel around his nose and forehead. His once silky red tresses had turned almost brown for want of washing, and the lower half of his face was covered in a three-day growth of ginger stubble. Whoever his human grandfather had been, the man had to have produced impressive facial hair.

Glimpsing himself in the glass beside me, Fanakel groaned. "Oh, this is a *disaster*," he muttered, running his hands over his cheeks and chin as if he could buff the offending hair away.

"I don't know," I said, "it blends with the sunburn."

He laughed, though it sounded more like a sob, and shook his head. "I can't imagine we'd look or smell any better had we been eaten by an Outsider and come out the other end. This is humiliating. At least they could allow us to wash before seeing Erianthe…"

"We're being assessed by the rightness of our cause, not by our beauty," Anji chimed in. "And what are you complaining about? I had a better beard at *ten*, lad."

"That was meant to be reassuring?" he asked, cocking an eyebrow.

"Would you settle for distracting? I hate to see a grown man cry over something so trivial."

"It's not *trivial*. Let me just take my shame out and parade it around—"

"Again," Mia interrupted, "hi, there, remember the human members of this party?"

"You're—"

"At least half and raised human, so if you'd quit whining like it's the worst fate imaginable, I'd feel *ever* so much better," she said, folding her arms. "And you can have an existential crisis on your own time, bub. We need you to go all-out elf."

Anji frowned. "For *what*?"

"You said yourself that our odds would be better if the Twins interceded with Daril," Mia reminded her. "How quickly does news travel around here?"

"News?"

"Of, say, our early departure from Nokan'ti with *him*."

Anji cut her eyes to Fanakel, gave him a long moment of study, then looked back at Mia with a sly smile. "Unless the Twins have spread the word with a maladeta...probably not that quickly. Crossing the desert takes time, and if there are Outsiders at large, one would take precautions. An armed band, not a lone rider."

"So, say, if a prince of Nokan'ti were to show up here tonight, and Daril was quickly convinced to free Suze..."

"They might break the bind before anyone was the wiser as to the Twins' true feelings," she finished, then met Fanakel's worried stare. "How much of an ass can you be?"

He cleared his throat. "Meaning—"

"The full True Child treatment. Can you do that?"

"I hardly think that constitutes being an ass," he began, then saw our expressions and paused. "Oh, come now, you must understand—"

"Don't *even* start that again," Mia interrupted.

"But—"

I managed to silence him when I grabbed his shoulders and looked him in the eye. "You come from a *weird* cultural place. We get that. But just because it's what you've always been taught doesn't make it right. And you know what else?" I said, leaning closer to him. "You're *better* than they are. I don't care why you're here—you're *here*, and you're trying to help me, and I appreciate the hell out of that. But with all that said, the 'True Children' are a bunch of jerks."

"We're not jealous of you," said Anji with a smirk. "We

just think you're insufferable idiots...and blasphemers, but that's a matter for another time."

"But you're all right," I added as I released Fanakel. "I mean it. And now, if you could act like a prince of Nokan'ti, that would be *swell.*"

"I, uh...I'll see what I can do," he mumbled, slumping, then gave Anji a sidelong glance. "'Insufferable idiots'? Truly?"

She shrugged. "Talk to a non-elf. You might learn something. Now, did anyone think to carry a comb?"


**T**he Darili throne room was less impressive to me than that of Nokan'ti, if only because it lacked the exotic factor of being part of a massive treehouse complex. As throne rooms went, it seemed perfectly serviceable—not that I had much experience to go on in making that assessment, of course. Stone walls dotted with arched windows rose to a peaked wooden ceiling painted like the sky: sunset over the door, a starry night in the middle of the long room, and sunrise over the gilded thrones at the far end. Statues of men and women in fabulously colored clothing were posed at intervals among the windows—Daril's garish answer to a royal portrait gallery, I surmised. They competed for space with the armed guards, who clustered near the royal dais and around the doors.

Though night had fallen by the time we were ushered inside and ordered to the front, the queen appeared to still be on the clock. I studied her as we drew near, or at least as well as I could from what I could see between the pair of guards who marched in front of us. She was handsome enough, maybe in her mid-forties, a thin woman with a head full of perfectly styled chestnut ringlets pinned around a tiara—a golden piece set with the blue-green gems I'd come to know so well. A coordinating gold necklace set with a large Aen crystal was draped around her neck. Her burgundy gown dipped low over her slight chest and flared into a skirt in which any little girl playing dress-up would have proudly twirled. From a distance, she appeared regal, calmly sitting on her throne and waiting for us to draw near. But as we approached, I saw the truth more clearly. Her face seemed unnaturally pinched, as if she'd been fasting for a month, and her blue eyes were too large above her prominent cheekbones. Her rouged lips pressed together into a severe gash, while her hands had tightened on the carved armrests as if they were the only thing preventing her from springing from her seat with her teeth bared.

The guards ahead of us reached the dais first and bowed low. "Your Majesty," the more senior of the pair began, "these are the captives we—"

She silenced him with a curt wave and stood, the better to stare down at the four of us lurking on her nice rug like refugees from a hurricane. "Who are you?" she said, her voice low and firm. "The gods demand truth. *Who are you*, and what you doing in *my* lands?"

Anji and Fanakel exchanged brief side-eyed glances, and she took the lead. "Queen Erianthe," she said, stepping forward and offering a polite nod to the throne. "I am Anjikora of Blackhorn Mountain. This was not the way we had intended to intrude upon Your Majesty, and I ask your forgiveness for that."

For a woman who looked like she'd been dragged halfway to hell and back, Anji was remarkably civil, and her soft tone seemed to put the queen slightly more at ease.

"This is Susan," she continued, beckoning for me to join her. "She's come from beyond the Crossing in search of help. Of *justice*. My father believes in her cause, and so he sent me to assist her—"

"Stop," Erianthe interrupted, then pointed to me. "Are you the Watcher, girl, yes or no?"

"Apparently," I replied, trying to adopt Anji's placating mode, and patted the sword at my side. "I came home three days after my uncle died and found *this* waiting. It won't leave me alone, and there's an endless parade of monstrosities coming after me. I didn't agree to *any* of this," I said, and hoped my bedraggled appearance gave my plea that much more pathos. "I didn't even know the Watcher existed until about two weeks ago. Now I can't leave my hometown...well, back beyond the Crossing, I mean. I'm stuck living in my uncle's lousy cabin in the woods so my old neighbors don't get attacked by Outsiders, and the damn things just *keep coming*. Every night, they come after me." I could hear myself speeding up, but I was in no position to practice my public speaking. "And they wouldn't bother us at all if you people hadn't made the sword and forced us to fight your battles for you. We're outside the Aen—they wouldn't come if not for you. It's not fair."

The queen stared down at me in stone-faced silence, and I tried again. "The sword is ruining my life. It trapped my uncle, and his uncle before him, and a whole line of people going back five hundred years. *Five hundred years*, now, you've had a reprieve at our expense. What did we ever do to you? What did *I* do to you?"

"The lass is young," Anji added. "Untrained at arms. Why Heart's Blood chose her is a mystery, but the fact that we rely upon a conscripted Watcher who gains nothing from the arrangement is unjust. Surely Daril must see that."

Erianthe ignored her, instead turning her attention to Fanakel. "And you are?"

I looked behind me in time to catch his raised eyebrow. Sure, it probably wasn't visible from the throne, seeing as his red hair blended so nicely into his sunburn, but the attitude was on full display. "I am of Nokan'ti," he said, his voice dripping with disdain. "And I have been *grievously* mistreated by your people, Erianthe."

I'd expected a reaction when he called her by name, but she seemed unfazed. Then again, I reasoned, if Daril had dealings with elves, she was probably used to it.

"Of Nokan'ti, you say?" Her mouth ticked into a brief smirk. "Surely not of a marriage bed."

"No," he replied, and examined his dirty cuticles. "Was that meant to insult me? Your ways can be so provincial—it's difficult to tell."

A flush began to creep into her cheeks, but Erianthe didn't rise to the bait.

"In any case," Fanakel continued, rubbing a bit of grime from one fingernail, "you're fortunate. Had I sprung from my father's consort, you would be facing the prospect of war for my ill-treatment. As the matter stands, you can still expect his severe displeasure. One does not abuse the True without repercussions, *especially* not those of us born of the royal blood." Buffing his nails against his shirt—which, truth be told, probably just made them dirtier—he finally looked back at the queen with utter contempt. "How does Daril intend to make amends?"

But she wasn't to be cowed. "And you?" she asked, pointing to Mia.

"The girl warms my bed," said Fanakel, lazily twirling a finger through Mia's tangles. "One should not travel without base comforts, and she..." He chuckled to himself. "Base, certainly, but comfortable enough. Isn't that right, little pretty?"

Mia, bless her, played her part. Casting her eyes at the rug, she didn't so much as stiffen when Fanakel snaked his arm around her waist and pulled her close.

I held my breath, but Erianthe seemed to buy the act and ceased her probing of Mia. "A younger daughter of Blackhorn Mountain, a bastard of Nokan'ti, and a runaway Watcher. A strange company—and a weak message from your fathers, *if* there is a message to be sent at all," she told Fanakel and Anji. "As for you," she said, turning her stare on me, "how dare you neglect your sacred duty? You have been ordained—"

"No, I *haven't*," I snapped, holding up my hands as if I

could push her off the dais. "And it's not a sacred duty. It's all of *you* deciding to shit on *us*. You made that decision, not some god. So don't lie to me like I'm a fool. *You* have the power to free me from this damn curse. Do the right thing."

A few of the guards stiffened, but Erianthe didn't flinch at my anger. "The right thing is to protect my people and this world," she murmured. "To honor the pact my forefather made to defend our lands. And now there are *Outsiders* in Kopaat? On this continent? In Daril itself?" Her voice began to rise as her own temper flared. "You deserted your post, and my people have suffered for it. How dare you?"

The guilt that had hounded me on the journey rose up to claw at me once again, but I slammed it back and stood my ground. "It's not my post! How dare *I*? How dare *you* try to force your problems onto me? If you want a Watcher so badly, assign one of your own soldiers to stand by the tunnels. Leave my people out of this!"

"Impossible," said the queen, resuming her seat as she replaced her mask of calm. "And unacceptable. You will return to the Crossing and do your duty. As for *you*," she said, pointing to Anji and Fanakel with two thin fingers, "you will remain here as my guests for the night, and I will see you escorted to the tunnel in the morning. I trust you can make your own way home from there."

"Your Majesty," Anji began, once more placating, "if you would just consider—"

But I was tired of begging. I was tired of the runaround, of blame for deaths I hadn't caused, of orders to roll over and do as my betters instructed me.

"*No*," I said, folding my arms, and locked eyes with Erianthe. "*That* is unacceptable."

She seemed taken aback—I suppose she wasn't accustomed to being denied to her face—but recovered quickly. "You refuse to do the task ordained for you?" she asked, holding my stare.

"*Ordained*, my ass. And the answer is no."

"Very well." Settling back against her throne, she smoothed her skirt, then quietly sighed. "This gives me no pleasure, but the administration of justice is seldom a delight. I hold you responsible, Watcher, for every death in this land caused by Outsiders. Before your arrival, the count was twenty-seven..." She paused as a guard jogged up the dais to whisper in her ear, then nodded and dismissed him. "Forty-three now, perhaps more. I understand that you allowed an entire town to be destroyed."

"We stopped to *help* them," Fanakel interrupted, indignant. "They might all have died had we not assisted them. And their thanks left us as you see us now! There is *vomit* on this shirt!"

She ignored his outburst. "Forty-three deaths, Watcher. I've had men executed for one."

"I didn't kill those people," I said, fighting the urge to grab the sword for reassurance.

"Your actions did. And since you have proven yourself unworthy of wielding Shadowbane, you will die at dawn, and the sword may choose a new Watcher."

"Wait, now," said Anji, "let's think about this—"

"Your father can do as he pleases," the queen replied, cutting her short. "*If* he is, in fact, your father."

Anji jerked as if she'd been slapped. "Do you doubt my word, Your Majesty?"

"I don't know. What I *do* know is that if Rokund and the Twins wanted to get my attention, they would have sent emissaries more prominent than a lesser daughter and half-blooded bastard—and the Twins, especially, would have sent their desires in writing, sealed," she added, giving Fanakel a withering look. "So to answer your question, if Rokund is indeed your father, then he may do as he likes. I choose to protect my people." She snapped her fingers, and half a dozen guards came running. "Take the condemned to a holding cell, and make our guests comfortable," she said, never looking away from my face. "And see that they don't go wandering in the night."

At least they left a washtub in my cell. The water inside was cold, and there was no soap, but hey, small mercies.

I hoped the others had been given guest rooms with real beds and toilet facilities better than a bucket in the corner. They deserved it after the hell we'd been through of late. As for me, I had a drafty room near the top of a tower that might have offered a lovely view were it not dark, the window not barred, and my mind not preoccupied with thoughts of death.

I'd never imagined that two weeks from my twenty-third birthday, I'd be passing the night alone on a straw-stuffed pallet, trying to puzzle a way out of mortal peril by the light of a single weak candle. Damp but cleaner than I'd been in days, I huddled in the corner of the cell, listening to the rain increase in tempo.

She was going to kill me. Erianthe was going to *kill* me. All I'd wanted was my freedom—my life—and she planned to execute me for the audacity.

Maybe, a tiny part of me suggested, I could reason with her. I could agree to go back to the Crossing and fight monsters for the rest of my days, just like Uncle Malachi...but what kind of life was *that*? I couldn't live that life. I *wouldn't*.

But what was the alternative? A swift trip through the end stages of the Darili justice system?

My musings were probably for naught, anyway. The queen hadn't been inclined to listen to reason, so all of this speculation was me banking on the hope that she'd feel differently about executing me after a good night's sleep.

Restless, I uncurled from the pallet and walked to the window. I'd left my sword in the corner of the room—the guards had taken it, but it had reappeared of its own accord ten minutes later like my silent shadow, still attached to its bungee belt. I knew I couldn't fight my way out of the cell—the door was thick and locked tight, and once it slammed, no visitation had followed.

They could have at least sent me a priest. Not that I knew jack about Darili religious systems, but it would have been nice to talk to *someone*.

Having passed a few hours in near darkness, when I peered through the vertical bars, I found that my eyes had adjusted sufficiently to make out the scenery below: a courtyard surrounded by the ubiquitous stone walls. It looked like a garden—not a manicured landscape like Versailles, but more like sculpted wilderness, the tops of tall trees and flatter patches that might have been grass or flowers, their colors and shapes obscured by night and rain. What caught my attention, though, was the serpentine gravel path gouged through the garden. It terminated at the wall...and as I strained for details, I realized that I was seeing the back side of one of the yellow brick patches. It seemed that the river had once flowed through the courtyard as a tamed, miniaturized version of the wide water outside the city, a decorative element in the faux woods and meadows of the castle garden. Given the river's current state, I could imagine why the castle's occupants had let the channel run dry.

Staring out at the night, I tried in vain to formulate an escape plan. The door was no use to me, nor the window—the bars were set too closely together for me to squeeze through, and in any case, my cell was at least eighty feet above the ground. I was no mountain climber, and even if I managed to get a few good handholds on the wet stone tower, I was guaranteed a long fall—painful at best, but probably fatal. The sword could set fire to an Outsider, but I didn't think it would be capable of burning through steel and morphing into a parachute.

I found no answers in the night, so I returned to my pallet, a canvas bag so poorly stuffed that I could feel the cold floor on my back. Frustrated and tense, I sat up and stared across the room at the sad washtub. I couldn't see its contents—which, considering my state before bathing, was for the best—but if I was still and focused my attention, I could feel the water's presence. Locked up as I was, I had time to experiment, and as it seemed like a better alternative to frantic sobbing, I decided to see what I could do in the few hours I had left.

Calling the rain had been a marathon, an endeavor that had taken mental strength I hadn't known I possessed. Bending the bathwater to my will was a one-mile fun run by comparison. A moment's thought and a touch of power pulled the water from the tub in a dark column that glinted in the weak candlelight. I separated a glob of water from its source like pulling off a bite of taffy and formed it into a rotating sphere, then split it into three and called the balls across the room to my bed. They hovered before me, and I reached out to cup one in my hands. The skin of the ball was damp and cool but left no trace of moisture on my palms—an impossibility, but yet, there it was.

I was still marveling at the spheres I'd made when I heard the tumblers in the rusty lock begin to squeal. Startled, I dropped the two floating spheres, which exploded into puddles on the floor, but the third remained cupped in my hands, quivering like a living thing. One makeshift water balloon wouldn't stop a determined executioner, but it would give me a moment to go for my sword.

To my surprise, however, it wasn't a black-hooded figure come to lead me to the chopping block. With a nod to the guard stationed outside my cell, Erianthe herself slipped through the door and closed it behind her. She'd exchanged her burgundy dress for a plainer number in pale blue—a nightgown, I surmised—beneath a heavy brown cloak, and she'd lost the crown over the course of the evening, though her waves were still perfectly coiffed.

"What are you doing here?" I asked as she blinked in the darkness. I'd seen a sliver of torchlight beyond the door, and Erianthe was probably relying as much on her hearing as her sight to locate me in the cell.

"I've been thinking." She crossed her arms and started to lean against the wall, then jerked away from the chill. "The dwarf was right—you *are* rather young. You've done a terrible thing, you know, but perhaps certain penalties could be lessened because of your youth."

"You're…letting me go?" I asked, trying not to get my hopes up even as my heart leapt.

"I will allow you to return to the Crossing and do your duty."

Disappointment grabbed my heart and yanked it back down. "That's hardly a better option."

"You've been chosen as the Watcher. It's a noble calling," she replied. "Live a life in service to a greater purpose. Your work will keep the peoples of our worlds safe and give them peace—"

"Oh, like the War of the True Children I've been hearing so much about?" I retorted. "I take away your common enemy, and you have loads of free time to kill each other."

Erianthe winced. "An unfortunate conflict, to be certain, but long since resolved. We are at peace now, and you can help maintain that. Help a generation of children yet unborn grow up in safety. Isn't that worth the sacrifice?"

I said nothing.

"A *noble* sacrifice," the queen insisted. "Your life will have great purpose."

"Then why not let someone who *wants* the job serve that great purpose?"

She shrugged beneath her cloak. "You were chosen. We cannot know the reason, but the sword selected *you*." When I didn't cheer at that, Erianthe tried a different approach. "You'll bring honor to your family. Your parents—"

At that, I couldn't hold back my incredulous laughter.

"My *family*? That damn thing has cursed my family for generations! My uncle, *his* uncle, back for hundreds of years. Let someone else's family have a turn with it!"

"Surely your family was proud of your uncle."

"My only family was my uncle and my dad, and both of them are dead. They never even *mentioned* the Watcher thing because they hoped it would spare me. So don't tell me how proud my family will be when this is the exact thing they didn't want to happen."

"What of your mother, then?"

"What of her?" I muttered. The watery ball in my hands began to spin as my agitation rose, and I tossed it into the air as I fidgeted. Solo catch was better than nothing.

"She would be proud of your service," said Erianthe. "A mother would understand sacrifice."

I snorted, caught the ball, and tossed it again. "If you ever find her, be sure to ask her. She abandoned me."

By then, the queen's eyes had begun to adjust, and she finally noticed what I was doing. "Is that…*what* is…"

"This?" I tossed the sphere her way, and she gasped as her hands closed around it. "Just something I've been messing with. Got a little talent with water, it seems."

She turned the ball over, inspecting it, and I caught the glint of candlelight on its surface. When she underhanded it back to me, she took a step closer, and her voice seemed oddly strained as she spoke. "Abandoned, you said?"

"Yeah." Tiring of the exercise, I tossed the sphere into the washtub and let it rejoin the dirty bath. "When my uncle found me, I was a naked, filthy newborn with a few ant bites, alone in the woods. Thanks for nothing, Mom."

I'd expected at least sympathetic noises from the queen, but her reply surprised me. "That explains everything," she said softly. "Why Shadowbane chose you. This is *fated*, Watcher."

"Huh?"

"Some years ago," she said, folding her arms again, "a

princess of Daril became infatuated with an elemental."
She hesitated, then murmured, "A *water* elemental. The girl
was young, naïve, she thought what she was feeling was
the first stirrings of love. And she gave herself to him."

Lost for words, I simply gaped and let her continue.

"Soon enough, she discovered that she was carrying his
child. A rogue elemental. Rather than allow
her...*indiscretion*...to bring shame to the throne and to
Daril, she concealed her pregnancy until her time had
nearly come. And then she took herself out of this world,
through the tunnels, and beyond the Aen."

My guts twisted as Erianthe told the tale. "You
mean..."

The queen spoke with as much emotion as if she were
reading a grocery list. "She went to the world beyond the
Crossing and found herself in a wooded place. And there,
all alone, she delivered the child, then made herself decent
and left it there to succumb. Couldn't bring herself to kill
it. She returned to Daril with no one the wiser."

Horrified, I sank onto my pallet before my knees could
buckle. "You...you think—"

"You would be of approximately the correct age. And
that *little* talent is anything but. Has anyone suggested to
you that you might be of elemental extraction?"

I was too stunned to think of lying to her. "Yes. An
elemental, actually."

"Then I suppose the princess was mistaken about the
fate of the child."

"What's her name?" I blurted.

I couldn't quite make out Erianthe's face in the
darkness, but she sounded perplexed. "Her name?"

"You think she's my mother, right? What's her name?"

"Why should that matter?" she replied. "She obviously
didn't want you."

"My father, then," I begged. "Does he know I exist?
Who is he?"

"He is none of your concern, Watcher—"

"*Susan*. My name is Susan. Please, I won't bother them, I just want answers, if—"

"You were your mother's great shame," she interrupted. "That is all you need to know. But don't you see how this was fated?" she continued, drawing closer to me. "A child of Daril now guards the Crossing. You were meant to die, but as you live, you can do your duty and erase some of your shame—"

"What *shame*?" I protested. "I've done nothing wrong! If my mother feels bad about what she did, that's her business. I'm not going to feel guilty for being alive."

"Then your sacrifice will restore some of her honor," Erianthe suggested. "You will protect your homeland and ensure its prosperity, and your life will have meaning. *Worth*. Wouldn't you like that?"

Gutted though I was, the spark of indignation within me flared as the queen cajoled me back into servitude. "My life had *plenty* of worth without this bullshit destiny being foisted upon me. You can't make me guard the Crossing. I *won't*."

"A pity, then," she said with a soft sigh, and headed for the door. "But you are young, Watcher, and I'll afford you time to think about your choice. At first light, be prepared to return to your post or to meet the gods."

"Wait," I began, but before I could run to stop her, she had left the room, and the key was turning in the lock. "Tell me their names!" I cried, hammering on the door. "I just want their names! Please, give me *something*!"

But there was no answer, and I was left to my racing thoughts and the rumbling thunder of the storm outside the tower walls.

# CHAPTER 17

The candle was burning low, but I barely needed it with the lightning storm, which periodically lit my cell like a bluish strobe. Wet wind whipped though the bars and swirled around the room, keeping the candle teetering on the edge of snuffing out.

I could have moved it to a more sheltered spot, had I only been able to bring myself to leave my pallet.

Snapshots of my childhood fantasies flickered and faded in my mind: my loving biological parents, a kingdom all my own, some great misunderstanding that had taken me away from the people to whom I truly belonged, from *home*. As dearly as I loved Dad and Uncle Malachi, I'd indulged the dream of meeting someone who looked like me, someone who would have all the answers as to why I'd been left in the woods. Someone who would reassure me that I was wanted, that I'd been wanted all along—that I hadn't been thrown away.

Just remembering those notions made me sick to my stomach with embarrassment. The only thing I'd gotten right was an alleged princess. If Erianthe had been honest with me, my father probably didn't know that I'd ever existed, my mother had left me to die, and there was no place for me in Daril.

Strange, frantic thoughts come to mind when one is hours from one's execution. That night, I wondered what would happen if I could find my mother. If Erianthe wouldn't tell me, surely someone in the castle had to know. I could find her, reveal myself, and beg her to help me. She'd do that, wouldn't she? Maybe she hadn't wanted a baby, but if I went to her as an adult, just asking for my life and my freedom, wouldn't she give me a hand?

Of course, I'd have to find her first—and before that, I'd need a way out of my cell. And if Erianthe wouldn't so much as name my mother, then maybe I *was* a great shame. Maybe she'd want me dead just to keep the truth under wraps.

Did she have other children? Princes and princesses, my brothers and sisters who'd never known that I drew breath? Did she love them? Was she a good mother?

Did she ever think of me and wonder?

And my father...

Erianthe had said he was a water elemental, which fit with what the air elemental had suggested. But how would he have met a princess...

My breath caught in my throat as a strong gust blew out the candle. Of *course*.

The Falova River hadn't just flowed near the castle—it had flowed *into* the courtyard. Anji was somewhere in her fifties, and she said she'd been about thirty when the queen married. Fanakel said the river had been dead for months by that point. I couldn't be certain, but considering that timeline and my age...

The pieces began to fall into place for me. Erianthe had a wayward sister or cousin, someone too important to exile but not so prominent that she'd be sorely missed during her pregnancy. Someone had discovered the baby's father and used magic I couldn't begin to comprehend to rip him from the river and drag him out into the desert, where he would never be able to tell anyone what he'd done with the princess. And the Fulquirs would keep their scandal under wraps...until now. I'd lived.

Why had Erianthe divulged what she did? She could have kept that secret...but maybe she had a heart. Maybe she didn't want to kill a niece or a little cousin. I could leave, never return, and fight monsters until the day I died, doing my part for good old Daril, and that would solve everything: she wouldn't have to kill a family member, and I'd remove myself from the equation.

But if Erianthe or someone else looking out for the honor of the family had kidnapped my father, didn't I have an obligation to try to rescue him? Especially if he was in danger of dying with every drought. Maybe he didn't know he'd gotten that princess pregnant, maybe he wouldn't want me around, but did that matter?

I'd have done it for Dad. For Uncle Malachi.

I had to try.

Of course, there was the *tiny* matter of my incarceration and looming choice as to exile or execution, and unless lightning blasted a hole in the tower, I wasn't getting out.

Or so I thought.


I had a minor heart attack when I heard the lock turn again—it was far too early for dawn, and I hadn't yet worked out how I was going to avoid my bad options— but to my surprise, when the door opened, it wasn't Erianthe or a guard on the other side.

"Dark in here, isn't it?" said Anji. "All right, lass?"

The torchlight in the hallway illuminated Mia and Fanakel right behind her…and a guard, slumped unconscious on the floor. "What…how…" I stammered.

Mia, who was wearing both of our backpacks, looked unusually smug. "Funny how Daril's royal security force is all male."

"Humans are *terrible* about not training their women for combat," Anji added.

"Such a pity," said Mia with false sadness. "And you know, I haven't eaten much at all in the last few days, and dinner tonight was meager at best, and you know how hangry I can get…"

My jaw sagged even as I laughed aloud. "You *didn't*."

"Oh, but she did," said Fanakel, mincing into the room

with a poor impression of a sultry pout. "And they were helpless. Fascinating, really—well, from an observational standpoint."

"Don't worry, you're off the menu," she replied, elbowing him in the ribs. "But yeah, I distracted them and made them tell me where our gear was and where you were being kept, and then Fanakel knocked them out."

"With *what*?" I asked.

He started to rub the back of his sunburned neck, then flinched and pulled his hand away. "Magic. Our talents are strongest on living things. It's, um…it's generally considered an affront to the Divine to use them in such a fashion, but under the circumstances—"

"Better to ask forgiveness than permission," Mia finished. "And for the ones who took too long to pass out, Anji is *scarily* good at improvisation."

"If they didn't want me to use heavy books, they shouldn't have left a library in my guest suite," the princess replied primly. "I'm afraid that a few of Daril's finest soldiers will have nasty knots on their heads in the morning, but that can't be helped." Glancing around my cell, she said, "This is atrocious. Shall we flee now, or would you rather wait for dawn?"

I snatched up my sword, then took my pack from Mia. "How are we getting out? And there's something *weird* I need to tell you—"

"Later. Come with us, we'll take the stairs back down…" Anji paused as we stepped into the corridor, hearing the sound of heavy boots and angry voices echoing up the spiral staircase. "High Queen have mercy, what *now*?"

"My stunning abilities could be better," Fanakel admitted, then pointed to a thick rope dangling from the ceiling. "Trapdoor. We can hide."

He and Mia yanked on the pull-cord, opening a panel in the wooden ceiling, and a rope ladder tumbled down. We scrambled up, tugging the ladder behind us, and closed the trap only a moment before the footsteps rang on the stone of the floor below.

"They'll find us soon," said Anji. "Mia, if you can hypnotize them, maybe—"

"Or we get out," I interrupted, and pushed a heavy wooden box over the trapdoor.

Fanakel frowned. "That won't stop anyone."

"But it'll hurt like hell. This way."

The room at the top of the trapdoor was barely a room at all—rather, it was a platform with a low wall at the peak of the tower, the empty space between the final floor and the conical roof. There was nothing to hide behind except a few narrow support columns, and as I peered over the edge at the stormy night, I saw nothing resembling a fire escape.

"There's nowhere to go," said Mia. "We're going to have to fight our way back down the stairs—"

"Trust me," I murmured, and closed my eyes.

If the washtub in my cell had been like a candle, the river beyond the wall was a wildfire, brilliant in the strange place behind my eyes that I was just beginning to explore. Coupled with the pouring rain, the potential was nearly overwhelming—and now, with no walls and bars in my way, I could stretch my limits. Fear made me strong—fear of capture, of death, of never answering the questions that had dogged me all my life—and when I called to the river, it answered.

I opened my eyes and smiled as an enormous ball of water rose and floated over the wall, then paused in its ascent just below me. Hoping I hadn't been overly confident, I stepped atop the wall, crossed my fingers, and jumped onto the watery sphere. It sagged beneath my weight like a waterbed, and I breathed a quick sigh of relief as it held. "Come on," I called to my flabbergasted rescuers. "Before they—"

A crash from inside the tower told me that the trapdoor had been pulled and my impromptu boobytrap sprung. That was all the encouragement the others needed to pile aboard my improbable escape vehicle, and with a prayer to anyone listening that I could steer the damn thing, I aimed us for the river. We dropped with stomach-churning rapidity, but we skimmed over the wall and landed with barely a splash—certainly nothing audible beneath the cacophony of the storm. Holding the ball together, I piloted us down the river, letting the current carry us away from the fortifications of Deoni and into the night.

After a rough ten minutes on the river, Anji pointed to an upcoming fork. The broader stream carried on in a roughly straight course, but the spur headed into the woods on the far bank, and I thought of what the elemental had suggested earlier that day. I steered us down the shallow stream until I could see no light behind us. "Get ready to land," I warned the others, then tried my best to gradually shrink the sphere. Unfortunately, my control being somewhat questionable, I succeeded only in dispersing the water in all directions, dropping the four of us into cold, hip-deep water—well, hip-deep for everyone but Anji, who found herself submerged almost to the chin.

"Sorry," I mumbled as we dragged ourselves onto the mossy bank. "That could have been better. Drier."

"Are you kidding?" said Mia. "That was incredible! How'd you guess that the sword could do that?"

"It can't."

"Huh?"

"In a minute." I walked a few yards away from the water, into the relative shelter of the trees, and spotted a small clearing. "There's room enough to pitch the tents here. Let's get dry, and I'll tell you everything."


My ability to repel the rain seemed somewhat useless by that point, considering how soaked we were, but Fanakel insisted it was better late than never. I held together an invisible canopy as he and Mia set up the tents and unrolled sleeping bags, and then we took turns changing into dry clothes before cramming into the tent that Mia and Anji had claimed for a debriefing.

We didn't dare turn on a flashlight, which made my job easier. Unable to see the others' faces well, I quieted my ravenous stomach with a granola bar and told them about everything: my private word with Kingkiller, my long conversation with the air elemental who had saved our lives, and my disquieting visit from the queen. "If she's telling the truth," I concluded, "I think my biological father is Falova. I don't know who my mother is beyond a Darili and"—I laughed at the absurdity—"some sort of princess, I guess, but anyway, that's why I, uh...I seem to have a talent for moving water around."

There was no response for a long moment, and then Anji broke the silence with a soft, "High Queen have mercy."

"Look, I get it," I said in a rush, "rogue elementals are supposed to be unpredictable, but I—"

"Not *that*," Fanakel interrupted. "I'm traveling with a female tekori—your father isn't our greatest concern right now."

"I told you, you're off the menu," Mia protested. "And I only went after the queen's goons because it was a matter of *life and death*."

"I appreciate that, but I did just witness what you can do on an empty stomach." He cleared his throat. "Susan, I...I'm not certain of the best way to tell you this, but the only Darili princess currently alive is Erianthe's youngest child, and she can't be older than fifteen. The last princess before her was Erianthe herself, and *she* had no siblings. It was thought that her mother couldn't carry a child to birth until Erianthe appeared."

"If she conceived by the Falova," Anji began in a low murmur, "then her marriage to Narod—"

"Would have been for naught," Fanakel finished.

My stomach lurched like I'd crested the hill of a roller coaster and plunged down the other side. "I don't...wait, I don't understand..."

"Erianthe and Narod were betrothed when they were young," Fanakel explained. "One benefit of the marriage for Cirivant was the promise of Narod's child on the Darili throne. But if you were Erianthe's firstborn..."

"Not legitimate," said Mia.

"It wouldn't matter. Most of the human kingdoms in Kopaat and Ga'besh put the ruler's eldest on the throne, no matter what the status of his or her birth. Erianthe's great-grandfather was born to a junior cook, you know. It was *notorious*."

"Which," said Anji, "if Erianthe was telling the truth, makes Susan the crown princess. High Queen..." She hissed between her teeth. "No wonder she was willing to execute you."

I understood the words coming out of her mouth, thanks to the damn sword, but my brain refused to accept the translation. "But...but no, Erianthe's the queen, if she'd gotten pregnant—"

"It's been rumored for years," said Fanakel. "Her father died, and she was crowned before her twenty-second birthday—I remember people speaking of how young she was, even for a human queen. They don't come of age until twenty-two," he said, shifting on Mia's sleeping bag. "She and Narod were meant to be married then, once he achieved majority—I believe he's slightly younger—but she postponed the wedding after her premature ascent, and then she was said to have contracted a dangerous illness. The queen mother ruled in her stead for months, if I remember correctly."

"That's what I recall," said Anji. "No one saw her for so long that it was rumored she'd become pregnant, but there was no sign of a baby when she emerged, and the marriage went through." She whistled low. "It makes sense. Erianthe's young, she gets pregnant, the baby would upend a marriage compact between two kingdoms—"

"And mark her as false in front of her people," Fanakel added. "Not a good way to start her reign."

"Not in Daril, anyway. So she confines herself when she can no longer hide the pregnancy, then sneaks to the Crossing and delivers...away from Daril, away from *Kopaat*, out of the Aen. She can't have imagined that you'd survive, leaving a newborn in the woods like that."

I felt Anji's hand land on my knee and squeeze.

"In sum," said Fanakel, "Erianthe's a liar, the heir to the Darili throne is a rogue elemental, the compact with Cirivant is broken, and the Watcher isn't guarding the Crossing. Well, now, *this* is delightful. What do we do?"

"We go back to my father," said Anji. "Tell him everything. He'll have to take Susan's side now. *Your* father is useless—Nokan'ti is too closely allied with Daril for him to interfere—but if Susan's truly the heir—"

"You think Rokund will jump in to defend the claim of a rogue elemental?" Fanakel countered. "Against *Daril?* If Erianthe calls for help, Nokan'ti is treaty-bound to assist, and do you really think your father is such a fool as to restart the war?"

"It's the right thing," she protested.

"And I love your idealism," Mia piped up, "but the elf's got a point. What if we go home and regroup? Fresh supplies, maybe some more guns and ammo..."

"Going anywhere near the tunnels right now is dangerous at best," said Fanakel. "Erianthe would be mad not to post a guard, and once she learns that we've escaped, I don't see her extending that offer of exile again. You're more trouble alive than you're worth, Susan, and I suspect the rest of us are as well."

"I'm sorry," I mumbled, overwhelmed and trying not to cry. "I...I'm so sorry, I never meant to get any of you into this..."

Anji's grip on my knee tightened. "Stop, lass. You didn't ask for this, and you didn't ask for my help. I gave it willingly."

"Ditto, Suze," said Mia. "And I'm not about to leave you to be killed by some bitch in a tiara."

Fanakel remained quiet for a moment, then sighed. "I'm here, aren't I?"

Lightning flashed overhead, and the boom of the thunder shook the trees around us. "Look," said Mia once the rumbling ceased, "it's been a hell of a week, and I think we could all do with a few hours' sleep. We'll figure this out in the morning, yeah?"

"Agreed," said Fanakel, and unzipped the tent door. "I'll leave you two alone. Coming, Susan?"

The idea of sleep sounded wonderful, but I knew I'd never be able to quiet my mind. "In a little while. I'll take the watch," I said, crawling out of the tent behind him. "It's the least I can do to thank you for the rescue."

I should have stayed close to the tents, but I needed to move. Walk. Run.

Scream.

And so I wandered back to the river, lost in my own head, and followed it downstream for a time as it meandered through the woods. The pouring rain didn't help my mood, but I couldn't bring myself to will it away.

Guilt pushed me to keep walking—to put as much distance as I could between myself and my sleeping companions, who, reassurances aside, had never signed on for this disastrous journey. Mia deserved to be back in town, pulling shifts at Antoinette's until her heart and head could agree on a destination. Hell, she deserved to be back in her own *body*, but there wasn't much I could do about that. Anji, kind as she had been, had done more than her share. She could go home to Heartfast with a clear conscience, and should her gods ever appear before me and demand a reckoning of her behavior, I'd give her top marks and extra credit for all the trouble I'd caused. And

Fanakel—*fuck*. He'd been coerced into our band, plain and simple. The poor guy had the bad luck to be on guard duty, nothing more. He didn't owe me any favors, much less his life.

That's what I was asking of them if I allowed them to stay near me: their lives. Back at the Crossing, I was a monster magnet. In Daril, I was a criminal at best, an international crisis waiting to happen if our suppositions were correct. If nothing else, I was a rogue elemental, and judging by the tenor of the remarks I'd heard on the subject, that was probably enough to get me killed.

I couldn't ask them to stick around. But where could I go? I didn't know Kopaat beyond what little I'd seen, and besides, who would help me?

And if no one was willing to free me from the sword, then what was the point of running? My options were clear: either go home and fight Outsiders until one opened up more than just my face, or skulk around Kopaat until someone killed me for abandoning my post. God knew how many innocents in the four worlds had died already because I'd gone on my little freedom quest.

That wasn't my fault. I told myself that I shouldn't carry their deaths, but I couldn't put that burden down.

What did that leave me, then? Kill myself?

Briefly, I toyed with the notion. I'd be free of the sword, and besides, what did I have to live for? My family in the Crossing was dead, and the woman who'd given me life had been prepared to take it back. No one wanted me, I was of no use to anyone, and the few people who'd stuck up for me were in danger.

But if I died, who would get the sword? Some random Darili? Someone with a family, marched off to an unfamiliar land forever?

*Mia?*

God, no. Not Mia.

And then, as lightning flashed off to my right, the answer blazed across my mind: I had to destroy the sword, even if it took me with it. No one else would be trapped as the Watcher, Mia could go on with her life, and the wayward royals could sneak home. But how to do it? The sword was tough, that was clear, but...

Thunder boomed in the distance, and I gasped as a wild thought struck me. Of *course*. The sword might do well with plain old fire, but surely lightning would be a different matter.

Screwing up my courage, I waded into the middle of the stream, trying to ignore the discomfort of the cold water, then held the sword aloft and waited for a bolt to find me. The blade was the biggest metal object for miles, and I'd planted myself in a highly conductive area—it *had* to work. I'd melt the sword, and if I survived, that would be a bonus. If not, at least I wouldn't be a danger to the folks around me who gave a damn.

A moment later, when lightning crackled closer, I almost lost my nerve. I was shaking—whether from the frigid river or my fear of imminent electrocution, I couldn't say—but something made me yell a challenge to the storm. "Come on!" I bellowed over the thunder. "I'm right here! Hit me! *Do it!*"

But the storm didn't answer my cries. Instead, I heard an unfamiliar voice pleading in my mind: *Stop, I beg you! Susan, please, don't!*

Startled, I dropped the sword, but I managed to snatch it before the current could carry it away. "Who said that?" I demanded, turning in a circle with the blade extended as I searched the darkness for movement. "Show yourself!"

*Can you hear me?* The voice sounded shocked. *You can! You heard me!*

"Yeah, I can hear you, so come on out."

*I can't.*

"Who are you?"

*I am myself.*

The voice seemed male, I thought, which limited the choices to air and water. "Elemental?"

*Exactly. Please, I'm begging you, don't destroy the sword.*

"Why shouldn't I?" I kept looking around, trying to spot the contours of an insubstantial body through the pounding rain.

*Because you'll kill me if you do.*

Understanding and horror dawned at once, and I froze in place, staring at the weapon in my hand. "You…are *you* the one the maladetas captured to make the sword?"

*I am.*

"But I thought you were dead!"

*Would have been kinder, but no.* He paused, then said, *Could we continue this somewhere that isn't the middle of a lightning strike zone? You're making me nervous.*

I obliged, slogging my way out of the river and onto the bank, and sheltered between two trees as I willed the rain away. Holding the sword in my lap, I practiced what the first air elemental had shown me. *You sound different than the others of your kind I've met.*

*Spend five hundred years with no one but humans, and you'd sound different, too.* I felt more than heard him sigh. *They trapped me in here. All of the magics worked to create and power the sword, they draw on me. Beyond the Aen, it was all I could do to maintain consciousness. But the pain is less here, and there's sufficient Aen now that I can make myself heard, and—*

*Pain?*

*Constant pain*, he replied. *Oh, it doesn't matter what you do with the sword*, he reassured me as my horror spiked again. *You can't make it any worse by using it. But it binds me—it's like red-hot chains running through me—and if I resist, it's excruciating. That's why I chose you*, he continued, speeding up. *I'm so sorry, I didn't want to—I <u>never</u> want to—and I held off as long as I could, but I had to choose someone eventually, and—*

*You knew about me*, I finished.

*In part. I sensed you were a rogue, and I thought you were my best chance at freedom. But Susan, I'm sorry, I shouldn't have done this to you. That's the last thing Malachi said—he told me to stay the hell away from you.* Odd as his voice was in my mind, I could still hear his guilt. *I didn't want to hurt you. Especially not you. But—*

*But you're desperate*, I replied, turning the sword over as if I might spot a face in the metal. *And you're in pain. And you've been like that for five hundred years.* Suddenly, my own predicament seemed less severe as I considered how much worse the Watcher's silent partner had it. "Shit," I whispered.

*I'm sorry.*

*It's okay.* Unsure what else to do, I carefully held the blade against my shoulder and gave the sword an awkward hug. *Tell me how to fix this.*

*I don't know. What I do know is that if the sword's broken, I die. The spells on it are strong, and they'll draw on anything they can to remain intact, and that would probably rip me apart. It has to be disassembled by magical means.*

*Well, unless you need me to splash something, I'm not sure how much help I can offer.*

I caught a flash of amusement mixed in with his overall remorse. *You brought me back within the Aen. That's closer to freedom than I've been since the day the maladetas grabbed me, so thank you. It's a beginning.*

I sat beneath my dry bubble for a long moment, my thoughts whirling, watching the lightning flash and counting the seconds until the thunder rolled.

It wasn't just me now. I held another being's life in my hands.

The elemental was trapped worse than I was, and he'd been imprisoned far longer. I couldn't go back to the Crossing—not until I figured out a way to free him. He'd come to me for help, and to be fair, the sword had saved my butt more than once in the last weeks. I should attempt to release him. I wanted my freedom so badly that I could taste it—I couldn't imagine how strong that yearning was for him. And as unjust as it was that I'd been tasked with fighting Outsiders, he was the one being actively hurt.

My despair burned away like fog as indignation flared

again. This wasn't right—*none* of this was right. And though I had no idea yet what I could do to fix it, I resolved to try.

*Are you there?* I asked.

*Can't exactly wander off.*

*I'm going to see what I can do to get us both out of this mess, okay? I mean, I haven't made much progress thus far, but I'll keep looking for a solution.*

*Thank you.* I knew I wasn't imagining the relief in his voice.

*So, uh…what do I call you? "Hey, you" just seems rude.*

*Whatever pleases you. I have no name.*

I thought about it for a time, silently going over the terms I'd heard people use for the sword: Heart's Blood, Bright Blade, Shadowbane. The sounds of the untranslated words rolled around in my mind, but nothing seemed quite right until I started picking them apart.

*What about Terj?* I asked, using the local term for "shadow" I'd heard in reference to the sword.

*Terj*, he repeated, as if trying it out. *Yes, I suppose that would suffice.*

*Okay, then.*

We sat in silence for a moment longer before he said, *Any interest in returning to your camp before you're attacked by a wild animal in the darkness?*

*Probably not a bad idea*, I replied, and pushed myself to my feet.

*You're soaked.*

*I'm half water elemental, remember?*

*Yeah, and the other half probably doesn't enjoy clammy leggings. Go on, dry off. I've put you through hell—there's no reason to make it worse, is there?*

Chuckling to myself, trying not to think of how close I'd come to doing something incredibly stupid, I picked my way along the riverbank toward my sleeping companions. *So, is this a one-time thing, or will I be hearing from you again?*

*Recall that part about how I was muzzled for five hundred years, Susan.*

*Is that a yes?*

*Oh, absolutely.*

I hated to ask, but the night was dark between lightning bolts. *Will it hurt worse if I make the sword light up?*

*No. And even if it did, I wouldn't object. I can't believe I almost got you executed...*

*If that's the worst that happens, I'll forgive it.* The blade's green glow lit the path before me, and I hurried back the way I'd come. *Thanks, Terj.*

*That is literally almost the least I can do.*

*But useful nonetheless*, I replied, and let him light the way to shelter.

Mia was the first to emerge at dawn, and she scowled when she found me sitting on a wet log, rubbing the stuck-on ichor and grime off the sword with a handful of wet moss. "Up the whole night?" she asked through a yawn. "You're going to be hurting in a few hours."

"I can do all things through caffeine," I replied, and nodded to the chemical heater I'd set up, which was bringing a pot of water to a boil. "Blade needed cleaning, anyway."

She grunted as she sat beside me. "As soon as there's less than a fifty percent chance that we're being hunted, remind me to clean the pistol."

*Malachi always liked that one. He'd be happy to see it used.*

Mia jerked and stared at me, wide-eyed. "Did you..."

I pointed to the sword in my lap.

"It *talks*?" she whispered.

"No, but the elemental trapped in it does."

*Hello*, he said. *I am called Terj.*

I was afraid that if Mia's eyes widened any farther, they'd fall out of her head. "But...but Kingkiller—"

*Was misinformed. I'm very much alive. Sometimes, I wish*

*otherwise, but this is the best I've had it since the sword was forged, so I shan't complain today.* He paused, then added, *You should probably blink, Mia.*

She took his advice, whether involuntarily or not, and leaned closer to inspect the sword. "So *you're* the one who fucked Suze over—"

"Mia," I began, but Terj was quicker on the draw.

*Yes. Regrettably, yes,* he said. *The magic worked on the sword makes me choose, and I thought my odds were best with Susan. Was it fair of me? No. Is any of this fair? Again, no. But if you lived as I have, there are few things you wouldn't try if it meant release.*

"His essence powers the sword, more or less," I explained. "Apparently, it hurts like hell. So Terj and I are going to figure out how to free us both. If you've had enough of backpacking, second puberty, and murderous parents, I certainly won't be offended if you go home, but—"

"Fuck that, you know I'm in. And is that tea or coffee on the heater?"

"It's water. Add whatever seems best."

She rose and dug in her bag, and soon, our campsite smelled of wet earth and strong, cheap coffee. Carrying over a mug for me and one for herself, Mia sat beside me again and sipped, letting the hot liquid mitigate the morning chill. "Know what else is unfair about this whole thing?" she asked.

"What's that?"

"How does everyone in our posse get to be royalty except me?"

*And me.*

"Okay, *thank you*," she said, dipping her mug toward the sword. "Two on three. Marginally better."

I laughed in disbelief as I scrubbed at a stubborn patch of unidentifiable stickiness. "At least your mother hasn't tried to kill you."

"Disowned me," she pointed out.

"But hasn't actually threatened execution yet, so point

goes to Janine Randolph."

"You say that, but remember that Janine screwed a stripper."

"Hey, Erianthe got freaky with an elemental, and I do *not* want to think about the mechanics of that."

We shuddered together and sipped our coffee.

*I've never attempted it, but it's probably not as difficult as you might imagine,* said Terj. *Not for a water elemental. Fire, now—*

"Dude," I muttered. "No."

*Why is it that humans are so distressed about their own creation? Wouldn't it more logically be an event to be celebrated?*

"Not just humans," said Mia, and waved as Anji poked her head out of the tent. "Coffee's this way," she called in greeting. "And would you like to have a nice chat about your parents' sex lives?"

The dwarf looked aghast at the notion. "I...I'm sorry, *what?*" she sputtered.

"Proved my point," Mia replied, and swept her free hand toward the sword. "Anji, Terj. Terj, no one wants to chat about their conception."

"Who is Terj?" Anji asked, creeping closer.

*Hello, Anjikora.*

What followed was a quick recap of my night's wanderings—minus the part about how I tried out my best impression of a lightning rod—then a second, quicker telling once Fanakel followed his nose into the morning mist. "So, you know, I don't have any idea what I'm doing yet," I concluded, "but I'm not dragging Terj back to the Crossing, and I'll understand if you'd rather be on your way—"

*Someone's coming.*

We stiffened and fell silent—even Fanakel paused with one hand halfway into the granola bag. *Who?* I asked Terj.

His answer, though brief, wasn't short enough to hide his anxiety from me: *Maladeta.*

I was on my feet in seconds, coffee forgotten, and held the sword out in front of me like I was searching for danger with a dowsing rod. *Where?*

*Left, left…yes, there. That direction.*

Standing my ground, I stared toward the river, looking at the path I'd trod during the night. Rustling and quick footsteps behind me told me the others were arming themselves, and when I spotted the top of a gray hood heading upriver along the bank, I gripped the sword and tried to affect a defensive stance. "Get ready," I muttered.

I heard Mia's pistol cocking to my right. "On it."

We held our breath and waited, listening as the approaching maladeta swished through the leaves and snapped twigs. I stared at the thin curtain of brush between us and the trail, hoping that the intruder wouldn't see us…but then she stopped in her tracks and said, in unmistakable English, "Is that *coffee* I smell?"

"Holy shit, that's—" Mia whispered, but I stopped her before she could head for the woman.

"Who wants to know?" I called back.

"*Susan?* Is that you?" Her words tumbled out with her excitement. "Oh, my goodness, girl, don't *move*, I'm coming."

Without further preamble, Ms. Quince smashed her way through the brush…and found herself confronted with three blades and the barrel of a pistol. "*Oh*…okay," she said, slowly raising her empty hands, "it's all right, I'm not here to harm you…"

Vaguely, I noticed that she'd switched languages, but the sword was doing a fine job of easing the transition for me.

Anji sidled closer and whispered, "You know her?"

"I thought I did. My old neighbor." Turning to Ms. Quince, I demanded, "Did you know?"

"You'll need to be more specific than that, dear," she began, then peered more closely at me. "Gracious, what happened to your face?"

"Outsider," said Mia.

Ms. Quince's eyes darted to her and bulged. "*Mia?*

What on earth—"

"Tekorish, apparently. Did you know about Susan?"

Shaken, Ms. Quince lowered the hood of her cloak, revealing the woman I'd known and trusted all my life. "What about Susan?"

"Rogue elemental," Anji offered, "and probably the heir to Daril."

"*What?*"

Her surprise seemed too sudden and genuine to be an act. This was Ms. Quince, I told myself, the nice lady who'd watched me pedal my bike around the street and sneaked me chocolate cookies, but I kept up my guard. A thought made the coffee rise from its pan and float toward me in a small brown sphere, which I left hovering between Ms. Quince and me. "Two elementals have suggested it, I've discovered a bit of a talent, and Erianthe told me a story about a Darili princess getting knocked up by a water elemental and abandoning the baby in the woods beyond the Crossing—while Erianthe was giving me a few hours to decide between death and exile, naturally—and those two filled in the gaps," I said, nodding toward Anji and Fanakel. "You didn't know?"

Briefly, Ms. Quince muttered under her breath. "No. No, of course not. Susan, honey, if I'd suspected, I'd have said *something*, I'd have gone home for guidance…"

She fell silent as Fanakel laughed. "*You?*" he said. "You mean for us to believe that the maladetas never heard the rumors? You hear of everything else, but not this?"

"What my sisters know and what *I* personally know are two different matters. I spent the last forty years with the Watcher—I received no news from home. Not even from our clan mother, and if any of the Taln'een know of Darili matters, she would be first among them. So no, Susan," she said, turning her attention back to me, "I knew nothing about this. And Erianthe was going to *kill* you?"

"Outsiders have slipped into Kopaat," said Anji. "Presumably the other worlds, too. We're all at risk with

Susan on the run."

"Unfortunately." Ms. Quince folded her arms and frowned. "You fled Deoni, I take it?"

"Wouldn't you?" Mia retorted. "And what the hell are you doing out here, anyway?"

She took her time in answering. "My people...we have ways of learning and sharing pertinent information."

"Magic?" I asked.

"Without going into specifics, it would probably help to think of it as a magical phone system connected to hidden cameras that no one else can access," she explained. "This pleases the other powers in our worlds to no end, as I'm sure you can imagine"—she paused as Fanakel snorted—"but it allows the clans to pass news. For instance, we received word that one of Rokund's daughters was with the Watcher and another...*presumed*...human. Last we'd heard, you were in Nokan'ti. My clan mother assumed you would try Daril if you couldn't find help from the elves—rightly, it seems— and sent me south to assist. She wasn't thrilled when I informed her that I'd told you the leash on the sword only bound you on *that* side of the Crossing, but she understood. She did her time with a Watcher, too. So now that you've left Deoni, I should send word—"

"Did you know about the sword?" I interrupted, keeping the point aimed at her.

Ms. Quince's brow furrowed. "Firebrand? I distinctly remember telling *you* about it, so yes."

"You knew about the elemental, then?"

She hesitated before offering a slow nod. "I was barely into my thirties when the sword was forged—*I* had no part in its making," she insisted—"but yes, I...I know what some of my sisters did. Other Taln'een. The effort killed them, it was so counter to the way our talents run. Still, sacrificing an elemental was the only way we could keep the sword together and functional beyond the Aen—"

*And whose sacrifice would that be, Ardielta?*

Ms. Quince stiffened and stared past us into the trees. "Who said—"

*That's what you're called, isn't it? Ardielta? Or do you still prefer Ardith?*

"Where—"

*Sword.*

She stared at the blade, her mouth moving into a silent *O.*

"He's not dead," I said softly. "But he's been in pain all this time. So I'm going to give you a chance to tell me how you're going to free us."

Stunned as she was, it took her a few seconds to produce words again. "I...I didn't know, Susan, believe me, I—"

"How do we fix this?" I asked, fighting to keep myself from shouting at her. "What will it take for you to undo the forging?"

I couldn't blame her for taking her time in answering me, considering the number of weapons trained on her, but she finally managed to regain a semblance of her old air of calm control. "I can't do it. I would if I could," she hurriedly insisted, "but I don't have that power. Even my clan mother probably doesn't have it. My clan together...perhaps, but overcoming the other types of magic on the sword may be impossible without assistance."

I glanced at the others, who nodded. "Sounds like the best plan we've got right now. Take us there."

"Like most things in life, child, it's not that simple. Will you let me contact the clan mother without turning me into a shish kebab?"

"A *what?*" asked Fanakel.

"Skewered meat. One cannot always depend on translators," she replied with a hint of reproach.

Though part of me feared she'd call the cavalry, I thought of Uncle Malachi. He'd trusted Ms. Quince—he'd probably loved her. Dad had trusted her, too. And for a member of a race spoken of with a touch of fear, she'd been *awfully* compliant.

"Okay," I said, and lowered the sword. "Don't make me regret this, eh?"

She smiled weakly and pulled what appeared to be a metal powder compact from the pocket of her long blue skirt. "Susan, dear, had I wished you ill, I'd never have sent you through the tunnels. Now give me a few minutes."

She took a seat atop our log and opened the compact, which held only a mirror on each half. Using two fingers, she traced a complicated pattern over the mirrors, frowning ever so slightly in concentration, and was rewarded with a flash of pale green light. Folding the compact until she could hold it in her palm and look into the top mirror, she waited, then dipped her chin. "Great Mother," she began, "I have news…" Pausing, she glanced over her mirror at her audience and shooed us away. "Pack your things, children. Hasn't anyone told you it's rude to eavesdrop?"

"Hasn't anyone told you it's rude to kidnap people and lock them into weapons?" I countered.

After the last two and a half weeks, Ms. Quince's reprimanding stare didn't pack quite as hard a punch as it once did, but I shrugged and helped Fanakel take down our tent as she murmured into her compact.

By the time we'd shoved and strapped the last of our things into place, she was hanging up—or whatever the magical equivalent was. "We're not strong enough to free you by ourselves," she said, sliding the compact back into her pocket as she stood. "Nor would our clan mother permit an attempt. We've been true to the pact we made with Firebrand's other creators, and she won't allow us to break faith."

"But—" I began.

Ms. Quince held up a hand to cut me off. "*But* she has an idea about how we might work around it. It's dangerous, and I don't like it one bit, but that's not my choice. So…how far are you willing to go?"

My left hand gripped the hilt of the sword hanging at my side. "As far as I need to."

"I'm in," said Mia.

"As am I," Anji added, "and Fanakel—"

"Hasn't run yet." He hoisted his duffel over his shoulder and adjusted its weight. "What would you have us do, then?"

"Follow the river north," said Ms. Quince, pointing to the watery ribbon beyond the sheltering brush. "All the way to the sea. You'll find our village there, a harbor. Ask for the great mother, and if anyone harasses you, tell them that Ardielta gave you leave."

"You're not coming with us?" Mia asked.

"I've been instructed to continue to Deoni and pretend that nothing's amiss. Let me see what I can learn of the queen and her plans for you. But this is where we part for now," she said, reaching out to grip my shoulder. "Go as quickly as you can, child, and be brave. I'll follow as soon as I'm able."

She surprised me with a rough hug, then hugged Mia in turn before pushing us toward the path. Without a backward look, she sped onward in the other direction, heading for the castle through the mist.

I started for the river and waited at the bank for the others to catch up. "Before we do something potentially stupid," I asked, "does anyone have a better plan?"

"Not me," said Fanakel, "and seeing as you have a *maladeta* on your side, perhaps we should give this town a try. Taln'een, was it?"

*I know the place. A deep harbor, well protected.*

"As if anyone would attack a maladetan settlement," Anji replied. "If they'll shelter us, we should be safe for a time. Long enough for proper bathing, I'd wager."

Mia chuckled at that but quickly sobered and patted my arm. "Up to you, Suze. What do you think?"

My stomach clenched at the realization that the others

were looking to me for answers, but I tried not to show it. Focusing on the river, I willed a small boat made of water to rise and sit atop the surface, then stepped aboard and took a seat at the bow. "I think we'd make better time if we didn't walk."

Grinning, Mia climbed in and sat beside me, then offered a hand to Fanakel and Anji. "How do you steer this thing?" she asked, examining the translucent seats.

"We're about to find out."

The river sang to me, a rushing channel of potential waiting to be tapped, and as I closed my eyes and opened my deeper senses to embrace it, I felt the faint tug of the distant sea.

*You can do this, Susan*, Terj whispered to my mind.

*I can, can't I?* I replied, and cast off from the shore.

# ACKNOWLEDGEMENTS

I started writing this book in July 2019, needing a change of pace after *Shadow of the Magus*.

Let's just say it didn't come easily.

Having by that point spent six and a half years exclusively playing in the *Stranger Magics* sandbox, I found myself struggling to once again build a world from the ground up. Eight long months later, I had a draft, and then I forced myself to press on to the sequel…but my heart wasn't in it. I abandoned ship about a third of the way through and shelved the project.

After the final two *Stranger Magics* books, all four volumes of *Hall of Thorns*, and the *Wild Hunt* trilogy, I finally found that spark again and dared to open the files once more. My sincere thanks go to the Novel Chicks, who kept periodically asking, "Hey, whatever happened to that book with the dwarves?"

And yes, here's to you, Mom and Dad.

# ABOUT THE AUTHOR

When not writing fiction, Ash Fitzsimmons is an appellate attorney and an unrepentant car singer.

Find her online:
www.ashfitzsimmons.com